A Penny For Your Thoughts

Bull Creek Book One

Amanda Marquardt

Silver Lane Publishing

Editing by Megan Carver

Proofreading by English Proper Editing Services

Cover art and design by Novel & Navy Designs

Paperback ISBN 979-8-9915280-5-4

EBook ISBN 979-8-9915280-4-7

DEDICATION

To my children.

Don't ever let someone tell you you're too much. They need to be bigger. You
never need to be smaller.

I love you.

CONTENTS

INTRODUCTION

Dear reader,

A Penny For Your Thoughts is book one in the Bull Creek series. It takes place after The Fallout Duet. While it's not necessary to read the duet first, there will be spoilers if you start here.

As you step into Leah and Nick's story, know that every step of the way they have chosen their own path. My intention was never to pair them up; it was a decision they made when I was drafting *When Sparks Fly*. I remember the exact moment, because I had to reconfigure the entire Bull Creek series afterward. Not only that, but in drafting *A Penny For Your Thoughts*, a singular comment was made that changed the series from three to four books.

I share all of this because they are so much more than "just" a romance story. I hope you love them, embrace them, laugh with them, and cry with them as much as I have. Leah and Nick are an exceptional couple.

This book is intended for readers 18+. It features an open door romance with explicit, on-page descriptions of sexual situations. For those who wish to prepare for what lies ahead, content notices are available in the next section. This includes reference to some current events, specifically a natural disaster.

Welcome (back) to Bull Creek!

CONTENT NOTICES

A Penny For Your Thoughts is a contemporary, open door romance, featuring on page sexual situations. All intimacy is consensual, including some kink exploration. The following can be found within:

- edging

- pressure play

- temperature play

- light restraint

- adult toy usage

Further, *A Penny For Your Thoughts* includes some heavy themes. The following topics are discussed and/or depicted:

- alcoholism

- substance abuse

- child neglect (a child is injured as the result of neglect)

- foster care

Special Note

In July, 2025, Texas experienced devastating flooding. My family, though safe, was impacted far greater than we could have imagined. Friends and family, and the community as a whole, experienced immense loss during this time.

Although Bull Creek is fictional, it's deeply rooted and inspired by my experiences and connections to the Texas Hill Country. Because of Nick's career, and the timing and location of this story, there is no way the characters would have not been impacted or attempted to help. Therefore, a scene late in the book mentions this event. It does not go into great detail, however as it's both fresh and deeply emotional I feel it's necessary to share for those who may wish to skip. If so, you may omit chapter 48, scene two. Scene three includes a passing comment at the start.

I've included organizations where donations can be made, in a section at the back of this book, for those who may want to support continued and future relief efforts.

Playlist

Here For The Party – **Gretchen Wilson**

Whatever She's Got – **David Naill**

you look like you love me (feat. Riley Green) – **Ella Langley**

America's Sweetheart – **Elle King**

Don't Ya – **Brett Eldredge**

Friends Don't – **Maddie & Tae**

Kiss Me In The Dark – **Randy Rogers Band**

Am I Okay? – **Megan Moroney**

Strong – **London Grammar**

To Hell & Back – **Maren Morris**

What My World Spins Around – **Jordan Davis**

Broken One – **RaeLynn**

CHAPTER 1

LEAH

The bed creaks as I attempt to stealthily roll over and shift to sitting.

"Where're you going?" Trevor's half-panicked voice comes from behind me.

I cringe, glad he can't see me in the darkened room. "I'm getting dressed."

My flavor du jour seemed promising on the front end but ended up lacking all of the flavor. I even let him bring a female friend along, because I'm an equal opportunity kind of gal, but she was clearly around for the big D just as much as I was. We had zero chemistry. And he had zero skills. The entire event fell flat.

"You don't have to go right now." He sits up, the woman slipping off his arm on the other side of the bed and groaning into her pillow.

It really is a shame it didn't go well, because he looks like every girl's wet dream. A firefighter cadet with cropped dark hair, hazel eyes, and shapely muscles. Dude is definitely one to catch feelings, though. The faster I get out of here, the better.

"I told you, I don't do sleepovers." I pull on my lace-up boots, shoving the loose strings inside, and stand, yanking my leather skirt up to my hips. His energy escalates palpably, and I anticipate him jumping out of the bed after me. "See you around," I say over my shoulder, swiping my shirt and bra from a nearby chair and dressing as I step into the hallway of his shared house.

I never bring anyone back to my place. I've seen enough documentaries to know what can happen to women living on their own. Not to mention, I don't need anyone who thinks they want a one-night stand—but ends up wanting more—showing up unannounced. And that's why I hardly date anyone in Bull Creek, opting more frequently for partners from the city. Even if I don't bring people home, I'm not hard to find in our small town.

These nights are getting old, though. Or my standards are getting higher. I don't need emotion, just someone who understands a woman's body. And maybe is a little rough around the edges.

The bell jingles as the door to Sadie's is opened, causing my skin to crawl and my teeth to clench. It's like a Pavlovian effect caused by a recent need for freedom from the Western store where I work. This time, Mr. Porter walks through.

"Mornin' Mr. Porter." My voice is unnaturally chirpy.

The funny thing is, I like people. The not-so-funny thing is that everyone who works in customer service believes the opposite. It's like the people on the other side of the counter forget we're human, too. More than that, though, I'm ready for a change. I always thought I'd leave town, then never did. Now, every time that bell chimes, I feel even more closed in.

"Howdy, Leah." Mr. Porter tips his hat at me, his swollen knuckles and thick, wrinkled skin keeping his hand from reopening fully. I reach for the second shelf on the back side of the counter, knowing what he's after before he says, "Should have a package here."

The glass countertop rattles in the loose fitting when I set the box down and open the lid in his direction. Inside is the custom belt he ordered last week. Not black or brown, but our house burnt orange.

"You have an eye for design. It's beautiful," he praises, gliding his crooked pointer along the hand-stitched thread.

With one hand, I twist all of my dark brown hair together and pull it over my shoulder. Wearing it loose is my signature style, but it has a tendency to add to my anxiety when I'm on edge, like a built-in noose tightening around my neck.

"It turned out very nice." His gaze catches on the leather initials. "Thank you, darlin'." He taps on the glass to signal his approval and I replace the top, handing the box over.

"Of course. Let me know when you're ready for the next one." I force a painfully pleasant smile. It's not that I dislike him, and chances are he's none the wiser to my internal struggle.

I'm just feeling stagnant. I'm ready to reap the fruits of my labor, to let my creative juices flow. Even though I helped Mr. Porter with his design plan, the store benefited from it. When I was an associate, I received commission for these types of transactions, but as an assistant manager, I don't get the same perk. Ironically, most customers look for me when they're ready to design anyway. It's always been a passion of mine.

Mr. Porter tips his hat again and heads out. The bell dings, and I shudder.

I've worked in this store for eight years. Never anywhere else. At sixteen, Bull Creek's main Western store, named for its owner, seemed like the perfect place to earn cash while embracing my love of fashion. Promotions came easily, the employee discount was reasonable, and the hours weren't the worst. So, I stuck around.

Until two years ago when I was promoted to assistant manager. That was my plateau. And nothing's changed since.

Ding.

I force another smile as someone makes their way back to the main counter from the front door. It's a simple setup, with the large, rectangular counter just short of the halfway point through the store. There's a smaller register at the very back of the store, close to our endless boot selection, but it hardly ever gets used.

The whole place smells like fresh leather. Kind of ironic that it used to be a welcome scent, like coming home; now it teases at giving me a headache.

When ice-blonde hair peeks through two racks of women's clothes, I release a breath and my tensed shoulders. My greeting comes out on a sighed, "Hi."

Izzy beams at me, her perfect teeth singing, "Well, hello to you." She scans the area. "Quiet today."

Somehow her powder-blue scrubs look crisp, even though they're covered in a day's worth of teeth cleaning. Fucking gross.

"Yeah." My voice lacks enthusiasm. There's so much I want to share about how I'm feeling, but I don't want us to get interrupted, so I leave it. "What are you doing here?"

A visit at work from either of my two best friends is always a treat. Izzy's schedule isn't especially flexible, given that dental hygienists work typical business hours. And Maci gets pulled in all directions between building up her photography business, learning the ropes at her fiancé's ranch, and prepping her late grandmother's home to become a bed and breakfast. I expected to see more of Maci now that she's living in town again, but that couldn't be further from the truth.

Izzy taps her fingers on the glass countertop, more of a thrumming thanks to her short, nude nails. "Well, it's Friday. We haven't had a night out in a while, and I need one after the week I've had."

I scoff. "When have I ever said no to a night out? All you had to do was send a text."

"Yes, but then I wouldn't get to experience your sunny disposition." Izzy flutters her eyelashes at me.

I'm not known for being the perky one of the three of us. Izzy is analytical, Maci is feisty, and I'm the free spirit. Wild, off-the-wall, foul-mouthed, yes. Happy-go-lucky? Not so much.

But maybe I'm a little more sour than usual.

"Well count me in." I blow an air kiss across the counter. "And make sure Maci is there."

"Yes ma'am." Izzy salutes me with a smirk. As she turns back toward the door, she gestures to my necklace. "By the way, I'm really feeling this piece. Yours?"

The fact that people identify my handcrafted jewelry as having its own characteristic style, even if it's just my best friends, means that my news tonight will be that much easier. "Yes. My newest."

"Love it. I want to be as cool as you when I grow up." She blows an air kiss my way. "See you later."

"Love you."

Izzy has an amazing knack for knowing what I need to hear. She's like the mother hen of the group in that way. Playful and vibrant, but still provides the perfect amount of support or ass-kicking that's needed. I almost ask if she has a sixth sense that told her to come by today.

Getting together with my best friends tonight is perfect timing.

CHAPTER 2

NICK

"Good afternoon, y'all." My voice startles the two men loading the back of a pickup. "State Game Warden. How are ya?"

The afternoon is crisp and overcast as I approach the open tailgate and the men, who are likely armed if the dead deer in the bed of the truck is any indication. They mumble greetings at me, and one shifts on his feet.

I was born and raised in Texas, not far from here. To some extent, that provides me with a southern accent many would automatically expect. Laying that on a little thicker when I'm in the field makes people more comfortable. The "good ole boy" isn't nearly as intimidating to most—presumed slow or stupid—and I like to think it's not too far off from my natural ability to relate to people.

Since it's never my goal to get one over on anyone, I'm happy to do what I can to facilitate calm conversations. It goes better for everyone involved. Unless I get the impression someone is being openly deceitful or my safety is at an elevated risk.

"Shoo, that's a nice one," I praise, assessing the antlers on the deer. The eight-point buck looks the appropriate size and age, but the man to my right still dances uncomfortably on his feet. I smile casually. "You guys have your huntin' licenses on you?"

The man to my left produces a license momentarily, while his companion shakes his head. "Who shot this buck?" I look between them.

"I did." The hunter without a license leans his forearms against the side panel of the truck, raising his pointer to indicate himself when he answers. He readjusts his hat, wiping at his brow.

As a law enforcement officer, my safety is always at risk. Nine times out of ten, I'm dealing with people who are armed—legally or illegally. So I take my ability to read people and judge situations very seriously.

It's not uncommon for people to *play* dumb, but it is uncommon if they *are* dumb, especially when it comes to the law. As nervous as he is, the man is being honest, so I'm hopeful that'll continue.

"Something tells me you know what I'm about to say," I say with a sad smile. The hunter hangs his head. After a quick conversation, I give them the good and the bad. "I'm only going to write a warning today, but I have to seize your deer, since it was killed illegally."

"Damn." The licensed hunter shakes his head. He kicks at the ground with the toe of his boot, studying it like it'll have better answers.

"Yeah. I bet you'll be more diligent about who you go hunting with in the future," I tell him with limited sympathy. After all I've seen, I'd find it hard to believe that he wasn't aware his friend was hunting illegally. "Give me a minute and I'll get you squared away."

After I've processed the warning and moved the deer into my truck bed, I dole out my usual reminder about hunting safely and hop into my department truck. While the men make quick work of loading up and heading out, I call a local homeless shelter to see if someone is available to receive the donated kill. The hunters might not be able to keep the illegally obtained meat, but that doesn't mean it has to go to waste.

Before heading over, I check my personal phone to find a text from my best friend.

Sutton:

The Spur tonight?

Nights at The Spur, Bull Creek's country bar and dance hall, aren't all that unusual. Though, it's not his favorite place to be. He'd rather host bonfires at his family's ranch.

In fact, we haven't been to The Spur since his fiancée, Maci, came into the picture last fall. They got caught up in her recovery and legal shit after a stalker situation. I'm glad it all worked out, though, because I'm pretty fond of the feisty brunette. And having her friends around adds a nice layer to our group dynamics.

Me:

Count me in.

As the only game warden in my county, I spend most of my time working alone. I have a small office just outside of Bull Creek, but the phone line forwards directly to a cell phone, since I'm in the field frequently.

I'm finishing up paperwork after dropping off the poached deer when my work phone rings. "Game Warden Foster."

"Hi! This is AJ at the Bull Creek Chamber of Commerce," the woman on the other end says. "Payton's assistant." I wonder if Payton told her to say that or if she does it on her own.

"How can I help, AJ?" I switch to speakerphone and set the phone on the desk, trying to kill two birds with one stone.

"The chamber is putting together our second annual bachelor auction for charity. We're looking for a few bachelors to volunteer."

My fingers hover over the keyboard. "Volunteer. To be auctioned."

"Yes," she says confidently.

"When is this?" The question is a stalling tactic, because honestly, I can't think of anything I'd like to do less.

"In February. The week before Valentine's."

"I see."

Maci joked once that hanging out with Sutton and me was like being with celebrities—people from town chat with us a lot. They always ask me questions about hunting, or in Sutton's case, cattle. I do lots of demonstrations and trainings for work, but truthfully, I am not a fan of being the center of attention. And being auctioned off feels exactly like that.

"Can we count on you, Warden?" AJ prompts when I don't respond right away.

"Can I check my calendar and get back to you?"

"Of course," she says professionally. Then, with a bit of small-town pointedness, she adds, "It's for a children's cancer research fund."

Well, that'd be shitty to ignore. "Count me in."

"Perfect. You can expect a call with details soon."

"You got it. Have a nice day." I'm not sure I'm going to like what I've been wrangled into.

CHAPTER 3

LEAH

There are two bars in town. The Spur, which is good for dancing, and The Wild Turkey, which is good for getting shit-faced alone in the dark. I'm a twenty-five-year-old woman who likes to drink, but I do it to have fun socially, so the latter isn't a place I frequent.

With any luck, I can solve my sex problem tonight. Or rather, lack-of-sex problem. It's been too long since I've been satisfied by more than my hand and a battery-operated friend. My last few trips to the city haven't gone to plan, and Bull Creek only has so many options, so the pickings are getting slim. Just because I like a good romp, doesn't mean nothing else matters. I still have standards.

I'm beginning to think it's Maci's fault. Ever since she came into town, I've been in a dry spell. Meeting Colt and Pete at The Spur did not work out in our favor. Not only did I not come out on top—or bottom—that night, but Colt started stalking Maci and shit went south quick.

I'll just have to make sure no biker bullshit gets in the way tonight.

With minutes to spare before I need to leave for The Spur, I choose the tightest tank and shortest skirt I own. The black cashmere top brushes against my skin like a warm caress. I pick a leather skirt that's tight as fuck, not too different from the one I wore when I met the firefighter cadet. He didn't deserve that outfit.

11

I feel like a million bucks, finishing off the look with my Western boots and black cowboy hat.

Smokey, my ragdoll cat, sits atop my dresser, swishing his tail at me. He stares me down, judging me with his pale-blue eyes. I scratch his head the way he likes. "Don't wait up."

His tail swishes again as I slip on one of my custom gold necklaces.

Despite the limited affection I bestowed on him, my black top is speckled with his white and gray fur. I quickly roll a lint brush over my torso before heading out and locking up.

The bar is packed. Maybe it's the gorgeous January weather, maybe it's just coincidence, but it feels like there are more people out than usual. The bouncer waves me in without checking my ID. "Hey Carlos," I greet happily.

"You good, Leah?" His massive arms are crossed over his chest, partially covering The Spur's logo on his black tee.

"Yep," I reply, wiggling my fingers in a wave as I dash in.

I'm the last of our group to arrive, and I find the girls, Sutton, and his friend, Nick, at a table near the dance floor.

I didn't even think about Sutton or Nick when Izzy came by, but Maci and Sutton are basically a package deal at this point. And there's no reason for Sutton not to tell his best friend about the outing. We've hung out in a group on occasion, and he's just about the nicest guy in town. I still tend to feel a little under the microscope when he's around.

"Hi, gorgeous!" Izzy has to shout over the music. The dance floor is full, and there are people crammed everywhere. Izzy and Maci take turns squeezing me in a hug as if we haven't seen each other in a while.

Maci used to be less touchy-feely, but ever since she shacked up with Sutton and started fixing her family issues, she's more affectionate. Izzy, on the other hand, has always been a lover.

"You're on fire!" Maci looks me over. "Fuck. If I wasn't straight and engaged, mmmm." She licks her lips seductively before laughing. I don't miss Sutton's hand sliding to the small of Maci's back.

"How are you, Naughty Cowboy?" I shoot a wink his way.

He shakes his head at me with a playful gleam in his eye, hiding his amusement as he often does. I don't think he's concerned about Maci and I crossing any lines, but I do think he's caught on that we tend to make questionable decisions together.

I steal a look at his friend from the corner of my eye. "Nick."

Nick dips his chin in acknowledgement before taking a long swig of his beer. If I was paying attention, I'd say he's hiding a smirk, but I'm not.

"No Liv?" I ask, quickly turning back to my friends. Maci's cousin often joins us for group events. We didn't spend a lot of time as a foursome growing up, but I've loved having her around more lately—if only to make her blush.

Maci shakes her head. "She had something else."

"What could be more important than us?" Izzy jokes.

"Nothing. Let's dance!" I call over the music, grabbing each of them by the hand and forcing them to the dance floor.

Three songs go by before Izzy shouts for a round of drinks, with Maci and I trailing her to the table. Sutton and Maci pair off to order the round, and Izzy nudges me, motioning that she's headed to the restroom. If we were in any other town or any other bar, we'd follow girl code and go together, but it's not a concern here. Having Sutton and Nick around is an added benefit.

When it's just the two of us, Nick takes a step closer. "How are you?" he asks casually.

"I'm good. You?" I ask, drumming my fingers on the glossy bar table.

"Good." He smiles.

Nick may be a beefy-as-shit State Game Warden, but he has that boy-next-door charm. The messy blonde hair, the cool-blue eyes, the easy smiles. Never mind that he's probably the safest man in this bar. And yet, our conversation is stiff, and I can't figure out if it's me or him causing it.

This all-but-forced friendship started on a night out with Maci, when I'd had entirely too much to drink. Nick carried me out to Maci's car and buckled me in like a damsel in distress. We never spoke about it again, but any time we all hang out, it's hard to miss his lingering eyes. Like he thinks I'm one step away from downing a bucket of beer at any given moment.

I'd love his funny one-liners, something I'm pretty decent at myself, if it weren't for the big brother act. I like having fun with the group, not feeling like the screw-up.

Nick's eyes fall to my collarbone. "Is that one of your pieces?"

"Yeah," I confirm, a little confused. I finger the thin chain. It looks simple enough, like a large Y coming down from each shoulder in delicate links, the center falling directly between my covered breasts. Every inch or so there's a tiny white stone knotted into the chain. "Did I forget mentioning my jewelry?"

"I heard you talking to Maci and Izzy about it once . . . Wow, that sounded creepy." He breathes a laugh.

His joke relieves a bit of the tension, and I laugh with him. "Not at all."

"You're talented," he adds.

"Thanks," I reply awkwardly. It's still weird getting a compliment from him, even if I know he's as genuine as they come.

He shoves his free hand into his front pocket, drawing my attention down. The man is built. His eyes are shadowed by his usual ball cap, and his navy tee stretches over his wide biceps. The tight-fitting jeans and matching belt and shoes complete the casual look. Although, looking him over like this feels anything but casual. I don't know what's sexier: his sculpted arms or his thick thighs. Both are mouth-watering.

Still, he's not my type. There's nothing rough about him, and you don't have to look hard to see all the ways we're complete opposites. He's a rule enforcer and I'm a rule breaker. I prefer one-and-done, and I've never seen him hit on a single person.

"Here!" Maci shouts, thrusting a drink at me. I jump, releasing my chain. She leans back dramatically at my startle. "Jesus, are you ok?"

My eyes connect with Nick's, and he turns his head to hide a grin.

Fuck, I need to get laid. "Yeah, I'm fine. Zoned out," I answer stiffly.

"Oh my god. That was the longest line I've ever seen." Izzy sidles up next to me, creating a physical barrier between Nick and me, which I couldn't be happier for.

Maci is still staring at me from the other side. I ignore her.

"You shouldn't have broken the seal. Now you're going to spend the rest of your night in that line." I bump Izzy with a shoulder, and she rolls her eyes. "You should get that trademarked," I tease, rolling my eyes back dramatically. She throws her head back laughing.

Izzy was all but spoiled growing up. The perfect parents, the perfect brother, stability, good grades, tons of hobbies that she was good at without trying. I've never understood why she's the serious one of the three of us. Getting her to laugh is one of my favorite things. Izzy deserves all the happiness there is.

"So, what's going on with you?" she asks gently, maintaining her soft smile.

"I think I'm going to make a change." My voice comes out stronger than I feel on the matter.

Izzy looks me over once. "What kind of change?" she inquires.

"I want to pursue my own business. With my jewelry." I look between my friends, gauging their responses.

"That's a great idea!" Maci's smile threatens to split her face. Sutton's hand is still tucked behind her, rubbing her back or drawing circles or something back there. It's a thing with them. There's no way anyone could doubt their love, the way they're constantly touching.

I've never witnessed anything like it before. And I certainly never expect to have it myself. I've seen far too many people betray, use, and disappoint each other to reach for that. I'm good with a free sample and moving on.

"It would just be on the side to start," I add.

"Don't make yourself smaller," Izzy chides, pursing her lips.

"What?" My brows scrunch tightly as I study her.

"You're already talking down about yourself before you've even started," Maci agrees.

"I'm just being realistic. I won't be able to live on it to begin with."

"That's a given." Izzy waves me off. "But don't sell yourself short. You have your trusty sisters from other misters to help you plan a way to scale quickly."

Maci nods excitedly, her bright green eyes lighting up.

I'm taken aback by her statement. Izzy is the first of us to think things through logically, and here she is making me sound like the responsible one.

"Am I missing something? What is with you two?" I look between them again.

"What if you had a show? To get your name out there," Maci suggests. Her energy is infectious. She sets her glass down on the table and begins talking with her hands, one step away from full-on ramble. "You could have one for ladies' night. Here, maybe! Show some pieces, have models. Everything could be for sale!"

My jaw goes slack as I take her in. It's like she's given this thought already, even though it's the first time I've mentioned it.

"We've talked about it," Izzy supplies, grinning.

Of course they have. I laugh and shake my head.

"Not in a bad way," Maci adds, her voice reassuring.

"I know." I lean my head on her shoulder, bumping her with my hat.

"We're just both so proud of you and your jewelry." Izzy places a hand on my arm. "You know we'll support you in any way that we can."

I offer a tentative smile. Yeah, I'm the spontaneous one, but I've never done something big with a career. Money never came easy for my family. My mom smoked all of our money away on drugs. My older sister realized she didn't have to work if she used everyone else for their money. Except that backfired, because all she managed to do was end up pregnant three times with three different men, who each bailed on her.

My financial situation is stable. Something my seventeen-year-old self craved. It's the one thing I don't play around with. I never have to be evicted again. I never have to be hungry while my mother gets drunk and passes out on the only bed in the house. Because let's face it, a pull-out couch is not a bed.

"Thanks," I say quietly and swallow the lump in my throat.

"Seriously, you should have a ladies' night here." Maci is still pressing the issue, and I raise my head. "I'll help. We'll talk to the managers during the week and see what we can set up."

"Oh my gosh, what about before Valentine's Day?" Izzy almost bounces on her feet. "Bull Creek is full of men shopping at the last minute. We could make it a couples thing!"

Their excitement over my new plan is exactly the support I need. These two are as much my sisters as Lily is. They may not know every gritty detail of my teen years, but they'd go through hell and back with me, just as I would for them.

"Ok," I finally agree.

Izzy and Maci grin at each other smugly.

My stomach does a weird topsy turvy maneuver, and I shove it away. I need a distraction.

It's odd that no one has come up to our table while we've chatted. Nick and Sutton have been carrying on a conversation, and a few people have made their way over to talk with one or both of the guys and then headed off, but no one has talked to Maci, Izzy, or me.

Granted, Maci and Sutton are obviously together. But the other three of us at the table aren't spoken for. And if my skirt gets any shorter, I'll be giving the goods away for free.

This town isn't that big. Whispers of Maci having to defend herself on her property last fall spread like wildfire. She was never charged, because it was quite obviously self-defense, but small towns love their tea, and hearing that a local's granddaughter had a one-night-stand turn stalker got the gossip mill flowing. It made finding out that her estranged father is President of The Falcons MC small news.

Then again, I've never heard any grumblings about the local motorcycle club before. Not until her stalker, Colt, came around.

I'm beginning to wonder if it's not Maci's situation that's caused my dry spell, but my proximity to the two muscular men I'm often grouped with.

"I need another drink!" I call out abruptly.

Maci and Izzy nod in agreement and begin to follow as I twist my hair over my shoulder. This hat was a bad idea. It's hot as shit in here with all these people, no matter how exposed my skin is.

Maci gives Sutton a kiss, but just before we walk away, Nick touches her shoulder and says something she nods to. At the bar, Maci orders our round from Tawny, the barely legal bartender, and motions to Nick. Tawny steals a quick look in his direction and sets to work on our drinks.

"What was that?" I nudge Maci in the ribs.

She scowls back at me. "Why do you always go for my damn ribs?"

I cover my grin quickly and cross my arms, waiting for a response to my question.

"Nick got our round."

I huff and lean my back against the bar, scanning the pickings for tonight.

"What?" Izzy asks, her eyebrows scrunching together.

"I need to get laid," I mutter.

She laughs, somehow hearing me over the ruckus of the bar patrons. I search the room for a willing participant. A willing participant that won't make me want to chew my own arm off in the morning.

I'm surprised none of the Falcons' members are here tonight. Truthfully, I prefer the bad boys to the cowboys that frequent The Spur, even more so than the surface cowboys—the ones who are all hat and no cattle, or however the saying goes.

I never told Maci, but I would've taken Colt up on any offer he made the night we met him if she hadn't. It's not that I couldn't tell her as much, but after he turned into a stalker and then attacked her at her grandmother's house, it no longer seemed appropriate to say. Not that I usually bother myself with appropriate.

Colt's friend, Pete, on the other hand, is sweet and fun and a decent dancer. Even though he's one of the Falcons, he's no bad boy.

"Dressed?" Tawny holds an unopened beer bottle in her hand. Nick's Dos Equis.

"Yes," I say, without thinking. Maci raises an eyebrow at me, but I don't acknowledge the look, turning back to the packed room.

"I didn't realize how Texan that is until we were in Hawaii," Izzy interjects.

"What is?" Maci asks.

"A dressed beer," Izzy explains.

"I do think it's mostly regional," I confirm.

"My brother ordered one while we were on vacation, and another tourist looked at him like he had three heads. Apparently, it's seen as feminine in some parts."

I snort. "I doubt Nick would give a shit if anyone thinks he's feminine based off his drink preference."

I swipe my drink as Tawny pushes the set our way. Maci claims hers and Sutton's, and Izzy reaches for hers, leaving Nick's. The lime wedge sticks out of the top with a heavy amount of salt covering the rim. I roll my eyes and grab the bottle off the bar, heading back to our table.

"Thanks," I say, lifting my drink and handing Nick his beer.

He smiles and opens his mouth to say something, but his eyebrows dip for the briefest moment and he looks back at me. "Did I say dressed?" He waggles the beer at me.

"No. I just knew," I say, shrugging.

"Mm." He removes the lime, squeezing the juice into the bottle.

"You know, they make some with lime and salt flavor, so you don't have to do all of *that*." I raise my hand, gesturing to his own movements.

He maintains eye contact as he takes a long pull.

I sip from my whiskey and soda, studying him as he swallows. Maybe a romp in the hay with Nick is exactly what I need. Sure, he's not my type, but he can't be any worse than what I've tried. Then again, I don't see women hanging all over him, so maybe he is. And it's not like I could ditch him after, since we're around each other so often these days.

Izzy grabs my arm, breaking the connection. "Come on! It's 'Copperhead Road!' How did you not hear it starting?"

CHAPTER 4

NICK

Saturday morning is humid, too warm for January. Texas is already hinting at leaving winter behind. I head out for a run anyway, popping my earbuds in and turning on a mix playlist. I enjoy the town coming to life, so the volume is only up halfway.

Most of my days are spent outside. Aside from checking hunting and fishing licenses, and other tasks surrounding wildlife conservation, I also assist other local law enforcement during natural disasters and serving warrants. I make a point to keep in shape to make that easier. Plus, it's a natural high I enjoy.

Today, I take the long way through town, weaving along the trail that follows the river. It's dotted with ducks (and duck shit), a few other runners, and the occasional mom with a stroller.

My shirt sticks to my back as soon as I leave the house. By the time I'm behind the library, my halfway point, I'm drenched. The steady thrum of my feet, the varied songs, and morning bird calls create their own symphony as I run, my heavy breathing accompanying me as I wind my way through town.

At River Road, I come off the trail and jog up to the street to run back along Main. The rising sun slowly casts shadows along one side of the street which hasn't fully come alive yet. The busiest place is The Filling Station, a coffee shop that carries Texas-grown coffee surrounded by gasoline memorabilia. The bold aroma wafting out of the doors as I pass is invigorating, even if I don't partake. I've never been a fan of coffee or energy drinks; water is my drink of choice. And sweet tea. There's no denying sweet tea.

"Morning, Nick." A woman's voice breaks through the bustle of the coffee shop patrons. I stop short, searching the shadows outside The Filling Station for the source. Payton is tucked under the large awning with a hot coffee in hand.

"Oh. Hey, Payton. How are you?" Like a good portion of the population, I've known Payton most of my life. We dated a couple of times after high school, but nothing ever came of it. Even if I hadn't left for college at the end of the summer, me and Payton weren't a long-term thing. I could never picture her in my world, or me in hers.

"Doing well." She speaks slowly, brushing a strand of blonde hair back from her perfectly-made-up face, before taking a step forward. She reminds me of the snake in *The Jungle Book*—intense but off base. "How about you?"

I shouldn't have stopped. "Good, good. Just, uh, finishing up my workout." With an earbud in hand, I gesture to the sidewalk ahead of me.

"Looks good on you," she says suggestively, making no attempt to hide her perusal of my body. "I can't wait to see you at the auction."

Ugh. I forgot all about that. "Uh, thanks."

"We should get together so I can give you all of the details." She takes another confident step forward.

"Wish I could, but I have to get into work. Just shoot me an email. Have a good day. Gotta run." I shove the earbud back in and jog off before she can respond.

Two blocks later, I turn left, enjoying the shade from the mature Texas Mountain Laurels that line the road on both sides. Come spring, their vibrant purple blooms emit a sweet, grape scent, which is kind of perfect for the sno-cone stand at the end of the street.

I cut across into a parking lot and jog along the storefronts of the shopping center. Most are still dark inside, but one—Sadie's—has lights on.

Damn, I missed her going in.

I'm not stalking Leah, I remind myself, because I feel like such a fucking creep.

I decided to extend my run one day and happened to see her opening the store. Then it became a habit to run this way. She doesn't have anyone looking out for her, except her two best friends. They're a tight trio and a lot of fun. On the few occasions we've all hung out together, we've all gotten along great. But I'll never forget Leah's almost-limp body the night we met.

I couldn't believe the biker she was hanging out with let her get that fucking wasted. There was no way Maci was getting her out to the car in one piece, so I stepped in. It wasn't that big of a deal. Buckling her in was a safety issue. And obviously if her head was bouncing around she'd risk damage or a headache, so I leaned her against the doorframe. Tucking her hair behind her ear was probably unnecessary.

And creepy.

God, I hope she doesn't remember that. Maybe that's why she always eyes me like she's uncomfortable when we make eye contact.

I make a sharp U in the parking lot and head back the way I came. Just as I pass the store again, I peek. It's a compulsion.

She's there. Reaching for something housed near the front window. Her jeans hug her ass and her white button-down tucks into her pants with a bold belt cinched at her waist. Her dark hair is loose and untamed. She looks fresh and fashionably professional, so different from last night when she was all but on display for the entire town.

It's hard not to look. She's a knockout in either scenario. But Sutton mentioning that she's got family shit and that her drinking may or may not be increasing doesn't make it easier for me to leave her alone.

She deserves for people to look out for her, too. Even if it's not really my place. She's a bit wild, but a fierce friend. A good one. And when shit went sideways with Maci, Leah was the one who held it together. So despite what she shows to everyone, I know there's someone more than capable inside.

My steps have slowed as I watch her. The moment is too intense—it feels like spying.

I turn back to my path heading home and increase my pace until it hurts, blocking out everything else.

Another perk of being a game warden is making your own hours. To an extent. I still have to check in with the captain of the region, but as long as I get my shit done, no one's worried about me. Which is great, because my dad scheduled a tee time for him, my brother, and me at the club this afternoon.

Bull Creek is small, but not small enough that we don't have a country club. It doubles as a resort, and my parents have had a membership there since I was little.

We all arrive in the parking lot around the same time. My dad shakes my hand. "Hey, son. How's work?"

It's always this way with him. Work and the club. My brother, Eli, and I had a fairly traditional upbringing, and he's made my parents proud with his business degree and starting the next generation of Fosters alongside his pretty wife.

Not that my parents aren't proud of me. They are. But my mom doesn't have to say out loud that she wants her oldest son to have a wife and babies for me to know it. And my dad doesn't have to say that he thinks I should've gone into business for me to know that, too.

"Work is good, Dad. I spent a little time out and about earlier, actually."

"Mm," he hums, which is code for "You wouldn't have to work Saturdays if you had gotten a business degree." Except that's not really true either. But since we don't say it, we don't have to bother arguing about it.

"Nicky!" my brother yells happily with a clap to my shoulder.

We couldn't look more different if we tried. While I got my father's facial features, my light hair and eyes came courtesy of my mother, whereas Eli got my father's dark hair and mother's facial features. The dark eyes are all his, though.

"Hey, Eli. How's the family?"

Elijah beams. "They're great. Peter Parker is walking now." The fact that my brother and his wife named their son Peter Parker Foster and insist on calling him by his first and middle name negates any superiority he may think he has over me. Not that he's ever acted that way. Despite my parents' attention to his work and family, he's never been anything but supportive of me.

"That's an exciting time," my father agrees half-heartedly. "How's the business?"

And that's the topic we stay on for nearly the entire four hours we're on the green. I respect what my brother and father do, but if I have to listen to much more about stocks, mergers, or the like, my ears are going to bleed.

When we reach the eighteenth hole, my mom calls. "Hello, dear," my father answers. "Oh yes, we're on the last hole." He pulls the phone away from his mouth a little but manages to inadvertently turn on the speakerphone, evident by the increased white noise coming from his hand. "Boys, your mother would like to meet us for dinner."

"I didn't plan on staying after, so you've got me in this," I remark, gesturing to my shorts and polo. The club has a few restaurant options, each with their own dress code.

Dad waves me off. "Oh, that's fine. We'll eat at the bar and grill."

My mother's voice echoes loudly. "Oh, I wish you wouldn't call it that, David."

My dad jumps at her volume. "That's what it is, Christine." He flusters trying to turn off the speakerphone.

"Erica and I have plans," Eli says.

My father relays the message and bobs his head while my mother speaks. "Ok, we'll finish here and meet you. Ok. Bye dear." He slides the cell phone back into his pocket. "Your mother would like you to send the family our love," he says to Eli.

After four hours on the course, another two hours solo with my parents is not how I wanted to end this night. I love them. I respect them. But I prefer small doses. It's no wonder my final hole is two over par.

CHAPTER 5

LEAH

My shift on Saturday is slow. January is often sleepy after the rush of the holidays. Plus there's a stock show two counties over, and being one of the last events before the annual championship, it draws a large crowd. It's amazing how much a turkey, pig, or steer can go for when ranchers are celebrating the students who've raised them over the last year.

I busy myself rearranging displays and marking down a few items. As a privately-owned business, our store doesn't have the overstock issues department stores do, so our clearance items are few and far between. When I was younger and money was tighter, I loved grabbing those pieces when I could. Especially because I could stack my employee discount. Now, I find myself shopping elsewhere or creating my own items.

The quiet gives me uninterrupted time to consider my conversation with Izzy and Maci. Although I was the one to bring up jewelry design as a business, I'm not convinced it will take off. My pieces always felt authentically me. Will anyone even want them?

This show could be an epic flop.

I'm still mulling over the work it would entail when I pull into my driveway and find my sister sitting in her driver's seat with my niece and nephew playing in the yard.

"Leah!" Roman cries, launching his sturdy four-year-old body into my legs when I get out of my car.

"Hey bud," I say with a ruffle to his dark hair. Annoyance creeps up on me. I hide that from him, because it's not his fault my sister is the most irresponsible person I know. Lily only shows up if she wants me to watch the kids or she needs money. I already know what's coming.

Savannah squeezes my legs as hard as her chubby toddler arms can, and I scoop her up for a big kiss. "Hey Banana. I missed you," I tell her quietly.

She chews a little finger as her unkempt, sandy hair falls into her face.

Lily climbs out of the car, wearing tattered jeans and a plain T-shirt. She has a full face of heavy makeup and her hair is straightened stiff.

"I didn't know you were coming," I say pointedly.

"My phone got shut off," she says dismissively.

I don't add 'again' to her statement.

"Leah, can I check your mail?" Roman looks up at me with big, round eyes and a hopeful smile.

"Sure, bud." He loves my mailbox on the sidewalk, unlike the shared room of boxes at my sister's apartment.

Lily looks anywhere but at me. "I need to work, and Mom won't watch them." She likes to put her problems onto everyone else, never solving things herself. Truthfully though, in the very unlikely chance I ever have children, our mom would be the absolute last person I'd ever ask to care for them. I lived that hell, and the fact that I made it through was all my doing and none of hers.

"You need to start scheduling these things with me, Lily. I have a life." I re-situate Savannah on my hip.

"Well, I would've if I had known Mom was gonna bail." She avoids eye contact as she increases her animation.

"Ok, but did you schedule with her?" It's hard to know who's in the wrong on this one. It's not uncommon for our mom to be too fucked up to be worth a shit, even after agreeing to do something.

Lily continues to avoid eye contact. "She knows when I work." She says it as if her schedule is set, but my sister's shifts at the gentleman's club fluctuate regularly.

Roman skips over, offering a small stack of mail to me.

"Thanks, bud. You hungry?" I know better than to assume they've been fed.

Roman bounces up and down. "Yes. Can we have grilled cheese?" I love how he can remind me of the simplest pleasures in life.

"Of course!" I grin down at him before tickling Savannah on her round belly. "Are you hungry too?" She doesn't remove the finger gently held between her teeth as she nods with a grin.

With my free hand, I yank my massive purse from inside my car and settle it on my shoulder. It's a patchwork leather and suede weekender bag with a wide strap and a small amount of fringe on one side. It feels like something Lainey Wilson might use, and I'm extremely proud to say I created it.

"What time will you be done?" I ask, turning to my sister.

Lily climbs into her car. "You know there's no way for me to plan that. Some nights are good; some nights are slow." The way she talks about men ogling her and sometimes attempting to grope is so flippant.

I don't think badly of her for her choices, though I do wish she'd choose something more stable for her family. Somewhere she can grow. But that's a reflection of her, not the job. There are plenty of women in her industry that make steady incomes for their family, and I'm reminded again of all the ways that my sister lacks drive.

I hitch my purse farther up. "Just let them stay over. But you *have* to be here by eight in the morning."

Lily slams the driver door closed and speaks to me through her open window. "You don't work on Sunday."

This bitch. "Sometimes I do. Not that I expect you to keep track. But like I said at the start of this conversation, I have a life." I don't waste my time waiting for a useful answer; I know my words go in one ear and out the other with her. "Come on, Roman. Let's go eat."

Neither Roman nor Savannah say goodbye to their mom as we head in. I squeeze my niece tighter in my arms. It's hard to admit to myself that they're so used to her dropping them at a moment's notice, they don't even bat an eye when she leaves.

I dangle the keys in front of Roman and he snatches them happily, working to fit the right one into the lock while I hold open the storm door. He giggles proudly when it opens and pushes inside, turning to offer me the key ring back. I drop my bag on the entry table and set Savannah on the floor.

"Can we play with Smokey?" Roman spins in a circle, searching for the ragdoll cat.

"He's probably sleeping on the bed in your room, but we need to feed him. Maybe when he's done he'll want to play a little."

The kids run off to my spare room and their soft, sing-song voices indicate I was right about where Smokey was resting.

Leaving the kitchen light off, I pull a hard seltzer from the fridge and take a long pull, holding the watermelon-flavored drink in my mouth longer than necessary before swallowing. The interaction moments ago still has my entire body tense as hell.

Light filters in through the large window above the sink and glows against the far wall as the sun sinks lower. I don't need this massive old country kitchen. It's not like I ever do any entertaining here. The linoleum floor is peeling, and there are chips on the Formica counters. The stark white cabinets could use a fresh coat of paint, and a natural patina covers the iron handles and drawer pulls. A typical, dated rental in Bull Creek.

But it's mine. My mom can't lose it to a habit, and my sister can't bail on it. Granted, she wants to move in, but there's no way I'm letting her. I'm surprised she didn't mention it today—how easy it would be for her to work if she had a built-in babysitter. More like how easy it would be for her to disappear at a moment's notice.

I take another long pull from the seltzer before flipping on the light. Giggles echo down the hall as I fill Smokey's bowl and give it a little shake. A loud thump and quick, soft feet on the floor precede him entering the kitchen with a loud meow. He follows me into the laundry room off the backside of the kitchen and hops onto the dryer where I set his bowl—a habit that stuck from when Roman was a baby. I give him a quick scratch behind an ear before washing up and making dinner.

When Lily does not arrive at my house by eight the next morning, I'm anything but surprised. She also doesn't arrive by nine. I'd call, but her damn phone is off.

What if there was a real emergency?

My agitation grows as the minutes tick past ten. I was hoping that giving her a false deadline would result in her showing up at a somewhat normal time.

When she finally rolls up, Roman and Savannah have had French toast and eggs, yogurt, three types of berries, animal crackers, and apples with peanut butter. Her brakes whine her approach and I meet her, standing behind the glass storm door as she climbs out of her car.

I'm overcome with a sense of wrongness. Of frustration.

Two years separate us. When I was halfway through high school, she was having her first baby. Neither of our parents did shit to help her, both useless in their own right.

Mom had sent Lily to live with our dad on the other side of the country a few months prior and they weren't speaking. When our dad found out Lily was pregnant at seventeen, and he and his wife realized she wasn't going to abort the baby, he refrained from shoving Lily onto the Greyhound back to Texas. But soon after she gave birth, they sent them both away.

You'd think, after being a teen mom herself, that our mother would've tried harder to teach us sexual education. Instead, she went for abstinence only. Since it worked so well for her.

Lily was happy when she came home with Jade. But she was young, and what she expected motherhood to be and what it was like to be a teen parent, with no education, couldn't have been more night and day. Our mom didn't offer much help, aside from suggesting a teaspoon of Amaretto when Jade would cry for over an hour.

Eventually, Lily decided that she couldn't provide a life for her. The adoption was complete by the time Jade was six months old. It was an open arrangement, but I'm not sure my sister has ever seen her baby girl.

AMANDA MARQUARDT

"I'm so fucking tired," Lily says, pushing past me into the house and throwing herself onto the couch. She doesn't sound tired at all. "Last night was so busy." Her clean hair and fresh eye makeup give away her recent shower. Good for her, even if it's outside of her norm to be so cleaned up.

"You're late."

"Yeah, my phone is off so I couldn't call," she huffs, as if the same tired excuse somehow negates her of any responsibilities.

"Lily, I was clear about time."

She hops up from the couch. "I don't know what you want me to do. Roman, Vannah," she calls, heading for the door.

They come out from playing and follow her path. My heart aches.

"Hugs," I say crouching down, and squeeze my niece and nephew tightly. Angry tears prick at my eyes. They don't deserve this from their mother. They deserve a mom who would move mountains for them. A mom who wants to be better for them. To give them everything.

It takes everything in me to let go. My heart is heavy with guilt that I haven't done more.

"Please call first next time. I'm happy to help when I know."

"Yep." Lily walks out without another glance.

Chapter 6

Leah

After Lily and the kids leave, I get changed for brunch at Maci's. We never need a real reason to hang out, but today is all about the upcoming nuptials between her and Sutton.

At the wrought iron gate, I key in the entry code. Izzy and I used to have to call up to The Big House to get in, where Sutton's parents live. They soon realized we come over so frequently, it made more sense for us to have alternate access. Sutton and Maci aren't the only package deal. She came to him with Izzy and I nearly attached to her.

Liv and Izzy's cars are parked in the drive when I pull in. Normally, Izzy and I carpool but I told her to come without me since I anticipated Lily would be late. At Nana's I never knocked, but I do at The Big House. Can't guarantee I will once Maci and Sutton's house is built, though. They'll just have to get used to me entering when I've been invited over.

Liv opens the door.

"You're the teacher, not the teacher's pet. Why are you answering the door?" I grin and hug her.

Her cheeks redden and she squeezes me briefly. "I just happened to be closest."

My steps feel lighter heading into the dining room. I can never get enough time with my girls. "The party has arrived!"

"Party's over. You missed it because you're perpetually late." Izzy steps out of the kitchen, blocking my path forward with a wide smile displaying her pearly whites. She has a serious thing for teeth health.

"Blame it on Lily," I grumble.

"Oh, you should've brought Roman and Banana." Maci knocks Izzy out of the way with a hip and hugs me with her arms extended, apparently having something on her hands.

"I didn't even think about that." I set the insulated bag I brought onto the counter, removing a fruit salad and cool whip.

"Aw, you didn't have to bring anything for later," Maci says, eyeing the cool whip and then laughs loudly at her innuendo.

"Only if I get to play, too," I say with a wink at Liv.

Her mouth drops open, maybe mortified, but smiling at least. I'm not sure she'll ever get used to our sexual jokes. If anyone will draw her out, it'll be me, but I haven't pushed the issue too hard since she's just started hanging out with us consistently.

"No dice," Maci says, washing her hands. "Sutton says no sharing."

"Sure, it was Sutton's idea," Izzy says, organizing trays on the round table in the dining room.

Maci pretends to think it over. "Ok, maybe I told him I'd cut off his cock before I share it with anyone."

"Jesus, Maci!" Liv squeals, her cheeks turning crimson as her eyes dart around the kitchen and living room. "His parents!"

Maci laughs loudly again. "They aren't here. I'm not that brazen. They're visiting Sammi and her family in Dallas."

Sutton's sister, Sammi, took us all in stride when she and her little family came for Thanksgiving. Her sweet baby, Viviane, played well with Savannah. I could see her being a strong member of our group if they lived closer.

"Well, let's eat and get down to business." Izzy snaps her fingers at us. The rest of us exchange faux annoyed expressions before we make our way to the table and gorge ourselves on delicious food.

When we're all stuffed, we start in on the wedding details.

Maci beams at us. "I think it goes without saying that you three are incredibly important to me. I wanted a clever way to ask you to be my bridesmaids, but then I decided you have no choice. So you're it."

Liv smiles and grips Maci's hand on the table.

"Whatever you need, honey." Izzy has replaced her plate with a notebook. She runs a hand through her blonde hair, fluffing her beachy waves. She's a gorgeous rodeo pageant queen and still the kindest person I've ever known. I'm not sure where Maci or I would be without her. For all her analytical prowess, she's fun, and friendly, and spirited. I always thought she'd be the first to get married. Life has a funny way of working out sometimes.

"You couldn't keep me from standing next to you if you tried," I challenge, crossing my arms over my chest as I settle against the back of the chair.

"Good. Sammi will also be a bridesmaid," Maci adds.

"That's so sweet," Liv says softly. While Maci is bold and takes no shit, Liv is all heart, like a quiet anchor. But their relationship doesn't have cracks—at least none that I've ever seen.

"Now that that's settled, as much as I love you, there's also probably a crazy amount of work. So, that's why I need two Maids of Honor." Maci presses her lips together to hide her continued smile, eyes bouncing between Izzy and me.

Izzy smiles proudly. "Honored, honey."

I nod with what feels like a vacant smile. Maid of Honor. I don't know a damn thing about weddings. I'm pretty sure Maids of Honor are supposed to organize them. I was thinking I'd only be here for moral support, but I'm not letting her in on that. I shove my doubts away as best I can.

"We're planning a pretty quick wedding," Maci adds.

"Unless you want your friends to bake in the Texas summer, you'd have to mean really quick," Izzy says. She grips her pen tightly as she stares at Maci with bated breath.

"Probably just after school's out," Maci admits sheepishly, her eyes darting to Liv.

"I beg your pardon?" Izzy's head juts forward on her neck. "That's what, four months?"

"Are you pregnant?" I tease. Maci gives me a nasty look, despite the joke.

"No, *Stephanie*, I'm not pregnant." Her dig, using her uptight mother's name, makes me return the disgusted face.

"How rude," I say in my best Stephanie Tanner impression.

Liv snickers. "Four months isn't *that* fast."

"Seriously," Maci agrees, giving her cousin an appreciative glance. "And we don't need a ton of people there," she adds, studying the wooden table with a wistful smile. "Sutton already told the guys."

"Nick's going to be his Best Man, right?" Izzy is steadily writing notes.

"Yes."

My heart drops into my gut. I always knew I'd be a part of Maci's wedding one day, and I'm honored she's asked me to be a Maid of Honor. Even though I have no fucking clue what to do with that role, I'll work that out later. Now my primary concern is the proximity I'll be forced into with Nick. And his ever-watchful gaze.

"Ok, so who's walking with who?" I twist my hair over my shoulder.

Maci tilts her head side to side, considering. "I think it could be fun if Nick walks with you *and* Izzy." A small relief. "Shane will probably walk with Sammi."

There's a tiny exhale from my left, and I sneak a peek at Liv, whose eyes widen in surprise when I look her way. Maci continues, "And Liv with Casey."

"We need to get you an appointment for dress shopping," Izzy says anxiously, whipping out her phone from her purse.

"Are we going wild for your bachelorette party?" I ask with an evil grin.

Izzy rolls her eyes at me—it's basically her favorite pastime.

"I don't think we're going to have separate parties," Maci replies, shaking her head at me.

I pull my mouth into another disgusted expression. "Why?"

She shrugs. "Just not our thing." Her eyes pop wide. "Oh, I just thought of something! The Lodge won't be open just yet. We should use it as a trial run and all stay there!"

Sutton recently acquired the property next to his family's ranch in a massive expansion. His parents have taken a step back, letting Sutton and Maci, along with the staff, map out its future. The Lodge is a grand, rustic house on the new property they're planning to use as accommodation for guests.

"Ok, but let us decide the menu with the chef. We'll cover the night," I counter. Maci doesn't get a chance to respond.

"I love that idea!" Izzy adds.

Liv nods. "It's the perfect test run, but still casual like you two."

"Ok, so where are you wanting to dress shop?" Izzy turns the conversation back to scheduling. "In the city? There are a ton of dress shops on the Riverwalk." She looks at Maci with an excited gleam in her bright blue eyes.

Maci stalls. "Probably not."

Izzy's smile vanishes as she visibly deflates before us, her shoulders and chest sinking. "What?"

"It might seem silly, but I'm trying to build a bigger presence here. For the ranch and for Southern Grace Photography. It just feels right to put money into the community of Bull Creek, not the city."

"It's *your* dress." Izzy's tone makes it clear that she doesn't agree with the choice.

"Are you inviting your mom to go dress shopping?" Liv asks.

"I hadn't considered that." Maci's eyes go vacant. "I'll think on it. I would like Sammi and Andi to come, if they want."

"I'm sure they will." Liv's voice is almost a coo. It's no wonder she became a kindergarten teacher.

I change the topic again. "What's the plan for the bridesmaids?" I'm not afraid of dressing up, and I trust Maci won't make us wear something ridiculous. It's too bad black isn't in for bridesmaids.

"When we go dress shopping I'll pick a color and y'all can choose a dress style you like from that. Sutton and I talked about it, and we're going to have the ceremony outdoors at Nopal Vista," she says, referring to the spot where she and Sutton are building their home on the ranch. "I just want y'all to be comfortable and everything to feel natural. We'll probably use a lot of cactus and wildflower elements, so a peach or sage color." It's the most she's said all at once about the upcoming wedding, and it's heartwarming. She should be excited. This day should be everything she wants. Sutton is an excellent partner for her and they're going to have a beautiful marriage.

She straightens. "Oh! Speaking of dresses, do you think Lily would be ok with Roman and Savannah being in the wedding?" Her question is hopeful.

The idea makes me smile. "They'd be adorable. I don't think she'd care normally, but she's mad at me right now." I try to keep my tone light, not to derail the subject at hand.

Maci purses her lips in a pout that's half concerned and half thoughtful. "I was thinking Banana and Vivi could wear the same style dresses as flower girls, and Roman could be the ring bearer."

"You're gonna trust him to carry the rings?" Izzy asks, her eyes widening in disbelief.

"They'll be fake." Maci waves her off with a laugh.

"There's no way Lily will go for buying a dress," I interject, "but I'll make sure it's taken care of."

Liv rubs my arm. She's starting to give Izzy a run for her money as the mother hen of the group, but I appreciate her kindness. There's a lot flying around right now and she seems to be picking up all the emotional tidbits and leaning into them.

Midday turns into afternoon before we clean up and call it quits. Air kisses go all around and then I head home to Smokey for some quiet.

CHAPTER 7

LEAH

Me:

I need to get laid.

Izzy:

Oh, so that's what's up with your attitude.

Me:

Nothing is up with my attitude.

Maci:

Didn't you go out with that firefighter we met at Granger's last week or something?

Me:

Firefighter cadet.

And yeah, I did. But it wasn't much to write home about.

Izzy:

They make toys for that.

Me:

You would know.

Maci:

Oh look, the attitude Izzy mentioned.

Me:

>rolling eyes emoji<

You guys suck.

I throw my phone onto the couch next to me. Smokey meows and jumps onto the coffee table, sauntering across and hopping into my lap. He bumps my chin with a purr and curls up, while I alternate between scratching and massaging his neck.

I need to be working on jewelry for the show—which is yet to be scheduled—but I feel like I downed a case of energy drinks. I don't know if it's the nerves of the show, which we still haven't discussed with management at The Spur, or something else.

Lily has shown up unannounced with the kids twice more since Saturday. Maybe I feel like there's electricity in my veins because she could show up again today.

It feels cliche, but my spirit still feels caged in lately, like my wings are clipped. Getting some fresh air, paired with some creativity, should help. I kiss Smokey's head before setting him on the cushion next to me. He lets out a displeased meow and contemplates following me, but drops his dark head instead and closes his eyes again.

I'm suddenly thankful for the beautiful supply box that Maci and Izzy got me for Christmas. It holds an ample amount of my jewelry-making supplies and tools. I double check that everything I need is there and head out to the car. If I'm not here, Lily can't drop her problems on me.

Just thinking it makes me feel guilty. I don't consider Savannah or Roman to be problems. I love them immensely. I just want her to start taking responsibility. And I don't know how to force that without letting them down.

It's freezing at the lake; the surrounding tables and playground are desolate, a welcome isolation. I place my items on a picnic table in the dormant grass and set to work in peace. Before long, my hands ache from the cold, and squeezing the tiny pliers is painful.

My phone buzzes in my pocket. It's a good excuse to set everything down and tuck a hand into my jacket's warmth while I check the message.

Izzy:

> **Let's stop by The Spur this afternoon to talk about the show.**

> **It should be slow since it's a Sunday.**

Me:

> **Yes ma'am.**

Maci:

> **I can't make it today, but keep me posted.**

"Ma'am, do you have a license for those pliers?"

I jolt from the unexpected voice behind me and drop my phone to the ground, whipping around before my brain has time to compute that it's Nick.

Nick, who I've never run into prior to meeting him through Maci. And now here he is, at the deserted lake in the middle of the day. How did I miss his truck pulling in?

"You scared the shit out of me!" I cry, standing up as if I plan to charge him.

His hands raise in surrender. "I didn't mean to startle you. I didn't realize you were so deep in thought. I'm sorry." He smiles softly at me, his eyes questioning as he gauges my response.

My heart rate returns to normal as he leans down to retrieve my dropped phone.

"Sorry, I shouldn't have yelled at you." I scan the parking lot and boat ramp. There's still no one else around besides me. And Nick. "What are you doing out here, anyway?"

"I could ask you the same thing. This isn't exactly a crafting space." He waves his empty hand at the picnic table and extends my phone to me with the other. His eyes are bright, and he works his jaw back and forth.

"I'm not—" I stop, realizing the joke, and cross my arms, tucking my phone underneath. "Ok, that's fair. I'm hiding from someone."

His stance tightens as the energy shifts. He crosses his arms, his biceps protesting against his sandy-brown, long-sleeved uniform shirt. It's a shame it's not blue. Navy blue is his color. Maybe it's the combination with his light eyes and hair, but it's just *his*. But the uniform, it's not bad.

"Not that kind of hiding," I say, laughing. "My sister keeps trying to pin me with babysitting without calling, but I need to get some work done. So I decided to get away from my house."

He frowns. "She doesn't understand what 'no' means?"

I cock my head in thought. "I've never actually told her no." *Not on this.*

"But you want to." It's a half question. His mouth tightens again.

"I don't mind watching my niece and nephew. I want her to be able to work and provide for them. I just wish she was more responsible about it."

He nods slowly then shifts his weight. "I'm checking fishing licenses."

A smile tugs each side of my mouth. "I don't see anyone fishing." The intensity of his eyes hasn't receded, and I know he's curious about my situation, even if he isn't asking.

His boyish grin appears. "You wouldn't. The boats go farther out. I'm actually meeting another warden at the next boat ramp so we can get out on the water. Just happened to see you when I was driving through."

"It's kind of a dick move, if you think about it."

"Which part?" Amusement plays across his eyes.

"Fishing. Especially catch and release."

He waits, and I drop my eyes to study his muscular arms. I don't see how anyone could find him scary, even with the bulky Kevlar vest beneath his sand-colored shirt. Everyone has to know he's a giant heart in a cage of muscle, right?

The cuffs have to be for show. He's probably never even been in a scuffle.

"You don't like fishing?" he finally asks.

"It's rude." I raise my eyebrows in challenge. "They're just minding their own fucking business, and then you come teasing them with a seafood dinner. *Then* when they accept, you stab them through the damn mouth! 'Ha ha! Gotcha, motherfucker!'" I throw my hands out in a big, wavy gesture.

Nick breaks into laughter, nearly doubling over. When he stands fully, his face is red and he wipes at his eyes. "I've never heard that interpretation before, and I've heard a lot."

"I can't be the only one to think it's an asshole move." I cross my arms again and jut my hip out.

"Maybe not. Just haven't heard the particular viewpoint." He shakes his head and I shrug. The quiet between us stretches a second too long, and I sense there's more he wants to say, but his expression changes. "I'll let you get back to it." He nods to the table, and I get the feeling he's giving me the professional version of himself. "See you around, Leah."

"Bye, Nick." I don't look away as he walks back to his truck. He fills out his uniform pants nicely. Men shouldn't look so good in desert-sand brown.

His truck faces the picnic table where I'm stationed and he makes eye contact as he climbs in. I turn on my heel and plop down on the bench. Whatever it is that my body thinks it needs from him, it needs to let go of it. Sleeping with people in the friend circle is off limits. All it would do is make shit awkward for everyone.

As anticipated, when Izzy and I head into The Spur, there are only a few people inside. Music plays lower than I've ever heard; the mounted televisions display a few football games and an old fantasy movie. A man with brassy blonde hair and wild blue eyes fills the screen.

"Different place in here during the day," Izzy mumbles as we make our way to the bar.

The only person behind the long counter is the manager, Gideon. Tawny and the other staff must have the afternoon off.

Gideon reminds me of Adam Brody with his short, dark curls and deep brown eyes. We've only spoken a time or two, and it's never been anything serious.

"Leah, Izzy, how are you?" he says with a wave. "What can I get you?"

"I'll take a water." Izzy slides onto one of the barstools and I sit next to her.

"Whiskey and soda," I add.

When Gideon returns with drinks, Izzy prompts me with a severe nudge. I scrunch my face up at her before turning back to him blankly. "So, how's business?"

He smiles as his eyebrows dip in confusion. "Fairly consistent."

"Good." I press my lips together and nod. Flirting, I can do. Small talk, not so much.

Izzy huffs and leans forward, pulling Gideon's attention to her. "You know, Leah, Maci, and I were discussing a ladies' night. Leah is opening her own jewelry business and we'd like to host a show here."

Gideon grins, his eyes scanning us one after the other as he processes. "How would it work?"

"It wouldn't be ticketed. Anyone could come. We can put together fliers." Izzy pulls her planner from her purse. "Maybe the week before Valentine's?"

Gideon's eyes come back to me, assessing my leather earrings. "Jewelry like your earrings?"

"Yeah. These are mine." I manage to avoid the compulsion to touch them. "The focus will be on some of my larger pieces." I unbutton my wool jacket and slide it off my arms, letting it pool around me in the chair. The gold necklace I'm wearing is wide and thick, falling just above the deep scoop collar of my sweater. Six additional strands dangle straight down, their bases hidden by the soft fabric that they disappear into. "Like this. I have back and arm pieces as well. I'll also have earrings, bracelets, and maybe a few rings."

His eyebrows rise gently, a pleasant smile breaking along his face. "I didn't know you were so talented. I'm no jewelry judge, but they look nice. What kind of help would you need on our end?"

"A stage," Izzy says quickly. "Even if it isn't elevated, something that's outlined or roped off in some way to make it apparent. Lights and music." She has the planner open to February.

I scan the bar area, visualizing what this could look like. Some bars have a dance floor centered in the room, but here it takes up a majority of the left wall, leaving seating in the middle instead. Having models walk to the dance floor would be odd in this case.

"If you could block off the back room so models could enter from there and have the runway come straight to the center of the room, that'd be ideal. Then we'll show off a bit, but we won't bother bar patrons or anyone who would rather dance."

Gideon eyes me again. The wheels are turning behind his brown eyes.

"If it's not the type of event you want here, that's fine. Just say so. It won't hurt my feelings any. I'll still come buy your alcohol and shake my ass on your dance floor."

His mouth pulls into a smirk. "Actually, it sounds like it could draw a crowd that may not normally be around during that time. Mutually beneficial."

"Perfect." Izzy writes in her planner before he's fully agreed. "So, Friday the seventh at 8 p.m.?"

"Sounds good." Gideon wipes the bar top absently. "We have an event on that Saturday, too."

I take a sip of my drink. Stupid tiny straws. "What event?"

"A bachelor auction?" he says, his voice only half sure. "The Chamber of Commerce is raising money for childhood cancer research."

"Who could be on the roster?" Izzy looks repulsed. When was the last time she dated someone in town? Or just someone?

I smirk and take another drink.

Gideon shakes his head. "No idea. That's above my paygrade. It'll be during the day though, and they're taking over the dance floor."

"Poor bastards." I snicker to myself.

CHAPTER 8

NICK

A ll Gussied Up is a one-stop shop for formal wear in Bull Creek. Soon it'll be packed with teens preparing for prom. Sutton informed the groomsmen that Maci is scheduled to get a wedding dress there, but today we have an appointment to pick jackets.

It's hard to imagine Maci and the bridesmaids in full-length gowns, because it's easy to picture them getting snagged on the rugged landscape of the ceremony site they've chosen at Nopal Vista. Thankfully, Maci's no Bridezilla—not that I expected her to be—and they've opted for more casual attire. The groomsmen will be in white button-down shirts and jeans with boots, plus our matching jackets.

The store is empty when we arrive, save the two women behind the counter. I'd guess one to be in her early thirties. She blushes deeply as she scans the four of us. The other is probably in her late fifties and doesn't bother hiding her thoughts.

She fans a hand at her face playfully. "You four don't even need to clean up and you'll do just fine." She smiles wickedly and Casey snickers. Heat creeps into my neck.

Sutton is still in the day's clothes from cattle wrangling, and Shane, Casey, and I are in respective work uniforms. We're quite the picture though.

A cowboy, a sheriff, a police officer, and a game warden. Sounds like the start of a politically incorrect joke.

Sutton extends a hand. "Sutton Strickland."

"You have a lot going on with an expansion and an upcoming wedding." She winks playfully at him, then sets her hand on her hip, looking us over in turn. "I'm Regina—this is my place. That's Caroline."

The younger woman hasn't moved. Her eyes flick erratically between us before settling on Sutton. "I'll grab a few colors for you to look at," she mumbles before hurrying away.

Regina doesn't acknowledge her. "And you're Sheriff Callahan," she continues as her gaze lands on Shane.

"Yes ma'am," he answers with a quick nod.

"I remember when your daddy was sheriff. Stubborn as a bull." Her pursed lips dare him to deny it, continuing to study him over the tiny glasses sitting precariously on the tip of her nose.

"That's still true." Shane isn't one to say much, but he's far from shy. He just chooses his words carefully. His own bride was a bit of a Bridezilla. She was just a zilla in general. I never understood how they ended up together, but I was even more surprised when she bailed.

"Yes it is," Casey, his brother, agrees.

"You must be Casey." The woman looks between them. "Well, you two don't look a bit alike, do you?" Her assessment of them is brief, having already compared Shane's dark hair, dark eyes, and massive build to Casey's light hair, light eyes, and average build.

"There's another one of you, right? A sister? She's not the one getting married, is she?" She looks sharply back to Sutton.

"No, ma'am." Casey speaks first. "That's Erin. She's in Dallas for college."

Regina barely bobs her head at Casey's response before turning to me thoughtfully. "You're the only one I don't know."

"Nick Foster." Her open assessment reminds me just how much I hate to be the center of attention. I dive into a little of my work persona to bring out the charm and lose the discomfort.

"Foster. I think your daddy has our insurance policy," she muses.

"That's likely true."

Already moving on to the next thought, she assesses us as a whole. "Well, it looks like a few of you are going to need to undress some to try on jackets. Or at the very least let us get some measurements. You can't very well slide all of that"—she feigns wiping the whole of my chest and shoulders—"into a dress jacket." Something like an owl hoot, which I think is supposed to be a laugh, bursts from her wide-open mouth and she shakes her head, walking behind the counter.

Caroline, hidden somewhere behind the counter, adds, "We have dressing rooms," as if to cement that we don't actually have to undress for her employer.

Casey snickers again. Shane side-eyes his brother without much of a response.

I like Casey. He's fun. When we were little, he got grouped into events with Shane, Sutton and me when we wouldn't have otherwise wanted him around. At some point the difference in age stopped mattering. Though he never has quite matured.

I turn to check out some of the mannequins in the window, which consist of several staged couples wearing tuxes and ridiculous amounts of white fabric. It's all comically grand.

Considering what a wedding for me would look like feels foreign. I dated more in college because I left Bull Creek. But here, there are so many women

53

that I knew from elementary school up. Women who are aware of my family's money, something I prefer to largely ignore.

Like Payton.

Jesus, that would really be a festival of fabric. I shudder at the thought.

An event like what Sutton and Maci are planning feels natural. Rustic, minimal, outdoors.

Through the window, wild, dark hair catches my eye. Passing cars on Main Street blur between us. Leah locks her white Acura and enters the store she parked in front of. A place that, despite living here my entire life, minus college and the academy, I did not know existed. Beads and Thimbles. Sounds straightforward enough.

Caroline returns with three jackets in tow. She starts telling Sutton about options. A casual glance our way has her cheeks coloring and her eyes widening again, but she forces her attention back to Sutton.

I frown, glancing at Shane and Casey, only to realize that the three of us are standing in an accidental row with wide stances and crossed arms. A straight wall of muscle.

This poor woman.

"Hey, I'll be right back," I call to Sutton.

Sutton checks me and nods, and I slip out the front door. Maybe a little less testosterone will calm the attendant down. At least that's the excuse I come up with as to why I think it's appropriate to chase Leah into this bead store and leave my best friend as he chooses his wedding attire.

The bell dings above my head as I enter.

"Fucking bells." There's no mistaking the gruff language that falls from Leah's mouth. She sounds close and I walk slowly, scanning the aisles to my right where the sound originated.

When I spot her, she's studying two handfuls of stones, her dark hair shielding her face from me. If I speak, I'm going to scare the shit out of her again, and I may take a rock or two to the face. But I also can't creep around without saying something.

"What's your problem with bells?" I keep to the entrance of the aisle just in case she launches projectiles at me.

Her head pops up and her full lips open slightly. "Nick," she breathes in surprise.

A tingle runs down my back. I don't know if it's the sound of my name falling out of her mouth, or the way it's fallen into a small O, but I push the sensation away as quickly as possible.

"What are you doing here? You definitely followed me this time. There are no fishing licenses to check here."

I breathe a laugh. "You got me. Only it's not as sinister as you make it sound." Though if she knew I watch her go into work most mornings, she may think differently. "I was across the street with Sutton and the guys. Jacket fittings." I hike a thumb toward the front door.

Her eyes follow the direction of my hand before returning to me, still not convinced. "Ok. That still doesn't explain why you're standing in front of me."

"We're friends, right?" I ask, as a preamble to my real question.

She gives me a one-sided shrug. "Sure, we're friends." She shifts all the rocks to one hand and pushes her hair to one side.

"I just thought I'd check on you. Last time I saw you, you seemed to be dealing with something."

Her face slackens. "I'm good, thanks," she says, her words tight.

It's the way she's trying to brush me off that tells me she's not good. I don't know Leah well, but character flaw or not, I have a tendency to study people—including her. "Ok. Good. But if you weren't, maybe I could do something to help."

Her mouth pulls into a smirk. She drags her gaze along the wall of rock-filled baskets to her right before slowly bringing her eyes back to me. "How can you help?"

Moving slowly, I begin to close the distance between us. Her hands clench the stones tighter. "Stress relief."

"Stress relief?" she repeats in surprise, and all of the stones fall into the basket dangling from her arm. "Are you propositioning me?"

"What? No!" I can't get the words out fast enough as my face and neck flame.

One of her eyebrows rises. "Cut the shit, Nick. What are you talking about?"

"Running," I explain.

She makes a disgusted face. "Running."

"Yeah, jogging. It's uh . . . a great stress reliever. Endorphins and all." My talk on the benefits of running is usually better, but I'm so flustered from her asking me if I was inviting her to bed that the words come out in a mess.

Leah takes a step forward. The basket almost presses into me as she inquires, "And you do this on purpose?"

"Yes?" She's been closer to me before, but my lungs threaten to seize because she's never looked at me in the coy way she is now.

"Not because something is chasing you," she states.

I huff a laugh, relieved at the broken tension. "No."

"Absolutely not. Hard pass," she says, her tone softening. Even with her face hardened and her arms crossed, the corner of her mouth teases at a smile. It begs me to kiss it.

I clear my throat and step back. "Fair enough. You change your mind, you know where to find me."

After a beat, she challenges, "I don't, actually."

"Sorry?"

"I don't know where to find you," she clarifies, cocking her head to one side as her lips threaten to purse.

My feet stay planted. I can't tell if she's fucking with me or not. She's never flirted with me in the past, and I just made an idiot of myself.

I reach into my front shirt pocket and remove a business card and a pen. It lists my work cell, and I add my personal cell to the bottom. "Here. You need anything, you call me."

She takes it, looking over both numbers. "Hard to believe, but there it is in black and white." She waits for me to take the bait.

"What's that?"

"Game Warden Nick Foster." She leaves her face tilted down but draws her eyes up to look at me through her lashes. "I guess it makes sense, though. You're such a boy scout."

"A boy scout?" I grin and shake my head. "I was never a boy scout."

"I don't believe *that*. Not for a second," she teases, shoving my card into the back pocket of her skin-tight jeans. "You have that whole boy-next-door vibe going on. I can just picture you camping and fishing, getting all of your badges." She gestures over my chest similarly to how Regina did, but it causes electricity to dance over my skin

I smile. "While none of that is true, you can count on me to find you if your wild ass ever gets lost on a hike."

Her laugh sends a spark through my veins. "And you can count on that never happening."

"No?"

"You'd have to pay me a lot of money to go hiking." She turns back to the wall of items, filling her basket with more of the items she was studying.

"You don't like to be outdoors?" I keep my tone neutral.

"Sure, if there's a pool or something. Just sweating my ass off? With big-ass bugs and shit that causes rashes? No, thank you."

"I'm in it daily, and I'm not covered in rashes or attacked by bugs."

She raises her eyebrows skeptically. "Yes, but you're covered from your neck down. And you're carrying thirty pounds worth of gear. It has to be like a swamp in there." She waves at my uniform again. "I hate to sweat. The idea of it trickling down my back or boobs—I don't think so."

The image of anything trickling down the places she's mentioned has me shifting on my feet. *Time to go.* "Fair enough."

She side-eyes me, maybe surprised that I'm not fighting harder.

"I should probably get back. I actually need to get that fitting done. Good to see you." I can't help my clipped tone. Leah has a way of making me feel like I'm crossing boundaries I need to re-establish.

Offering a half wave, half salute, I turn to go.

"Hey, Boy Scout?"

I grin, telling myself not to turn in response but do so anyway. Her hazel eyes are intense as she peers at me.

"Is your favorite color navy blue or green?"

Her question catches me off guard. "Why would you assume either of those colors?"

"You wear a lot of blue, aside from your uniform. But you feel like a green."

I feel like a green? What does that even mean?

She twists to face me fully again, answering before I can ask. "You know, fresh and vibrant, steady like the plains."

"Green," I confirm. Anything else feels too deep.

She drags her teeth over her bottom lip before responding proudly. "Thought so. Have fun at your fitting."

"Later, Wild Thing."

I'm driving home from the fitting when my cell rings. I could link the phone to my truck via Bluetooth, but it only makes all of my conversations loud enough for everyone to hear—something I think most people don't realize when they're having personal conversations in the grocery store parking lot. Instead, I pull onto a side street and answer on speaker.

"Warden Foster."

"Hey Nick, it's Payton." Her voice comes through casual and a little sultry.

To say I'm confused would be an understatement. Did Payton really go out of her way to get my personal number? "Oh, hi. How can I help you?"

"I'm calling about our date," she says confidently, as if I should've been expecting her call.

"Pardon?"

"The date auction for charity, silly." Her voice turns sickly sweet, and it's having the opposite effect of what I think she's going for.

"Oh, right." As if the idea of being auctioned off isn't weird enough, knowing Payton has her hands in it makes me even more uneasy.

"You are going to draw so much money. I can't thank you enough for participating."

I can't bring myself to respond. Even if being the center of attention wasn't an issue for me, I'd still be uncomfortable with what she's saying.

She doesn't seem to notice since she continues speaking. "The auction is Saturday the eighth at two. It'll be at The Spur. The dates will take place on the thirteenth."

"You're kidding." How did I manage to get roped into a Valentine's date?

Her voice hints at a wide smile. "No, it'll be fun! The men will prepare a date beforehand, and we'll share the details during the auction."

"The date is at our expense?" I guess.

"It's tax deductible," she replies, her tone saccharine.

I frown. "I don't think that's how that works, Payton. "

She's quiet for a moment before she responds flatly, "We can figure it out."

I don't like her use of "we." Images of the bridal store flash through my head, followed by a vision of Payton and me standing as wedding cake toppers, wearing entirely too much fabric and hair gel. I gag. "I'll come up with something."

"Something romantic, hopefully."

I don't respond.

"If any of your friends are interested, let me know. We still have room on the roster," she adds sweetly.

"Will do." Half of me thinks like hell I'd subject someone else to this. The other half is wondering who I can strong arm into the craziness with me. I bet I can talk Casey into it.

"Do you have any questions?"

I rush my answer. "Nope. Pretty straightforward. All right, well, I've gotta run. If you think of anything else, just give me a ring." I hope she doesn't. "Ok. Bye, Nick. See you soon," Payton drawls.

Chapter 9

Leah

The idea of being a designer by trade is foreign to me. Yes, it was my idea to start selling my jewelry, but I've never considered a *fashion show* before.

Since our conversation with Gideon, my mind has been running a mile a minute, trying to imagine what this will all look like. A flutter of anticipation rushes through my chest. Can I really do this? I didn't really expect it to be a jump-in-with-both-feet thing, and it's already feeling way bigger than I planned.

It's not like I'm quitting my job tomorrow, but there's a new pressure building now that my little dream is out in the open.

I have a plan for pieces and a tentative order. The only problem is models. Maci, Izzy, and Liv have agreed to walk in the show, but I need at least six more.

I also haven't told my boss the plan. Not that I owe the store any information about my personal life, but they're bound to find out sooner or later—like when we put up flyers—and I'd rather they don't think I'm hiding something.

"Morning Leah," Abigail says as she enters the store.

"Hey Abbykins," I reply with a smile.

I hired Abigail two years ago in what was supposed to be a seasonal position. After the holiday rush was over, she was the only temporary employee that we kept around, and she's been a permanent fixture ever since.

She pauses on her way to the back of the store to drop off her things. "What's up?" she asks, her eyebrows pinching together.

"Chillin' like a villain." I continue dusting the perfumes in the front case.

"Ew. Don't ever say that again."

Less than six years separate us, but I enjoy exploiting my ability to make her cringe.

"What's wrong?" she presses.

"I'm good. You good?" I say casually. I stand fully behind the counter and cross my arms, plastering a fake smile on my face.

Abigail isn't a southern belle; she's a rough-around-the-edges teen that will probably move into the city as soon as she scrapes up enough money to do so. She's attending courses at the community college in the city, and she reminds me of myself in some ways.

We aren't friends outside of work, but I enjoy our shifts together and we've come to read each other well.

She chews the inside of her lip. We both know I'm lying, but she's learned better than to push by now. "Suit yourself," she mutters, turning on her heel and disappearing around a new jean display I set up this morning.

"How do you like the Wranglers?" I shout after her.

"Fabulous." She barely raises her voice, and the single word holds the same annoyance as her previous statement. I grin to myself.

The morning drags on. I remove all the candles from the front display, wipe down the glass shelves, and put them all back in a new order. Abigail restocks shoes and makes sure everything is organized by size. She's making her way up front around lunchtime when the owner, Sadie, sashays her way into the store.

"Good afternoon, ladies," Sadie singsongs when she spots us both behind the counter. She peppers us with questions on the status of the store before Abigail disappears into the back again.

I lean my ass against the older countertop that serves as a desk. "You sticking around for a few minutes?" I ask.

When I was younger, Sadie spent a lot more time in the store. Over the years, she's backed off. She studies me from the desk chair. "A bit longer," she answers, her Texas drawl thick. "Got somethin' on your mind?"

My stomach clenches. It's not that I'm worried about being competition for the store. And Sadie's never given me reason to worry about my job. She's always pulled me in close when it comes to happenings at the store. But I don't want to mess up the one stable thing in my life. "Um, I need the second Saturday in February off."

Her lips press into a thoughtful pout, and she shoves the chair back from the desk with enough force that it almost careens into the rolls of wrapping paper in the counter behind her. Giving me her undivided attention, she says, "Leah Charlotte, you make the store schedule; what're you gettin' at?" Sadie is the only person to ever use my middle name, and it still catches me off-guard. Almost like a forced connection. I've never returned the favor.

"You know how I make jewelry on the side?" I cross my arms. I'm not sure how it reads, but it feels stiff. An outward reflection of the figurative rod drawing up through my body.

She cocks her head to one side. "Sure. You have pretty designs." Her gaze drops to my necklace momentarily.

"Thank you." My tongue sticks to my throat. "I'm having a show. To share my jewelry."

Sadie nods absently as if she's waiting for the punch line.

"It's on that Saturday," I add, as if she hasn't made the connection.

"That sounds like fun," she chirps with a broad smile. Her teeth are glossy and white and, together with her unnaturally blonde hair, give her a sunny expression. Even if it doesn't seem overly supportive.

I press my lips into a flat line and nod, tamping down my sudden annoyance. I'm relieved Sadie's not concerned, but she also doesn't seem to give it much merit. "Yeah."

We aren't friends, and I've never wanted as much. She keeps me and the rest of the staff at arm's length, the same way I've mostly done over the years. Maybe my distance hasn't been about my own boundaries at all.

I keep myself busy around the store while Sadie continues to work. When she heads out, there are no customers in the store and she hollers, "Bye Abigail!" toward the back, then waves happily at me. "Bye Leah."

Shortly after, Abigail comes up front and I leave for lunch.

I don't know what to do with myself as frustration builds at Sadie's lack of enthusiasm. What I want is a strong drink to take the edge off, but I refrain since I have to come back. Instead, I climb into my car, locking the doors out of habit, and turn the radio up as loud as I dare without bursting the speakers. I'm parked in the farthest spot from the entrance and there aren't many people around, so I throw my seat back into a nearly flattened position.

With my eyes closed, I let the heavy beat and strong melody wash over me, willing away the negative thoughts roiling inside me. By the time I have to return, I at least feel ready to be around people again.

Abigail steals glances at me every chance she gets for the rest of the afternoon. The scrutiny adds to my growing irritation. She's practically stalking me as I walk toward the jean display when I finally cave. "What is it?" I barely manage to keep the bite from my question.

"Something's up with you. Just tell me already."

"I'm good," I lie. "Isn't your shift over?" I make a show of checking my watch.

She grins. "You're right. It is. Guess I'll see you tomorrow." As she turns for the back of the store to collect her things, she swipes her hip to the side, knocking a stack of jeans off the end of the table. "Whoops. Sorry to make more work for you."

"That table has been there all day, and you've managed to avoid it." I frown.

"I can't help that I'm a klutz sometimes," she says coyly, her grin laced with sarcasm.

"You're such a child," I tease and huff, picking up the jeans. I know exactly what she's doing.

"So, what's really going on?" She perches against a boot display with her arms crossed. I don't respond. She jostles the display with her hip. "Oh darn it, I'm so klutzy today."

"Do. Not." I pin her with a less-than-stern glare as I set the final pair of jeans back in place.

"I can knock stuff over all day," she threatens.

I heave a sigh. "Fine. I just have a lot going on personally."

"Oh, well *thank you* for clearing it all up." She lifts a foot and rests it against the front stack of boxes on the display in another silent threat.

"You're a menace." I cross my arms and jut a hip out in faux annoyance, even though I'm realizing it's disappointment that I'm dealing with. "I told Sadie about a jewelry show I'm having in February, and she didn't bat an eye."

Abby perks up. "What kind of show? A fashion show?"

My heart skips a little at her choice of words. "Something like that. At The Spur. I told Sadie because I was letting her know that I needed the date off, and she said it sounded 'fun.'" I add air quotes.

She curls her lip. "Yeah, 'fun' does seem a bit dismissive. Can I come? Ooh ooh! Can I be a model?" Her pitch increases with each sentence.

"It's a bar," I tell her flatly before chewing my lip as I mull over the idea. "But I could use another model ." I wonder if Gideon would allow a minor in for the night.

She offers an exaggerated pout and puppy-dog eyes.

"I'll see if I can pull some strings. You can pretend to be a bad bitch for the night." I wink. "Now get out of here."

After work, I head straight to All Gussied Up for dress shopping with Maci.

"We're all here now," Maci says to the two women behind the counter as I enter. Andi, Maci's soon-to-be mother-in-law, and Sammi, Sutton's sister, stand nearby. Even Maci's mother, Stephanie, has made an appearance, though she has her typical stick up her ass.

"Leah bringing up the rear, as usual." Izzy bumps me with a hip.

"Don't tease me with ass play, Blondie." I curl my lip in an attempt at a forced smile, but even I can feel it doesn't quite hit.

"You good?" she asks so only I can hear.

Liv's inquisitive gaze bores into me from the other side as Maci chats with the older of the two women.

"Long day," I offer. I think I'm making a bigger deal out of the Sadie thing than necessary, and I don't want to discuss it with an audience.

The younger woman steps out from behind the counter. "You'll have some privacy tonight. Follow me." Her tone is almost curt, and she leads the seven of us into an expansive room to the left.

The area is styled completely different from the entrance, which has worn, beige carpet and mannequins dressed in traditional wedding attire. Twinkle lights beneath sheer cream fabric create a sort of starburst dispersing from a rustic, glitzy chandelier in the center of the room. Beneath it, a chocolate-colored leather couch sits with a matching chair on a massive, faux cow-print rug. A runner leads from the seating area to a single wide door, which I assume to be the dressing space. It has all the elegance of a wedding shop, with all the charm of our small town.

Racks upon racks of white, cream, silver, and rosy-pink dresses line the room. There are even fresh flowers on gorgeous wood tables throughout. Once again, I feel completely out of my element. Izzy lights up next to me, and I think I hear Andi sniffle. As Sammi wraps an arm around her mom, I check on Maci.

"What do you think?" I squeeze between Maci and Stephanie. "I never even knew there were this many fabrics."

Maci's face spreads into a grin and her shoulders soften. "It really is a lot."

I spot the younger woman's name tag—Caroline—as she speaks. "What are you thinking for your perfect dress, Maci? Do you have a style or fabric in mind? White, I assume?"

My lip lifts at the insinuation. Our friend group may be progressive, but we're still in small town, Texas. Her eyes dart my way before returning to Maci.

"Actually, off-white or cream, I think. Something light and airy. Probably sleeveless. Lace, maybe. Is bohemian vintage a thing?" Maci trails off.

The woman nods. "I think we have several dresses that fit what you're looking for. I'll pull a few that work with the timeline and budget you gave us." She scans the rest of the group. "Make yourselves comfortable. Would anyone like a drink?"

A few in the group ask for water while Stephanie moves to sit in the single chair near the couch. Despite knowing Maci since we were all about twelve, most of our family time with her included her late grandmother, Nana. Though, Stephanie's cold demeanor is hard to forget. She's stiff and judgmental on a good day, and while I know she and Maci are trying to work through their strained history, I can't help but think she's still maintaining the same distance.

Andi sits at the end of the couch nearest Stephanie, striking up a conversation in a friendly tone. We should all be so lucky to have a mother-in-law like her. If anyone can break through Stephanie's ice-cold exterior, it's Andi.

I don't bother with the couch but plop onto the floor in front of it. Liv and Izzy sit behind me, and Sammi drops to the floor next to me. "Can I sit at the kids' table with you?"

"Happy to have you." I lean my shoulder into hers.

She reaches into the tiny purse slung over her body and pulls out a circular pink perfume bottle with a faux crystal cap. Before I can ask about it, she unscrews the top, takes a swig, and winks at me.

My eyes widen and she offers me the bottle. "Oh, now I'm extra happy to have you." I take a sip and replace the cap before returning it. The whiskey coats my throat on the way down, and I relish the slow burn that follows.

Sammi places a finger over her lips and stashes the bottle again, just as Andi chimes in, "What are you two whispering about?"

Izzy speaks up before either of us can respond. "Knowing Leah, it's probably not family friendly."

I shrug. "That should be my disclaimer." I manage to catch a glimpse of Maci slipping into the dressing room, despite not seeing any dresses go in with her. A moment later, Caroline returns with the waters.

"So, Izzy says I'm walking with Shane," Sammi says as small conversations pick up again.

If Sutton is a man of few words, Shane is practically mute. "He doesn't say much, does he?" I ask playfully.

Sammi juts her bottom lip out in thought. "Yeah, he's always been that way. Very dry exterior, but he's a good guy. Who are you walking with?"

"Nick," Liv supplies in a teasing voice.

I twist enough to spot Liv's teasing grin. "What she said."

Sammi looks between us. "Nick is the best," she says expectantly, waiting for Liv or me to say more. But Liv only grins and I keep my mouth shut.

The door swings open to the dressing room and Maci emerges in layer after layer of lace. The cream dress plummets into a deep V between her breasts and cascades over her lower half. Her mouth is pulled tight as she wades our direction.

She steps onto the round dais before us without turning to take herself in. The triple mirrors behind her give the dress an even larger appearance. Without saying anything, I know she hates the dress.

"What do you think?" Izzy asks delicately.

"This isn't it," Maci states, her tone all business.

Caroline tuts around the bottom of the dress, fluffing the layers and extending them out neatly. "What don't you like about it?" she asks when she's finished, her tone almost challenging.

"It's too big," Maci answers quickly.

I snicker. "That's not what you said last ni—" A sharp jab to my back stops me short. I shoot a look over my shoulder to find Izzy glaring at me with all the venom of a mother in church, quieting her restless kids.

Maci's face holds far less annoyance when I turn back. She grins at me before continuing. "I need something simpler."

"Ok, we'll keep trying." Caroline ushers Maci toward the dressing room, and quiet conversations pick up again.

Maci returns twice more with similar results. Too showy. Too traditional.

"I think the first one was beautiful, Maci Grace." Stephanie's crisp words cut through the softness of the evening. Her tone hints at annoyance, and I suspect she thinks Maci is being too picky. Stephanie has always had a way of making Maci feel like she's too much or too little of something. A feeling I've always been able to relate to over the years, unfortunately.

"I'm surprised to hear you say that, considering the amount of cleavage I had on display," Maci states, her tight face full of annoyance.

"It only matters if you like it," I interject before the two of them can get started.

As if orchestrated, Izzy and I stand at the same time, each grabbing one of Maci's limp hands. "What is it, honey?" Izzy asks.

"None of these feel like me," Maci whispers. She picks at the hem of the dress without looking at us.

I give her hand a squeeze. "So you keep trying, or we go somewhere else. There isn't a rule that you have to choose a dress today," I tell her.

Izzy leans in, speaking in a firm, quiet tone. "She's right. This is about you. You set the rules."

Maci squeezes our hands. "I have one more. If it doesn't work, I'll schedule another time." She turns and heads for the dressing room again.

"At this rate, she's going to need a custom dress," Stephanie chides.

Before I have a chance to tell her to fuck right off, Sammi speaks. "I'm pretty sure I tried on ten or twelve before I said yes to the dress." Her tone is soft—which I'm thankful for, because it brings down my own rising anger—but the message is clear.

Andi chuckles. "I was beginning to think you'd be married in a potato sack." She smiles proudly down at Sammi. "And you would've looked lovely in it, if that's what you chose."

Sammi shakes her head. "Never."

"Ugh. I'm so glad I never have to worry about this." My words are meant for me, but I speak them too loud.

"Dress shopping?" Liv prods.

"Yep," I say definitively. "I'm never getting married."

"Never say never," Sammi says confidently. "Crazy things happen."

I shrug. "Maybe. But I can't imagine finding someone to be attached to for the rest of my life. People are too selfish. Me included."

"You aren't selfish at all, Leah," Izzy argues quietly. "Far from it."

Quiet falls on the group. Liv, who's been near-silent the entire time, is the one to break it. "How does Justin feel about not being in the wedding party?" Her reference to Sammi's husband reminds me of the processional lineup which was mentioned earlier.

"Oh, he's not getting off that easy. He's the flower girl handler for the event," Sammi tells her.

"Oh good, I'll put him on duty for Roman and Savannah, too," I joke, laughing as the door to the dressing room opens again.

This time when Maci comes out, a smile lights up her face and she practically parades toward us.

"Oh, my." Andi breathes behind me. An excited electricity takes over us as Maci climbs the step to the rounded dais again. This time she assesses herself dreamily before the three mirrors. The dress is just shy of white and made of a stunning lace design. It's as if it were crafted at once from a single, perfect sheet. The straps are just right for an early summer wedding, and I can already picture her meeting Sutton in the wildflowers on their property.

"Damn," I choke out. Confidence radiates from her.

Maci swings the dress back and forth before turning abruptly with an infectious grin. "This is my dress."

CHAPTER 10

LEAH

Lily hasn't bothered to get her phone turned back on. Or if she has, she hasn't told me, which I wouldn't put past her either. Instead, I hear from my mom that she needs me to pick up Roman and Savannah from her place after I'm off work. I don't bother arguing. It wouldn't do any good, and it wouldn't be fair to the kids.

When I show up to my mom's run-down duplex, Roman is playing in the front yard. I release a heavy sigh into my closed car instead of the scream I want to let loose. I shouldn't assume the worst, but given my mom's track record, I do.

The neighbor, an eighty-something-year-old woman, sits on her front porch in a broken sun chair, smoking a cigarette. She doesn't seem to notice Roman or I even exist.

"Leah!" Roman runs over and squeezes me around my middle, his tiny arms stronger than one would expect.

"Hey Bud. Where's Banana?" I say as I slide out of my car.

"She's inside with Bunny."

Bunny. The "grandma" alternative my mom came up with. I conjure a woman with Texas-high hair, equally high pink heels and leggings, and a thick, Jersey accent.

My mom is none of these things. Her fried voice box betrays smoking two packs a day. Her hair hardly ever comes out of its short, messy ponytail. And she hasn't worn more than what can be considered a muumuu and house shoes in several years.

"Ok. I'll be right back." I don't spend much time here. When I was younger, the lingering smoke on my clothes was an embarrassing hassle. I keep Roman outside to avoid the same dilemma, even though it's too late.

He leans against the still-warm front of my car with a sweet smile.

"Hey Mom," I say, pushing through the screen door.

Savannah is perched on the couch watching a show about underwater creatures that's far from educational. My mom is nowhere in sight. Crushed beer cans litter the coffee table, alongside a full ashtray and bits of paper. A mess probably left from Mom's current boyfriend, who I have no desire to run into.

"Hey, Banana," I say quietly, leaning down to kiss her head.

She looks up at me with glazed eyes. My heart cracks.

"Where's Bunny?" I whisper.

Savannah looks around the room as if contemplating this for the first time herself. She turns back to the television and a yelling squid without responding.

My heartbeat quickens. I scan the living room and kitchen, an open concept in the duplex unit. There's only one bedroom, and the door hangs open. The fact that fresh smoke doesn't waft from its opening is a small surprise.

I hold my breath, steeling myself for what I might find as I head toward the bedroom. A loud snort makes me jump just as I reach the threshold.

"Mom," I say firmly. Her snoring continues. She's splayed flat on the unkempt bed, the dated comforter stuffed to one side and the fitted sheet loose and crumpled around the middle. A medicine bottle is tipped over on the table with small, white escapees spilled out. My stomach clenches.

These kids shouldn't be here.

When she doesn't stir, I take one full step into the bedroom and speak louder. "Mom!"

She snorts again and startles. "What?" Her voice is gruff, angry that I scared her awake. When I was younger, I may have gotten slapped for such a thing.

"I'm taking the kids." I hate this. I hate being here. I hate seeing her like this. I hate the kids being anywhere in the vicinity.

"Ugh," she growls, clearing her throat and rolling onto her side so she can sit up. Her feet brush the discolored floor and a small part of me wonders when it was cleaned last. She presses a hand to her lower back as she stands. "My ass is on fire."

A disgusted exhale whooshes from my mouth.

After Lily moved to live with our dad, my mom and I were in an awful car accident. She's had pain in her back ever since, especially her lower back. It made her even more dependent on alcohol and pain medication, substances she was already happy to partake in.

I ignore my mother hobbling to the only bathroom in the unit, hidden in her room, and turn for the living room and Savannah. I want to feel badly for her. When it comes to the pain, I do. If only that's all it was.

"Come on, Banana." I scoop my niece from the couch, ignoring the squirrel with a twang from hell screeching on the TV.

My mom says nothing else as I exit the front door.

Roman paces in the gravel drive. His face brightens as I come out with his sister. I open the back passenger door for them to climb in. The smoke lingering in Savannah's hair wafts into my nose with the breeze.

"What do you say we grab some burgers and go to the playground?"

Roman buckles himself into the booster in my car as I slide Savannah into the car seat, tightening the straps over her chest.

"Are we spending the night?" he asks.

"Yep. That ok?" I pause with the door open.

A small smile blinks across his face. "Yeah."

"What is it, bud?"

"I like staying at your house." His speech is getting better as he nears his fifth birthday, another reminder of his ability to see more truths in the world. Does he know why his grandmother was passed out in the bedroom? Who turned on the television in the first place?

"I like when you stay with me," I agree, keeping my voice soft.

Savannah looks between us.

"I wish we could stay more," he says, tucking his hands into his lap and staring at them with heavy eyes.

"Your mom would miss you if you came over too much." I grin at him, trying to lighten the mood.

He doesn't bother looking up. "No she wouldn't."

I want to argue. To tell him, "Of course she would!" But the words won't come. I can't bring myself to lie to him.

I know my sister loves her kids. They're her babies. She just doesn't have all the tools to show it. To deal with her struggles and remind them how perfect and special they are.

But she absolutely loves them.

She loves them.

CHAPTER 11

NICK

I've spent the better part of the afternoon checking fishing hauls at a local park. It's an area of the tributary that fishermen often mistake as being included in the state parks system, and therefore free of a fishing license requirement. Coincidentally, these same fishermen are notorious for choosing to keep fish that are too small. Thankfully, unlike the deer I had to seize recently, the fish can usually be put back to grow and breed if we catch them in time.

I'm heading back to my truck when I spot familiar, chocolate-colored hair. At first it doesn't make any sense, because this woman is pushing a toddler in a swing at the adjacent playground. A little boy stands in the seat of the child-sized swing next to her, and though I can't hear what he says, the woman throws her head back and laughs loudly.

A couple of parents in the area look her way.

Leah.

I course correct, heading for the swing set.

Her attention swivels between the two children, her gorgeous smile never wavering. Their chatter continues until the little boy targets me from his place on the swing. I smile broadly, but he drops to a sitting position and slides off the front.

"Is dat a cop?" Fear coats his small voice.

Leah's head snaps my way. One shoulder drops and her hip kicks out on the opposite side. "No, Roman. He's not a cop. He's a boy scout."

There's no stopping my grin as I step down into the swing area. Gravel rearranges and crunches under my boots.

The boy stares at me. "He looks too old to be a boy scout."

"Troop leader?" Leah supplies, looking proud.

"Hey, man," I say with a big smile when I'm close. "Neither of those are true, actually. I'm a game warden."

His upper lip lifts in confusion. He assesses my uniform and his eyes halt on my badge. "Dat sounds made up."

Leah laughs again. The toddler peers over her shoulder at me. If I didn't suspect relation to Leah, I'd assume they were children from two different families that she was babysitting.

The boy has short, dark hair and curious deep-brown eyes. The girl has sandy hair and crisp-blue eyes. There isn't a single feature—eyes, nose, mouth, cheeks—between them that looks similar.

"This is Nick," Leah says.

The boy extends a hand. "I'm Roman. Dat's Savannah. She's one; I'm four."

"Four? I thought you were six." His eyes light up at my words. I shake his outstretched hand.

"My birthday is in June," he says proudly. "Savannah's is March."

"What are you doing here, Boy Scout?" Leah's face remains amused despite the interruption.

"You're always asking me that, but I'm beginning to think it's you who keeps showing up where *I* am, and not the other way around." I lean against the pipe supporting the swing set on one side.

She gives me a slow blink, unphased. "You like tater tots?"

"Uh . . . yeah?"

"There's some left in the bag." She gestures to a bench with the tip of her head, where a takeout bag sits.

"I'm good. We had a work lunch that ran late. Thanks, though." Chili cheese tater tots are a guilty pleasure. But even if what's in the bag is plain, I'm not lying about lunch.

Roman leans over the swing on his stomach and swoops his arms out airplane style, his assessment of me finished. Savannah kicks her legs as she shouts, "Faster!"

"You mean higher," Leah tells her, shoving the seat with gentle force.

"Faster!" the toddler yells with a toothy grin.

Leah snatches the front of the seat, stopping it in midair, and her free hand dives under the girl's chin. Squeals erupt. "You don't yell at me, missy," Leah says, laughing. She releases the swing into the air.

Savannah's giggles continue as she pendulums between us on either side of the swing set.

When Leah's eyes return to me, some of the mirth leaves. She's good at covering things up. Better than most. But in between her laughs and smiles, her brassy comments, her flirty attitude, there's a woman who's dealing with shit. It's in the tightness of her mouth and the heaviness of her eyes.

I want to question her, find out what's crawling beneath the surface, but the time isn't right. "What do you have going on this weekend?" I ask instead.

Thankfully she takes it for the casual question it is. For once. "I have a show Friday."

"A show?"

"Yeah." She hesitates, pushing the swing again. Another peal of laughter splits the cool afternoon air. "A jewelry show."

"Oh? For yours?" I say, gesturing to the jewelry she's wearing. She has on two necklaces of different lengths and a matching bracelet. An oval turquoise stone is central on one of each.

"Yeah. Crazy, right?" she jokes.

"I think it's pretty damn cool."

A reserved smile lifts her lips.

"Sorry," I add, referring to cussing around the kids.

She brushes me off with a tiny wave and shake of her head. "You should hear how my mom speaks. I'm surprised their first words weren't R-rated."

Roman pushes his arms directly in front of him and slides backward off the swing before standing. "I'm going to duh slide."

"Ok," Leah says, watching after him as he runs off. "He's getting so big."

"Has it been better with your sister?"

She snorts. "Not even close. The more I do, the less I feel like I'm doing. Today, I—" She stops speaking abruptly and her eyes meet mine. Something like fear dances across them. Releasing her breath, she pushes the swing again. "Sorry, don't mind me."

"You can say whatever it is you were going to say."

Her mouth tightens and she shakes her head. "It's fine. Just my family being difficult as usual."

My friends aren't exactly chatterboxes. Sutton is often closed off, and Shane doesn't say much either, unless it's important. Still, I can get them to open up to me when the need arises.

Leah feels different. I want her to be comfortable, but she gets so tight-lipped when she shuts down; it feels like pushing would have the opposite effect. I have to figure out a way in.

I don't know why I feel such a need. She has friends. She doesn't need me. Maybe that's what she's trying to say.

Back off, Nick.

"Down! Down!" Savannah cries.

"I guess I should get them home and bathed." Leah's entire demeanor has changed, any progress we may have made erased. "Good to see you, though." She waves past me at Roman coming off the slide.

His running steps clatter against the park gravel as he approaches. "I'll see you Friday," I say.

"Friday?"

"At your show." I turn and wave at Roman. "See ya, man."

"Bye, Nick," he says happily.

"You don't have to do that," Leah says as I start walking away.

I smile over my shoulder. "See you Friday, Wild Thing."

CHAPTER 12

LEAH

Wednesday afternoon, I stop by The Spur to talk with Gideon about Abigail helping out with the show.

"Hey Leah," he says when I seat myself at the end of the bar. There are way more people here than I'd expect for a weekday afternoon. "Whiskey and soda?"

I grin. "Yes, please. How's it going?"

"Same old, same old." It's a useless statement, because I don't know what regular looks like for him, but I bounce my eyebrows like I do. He slides the glass across the bar top to me. "Is your visit business or pleasure?"

I can't help myself. "Can't it be both?" I tease, removing the tiny straw and drinking from the glass.

Gideon leans his weight onto his hands against the glossy top. "It can be whatever you want."

"Good to know." I swish the ice in the glass. "Actually, I do have a question about the show."

"Shoot." He moves to lean casually against the back countertop, crossing his arms over his chest.

"One of my potential models is nineteen. Think we could let her in for the show?" I ask and tilt my head playfully.

"I'm happy to let her come for the event. But she has to see me first. I'm gonna put a big-ass 'X' on her hand and she needs to leave right after." He holds up a fat marker.

"That's fine."

"And don't let anyone give her alcohol back there." He nods to the back room.

I smirk. "Yes sir."

His eyes narrow.

I change the subject quickly. "Also, I'm going to have everything for sale that night. My thought is to use a sign-up, that way I can package it all later and get it to the right person. Assuming anyone is interested. You don't need to do any invoicing, but maybe you could manage the sign-up?"

"Yeah, no problem. But why not just sell them at the show, if that's what you want?"

"It just seems weird to take them from one body and put them on another or into a box."

He tips his head side to side. "Yeah, I guess. I'm happy to get sign-ups. Who knows, you may have a bidding war over pieces," he says with a grin.

"I'm not counting on it. We did put the flyers up though, so hopefully we'll see a decent turnout." I finish my drink and stand, putting some cash on the bar. "Thanks, Gideon."

"See you Friday." Gideon winks salaciously.

Me:

Gideon is letting Abigail come to the show so she can model for me.

Now I only need five more.

Izzy:

I forgot to tell you! One of the other hygienists wants to help.

Me:

Really?

Izzy:

Yes! She saw the necklace you made me for my birthday.

Me:

Damn. Cool. Give her my number.

Maci:

'll see if any of the teachers Liv works with want to help.

Me:

Ok.

Maci:

Don't worry. We'll figure it out.

Me:

I'm starting to freak out a little.

Izzy:

> **It's gonna be amazing.**

Maci:

> **FUCKING amazing.**

I stare at the phone. But is it?

Izzy:

> **What she said.**

This is the biggest thing I've ever done. I have most of the collection done, but I'm starting to doubt anyone will have any interest in these pieces. Pieces of me.

Aside from my best friends, no one has tolerated the broken, jagged shards of who I am. The sweet and the sour. The reckless choices I make to feel something other than disappointment and hurt.

But have I ever let anyone else in? Given someone a glimpse of the whole me instead of bailing before they could?

Chapter 13

Nick

My personal phone rings as I'm unlocking my front door. Quite honestly, I could leave the damn thing unlocked. No one is coming out to my place without knowing where it is. Sutton may have a ranch over ten thousand acres, but I have my own piece of heaven outside the city limits with an old farmhouse and a gorgeous view of the hill country.

"Game Warden Foster," I answer.

"Hey, Nick," Payton says, and my jaw clenches.

Fuck. I made the mistake of not saving Payton's number last time she called, so I didn't think to screen it.

I opt to play stupid. "This is he."

"It's Payton."

"Oh. Hey, Payton. What can I do for ya?" It's an effort to maintain a neutral tone.

I can hear her too-wide smile through her words. "I'm calling because I need to get a photo of you."

I shut the door behind me a little too hard. "What kind of photo?" Has she lost her damn mind?

"It's for the chamber website. We're posting the bachelor roster for virtual bids and additional interest," she explains.

Ok, maybe that's a little better. "Ah. I can send one over."

"In your uniform?" she prompts.

I pause taking off my duty belt. "Uh, yeah, not a problem."

She makes a noise akin to a happy squeal. "Wonderful! Oh, Nick, I can't wait. This year is going to be great."

"Glad to do my part. Where should I email the photo?"

She rattles off her assistant's email and I hurry her off the phone. It's just one day, I remind myself. And it's for charity. For the kids.

After getting comfortable and grabbing a quick bite to eat, I head onto my porch and call Casey. I have to get someone else in on this gig with me.

Lucky for me, he's already roped in. "Payton got some of the PD officers in on it. Me and two others signed up."

"Man, it's going to be law enforcement heavy."

"Women love men in uniforms," he says, like it's common knowledge.

"It's not like we'll be in them," I argue.

"We could!" he offers with a lilt to his voice.

Hell no. "Uh. No thanks." I laugh. "You do you, though."

Casey chuckles. "No, I don't think I'll do that. Some woman might want to cuff me instead." His laughter continues and I'm thankful he can't see my face, because being cuffed isn't the worst outcome I can imagine.

"Good point. Well, I'll see you there then."

"Do you have your date figured out yet?" he asks.

"Yes and no. It's not a one-size-fits-all kind of thing." How do you plan a date for someone you don't even know? Romance means something different to everyone. This is why I've never been a fan of blind dates.

"Damn, dude. That's going a little deep."

I laugh to cover my discomfort. "Probably so. Anyway, I'll see you Saturday."

"Bye."

After we get off the phone, I stare into the hills for a bit, lost in my thoughts. A group of deer move out of the tree line on the south. It shouldn't be a bad thing to be deep. To place value on something important. Maybe this auction isn't actually in line with my love life, but I'm still not going to compromise on the things that I find beautiful.

Chapter 14

Leah

Of all the times we've been to The Spur, I've never entered through the back. When we arrive an hour in advance of the show, Gideon has the exterior door on the back of the building open for us. Unlike other fashion shows, I assume, the preparation for this is minimal. I've talked through outfit choices with the models so they'll showcase the jewelry, but instead of directing their attire or hair and makeup choices, I told them to dress for a date night. I'm not some fancy designer—I just create fun, everyday pieces.

The door between the back room and the main room is closed, but otherwise nothing looks different here. It's a little odd to be prepping for a mini fashion show among pool tables and dart boards.

I pull a tiny flask from my bag and take a long pull before stowing it away again as footsteps approach on the sidewalk. I don't need any external commentary on my drinking.

Maci groans and shudders as she enters behind me.

"You good?" I ask curiously.

She closes her eyes through a second shudder. "Yeah. Bad memories."

My eyes pop wide. "Ohmygod, is that where you and—"

"*Don't* even say it," she says, putting a hand in front of my face. "I'd prefer to erase it from my mind."

I can't help but grin as I tease her. "Aren't you supposed to be confronting your emotions instead of burying them?"

She rolls her eyes.

If things didn't turn out the way they have, I wouldn't be joking with Maci about her at-home therapy technique attempts, one of which is exposure therapy. "Sounds like we'll each have our own firsts tied to this place."

"I love you, but sometimes you need to learn when to shut up," she growls, before her mood shifts to excitement. "I'm overriding my bad memories with this one, anyway. Are you so excited? I can't wait to strut my stuff." She shimmies her shoulders for effect.

I cackle. Maci has never strutted her stuff.

"Well, then let's get your sexy ass into some jewelry," I say, setting my box on a covered pool table and pulling pieces out. Maci follows me around in a circle as I unpack and display each item on the table.

"Oh Leah, these are beautiful." Her bottom lip juts out and she looks at me with full, wet eyes. "I'm so fucking proud of you," she whispers.

My heart swells. "Nothing's even happened yet. This could be a massive flop."

Her hands find her hips. "Are you serious? I can hear the noise from the other room through that closed door." She hikes a thumb over her shoulder. "And even if none of those people are here for you and no one buys a damn thing, I'm still proud. Look at what you've created! These pieces are delicate, and fierce, and sexy. You've captured everything women want to be."

"Thank you," I reply, running a hand through my hair and sweeping it all to one side.

"So, which one is mine?" Maci grins devilishly.

I point to the far side of the table from us, where I've laid a set of twin armlets. The cuffs are made of gold metal, which start and end in swirls and align one atop the other. They'll contrast perfectly with her black sleeveless dress.

She slides each one up an arm until they're in place, studying them carefully. "These are awesome. I've never worn anything like this."

"Wowza!" Izzy yells from the doorway as she enters from the back. "Look at you two!"

Unlike Maci in her floor-length maxi dress, I have on a caramel-colored suede skirt and a T-shirt from one of my favorite rockabilly bands, tied in a knot on one side. My accessories are various leather pieces I've created, including my earrings, a few wide band bracelets, and one gold wire ring that has a feather on the front.

Izzy hugs us in turn, smiling widely.

"Don't act like you're not dressed to kill." Maci gestures to Izzy's outfit. Her blonde hair is piled on top of her head in a perfect messy bun, paired with a cropped spaghetti strap top and a calf-length, leopard-print skirt. The skirt has a slit to her mid-thigh, exposing the tops of her cream suede boots.

"Damn, you ladies really dressed up for this." I pull two necklaces from the table and start securing them around Izzy's neck. One is a silver choker threaded with turquoise beads. The other is longer, stopping just above the deep V in her top, made of a delicate silver chain and wrapping around a large, pale pink stone in a mess of wire.

"You knew what we were wearing," Maci says, as if I need the reminder.

"Yeah, but seeing it in the flesh is different. It's real."

"Need me to pinch you?"

I swat at her and she snickers. "Don't even."

Izzy heads over to the door between the two rooms and cracks it open. Loud music from the jukebox blasts through the space, accompanied by an array of voices. "Holy shit, it's filling up fast." She waves us over, keeping her eye pressed to the gap.

Maci hurries to her side, but I hang back. "I don't think I can look."

My friends turn to me sharply. Maci's pitch jumps an octave as she cries, "What? Get your ass over here. This is amazing!"

I swallow my heart, which is trying to escape through my throat, and sneak up behind them. I knew the parking lot looked fuller than usual when we arrived, especially for the early hour, but the number of people is still shocking. The dance floor is busy, and the three bartenders hurry back and forth behind the full bar. Gideon is busy greeting more patrons with the bouncers.

I pull back. "Holy hell."

Liv bursts through the back door. "Oh my god, this is insane. I had to park in front of the Chinese restaurant next door." The buildings share a parking lot, but that's farther than I've ever had to park to get in.

She hugs me as she approaches and looks over the remaining jewelry. "Leah, these are gorgeous." Her fingers trail the covering on the pool table, never touching the pieces. She lays her jacket on a cocktail table. "I think I might puke," she says, clutching her stomach. "I'm so nervous."

"Me too," I murmur, taking in her outfit. It's as she said it would be, only more. "Fuck, Liv. You're a little baddie." Liv promised me a black, long-sleeve, full-length dress with a brown belt and brown boots. She delivered, only each side also has a slit up her legs to her hips, and her breasts threaten to spill out of the deep neckline.

Her cheeks redden. "Hush."

Still standing at the door to the main room, Maci turns. "Leah, you're right. We really need to keep an eye on the teachers around here," she teases, referencing a joke I made at Liv's expense in the fall.

Izzy whistles loudly. "I didn't know you had it in you."

Liv's face is a dark crimson. "Shut up. I'm leaving." She buries her face in her hands.

"Well, what did you expect to happen with that dress?" I ask, lifting my hand at her outfit.

Liv adjusts her cream Stetson over her braided hair, as if it might somehow conceal her face. "I just thought it was the best option to cover up my extra curves."

"Um, no ma'am." Maci steps into her cousin's space. "A. Your body is stunning and do not let anyone tell you otherwise. B. This dress does not cover. It teases. It hugs. It showcases. Daddies are going to be drooling out there."

"Oh my god, Maci!" Liv's blush renews. "I didn't even think about parents being here!" She turns to me, her mouth agape and true panic creeping into her eyes.

"Cat's out of the bag now. Ms. Liv is a hottie." I can't help but continue to tease.

She runs a hand over her face.

"These are for you." I gather several rings of varied widths, a pair of earrings, and a sturdy necklace. The necklace isn't a continuous circle, instead opening to the front like a rounded horseshoe. All the pieces contain a mixture of silver, turquoise, and several other stones I picked up during my conversation with Nick. Which reminds me—

"Oh." The word falls out unintentionally.

"Everything ok?" Liv studies my face as I finish placing the necklace.

"Yes, I just remembered something." With the door to the main room closed again, Izzy and Maci hang out near my makeshift staging area. I pull a notebook from my bag and open it to the page with jewelry listings for tonight. "If any of the other models show up, will you make sure they get the right jewelry? I have to run out and do something."

"Of course," Izzy says, but she eyes me curiously instead of looking at the notebook.

I dig through my bag, finding the small box I'm looking for, and take it with me into the main room. Several people glance as the door opens, and I do my best to ignore them as I make my way through the crowd. Having attention as the party girl has always been my gig—having it for another reason feels more like judgment.

I spot Sutton first. His chocolate-brown cowboy hat stands out despite the sea of hats. When I see Nick to his right, my mouth goes dry. He's swapped his standard tight tee for a plaid button-up tucked into his jeans. One hand is tucked into a front pocket, the other against the dance floor fencing. He stands fully when he sees me coming.

"Hey Sutton. Nick," I greet. My voice feels quiet in the boisterous room.

Sutton gives me a side hug. "Congrats."

It's the first time he's initiated any kind of physical contact, and a zing of happiness shoots through me over his familial acceptance. "Thanks."

Nick leans forward and wraps me in a one-armed hug. My arms loosely wrap around him, his fresh scent washing over me as I get close. "Looking good, Wild Thing," he says into my hair.

I suppress the shiver that runs down my spine and lean back to open the box I brought. "I have a favor to ask." My eyes move to Sutton and back to Nick. "My focus is women's jewelry, but I'm not leaving the men out."

I offer a braided leather bracelet to Sutton. Like the women, I've tried to pair them with pieces that feel like something they would naturally wear. He accepts the offering curiously and slides it on, tightening the metal clip to the right length.

"It's softer than I expected," he says, his thumb and forefinger rubbing back and forth over the grooves. "You may not get this back."

I smile, genuinely warmed by his response. "Fine with me."

The second bracelet I pull out is my own version of a paracord bracelet, made in a green that I think Nick would like. I've woven in a few tiger's eye beads. "This one is for you."

Nick looks at the bracelet and then into my eyes, opening his hand for me to drop it in. "Green."

I clip the bracelet around his wrist instead of letting it go into his hand. "Green," I confirm. "The tiger's eye is for protection."

"Protection?"

I shrug because I can't offer more.

He drops his chin and lowers his voice so it's almost too hard to hear in the crowded room. "Have you been planning this the whole time?"

I hold his inquisitive stare. "Maybe," I say quietly, biting my lip to hide a smile. His hand grows heavy in mine before I feel Sutton's eyes on us and pull back. "See y'all after." I wave and hurry away.

Gideon is waiting at the entrance to the staging room. "You still good on time, gorgeous?" I don't miss his eyes trailing down my body, or his suggestive tone.

He's cleaned up tonight, wearing a sharp black button-down. I take a step forward. "Yeah, we're good. I'm going to check in and make sure everyone's here and ready to go."

"Awesome." His eyes drop to my mouth. "I'll get the microphone ready to go. Give me a two-minute warning and I'll intro you. Then you can take it away."

My heart flutters in my chest. This is really happening. "Thanks, Gideon. I really appreciate you letting us do this here."

"You bet." He flicks the knot in my shirt with a finger, gives me a wink, and heads back to the bar. Maybe my dry spell is coming to an end.

In the staging room, all the models have arrived and everyone has jewelry on. My throat threatens to close, and I take in the moment to look at all these women who agreed to help me display my creations.

There's no going back from this moment. No matter what happens during or after the show, I will have fully showcased my passion to our town.

During one last pass, I check for any issues with the pieces before stopping to take them all in.

"Look at you," I say to Abigail at the end. "A baby in a bar."

"You're a terrible influence," she responds, grinning.

I squeeze her in a quick hug. "Don't get into any trouble tonight," I say low enough that only she can hear.

The women go quiet, waiting for me to speak. Like when all eyes turned on me a moment ago, it feels surreal to be seen as someone important. I haven't decided if I like it or not. "Y'all look fucking amazing. Thank you for supporting me in this. For taking time out of your schedules to join me as I jump into something new. Especially my besties, Maci and Izzy, for forcing me to do a show when I was convinced I wasn't ready."

Maci and Izzy hug each other, watching me from the opposite side of the room.

"Let's do the damn thing," Maci says with a grin.

"Ok. I'm going to put you in order, and then we'll get started." I clap my hands together like an awkward teacher. This is going to take some getting used to.

Once we're ready with Izzy leading the line, she pokes her head out and signals Gideon. It's only a few seconds before his voice filters through the speakers in the main room and the overall noise dies down. His words are garbled, but I catch him telling everyone it's going to be a great show and then leading into something else when he shouts my name.

The ladies in the room with me clap and hoot, and I slip through the door onto the makeshift runway. Thankfully there's no red carpet. Instead, it's lined on both sides by galvanized buckets containing The Spur's parking signs in concrete.

Suddenly, I feel so tiny, the reception from our little town more than I could have imagined. Wishing I'd done a couple more shots in the staging area, I pull up my metaphorical boots and start speaking. "Hey everyone! How are you tonight?"

Cheers, claps, and a few whistles round the room. The jukebox still plays as Ella Langley sings about a cowboy in a bar. I find Nick in the crowd without trying. The soft smile he wears and the intensity of his eyes hint at pride. And I have no idea why; it's not like we're close. Yet again, he's showing that he's just a really good guy who always shows up for his friends.

"Thank you all for coming out!" I manage to continue. "All the jewelry you'll see tonight has been handmade by me. I hope it feels like home, like Bull Creek, like the Hill Country. There's a mixture of textures, colors, and styles that are accommodating for everyday wear or a date night on the town.

"All of the pieces are for sale, so if you see something you like, see the man in black." I toss a hand to where Gideon leans against the bar top, his eyes pinned on me. He grins and waves to the room.

I scan the room in hopes of appearing inviting. "This show wouldn't be possible without the amazing women of Bull Creek. Please show them lots of love. They're the perfect models for this collection, and they look fucking amazing!"

The room erupts in cheers again, and I give a tiny bow before turning and heading back into the staging room.

Holy shit. That really happened.

Here goes nothing.

"You ladies showed up tonight!" I yell when we're all in the back room at the conclusion of the show. One by one they return their modeled jewelry, their hugs and congratulations adding to the excitement bubbling within me.

"Oh my god, what a high!" Maci cries as she wraps an arm around my waist, with Izzy on the other side. "You need us for anything?"

"No, you've both been amazing. Go enjoy your night."

"I'm taking my leave," Liv says with a chuckle.

I wave and catch sight of Abigail waving as she heads out the back door. "Thanks Abbykins, you're a rockstar!" I yell after her.

"You're coming, right?" Izzy says, giving my waist another squeeze.

I unwind myself from them and begin closing the large carrying case. "Yeah, I'm going to touch base with Gideon real quick."

Maci raises an eyebrow. "Is that what we're calling it now?"

"Oh, hush." I laugh. "That man is sexy, and if he wants to show me what he's made of, who am I to turn him down?"

Izzy shakes her head. "Hope it's worth it."

"Me too," I say with a grin as they head into the main room. I lock everything up in my case and take it all to my trunk before coming back through the front door. Several people stop me to say how beautiful my pieces are, which feels weird. I chat as casually as possible as I make my way toward the bar. Gideon mingles with patrons against the wall at the far side, smiling when he catches me walking toward him.

"Hey Boss," he says as I approach, and the two people he was talking to wander off.

"Hey. Thanks again," I reply, stopping a little closer than necessary.

He stands fully. "It was great. I'm glad you asked me about it. The turnout was awesome." He reaches over the bar and grabs a clipboard. "You sold out."

I stare at him as my brain processes. "What?"

"Yep." He hands me the clipboard with the list of jewelry by model, a copy of my own list. "Look at the next pages."

Flipping through the several pieces of copy paper, I find each one filled with personal details of people requesting the jewelry. The final page is a waitlist.

My eyes fly up to his, and he grins widely at me. "A waitlist?"

He nods slowly for effect. "You may need to quit your job to meet the demand."

I laugh and shake my head at him. "I wouldn't go that far." Looking back at the list, I murmur, "This is insane."

"What are your plans for later?" This time, he moves closer.

I pause, looking from the clipboard to Gideon. It's clear what he wants, and call me a needy wench, but I want it too. "Well . . ." I start coyly, and chance a look over my shoulder, looking for Maci and Izzy in the crowd.

When I look back at Gideon, he's followed my gaze. He takes a step back and shoves his hands in his pockets. "I'm sorry, Leah." His eyes ping pong once more between mine and my friends somewhere behind me. "I didn't mean to overstep."

My eyebrows scrunch. "What?"

"Have a good night. Congrats." He turns without another word and walks off. My eyes trail after him as he heads into his office, closing the door behind him.

What the fuck just happened?

I flag down Tawny for two drinks when she comes by, downing the first before heading to the table with my friends.

"There she is!" Izzy yells.

Maci frowns. "What's wrong? It looked like it went well."

"It did." I set my drink on the table and hand the clipboard to Maci. "I sold out. I have a waitlist."

A deep smile fills her face as she glances at the list. "So why the face, then?"

"It's Gideon."

Izzy angles closer, lowering her voice. "I thought that was a sealed deal."

I shake my head. "You know what they say about assuming. Except, I'm the only ass this time. I don't know. One second he was coming in hot, and the next he apologized for crossing a line."

"Did he kiss you or something?" she presses.

"No. He asked if I had plans. Then totally bailed." I chew my lip.

"Fuck him," Maci declares and sips her mixed drink. "Let's dance. You need to celebrate."

"You're right." I angle my body toward the dance floor, taking a quick pull of my drink. When I set it down again, Nick's green bracelet catches my eye where his palm rests against the tabletop.

Nick.

My eyes jump up to his face, finding him already looking at me.

"Badass show tonight," he says, giving me one of his easy smiles, his eyes thoughtful and kind.

"Thanks." I can't help the suspicion rising within. Did he give Gideon a look that I missed?

"Leah?" A familiar voice behind me breaks through my trance.

I turn sharply. Pete, one of the Falcons, moves into the place Maci and Izzy vacated. I had planned to follow them. Now I'm standing here with Sutton and Nick, staring at him like an idiot.

"Great show. I had no idea you were so creative." He smiles widely. He wears a black cap on backward, the logo matching his MC vest, and a black T-shirt and jeans. Not like Sutton and Nick's—boot cut and tight through the thighs. Just casual, rumpled jeans.

I force the playful smile that I would normally give him. "Thanks for coming." I look to the guys. "You know Sutton and Nick."

"Uh, yeah. Hey man." Pete shakes Sutton's hand, but only offers a nod from across the table toward Nick.

For the first time, Nick's jaw is hard and his eyes narrow. "How ya been?" The words are the least friendly I've ever heard from him.

Pete swallows and wets his lips. "Good, thanks for asking. It was good to see you, Leah. I've got a club thing. See you around." His nervous eyes soften for a split second. He salutes a wave at Nick and Sutton and makes a straight line for the front door.

I stare at Nick. His features have softened, and he takes a long drink of his beer as he brings his gaze back to mine. I grab my glass, and my drink goes down quickly as I stare back, my stare hardening by the moment. Sutton clears his throat.

"I'm going to find Maci and Izzy," I state, my voice stern as I turn for the dance floor. My timing is perfect because my favorite song comes on, and I let myself get lost in the music for a while.

During a break, we grab another round of drinks on my tab. I finish a drink before we leave the bar, leaving me a free hand to bring Nick a beer.

This is exactly the shit that warns off other guys.

"Here, Boy Scout." I thrust the beer at him a little forcefully when we reach the table.

"You good?" He pulls the lime wedge from the mouth of the bottle but waits for a response before squeezing the juice inside.

"Yep. Just need to get laid." I lean against the table backwards, our arms nearly brushing. Nick sidesteps slightly, creating more space. "It's ok if you don't know how to ask."

I hold his eyes as I take a drink.

His bottom lip pops out in thought for a split second. "I'm not following."

"I'm not sure exactly what's going on, but you've managed to scare off two men who were interested in me tonight. And you're not giving off big brother vibes, so if you're interested, just say so," I demand.

A muscle in his cheek twitches. "I haven't said anything to anyone. I'm sorry if I interrupted your night," he says, his voice low. The hidden smirk reads more amused than apologetic. "Didn't realize you had anything going on after."

"Don't judge me, Nick," I say sharply, standing upright and pressing a finger into his sternum. His blue eyes bore into mine, even though I expect he'll back up and relent as he usually does.

He doesn't.

Instead, he takes enough of a step forward to press his chest firmer into my finger. His chin tucks so he's looking down on me, crowding my space. My skin, which was sticky and warm from dancing moments ago, is scalding.

"I'm not judging you, Wild Thing. I never have. Never."

There's so much honesty in his eyes, it's overwhelming. I drop my hand and shift my weight the opposite direction.

"I have no desire to ruin your night. I was a little cold with Pete, but I won't apologize for that. And if you don't understand, that's fine. Because he does." He glances at the door like Pete may return.

"You don't have to do that, you know," I mutter.

Nick shifts his body in front of me, loosely cutting off the rest of the bar. "What's that?"

"Watch out for me." I hate acknowledging it, but it needs to be said.

The corner of his mouth tips up, but it's not a smug gesture. I can't imagine Nick smug. "Who says I am?"

My eyes lift to the ceiling as I determine what words to use. I'm not verbal like Maci and Izzy. I'm honest. Brazen even. So being polite as I say this doesn't come naturally. I meet his gaze again, trying to reel in my frustration as I speak. "Despite what you may think based on the first night you met me, I'm not shy or weak. And not usually stupid, either. You don't need to look out for me. I can handle myself."

Nick waits for a few beats. When I don't continue talking, he takes another small step forward. At a stacked six-foot-two, he could swallow me whole if he wanted. Even in my boots, I'd be pushing it to say I'm five-eight, but I don't move. I only shift my eyes up to hold his stare.

"I've never assumed you to be weak or shy. I'm not sure anyone would argue that you are. And I certainly don't think you're stupid. Maybe a little reckless sometimes." He drags his teeth over his lip with a playful grin.

I cross my arms.

He lowers his voice and leans in, the scent of his cologne washing over me again as he speaks. "You matter. You're important to Maci, and she's important to Sutton, and they're both important to me."

There he goes being the boy-next-door again. So, he's watching me as a favor to Maci. Wonderful.

"I'm sure Maci will be fine if you take a break from babysitting me."

He laughs, rubbing his face with a large hand. "I'm not babysitting you. I'm sorry if I've made you uncomfortable."

"I'm not uncomfortable." The words spill out too quickly. "I just don't want to be a burden. I'm fine. And quite frankly, I think you're throwing a wrench in my game."

Nick chews the inside of his lip. "Got it. But for what it's worth, you could never be a burden." He tips the neck of his beer my way. "And anyone who would put you in jeopardy doesn't deserve you."

Lightning zaps my heart.

There's an easy solution to this. Yes, Nick is in the friend circle, but I'm a one-and-done kind of girl. Nick never has anyone hanging around, so he's either not into strings or he's not that great in bed, in which case I won't be any worse off than I already am. Sleeping Nick out of my system seems like a really logical way to handle all of this. Whatever tension is between us will be taken care of, and we can both just move on.

There's hardly any space between us now, but I close what's left and poke him in the chest again. This time, I'm not backing down. "Nick Foster, do you have a crush on me?" I ask in a low voice, hoping to ruffle his composure.

He stills, and I'm convinced he stops breathing.

"It's fine. You're not the first. I usually try to keep my extracurriculars separate from the friend group, but I'm up for no strings attached, if you want," I drawl.

He inhales deeply and lays a hand atop mine on the cocktail table. It's gentle, and I will myself not to stare at the connection. "Leah, I think you're beautiful. Anyone would be lucky to spend time with you. But I'm not what you're looking for."

My stomach knots and heat floods my cheeks. I'm thankful for the darkened room. I can't remember the last time I was turned down. That usually works the other way around.

He takes a swig of his beer and sets it on the table. "Don't sell yourself short. You're worth more than one night." His fingers tap next to mine and he turns to the others. "I'm out, guys."

Maci and Izzy take turns hugging him, before Sutton shakes his hand and they say their goodbyes. He looks at me once more before he leaves. "Great show, Leah. Congratulations."

Fucking fabulous. Not only did I get turned down, but Nick was so uncomfortable by my proposition that he left.

Smooth move, Leah.

Chapter 15

Leah

I wake to the sound of my phone jingling on the nightstand. My head pounds as I unlock the screen.

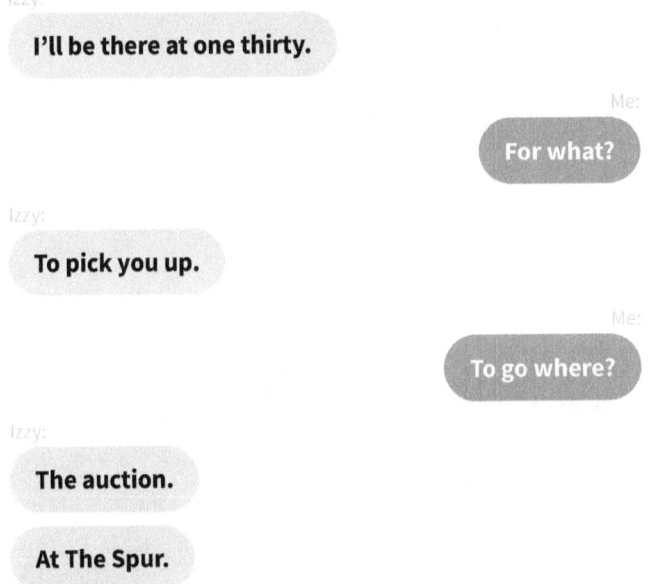

Izzy:

I'll be there at one thirty.

Me:

For what?

Izzy:

To pick you up.

Me:

To go where?

Izzy:

The auction.

At The Spur.

I stare at my phone. Did I agree to this? I vaguely remember hearing about it. I send back a question mark.

Smokey trots in from the living room and pounces onto the bed, bumping me twice with his soft head to request breakfast. He's insistent with his rubs and vocalizations as my phone vibrates again in my hand.

"Ok, sweet boy. Come on, I'll feed you." He winds around my legs on the way to the kitchen, not trusting I'll go straight to the bowl.

I wash a couple pain relievers down with some water. My phone chirps again.

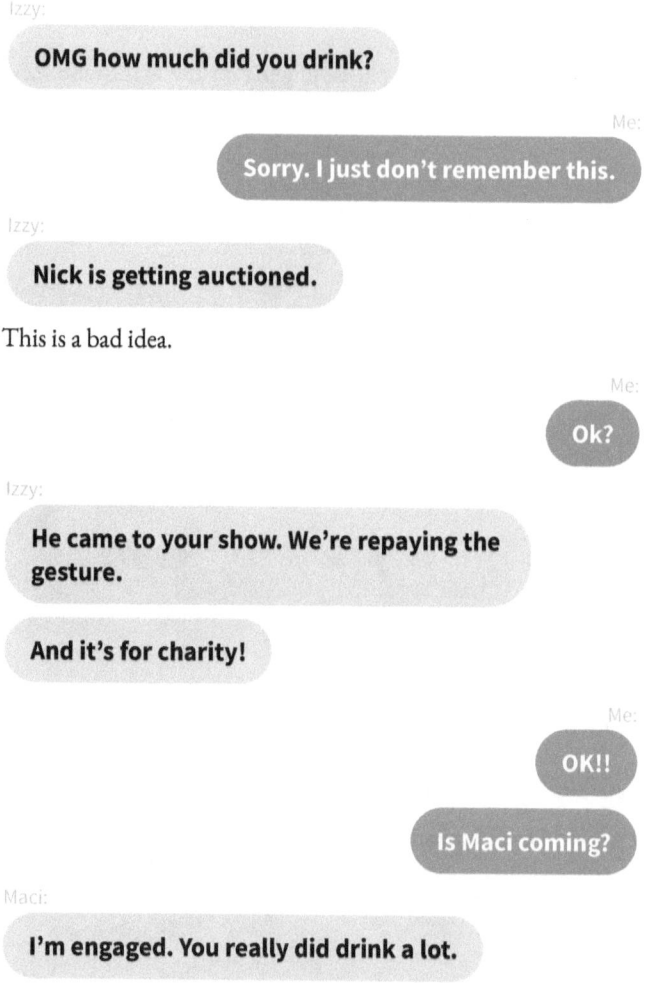

Izzy:

OMG how much did you drink?

Me:

Sorry. I just don't remember this.

Izzy:

Nick is getting auctioned.

This is a bad idea.

Me:

Ok?

Izzy:

He came to your show. We're repaying the gesture.

And it's for charity!

Me:

OK!!

Is Maci coming?

Maci:

I'm engaged. You really did drink a lot.

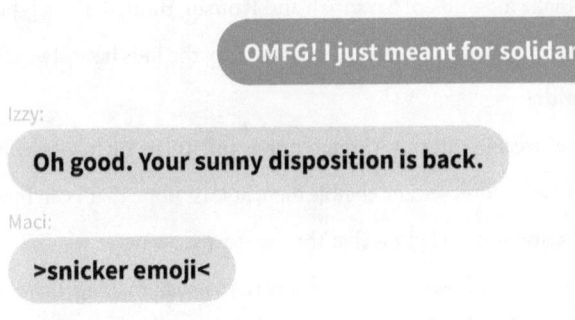

Me:

OMFG! I just meant for solidarity.

Izzy:

Oh good. Your sunny disposition is back.

Maci:

>snicker emoji<

I don't have a clue what the dress code is for this thing. Yeah, it's for charity, but it's a bachelor auction at a bar in Bull Creek. They have to know their audience. Right? Aside from the overwhelming number of blue-collar workers, ranchers, and law enforcement officers, there can't be more than a handful of "eligible" bachelors.

My version of a date day is a black mini dress with thigh-high black boots and an oversized denim jacket. They can take it or leave it. Who says I'll even bid on anyone?

Next to Izzy, my oversized denim jacket looks like a trash bag. And that's not downplaying me, because I look fucking hot. However, she's managed to make an all-denim romper and white boots look like a pin-up model. Her blonde hair is in bold waves, loose down her back. I link arms with her as we enter The Spur behind several other women from town.

For once, I appreciate that there's an entry fee. Even if I don't bid, I won't feel like I totally sucked out on kids with cancer.

It does make me think of Savannah and Roman, though. For all the shit we've gone through with my sister, I'm glad to say the kids have always been relatively healthy.

There's a sizeable turnout, though not as full as last night—which I'm secretly proud of. I don't see any eligible men, at least none that I can imagine are part of the auction, so I guess that they're stowed away.

The women are dressed more modestly than usual, making Tawny look especially out of place, with her plaid shirt tied between her breasts as usual. Someone is going to pop off with a "bless your heart" at any moment. There are way too many southern belles in here today.

I open my mouth to order and Tawny taps a tiny chalkboard menu on the bar top. "Specials today."

I clock the menu and then look back at her. "Uh. Ok?"

Izzy snickers. "They limited the drink options."

Tawny's face is fixed with an annoyed expression.

I scrunch my face. "I'm paying. Why can't I buy what I want?"

Tawny shrugs. "Ask Payton."

"Who's Payton?" I ask, irritation lining my voice.

"The one in charge." Her heavy eyelids and straight mouth indicate that she's in no mood to argue with me, or *for* me, for that matter.

Izzy grips my arm. "Maybe don't."

I give her a coy sideways glance. "I'm not doing anything."

"Play nice today," Izzy orders and turns back to Tawny. "Two mimosas."

Turning away from the bar and leaning against it, I cross my arms. "I always play nice."

Izzy shakes her head. "You know what I mean."

The door to the back room opens and a blonde woman slips out, her entire vibe screaming southern belle. She wears a strapless maxi dress in a bold floral print with a ruffle around the top. Her hair is in a fat, loose bun on top of her head with ringlets pulled out around her temples. A beaming smile splits her face as she hurries over to the end of the bar, where I half expect her to yank out a black card and wave it around.

Gideon turns his ear her way, tuning in to whatever she's saying. He nods and smiles at her, responding in kind.

Her over-the-top laughter rings out above the chatter around us. As if she can't manage to stand on her own, she grips his bicep as she quiets.

"Wonder if he's on the chopping block."

"Do you mean auction block?" Izzy asks, before sipping her drink.

I side-eye her, reaching for my own drink, and we head deeper into the crowded room. We find an empty table toward the back corner of the dance floor. All we'll see from here is asses. Fine by me.

"Who?" Izzy inquires.

I sip my drink. "Who what?"

"Who's on the chopping block?"

I grin. "I was being facetious. Gideon."

The room is warm and I'm debating removing my jacket, but I don't have anywhere to put it because they've put the chairs away and I don't want to drape it over a table.

"You're still upset about that?" Izzy asks.

Before I can respond, Blondie grabs a microphone from Gideon and makes her way to the center of the dance floor. Her over-the-top smile almost gets there before she does, and she wiggles her fingers in tiny waves at people as she passes between them.

"No," I finally say, crossing my arms over my chest and leaving my drink on the table. My eyes never leave the dance floor.

The music gets turned down and chatter in the room lowers. "Hi everyone!" The blonde says in an overly-animated way, which may be captivating if you like her sort of vibe. "Thank you so much for coming out today! We are so excited to support Heroes for Children for the second year in a row. We had an amazing turnout last year, and we have high hopes for this go around. So, open your pocketbooks and hearts, and *pocketbooks.*" She pauses for effect and people giggle.

"I'm a hype girl, right?" I murmur to Izzy.

She shuffles next to me. "Um, yes? Why wouldn't you be? You totally support other women."

"My name is Payton, and I'm the Special Events Coordinator at the Bull Creek Chamber of Commerce. I'm so excited to emcee this event and maybe play a little matchmaker today!" Payton shimmies her hips and her shoulders scrunch up in excitement.

"I'm a hype girl," I say to myself this time.

Izzy scoots closer to me. "Is this about Gideon?" she asks, her tone laced with confusion.

"No."

She continues to stare at me, waiting for me to elaborate. I can't take my eyes off the dance floor. I only say, "I hate her."

CHAPTER 16

NICK

When I was little and I had a bad day, my mom would tell me to "sleep on it" and it would look better in the morning. It was one of the few comforting lines she had.

Sleeping on my conversation with Leah does nothing to curb the unease that lingers from last night. And it's not like she didn't give me a chance. Seriously, what the fuck was that? That's twice that she's mentioned me wanting to somehow get her into bed.

But I don't see her that way.

I'm a man. *I see her*. I just don't see her as one and done. But I still can't determine if that's more about me or her.

I crave. I have desires. But I don't need different women all the time. In fact, I prefer to be with a woman who wants me for more than a lay. And that's why I haven't taken Leah up on an offer.

Leah's sexual prowess isn't a secret. She's open about her desire for pleasure. Jokes about it like it's all in fun. And for some reason she thinks I've judged her about it, but I haven't. She could sleep with half the town and I wouldn't judge her. Though, I'm beginning to realize I may be jealous.

After my run, intentionally not going past Sadie's, I shower and plan out this "date" that's supposed to be auctioned off with me. I'm torn between treating this like something disposable and trying my best.

Who am I kidding? Leah may have been off base about me being a boy scout, but striving for excellence was drilled into me by my parents from a young age. There isn't an option where I don't give it my all.

My thumb runs along my fingertips in an erratic rhythm as I enter The Spur. Payton waves excitedly as soon as she lays eyes on me. It's not needed, but I turn on the charm. May as well get into character now—it's for charity, anyway.

"Payton, how are you?" I ask politely.

She approaches with a broad smile and leans in for a hug like we're old friends. I release her quickly. "You smell delicious," she practically purrs.

"Uh, thanks. Where would you like me?"

Her eyes light up, and I regret my phrasing.

Shit. Can she bid on me? This could go sideways fast.

"All the bachelors are in the back room."

"Cool. I'll join them," I say, stepping to one side.

She places a firm palm on my bicep. "You don't have to hurry off."

"You have a lot to do. I'll just be in the way. Thanks for having me," I offer, quickening my pace as I walk away. In the back, I see a few friendly faces, including Casey.

"You made it!" Casey cheers.

As if I had a choice to back out. It's like the guy hasn't known me his entire life.

"I made it." I smile anyway.

"What'd you decide on?" he asks.

"For the date?" I look around the room. I recognize the other two police officers that Casey mentioned. One was at Maci's grandmother's house the night she was attacked. His personality leaves a lot to be desired, and Sutton came close to knocking his teeth out. I turn my attention back to Casey and answer, "An outdoorsy thing."

He raises an eyebrow. "Damn. You're brave."

I chuckle. "Why?"

"I figure you have two options here in town: women who know how to shoot, and women who know how to point their finger. And I think it's the latter showing up today." He grins like he's solved some kind of mystery.

"I guess it's a gamble."

When the last of the bachelors arrives, Payton slides in the room to get everyone organized into a particular order. Somehow, I'm last in the lineup. What are the chances?

Now I have the entire thing to work myself up over being a piece of meat for sale. And everyone will be watching.

We watch from the wings, so to speak, as one by one our fates are left in the hands of local townspeople. Casey manages to bring in two hundred dollars, which seems to be the number to beat, but I don't have a chance to see how he feels about being auctioned off to a widow twice his age.

At least it's for charity, right?

It's one fake date. I can certainly pull it together for that.

Payton gears up for me to come out. "Our last bachelor this afternoon is certainly not the least! He's our county game warden, a lifelong citizen of Bull Creek, and handsome to boot." Her arm extends my way, and she smiles bigger than before. Being on display and talked about like cattle is such a surreal feeling.

Movement behind Payton catches my attention, and then my breath. Leah and Izzy are talking on the other side of the dance floor. How did I miss them until now?

Leah's fresh and spirited, and looking casually seductive, which is on brand.

"Nick Foster!" Payton hollers happily.

Swallowing, I walk through the door and then the crowd before meeting Payton on the dance floor. Standing in the middle, I can't even get a glimpse of Leah. I wonder what she thinks of me out here, being objectified.

Maybe she likes it. It fits with her tendency to enjoy one-off trysts. The thought feels mean, because I know there's more to her than that. I've seen plenty of her wild side, but outside social settings, she's more reserved, thoughtful. Something just doesn't add up.

"Nick, why don't you tell us about the date you've planned?"

I clear my throat and lean toward the microphone she has outstretched. "Like you said, I'm a game warden and both my career and passion center on protecting our wildlife and natural habitats. I really enjoy being outdoors, even when I'm not working. So I thought it'd be fun to visit one of our local cave systems for a tour and then have lunch at their museum."

"You heard it, ladies. You can trust this one to catch you if you fall. In more ways than one!" Payton leans against my arm, wrapping her hand around it, and almost yells into the microphone. "Let's start the bidding at seventy five dollars!"

The bidding has picked up slowly in each round. Payton started most of the bidding at fifty dollars— I have no idea how she planned the numbers—so at first, I assume the bidders will call out smaller increments. But I'm wrong. The second bid is a hundred bucks.

Noise escalates rapidly and women bounce on their feet, yelling to the dance floor and in between tables. I run a hand over my face. What the fuck have I gotten myself into?

We live in a small town, but that doesn't mean I know every woman here. I'm realizing now that there are many I've seen in passing, but I don't know a ton about them personally. Some I'm familiar with from high school, others from arrests or warrants I've helped serve.

Please don't let me get picked up by some woman with a husband in jail.

Payton yells something into the microphone, and I home in on the words "two hundred." Two hundred already?

Someone screams in the crowd. The women are screaming like teens at a boy band concert.

Gideon leans against the shelf behind the bar with his arms crossed, eyeing me with disgust. I don't understand; he agreed to this event, so I don't know what he could be upset about.

The bidding slows. "Two fifty?" Payton seems optimistic next to me. No one responds right away, and she says, "I may have to outbid you, Carla, because Nick is a catch. It's for charity, after all." She laughs loudly. I pray again that she won't actually do what she's threatening.

From my right, I hear a strong voice call out, "Two fifty."

Payton and I both whip our heads in that direction to find Leah holding cash in hand between her thumb and first two fingers. Her eyes land on me briefly, a coy smirk on her mouth, before shifting to Payton. There's a dare I can see even from here.

"I have two fifty." Payton's clipped affirmation is tinted with annoyance. "Do I have two seventy five?"

There are a few murmurs that go around, but no one else bids. My heart thumps hard in my chest.

Payton's grip on the microphone tightens and loosens several times. "Two hundred fifty going once." She scans the room, as do I. The noise has lowered even more. "Two fifty going twice."

My eyes return to Payton, willing her to make the call. Instead of making eye contact with me, she glances briefly in Leah's direction.

"Sold to the girl in the jean jacket for two hundred and fifty dollars. Congratulations," she says with a stiff smile. There's something about her use of "jean jacket" that feels like a dig.

This time I look Leah's way, but she's already cutting a path around the outside of the dance floor to its entrance.

"Thank you to everyone for coming out today! If you'd like to make an additional contribution, please see me before you leave. Make sure to check our website for all of our upcoming events!" The crowd is already dispersing as Payton yells louder to share the last bits of information.

We move to exit the floor as Leah hits the threshold.

"Oh, you don't have to—" Payton puts her hand up to stop Leah.

Leah tucks the money into the elastic at the top of Payton's dress. "Sorry, I don't like to wait on my merchandise." She tangles her cool fingers with mine and pulls me behind her toward her table.

I consider pulling her against my side in a friendly hug. As if hearing my thoughts, she drops my hand and moves around the table.

"Damn! Top earner!" Izzy grins and hugs me.

Leah drinks from her mimosa, looking less than pleased.

"Thanks," I say, distracted. Something feels off.

Izzy's eyes dart between Leah and me. "I'm running to the bar for a refill. Want anything?"

Leah cuts her eyes at Izzy from the side. "No, thanks. I've reached my quota of orange juice for the day."

Izzy drops her head back to look at the ceiling in exasperation. "Nick?"

"No, thanks." She starts to walk away as I continue, "I have a date to get to." Never mind that it's actually scheduled for next weekend.

Leah shakes her head. "Don't worry about it."

"Don't worry about what?"

"The date," she mutters, waving a hand dismissively. "I didn't bid for that."

"You mean you didn't bid for me to woo you with my knowledge of cave systems and local geography?" I smirk at her, but she doesn't return the gesture.

"I did not." She looks at me for a split second, barely meeting my eyes.

I step in front of her. She's ignoring me for some reason, and I'd like to know why. "What's going on?"

Her next sip brings forth a disgusted face before she schools it. "Nothing."

"'Nothing' is like when a woman says 'fine.' It's not either of those things." I slide my hands into my front pockets, which draws her eyes down.

She drags her gaze from the floor to where my hands are tucked into my pockets, lingering briefly before slowly raising them to my face. "You made it clear how you feel. I didn't want you to think that I was trying to force the issue. And anyway, you know my stance on sweat." For just a second, I can see the Leah that she keeps hidden. Something insecure peeking through behind her gorgeous hazel eyes. But she blinks and it's gone.

"Force the issue?" I tuck my head, still trying to get her to look up at me again. "Wait. Is this about last night?"

She doesn't respond.

"Leah, if I offended you, I'm sorry. That's not what I meant at all."

She scoffs. "You're really good at apologizing, Nick. But stop. I'm not offended, I just understand the line and I want you to know I'm not crossing it."

I drop my head back and sigh. This isn't how this was supposed to go.

She keeps talking. "Maybe I read the signs wrong, but it looked like Blondie was about to sink her claws into you, and I thought maybe you didn't want her to."

My eyes jump as if she'll hear, accidentally finding Payton studying me from the bar. I adjust my stance, placing my back to her as I face Leah. "You're right."

"Good. Then, we're good. The money was for charity, and I did something good for a friend."

I release my hands from their pockets and grip her shoulders softly. Her eyes slowly meet mine. "Please don't say good again."

This time, the tiniest bit of color comes to her face, and she stifles a grin on one side. "That was a lot."

"Caves are cool," I state.

Her thick brows pull together. "What?"

"Caves tend to be cooler than outside. You won't be sweating." I slide my hands down her arms, brushing her fingers as I release her.

Her denim jacket swallows her frame as she laughs. Even in something oversized, she's enticing. "Whatever you say, Boy Scout."

"What would you choose, then? If it were up to you, what would an ideal date be?"

She shrugs. "I'm easy. Pizza and beer."

I pretend to look distractedly around the room, as if I'm not wholly focused on her. "Don't tell me you like pineapple on it," I joke.

"Nick Foster, if you come for my pineapple, you're losing a patch." She pins me with a challenging stare.

I throw my head back and laugh. "For what?"

She shakes her head. "I don't know; I'm not up on my boy scout patches. But believe me, one is getting taken. What happens when you get in trouble in boy scouts? Do you get demerits? Maybe that's cheerleading."

I laugh again. "I have no clue what that is. Remember?" I point to my chest. "Not a boy scout."

She cuts her eyes at me. "Liar."

"Wait. What do you know about cheerleading?"

"Nothing. Izzy was a cheerleader in middle school for a year."

Izzy arrives then and sets three drinks on the table.

"I said no," Leah says, her face more angry than her tone.

"And I ignored you. Take a drink. You too," Izzy demands, jerking her chin at me.

I sip the beer. It's not dressed, but I don't complain. "Is she always so bossy?" My stage whisper to Leah brings out another small grin.

"Always," Izzy replies with a knowing smirk.

CHAPTER 17

LEAH

Me:

Sorry about the other night. It was crazier than I expected. Thanks for coming to my show.

T hree dots light up on Pete's side of the conversation and then stop.
Twice.

Fucking Nick.

A few days after the show, not only am I still horny as fuck, but everything just feels out of sorts. I shouldn't feel this way after what was an epic night. All of the jewelry from the show has been settled and delivered, and I've started working on custom orders.

Unlike any of the other guys I've given my number to, I've known Pete for months and never slept with him. And I've never blown him off. Not permanently. I've always kept him at arm's length. But for some reason I can't figure out, he keeps sticking around.

I wouldn't blame him if he's reached his limit. In fact, I'm not sure I'd sleep with him if he responded now. He just seems like a nice guy with a good heart, and those types don't come along very often.

Me:

I'm sorry about Nick. He's still a little salty about that night at the bar.

The dots appear and disappear again. I throw the phone onto the couch and grab a pillow from next to me to yell into. I hate feeling like a stranger in my own skin.

Skin.

A new tattoo would cheer me up.

I clean up quickly and throw my phone in my bag as I head out the door. My favorite tattoo artist is in the city, and if I hurry, I can be there when they open.

There's a notification on my phone when I park.

Pete:

No apologies necessary. Ur a boss.

A tiny smile tugs at my mouth.

After I finish my tattoo, a tiny monarch butterfly on the underside of my wrist, I text Pete again.

Me:

What are you doing right now?

Pete:

I'm at the clubhouse having a beer.

I stare at the phone. Not what I was hoping for. I don't know why I suddenly want to hang out with him, except that it's different from my usual, and I need something to break up what's going on. A reset, a change. Something.

Pete:

U wanna come?

Me:

To the clubhouse? Aren't there rules against that?

Pete:

No. I can bring whoever I want.

Do motorcycle club members gossip? Because this is already a small enough town, and enough shit gets said to my face and behind my back that I do not need to add another layer to it.

The Falcons come to The Spur occasionally. Usually only a few at a time. Otherwise, I've seen them on rides in various numbers. I assume they mostly hang out together wherever this clubhouse is.

Maci's been there to see her dad since he lives there, but she's never taken me, and I've never asked. It didn't seem appropriate—not that I'm the queen of that.

Me:

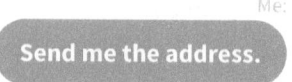

Send me the address.

The drive is easy once Pete tells me where it is. When I arrive, he's outside near a chain link fence that encloses the parking lot. He chats with an older guy at the gate, and it rattles open.

Pete motions to a space up front for me to park and opens my door before I have my seatbelt off.

"Hey gorgeous," he says, wrapping me in a hug.

There's something comforting about his arms. "Hi."

The club is like a barndominium, with a large garage on the backside of the parking lot. It has a masculine, rustic feel with dark metals, intentionally charred wood, and concrete. Inside, Pete gives me the shortest tour ever, which is basically the main room. Much like The Spur, there are pool tables and a bar, but there's a sophisticated aesthetic that I didn't expect.

A pair of French doors next to a set of stairs on the far wall partition off what I assume to be a meeting room.

We take up chairs at the bar, next to a guy that Pete introduces as McCoy. He's a few years younger than me and looks familiar, but I can't place how.

People assume in small towns that everyone knows everyone. And in some capacities, that's true. But there are still plenty of opportunities for us to miss each other. Especially if we don't run in the same circles. Or, if you're like me—and probably McCoy—and you come from basically nothing, you do your best to avoid the toxic limelight your family shines on you. At least until you can outshine them in some other way.

"Don't ask me for some fruity cocktail," the bartender says, eyeing me skeptically. Her auburn hair is pulled into a ponytail with her bangs teasing at covering her eyes and large gold hoops adorning her ears.

I smirk. "You're Ginger. I see it now."

Her eyes slide to Pete, annoyed that he's been running his mouth, but in truth it's Maci who's told me about her.

"Leah." She stares at me as if to ask why my name should be important. "I'm Maci's best friend."

A slow smile spreads across her face. "So keep the whiskey coming, then?"

"Absofuckinglutely." I slap the bar top.

Once we both have drinks, Pete chatters away about his new bike. I don't get a word in for a while, but it's not a bother. His energy is infectious and just what I was looking for to escape the anxieties of life. The whiskey helps, too.

He doesn't stay as close as before. Maybe it's because I was blackout drunk last time we hung out and he had to hand me off to Maci, Sutton, and Nick. Or maybe it's that I haven't been eager for his advances. Or maybe it's the way Nick treated him the other night.

"So, how's life? You're a big designer now." He swigs his beer through a grin.

My smile feels heavy. "Getting there. It took off faster than I anticipated, but there's still a long way to go."

He nods, giving me time to elaborate, but I don't. My girlfriends have to pull the bullshit out of me; he's certainly not going to get much.

"So why'd you text tonight? I'm usually the first to reach out."

And just like that, the smile is gone. Of course he'd question me. It's only fair. "Colt kind of screwed you."

Pete's face drops. The mention of his late friend is as unexpected to him as it is to me. I never planned to bring him up. "I don't think I'm following."

"The night we met at The Spur— you and me, Maci and Colt—I would've fucked you then."

He chokes on his drink, releasing the bottle and setting it firmly on the bar.

I smirk but continue. "If Colt hadn't ruined it with what happened with Maci in the alley. Maybe I would've slept with you the night I got wasted, if I hadn't. I'm not afraid of a one-night stand, but that's it. And you kept checking in after. Even if only through Maci. You're so nice—"

"Nice," he says flatly, interrupting. It's the most defeated he's ever been.

"You *are* nice," I insist, my cheeks heating uncharacteristically. "It felt good when you reached out. It's been a hard few months, and I didn't want to ruin it by dropping you after we fucked. Because that's the truth of how it would've gone down."

He stares at me quietly as a myriad of emotions pass over his face. I don't know what the fuck's gotten into me. When did I become vulnerable and honest? I sigh, turning to face the bar and downing the rest of my drink.

"Ok, then," he says after a minute. "So . . . friends."

I peek at him from the corner of my eye. "If you'll have me."

"Fuck." He breathes a laugh, shakes his head, and takes another long pull from his beer. "Yeah."

"Thanks, Pete." I want to grab his hand, give it a squeeze to indicate how much it means to me, but I don't. I know it's akin to pouring salt in his open wound.

I stay much longer than anticipated. I can see now why Ginger and Maci didn't quite get off on the right foot. Ginger is gruff and harsh, and she doesn't have to tell me that she comes from nothing. I think our families lived near each other in a trailer park when I was really little, but she's got several years on me, so I'm not positive it was her. And it doesn't feel like the right place for me to ask, anyway.

Eventually we run out of chairs at the bar as more and more Falcons show up. The alcohol has been flowing for a while, and Pete makes a joke about me sitting in his lap. Instead, I lift myself and sit on the bar top.

"What the fuck are you doing?" Ginger says, laughing. "Get down from there."

I've had entirely too much to drink to listen to anyone. I lift my heels and spin around on the slick surface, doing a one eighty so I face Ginger directly. "Make me," I say playfully.

She grips both sides of my flannel and yanks me off the bar toward the liquor-lined shelves. I bump my ass as I bounce down—thankful I was directly over the beer cooler—and land on my feet in front of her.

"Don't sit on my bar, Leah." Her words are serious, but she drops her eyes to my mouth. I know there's more to it than that.

Quickly, I reach into her auburn hair and yank her to me, slamming my mouth into hers. It's got all the makings of a drunken kiss, even though she hasn't been drinking. It's messy and wet and our teeth clash together.

But it's also safe. Just a release. Truthfully, being open to women or not, Ginger just isn't my type.

She laughs when I pull back. "You're wild."

I wipe under my lip, fixing whatever's left of my smeared lipstick. Then I turn to exit the space behind the bar. Pete and some of the other guys stare silently; McCoy looks disinterested. I grin at Pete as I walk back around the counter, but someone clears their throat, pulling my attention.

"Leah." A subtle Irish accent greets me.

James, Maci's father and the President of the MC, stands midway across the room, apparently unimpressed with my behavior. He's mysteriously calm all the time. I know he'd be a good fuck, and Maci's mom would shit a brick if I accidentally let that one slip. Honestly, it would make the experience that much better.

It really sucks that he's my best friend's dad because, once again, that's a line I won't cross. I guess that's karma for Pete.

"Hi, Da—James," I say, wiggling my fingers and cringing internally at almost calling him Daddy out loud. I like to mess with Maci about it, but she never seems bothered. Izzy and Liv both turn crimson when I say it though, which is always a win.

James scans the inhabitants of the chairs at his bar, then checks his watch. "Time to go." His words are directed at me, and he waits for me to acknowledge him.

"Can't drive like this," I say with a thick tongue.

"No, you can't. And neither can this lot. I'll take you."

Fuck.

He gives a cursory look to the front door, his cool demeanor nowhere to be found. There's a seriousness coming from him that I've never witnessed. Though, in his defense, I've only met him a couple times.

Pete's warm arm wraps around my waist. He tucks his mouth against my ear, but it's not seductive, just private. "You don't need to worry," he promises quietly. "James would castrate a motherfucker on the spot if they tried any bullshit with you. He'll get you home in one piece. He basically never drinks anyway."

I nod, only looking at him in my periphery. I'm not afraid of James, but I don't like the hint of protective nature he's exhibiting either.

"Yes, sir." I salute James's way and head for the door.

A whistle catches my attention, and I snap my head toward the group. Ginger rounds the bar, holding up my bag, and extends it to me. "Don't be a stranger." Her wink is more friendly than anything.

I step into the cool night air and wait for James to appear.

"This way," he says as the door closes behind him. The gravel crunches loudly in the quiet as I trudge across the lot behind him. He reaches the garage before me, opening a massive metal door and pressing a button inside. The first bay opens and a muscle car that I'd guess to be in mint condition sits waiting. Not that I know a fucking thing about them. It's a black beauty, though.

"Well, that's unexpected," I say, swaying on my feet as I study the car.

"In you go," he says, his Irish lilt thicker. He opens the passenger door and waves me to the seat.

I don't know his history, or if his accent is something he attempts to hide. Maybe years of living here causes it to ebb, but I imagine he can get a lot of people—men and women—to do exactly what he wants if he uses it properly.

I slide into the seat and he shuts the door. Resting my head against the cool window, I doze while he drives. It's not until he's pulled into my driveway that I realize I never told him where I live. I really need to cut back on the drinking.

"Be careful, Leah. Maci'd be real upset if something happened to you." It's about the nicest thing he could've said. And at the same time, it's the equivalent of a parent saying they're disappointed in you—a parent you respect. With the simple phrase, he's sealed his place in my life as just that.

Still, I can't bring myself to say much besides, "Thanks," because I'm suddenly feeling very in the spotlight about my behavior at the club. And not in a good way.

I slip out of the car and shut the door behind me. His lights stay pinned on my porch until I'm inside, and then I watch them recede from the living room window.

I seriously need to get my shit together.

Chapter 18

Leah

Before I know it, another week has gone by. Lily still doesn't have her phone turned on, despite me watching the kids two more nights. If anything, her habits are getting worse, not better. When she showed up on Thursday, the kids were dirtier than usual, so I got them into baths as soon as dinner was over.

On Friday, she's waiting for me when I get home from work. Roman hands me the mail as I get out of my car.

"Lily, if this is going to be all the time, we need to discuss it."

"Take it up with Mom." She jingles the keys on her fingers and avoids eye contact as usual. "You know I have to work tonight."

I widen my eyes and shake my head at her in confusion. "What would give me that assumption?"

She looks at me like I'm an idiot. "Tomorrow is Valentine's Day."

"Is that supposed to mean something to me?" I ask, annoyed.

"Um, yes. Lonely guys are dying for someone in their lap."

I put a hand up to shush her and curl my lip. "I don't need any more details. I work late tomorrow, so just plan to leave the kids tonight. But you better figure out something with Mom for tomorrow night, because I won't be here if you show up." I stare at the side of her head as she continues to ignore me.

"I'll talk to her. See you in the morning." She kisses Roman on the head as she walks past him to her car. "Bye, Vannah."

Savannah waves with her tiny hand extended from where she waits for me on the front porch.

"What are we gonna do for dinner tonight?" I ruffle Roman's hair as we walk up to the porch and unlock the door. Shoving it open, I let them run in ahead of me.

"Pasta!" Savannah hollers and runs straight for the kitchen.

Smokey perches atop the back corner of the sectional, waiting for us to enter. He greets me with a happy purr as the kids rush by. "Hey sweet boy, how was your day?" I drop my bag on the table and scoop him up in my arms. His fur is perfectly soft as I tangle my fingers through it and scratch his chest.

"Can we have pasta?" Roman stands by the pantry, waiting for the ok to open the door.

I lean forward, letting Smokey jump down from my arms. He winds around the kids' legs, throwing himself onto his back as Roman ignores him.

"Sure. See what you can find in there. I'm going to have to do some more shopping with all the meals you two have here." I grin at them so they know it's not a bother.

Roman returns with their favorite pasta shape and jar sauce. Savannah trades places with him, dragging the wooden stool out and across the room, the legs squeaking loudly on the linoleum floor. When she has it butted up against the counter, she climbs up beside her brother.

My heart tightens at what's becoming a bit of a new normal for us. I've always loved having the two of them over, but they've been spending more and more time here. It's made the nights less quiet.

"Pull the medium-sized pot from under there," I instruct, pointing to a lower cabinet. Roman yanks the pot out, offering it to me. "You two are pretty good kitchen helpers."

Savannah giggles and pretends to double over in exaggerated laughter as I fill the pot. I set it on the stove and lean down to her. "I need to get you a chef's hat." I tickle her belly and they laugh together.

"Ok, I'm about to turn the burner on, so what now?" I leave my hand on the knob without turning. Savannah waits with wide eyes and Roman purses his lips. "Pour in the pasta?"

"Well, first the water has to boil. But remember, I told you when the burner is on, you can't touch the stove. It will hurt you."

Savannah nods seriously, even though I'm positive she's not really absorbing anything, and Roman thumps his forehead with an open palm. "Oh yeah! I forgot dat part."

"It's really important. Never touch the top when it's on or after we're done. It stays hot for a long time."

He nods. "Ok."

After we make dinner together, they eat on the living room floor around the coffee table, because I've never bothered with a dining room set. I'm realizing it's becoming a necessity as of late. As well as several other things.

The kids help me clean up, and then I get them into baths before snuggling them into the bed in my spare room. Smokey curls up between them, purring contentedly, making me wonder who enjoys who more.

Just as I'm slipping out of their room, someone knocks on the front door. Smokey stays put, only turning his head to acknowledge the sound.

Unless Lily got sent home, I don't know who could be here. I don't bother checking before I fling the wood door open.

Nick stands on the other side with a pizza in one hand and a six-pack of canned whiskey cocktails in the other.

"Um, hi?" I ask, pushing the storm door open. Saying I'm confused by his presence is an understatement.

He doesn't move at first. "I owe you a date."

Crossing my arms to hide that I've already taken my bra off, made more obvious by the crisp February air, I lean against the open glass door. "You don't owe me anything."

"If it's not a good time . . ." He glances past me into the living room for a second.

"My niece and nephew are here, but you're welcome to come in."

"Are you sure? I don't want to interrupt family time."

"It's fine." I wave him in with a free hand and move out of the way. "Come in. They're asleep."

Finally he enters, and I watch as he scans the living room. "Wow. This isn't what I was expecting."

A large, cream sectional faces a massive television mounted above my fireplace, which is really more for show. It's too much work for the few days of the year we'd actually need a fire. The built-ins on either side of the fireplace house picture frames of me and my best friends, or Roman and Savannah. There are two necklace displays with my first two creations. A plush rug and rectangular coffee table fill the space between the couch and fireplace. It's just a comfortable room for living. Nothing exciting.

"You were expecting a mechanical bull in the corner and a jukebox?" I supply.

He turns with a grin. "No. I think I expected something . . . darker."

I draw my eyes up the walls. "Yeah, I guess it's pretty light. But it's a rental." I gesture to the couch. "Make yourself comfortable."

"I hope you like mushrooms," he says, sliding the pizza across the coffee table as he seats himself on the far side of the sectional.

"Boy scouts shouldn't lie. I can smell the pineapple from here." Calling him out on his fib is more to distract myself from how I feel about him remembering that I like pineapple on my pizza. And that he made a point to get something I like—even if he doesn't.

Popping the top on a can from the case, he offers me the drink.

"Thanks. So really, what's up?" I sip the whiskey and grapefruit combo. Not my first choice, but it'll do.

A gentle smile rests on his face, and he looks at me softly. He's like the epitome of loyalty. "I told you, I owe you a date."

I tuck myself tightly onto the opposite side of the couch from him.

Having Nick taking up space in my home is odd. He looks reasonably comfortable, and it seems too easy to crawl into his lap and kiss him. And yet, there's nothing in our history that says I should. Or that he wants me to. More importantly, he all but told me to back off. Which is why I can't figure out why he's here.

So instead, I lace my fingers together over my legs to keep them occupied.

When he offers me a slice of pizza, I hesitate. My eyes slide up his toned arm, the forearm defined even just holding a simple dinner. His eyes are encouraging.

I don't want to do this. I don't do casual. I do easy, yes. But easy and done. No strings, no bullshit. No pizza and chilling on my fucking couch with my family in the other room.

Keeping it all quietly tucked away, reminding myself that this isn't what I'm making it out to be, I accept the slice and take a bite. It's still warm, and the pineapple adds the perfect amount of sweetness on my tongue.

"Is it ok?" His voice is more confident than the question.

I swallow the bite, nodding. "Yes," I manage.

Nick grabs his own piece, chewing thoughtfully as he sits back. "Mmm."

I cock my head, a silent request for an explanation.

"Ok, fine. The pineapple isn't the worst thing," he mumbles.

"Never doubt me."

"Never, Wild Thing." He holds my eyes while taking another bite.

He's dangerous.

I might call him a boy scout, but I don't actually dismiss him as such. He's more like a Swiss Army Knife. He's capable of things I can't even imagine, and I'm afraid if I use it, I'll be lost without it.

"Penny for your thoughts," he says after swallowing.

The smile that overtakes my face is genuine and deep. "I haven't heard that phrase in a long time."

He waits.

"Maci's grandmother, Nana, used to say that to us," I add. I set the half-eaten piece of pizza back in the box and re-tuck my legs, wrapping my arms around them.

"Y'all were close. With her grandmother, I mean."

I nod, staring at the pattern in the rug. "Yeah. We met when we were in middle school. Maci's mom had just started dating her stepdad." I don't have to dive into what a fucking train wreck that was. We all lived the repercussions of it in the fall. "And my family has always been a disaster and a half. Izzy's family is perfect, but her parents are older and her grandparents passed when she was young. We all met at the city pool once, and we were inseparable after that."

Nick doesn't interrupt as I reminisce.

"My mom had a habit of making bad choices, and middle school is hard for a girl anyway. So as we grew, it wasn't uncommon for me to be dealing with something. Nana was always really good at checking in. She was probably the most solid adult I had in my life."

"Wow." Nick leans back and spreads his arms along the couch. It's not imposing or smug. Just casual.

I think he could be easy to love.

And that's scary as shit. I don't do love. Not that kind.

Smokey gives a trilling meow as he comes into the living room, but his pace slows when his eyes land on Nick.

"You have a cat," Nick observes with a smirk.

"Yeah. Surprised I can take care of someone besides myself?" It's a self-deprecating joke, hinting at the first night we met, but even rolling off my tongue it feels weird.

He shakes his head and his eyebrows dip for a second. "Not even a little."

Smokey sits like a statue on the opposite end of the couch from Nick, out of reach of me. His usually soft eyes are pensive.

"So ,what's next?" I ask, peering at Nick over my legs.

He drags his teeth over his lip. "You never answered me," he says playfully.

"I don't remember." The lie rolls off my tongue easily.

His leg bounces and he drops his eyes to the rug for a moment. When they come back, there's something new. Something hard. "Now who's lying?"

My breath catches. Him calling me out sends a zing of desire through me. I grin, unable to stop myself. "I don't know what you mean."

He twists to face me on the couch, scooting closer. "Mkay. Whatever you say. Anyway, it was your date idea. What comes after beer and pizza?" His head falls sideways to the back of the couch and he looks at me again, his gaze soft.

Despite the voice inside telling me not to—screaming really—I feel myself leaning forward. Drawn to him. His warmth, his honesty, his loyalty. His eyes bounce between my mouth and eyes.

My body continues to tilt forward with him leaning to meet me halfway. The warmth of his breath skates over my mouth, and I open my lips to warn him again that this isn't a good idea, I don't do repeats, when a loud screech rings out.

Both of us jump at the sound from the spare room. I haul ass into the hallway to find Roman sitting up in the bed, panting. "It's ok, you're safe. I'm here." I wrap my arm around his tiny, shaking body. He cries against my chest. "Did you have a bad dream?"

He nods against me. "I tought I was alone."

"No, bud. I'm here with you," I tell him quietly, squeezing him tighter in my arms.

Savannah is undisturbed, gently snoring next to him. After a minute, he scoots back down in the bed and rests his head on the pillow. I scratch my fingers through his dark hair.

"Leah?" Roman's eyes are closed and he speaks quietly. "Will you stay?"

"Sure, I can stay a few minutes." I continue stroking as his lids get heavier.

"I mean all night," he mumbles.

I chuckle. "It's my house; of course I'll be here all night."

"Mom leaves sometimes." His words are thick with sleep, and at first I'm not sure he said what I think. My hand stutters before I right it and continue my slow scratching through his hair. The thoughts in my mind are frantic.

Surely my sister isn't leaving her children alone at night? Four-year-old me starts to panic. *The dark is closing in, the thunder booms outside the window, and the rain falls in sheets.* She's not that far gone, is she?

When his breathing is heavy again, I sneak out the door to their room. My cheeks are wet with tears, and I wipe at them hastily.

Nick isn't in the living room when I round the corner, but he comes out of the kitchen as I enter, nearly running into me. "Hey. I put everything in the fridge. I can head out—" He's hiking his thumb over his shoulder as he takes in my face and pauses. "Are you ok?"

I nod but don't say anything. I'm not sure I could keep it together if I tried.

Indecision coats his features, the tight brow and pursed lips, his tense jaw. "I was going to say I should go. I know you have the kids here and I don't want to take you away from them. But now . . . I'm not sure I should."

My bottom lip wobbles and heavy tears fill my eyes. "I'm sorry. Just bullshit from my childhood."

He drops his chin lower, trying to get me to make eye contact. "You may not know this yet, but I'm a really good listener."

I wipe at my eyes again, trying to remove the makeup I assume is smeared. But something is crumbling, and I can't hold anything back. The idea that my sister would leave her babies, just like my father left his babies. My breathing won't steady, and a disjointed inhale sticks in my chest.

Nick slowly closes the distance between us and wraps his arms around me, and I start sobbing, tucking my arms between us. Four-year-old me is heartbroken, terrified, panicking. I let the tears fall until I can breathe normally again, or as normally as a swollen nose allows. Nick doesn't pull back until I gently push away.

"I'm sorry. Just give me a minute." I walk past him into the kitchen and grab a thick paper towel, wetting it under the faucet and cleaning up my face.

Nick is rooted in the same place when I return. He assesses me slowly. "Do you want to talk?"

I gesture him toward the couch. "You just let me sob into your shoulder. I guess I owe you a little explanation."

"You don't owe me shit. Or anyone else," he says firmly, but he moves to the couch.

Pressing myself into the fat pillows, I pull a blanket over me. Nick says nothing, keeping his face blank. I take a deep breath. "My parents have been divorced forever. My dad moved away when Lily and I were little. We still went and saw him, but it wasn't very frequent. A couple weeks twice a year or so.

"He drank a lot. He wasn't mean or anything. Didn't yell or hit us. He was just consumed with it and didn't pay attention to anything else. When I was four and Lily was about six, we were there visiting in the summer. We went to sleep and a little bit later I heard him leave. I didn't know it at the time, but later we found out he went to the bar."

"He left you alone to go to the bar?" Nick asks as his face tenses.

"Me and Lily," I confirm. "There was a storm. A huge thunderstorm. The rain was crashing into the windows, there was so much lightning. The power went out. I remember sitting on the bed sobbing, calling for my dad, and Lily kept telling me to be quiet and go to sleep." Tears fall again. Not heavy ones. Just the ones that seep and never stop. The tired, heartbroken ones. I use the fresh napkin I brought to dab under my eyes. "I cried myself to sleep. It took a while. My dad didn't come back until midday."

Nick shifts forward. "Leah, I'm—" He stares at me for a moment. "I don't think I have words for how fucked up that is. What happened to him?"

I shrug. "Nothing. We were kids; what were we gonna do?" I frown. "Our mom didn't care. She was hardly any better. Just because she was around doesn't mean she was present. I'm not getting into that," I say, waving my hand in the air. "I just— I got upset just now because Roman was scared, and he asked me to stay. I thought he meant until he fell asleep again, but he told me not to leave like his mom."

The crying renews. I bury my face in my hands, the uncontrollable sobs escaping my heaving chest. Nick's arms wrap around me again. I'm not sure he even knows what I say as I cry, "How could she do that? She couldn't, right? She wouldn't do what our dad did? I mean, I'm here. I've been helping. I can't do much more. Her phone is off, she never calls, she never warns me. They aren't mine, but I'm doing the best I can. But that, *that*. It's unacceptable." Anger takes over the hurt as I clean up again.

Nick releases me and leans back. "I don't know what she's capable of." He brushes hair over my shoulder. "Fuck. I'm sorry. I can't imagine what any of that must have been like." I sit with his words. Then he adds, "I'm glad you're able to help give the kids some stability. Do you really think she's leaving them?"

I sniff. "I don't know. They haven't said anything before, but Roman's just old enough to say something."

He nods.

"Not really the date you expected, huh?" I say, laughing to cover the embarrassment creeping in.

He winks. "It wasn't a date, remember?"

"Yeah." I chew my lip.

"I'm glad I came."

I can't look away this time. He's studying me, maybe waiting for confirmation. "Me too."

He glances down at his watch. "Are they early risers? Maybe you should get some sleep." He stands. "I can tuck you in. Snug as a bug in a rug."

I laugh. "I believe that, Boy Scout," I say, standing as well. "Thank you for coming tonight. For the pizza and for being a literal shoulder to cry on. Sorry about your shirt." I wipe at the wet area near his pec.

Nick clasps my hand with his, stopping my useless movements. "You don't need to apologize. Shirts get washed." For a long moment, we only stare at each other. Then he releases my hand and starts walking to the door.

I follow, holding the storm door open once he's outside. He turns around, illuminated in the yellow porch light. "Good night, Leah." There's one more long beat before he turns and heads for his truck.

"Night." I let the storm door fall closed, waiting until he's left the driveway to close the main door. I lean my forehead against it, drained.

CHAPTER 19

NICK

M y morning run is long and brutal, and all because I'm doing it to myself. As if the pounding asphalt could alleviate some of the tension and anger I hold from last night.

My conversation with Leah lingers in my mind. Knowing what she's doing with her family, knowing what they've done to her, what they continue to do to her.

She's got a tough exterior, but she's not unbreakable. Her ride-or-die friendship with Maci makes even more sense. They're two peas in a pod, in good *and* bad ways. I'm beginning to see her circle of trust is extremely limited. The reason she treats sex and romance the way she does is so much clearer.

People form so many beliefs about love and intimacy from experiences they have as children. And all she's seen is how people fail each other—and her. Show her that she doesn't matter. That they can't be trusted.

The pavement takes as much of a beating as it beats me. Last night was crisp, but the morning is warming up fast. I take all the trails and avoid Main Street, getting lost in my thoughts.

It's the longest run I've gone on in a while. I finally find myself at the end of the city trail behind The Spur. I jog up the sidewalk and turn at the corner to head back through town when I hear a door slam in the parking lot, drawing my attention over my music.

It's Gideon arriving for the day. I wave at him as I pass, doing a double take at the expression on his face. Like at the auction last week, he scowls at me, his mouth pulled into a deep frown.

Even though we aren't friends in the traditional sense, we've always been friendly toward each other. I don't know what's changed. And despite it not being my place or the norm for us, I turn and head his way to check in. "You good, man?"

"I'm good. You good?" His tone says otherwise. He crosses his arms and widens his stance.

I'm not sure why it bothers me so much that Gideon's demeanor toward me seems off. I'm not usually concerned with everyone in town. "I can't help but think that's not really the truth."

He arches an eyebrow and pulls his mouth forward in a smug expression. "I just don't get you, man."

Now I'm even more confused. "You're going to have to elaborate."

"I don't know if Leah told you the other night, but I apologized for overstepping. I didn't realize you two were a thing." His statement catches me off guard, but I don't have a chance to respond as he continues. "But then you show up the next day for the bachelor auction. Seems shitty to me."

"Well, I'd think the same if that's how I saw things, too. But you've got it wrong. Leah and I aren't a couple. I came to her show to support her as a friend. And she came the next day for the same reason."

"She bid on you. Quite high, if I recall," he challenges, his blank face a giveaway to his disbelief.

"Yeah, she did." I can't determine how forthcoming to be about why Leah bid so high, so I settle on a partial truth. "She thought she was helping me out. As a friend."

"Well, fuck." He scrubs a hand over his face. "Then maybe I didn't read all the flirting wrong after all."

My hands clench and unclench at my sides. I do my best to squash the rising jealousy at the idea of Leah flirting with Gideon or anyone else. It's likely fueled by a desire to protect her, and I lean into that. It doesn't matter that we had a moment last night, or that she opened up to me in an extremely vulnerable way. I've always known she could use a strong friend, and that's all it is. I don't get to be jealous.

"Yeah, maybe," I manage.

"Sorry, man." Gideon extends a hand, and I shake it quickly.

"No harm, no foul. I gotta finish my run. See you around." I hurry off before any more surprising feelings or news can come up.

My unusually long run, and the conversation with Gideon partway through, has me running late. I'm rushing out to the truck after a shower when Sutton calls. We haven't spoken since Leah's show and I answer from the dash, knowing I have a long highway drive ahead of me.

"Sutton! What's up, man?"

"Hey. You working?" he asks.

"On my way. What's up with you?"

"It's been a busy week, but I was calling to check on you. You want to tell me what happened last weekend?"

Sutton and Shane run a close tie for "Man of Fewest Words." Though, since meeting Maci, Sutton's really leaned in. He's much more involved in different friendships. I don't know if it's because of Maci, or because of almost losing her and all that transpired after. Either way, I've never needed him to prove his loyalty to me. And I have no idea what he's talking about.

I pull onto the county road, trying to bring to mind what he may mean. "I usually follow you pretty well, but I'm lost. What happened last weekend?"

"With Leah," he prompts suggestively.

I clear my throat.

"Uh huh." He chuckles.

"I think you misinterpreted that," I argue.

"Doubtful. But please, tell me what I got wrong. Or maybe what I got right. Because one minute you two were staring at each other like one or both of you was going to spontaneously combust, and then the next y'all were on your own roller coaster." I open my mouth to speak but his quick inhale stops me, and he continues. "And don't think I missed the way you watched her at the bonfire."

"Whoa. You've been holding onto that one for a while," I mutter. The bonfire at the ranch around Thanksgiving was one of the first times we all hung out together socially. And after the incident at The Spur with Leah basically passed out drunk, I couldn't help but feel protective. Then fucking Casey wanted to try and match her drink for drink.

I rub the bridge of my nose, suppressing my unwarranted frustration with Casey and composing my thoughts.

"Leah and I are friends." It doesn't feel like enough of an explanation, and Sutton says nothing as he waits for more. "We've run into each other a couple of times recently, and the night of her show she seemed to think I was hitting on her or trying to cockblock, or something."

"Kay. And then?"

I shake my head in the empty truck. "Then nothing. I let her know it wasn't like that."

"So why did she bid on you at the auction?"

His pointed question causes me to silently curse those women. "I'm assuming that came from Maci. I'm also assuming she told you it's because Leah was helping me out."

"Helping how?" I don't miss the skepticism in his tone as I turn onto the state highway. A shudder runs through me at the thought of Payton bidding on me.

"Payton ran the auction, and she was joking about bidding on me."

"Payton from high school?" This finally seems to catch him unprepared.

"Yep."

He scoffs. "Man, she's been holding on a while, huh?"

"I guess." I exhale heavily. "So it was all a big misunderstanding. Leah was trying to help so I wasn't uncomfortable. She made it clear that it wasn't about a date, especially after I told her . . ." I realize my slipup too late.

"After you told her . . . ?" Sutton prompts.

"Just that I wasn't hitting on her."

I can see Sutton's signature stare in my mind's eye. "Something isn't adding up. I remember a conversation like this recently. Only I was on the other end."

"No. No way. This isn't like that. For one, you shut me out."

"Or maybe you didn't ask the right questions," he teases.

I laugh. "I don't know what you want me to say! I answered your questions. Leah and I are just friends."

"I thought you were lying to me, but you're lying to you. I saw you."

"I'm not. Look, I think she's gorgeous, and fun, and creative, and a fucking great friend and aunt." I realize I'm not getting to the "but" part of the equation fast enough. "But that doesn't mean I want to date her. And even if I did"—my words are coming faster now—"we aren't right for each other."

"Now we're getting somewhere."

"Don't you have a wedding to focus on? Why are you suddenly trying to play matchmaker?" I grip the steering wheel harder. This conversation is making me itch.

"Fine. Deflect. I'll let it go for now. But you better come clean to yourself. Maci hasn't said she's noticed anything yet, but I know she has. If you think my questions are tough, wait until Leah's two best friends start digging."

CHAPTER 20

LEAH

Instead of meeting Lily at the door with the kids in the morning, I wait outside. I pick at weeds growing in the planters around the front porch—the only things that seem to grow in them.

She arrives around ten, which has been her normal when they stay over no matter what time I advise her to show up.

"They still sleeping?" She shuts her door when she gets out but leaves the car running.

I wanted to handle this calmly, but anger bubbles out of me. Like a boiling teapot, I all but scream, "Have you been leaving them alone at night?"

Her face pulls in disgust like I'm an idiot. "No! Why are you always looking for something to pick about? I'm doing the best I can!" Her hands swing as she talks like she's frustrated, but she has no other signs of being concerned or stressed.

"Oh, are you?" I ask, sarcastically.

"Yeah, we all know you're the good daughter, Leah. Fucking Christ, just send them out." She leans against the driver door, looking out into the street.

She's older, but I have about two inches on her these days. When I was little and she was bigger, she'd beat my ass if I stood up to her. I was close to ten before I matched her in size, and by that point I didn't fight back. She'd knock me around on occasion, but I assumed it was all normal sister shit.

Today, I use my size to my advantage. "Don't treat them like that!" I shove my finger in her face and nearly press my body against hers at the car.

She doesn't flinch or acknowledge me.

"They're kids! They're innocent! God, I'm helping you, right? What the fuck could you possibly need to do that would make you leave *children* alone?"

"Oh my god, Leah, it's not that fucking deep." She stands up straight and pushes her chest into me. She's petite, but it didn't stop her from breaking another girl's nose in high school and getting arrested. Anger management classes didn't go well because her coping skills were set by that point. A tiny kernel of apprehension embeds itself in my chest. "Occasionally, when they're asleep, I run up to the corner store for a soda."

"Nothing is worth leaving children alone. How could you? After what we went through?"

"What *we* went through?" She nearly spits at me. "You cried like a baby any time someone so much as looked at you wrong. So *I* had to be the one to take care of you. How many times did Mom hit me instead of you because you were crying? I got stronger and you got to play the fucking victim."

"That's not my fault. It's theirs." I don't have to call our parents out for her to know who I'm referring to. I may not remember the abuse she's talking about, but I believe it happened. Our mom wasn't equipped to handle us.

"Nothing's ever your fault," she quips, shouldering past me toward the door. "And then, after everything we did for you, you constantly judge people."

"Judge people? Mom is a drug addict who got us evicted multiple times while we were growing up. She encouraged me to do illegal drugs! Those are facts! And *you*. You can't take accountability for anything, and you're leaving your small children alone at night."

Lily whips around. "I told you it was to get a drink!"

"You're lying," I say flatly, trying my best to lower my voice as we scream at each other in my front yard for the whole town to see.

"What!?"

I shake my head. "You're lying. You always have. It's such a part of you that you probably don't even know what reality is anymore."

"Fuck you and the high horse you rode in on, Leah."

She disappears inside the house while hot tears fill my eyes. Angry, defeated tears. I can't believe she's doubling down on this, but of course she'd turn it around on me.

I'm at a complete loss. I'm doing my best to help everyone. But I can't make her want to be better.

Moments later she shoves my door open and all but pushes Roman and Savannah outside. I help buckle them in the car despite the anger and hurt battling inside. After Savannah is in snug and I step back to shut the door, I realize Roman is staring at me with wide, worried eyes.

My heart cracks. "I love you, bud," I whisper, though my throat is threatening to close. "I love you, Banana." Savannah looks at me blankly, and I blow them both a kiss. Lily hardly waits for me to close the back door before she reverses out of the driveway; I barely make it inside before I collapse against the door.

Last night's cry fest depleted most of my tears, but some still eke out while my breathing becomes painful and erratic. Racing thoughts fight for priority. How is it that nothing and no one is around and still everything is so loud?

I need to pull myself together. To find something to take the edge off.

There are still some whiskey cocktails left in the refrigerator. I swiftly open one and drink deeply. Leaning against the kitchen counter, I alternate between controlling my breathing and taking long pulls from the can until it's empty. My chest still hurts, but I convince myself it's residual, and if I distract myself with getting ready for work, I'll forget about it. I exchange the empty can for a fresh one and head into the bathroom.

My phone chirps on the counter as I'm finishing my makeup.

Maci:

Happy Galentine's Day!!

Izzy:

Wasn't that yesterday?

Maci:

It's whenever I say it is!

Izzy:

Whatever you say.

Maci:

Ma'am, what is your problem?

Izzy:

You interrupted my date.

Maci:

With your toy?

Izzy:

I don't kiss and tell.

Maci:

That's a different opening.

Maci:

> **And I don't know if you know this or not but you can silence your notifications.**

Izzy:

> **You broke through the barrier.**

Maci:

> **Yikes.**

I can't help but laugh to myself. The sound provides a release and interrupts the battling emotions within. I look back at the mirror, staring at my reflection. She looks made up while I still feel a mess. She whispers that I'm slipping. That things are getting worse.

"It's fine." My whisper escapes into the bathroom. "I've got it under control."

We both know I'm lying.

My phone beckons again.

Maci:

> **Leah, are you on a date, too?**

Me:

> **No. Getting ready for work.**

> **Happy Galentine's.**

CHAPTER 21

LEAH

Valentine's afternoon and evening is uneventful at work, aside from the rage and despair festering inside me. After I get off, I pull through The Beverage Barn, a drive-through convenience store, to replenish my alcohol stores. The cashier, a woman in her late forties, looks vaguely familiar. Her full mouth and dark eyes remind me of someone I can't place.

"You're very pretty. It won't always be Singles Awareness Day," she says with a wink.

"Oh, believe me, that's the least of my concerns." I heft the bag into the passenger seat as she pushes it through the window. "Have a good night."

At home, I mix myself a drink and continue to refill the glass until I get too drowsy to fight sleep anymore, passing out on the couch.

Early in the morning, I wake from a nightmare drenched in sweat. The images linger as I make my way into the bathroom to shower and brush my teeth. *A thunderstorm, alone in a dark room. When the lightning cracked, my small form morphed into my nephew, terrified in the dark.* The memory makes my stomach turn.

I have to work again today, so I only make a small drink to take the edge off my growing headache. I can't stomach anything else.

Abigail arrives just as I've finished counting and opening the two drawers. "Morning, Leah!" she sings. Her smile is brighter—and louder—than ever.

I cringe. "Hey, Abbykins."

She stops short. "Uh, what the fuck?" Her volume continues to increase.

I close one eye to compensate. Fucking light. "Sorry, I couldn't understand your shouting. What's the problem?"

"My problem? I was going to ask you the same thing." She fails to lower her volume.

I wince. "Just a little headache." I ignore her stare, sitting down to work on next week's schedule. A few seconds later, she disappears into the back.

We don't speak for the majority of the shift. I feign total focus on scheduling, getting up to help the few times that Abigail ends up with a line. She works on new mannequin attire and a front table display.

When she's run out of things to do, she makes her way back to me, moving around doing a whole lot of nothing. "I wonder if Sadie would stock your jewelry. Have you asked her? She supports local artists." Her point is valid, especially since I never considered asking.

"I haven't asked," I say softly.

"Wouldn't hurt."

"It's a good idea." I offer her a small smile and a nod. It's the best I can do.

I want to talk to Abby about my jewelry. About anything, really. But all I can think about is my selfish sister and her innocent children. How she's breaking them piece by tiny piece. And how I hate myself for not doing more.

Lily asked me to let her and the kids move in. Tried to say it would save us both money, but that's not really the gig. She just wants someone accessible all the time. And it's not like I wouldn't help her every chance I got, but I have a life, too.

But even that feels selfish. Because instead of me being forced into permanent babysitting duties, Roman and Savannah are suffering.

I suck.

I still have plenty of alcohol at the house, but I don't want to drown my sorrows alone. My friends will just try to cheer me up, but that's not what I need. I need to wallow. Which is how I end up at The Wild Turkey.

My mom used to play cards here when I was younger. I never saw a person under fifty. It's all dark corners and sad jukebox music in a beat-up old cinder block building.

It's perfect.

I park my ass at the bar, which is mostly full, and order two shots and a whiskey and soda to start. The bartender, a woman pushing seventy, eyes me speculatively. "Bad breakup?"

"Nope." I down the first shot. "Just shitty family." I down the second shot. "Though, I'm partially to blame."

"Aren't we all," she says wryly.

"Might as well leave the bottle," I mutter, pulling the straw from my glass and drinking it down quickly. The faster I get drunk tonight the better.

Mag, which I learn is the bartender's name, does indeed keep the drinks coming. After round four of the same, or maybe it's five, she asks, "You got a ride, darlin'?"

The edges of my vision are fuzzy, but I still feel the anger and hurt, so I'm not done. "Yep," I lie. I do need to consider how I'm getting home. I could call Nick, but the idea of him looking at me with pity or something similar threatens to make my drinks reappear. I could call Maci or Izzy, but they'll want to talk this shit out, and that's exactly what I'm trying to avoid. Pete might be an option. But I'm not convinced I'll be able to hold on for the ride home.

The image of me falling off the back of his motorcycle and getting run over on Main Street flashes through my mind. I snort. That might actually turn out ok.

Mag takes too long looking me over. "Not sure I believe you, doll."

"Don't care if you do," I mumble. I slap the bar top for another round. "One more, Mag. You're the best."

"Leah?" a familiar voice comes from behind.

I swivel too quickly on the chair, trying to see who's behind me. Ginger stands with her hands on her hips. "Ginger!"

She smirks at me. "What are you up to here?"

"Washing away my problems?"

"That's not how that works."

"D'you know her, Ginger?" Mag asks.

"Yes, aunty. She's a friend of a friend." Ginger looks past me to the woman.

"Aw, aunty. Is bartending a family thing?" I ask with a thick tongue.

Ginger's eyes slide to me. "Not exactly. How are you getting home? It's time to go."

"I'm not done yet." My voice is too high and a little whiny. Maybe I am done.

"Said she has a ride," Mag offers.

"Doubt that's true," Ginger says without looking her way. "I'll take her. Let's go, babe." She extends an arm to me in encouragement.

I huff. "Buzzkill."

"You'll thank me later."

"Wait! I have to pay Mag." I swivel the chair back around and nearly slide off. Ginger's hands cinch at my waist. "Whoa, shit!" Hysterical laughter bursts free. Laughter is exactly what I need.

"You already gave me your card, sweetheart." Mag reaches across the bar, extending my debit card.

"Oh." My mouth drops open heavily. "I completely forgot. See, I told you you're the best."

She sets a hand on her hip and smirks. "Don't know what you're going through, hon, but I hope you get it worked out. Men aren't worth the headache."

"What about sisters?" I ask too quickly.

Her eyebrows rise and she purses her lips. "Can't say."

"Let's go," Ginger says, helping me down from the stool.

"What did you come here for?" I ask on the way to the car.

"It's my night off. And I don't need cowboy bullshit at The Spur. Sometimes I like to drink quietly by myself. Though maybe not as much as you." She smiles, shutting the door after I sit in the passenger seat. "Where am I goin'?"

I give the address and pass out before we get there.

CHAPTER 22

NICK

E very month I have to spend a week supporting a game warden in another county. Sometimes more frequently than that, depending on the needs in the area. It doesn't bother me to have fresh landscape, and the entire week is considered overtime, so it never feels like a hassle.

Only this time I contemplate stopping by Leah's to check on her before I leave.

Even though I've given her my number, she hasn't used it. Asking for hers seems like the opposite of maintaining the boundary I set. The boundary I muddied by taking alcohol and pizza to her house unannounced. And almost kissing her.

Showing up to her house unannounced again in the middle of the afternoon feels like making myself at home. Or a nuisance.

It's a risk, but I decide to see if I can get some information out of Sutton without directly asking.

Me:

> Headed to the valley for the week. You guys need anything before I go?

Sutton:

> **Did you mean for this to come to me?**

> **Kidding, man. We're good.**

I stare at the phone, contemplating being more direct. He already thinks something's up.

Sutton:

> **How's Leah?**

I'm both annoyed and relieved that he's posed the question instead of me.

Me:

> **That's a good question. Know something I don't?**

It was the best in I was going to get. Unlike the first few messages, he doesn't respond right away. I'm loading the truck when my phone pings again.

Sutton:

> **Nope.**

I can't decide if his message is helpful or not. If there was something catastrophic, he'd have to know. I don't get the impression Maci keeps much from him. Unless Leah isn't telling her.

A pit forms in my stomach. How much is she keeping locked up?

Fuck.

She can tell me to get lost if she wants, but I'm not leaving without checking on her.

Leah's house is shut up tight. There aren't any other cars parked in the drive. If the kids are over, they're quiet.

I knock and question if this was the best idea while I wait for her to answer.

The wide, white door swings open and Leah stares at me from behind the storm door, looking pale. Her hair is in a wild mess on top of her head, posted over droopy eyes. Smokey greets me from behind her, jumping gracefully to the back of the couch and meowing happily, but Leah's face doesn't brighten.

"Hey," I finally say. Something tells me that coming by was a good thing, except I don't think she's going to see it that way. "You good?" I turn up the charm, letting the words fall out casually like I would greet her any other time. Not like I'm convinced she's self-medicating and drowning in her sadness.

"Peachy." She doesn't invite me in as she turns and saunters away from the door, but she doesn't close it either. As I step inside fully, the cat bats at my arm, pleading for attention. I give him a quick scratch behind the ears and shut the door behind me.

Not a single light is on. All the curtains are shut. I don't hear anything in the way of music or television noise. The air feels stiff, stagnant.

Following Leah's path, I walk into the kitchen. She pulls something from the fridge and pops open the top of a drink as the door lazily swings closed. A whiskey cocktail. A couple used glasses sit by the sink, along with an empty bottle.

I don't have a baseline to judge her drinking habits. I've seen her drink socially—and she can put some shit away—which tells me she had a fuck ton the night we met. But I don't know if she's a daily drinker. I only know that Maci said there has been an increase.

"Want one?" she asks, her voice heavy with fatigue. She gulps the fresh drink.

"No, thanks. I'm actually headed out of town for work."

Her head tilts slightly and she finally catalogues my uniform. At least there's some interest there. "Did something happen?"

"No. I have to support another county once a month." I lean my weight against the doorframe of the kitchen. She's not coming out of here without giving me some better answers. "So, let's try this again. Are you ok?"

Her hazel eyes never leave mine as she drinks deeply from the can. For once, I don't think she means it as a challenge, even though it feels that way. "Yep."

"I can't say I believe you."

"Can't say I care," she says curtly, staring angrily at the floor.

"Are you talking to Maci and Izzy about what's going on?" I press.

Her face jerks up. "What's going on?"

I scrunch my face. "What Roman said." *What else could I mean?*

Her chest seems to deflate slightly. "I haven't had an opportunity."

"You're lying."

At that, she turns her anger on me, stalking forward from the fridge. "You don't know anything, Nick Foster." She pokes me in the chest with a finger. Last time she did this was far more pleasant. "And don't call me a liar."

I smirk. "I didn't call you a liar, Wild Thing. I said you're lying." She crosses her arms, squeezing the can in one hand, her nude nail polish chipping at the edges. "You need to lean into your friends," I continue. "They'll do anything for you."

"Yep." Leah turns and downs the rest of the drink before tossing the can into the recycling. The green bin is overflowing with cans and bottles, and not one item seems to be anything other than alcohol. Then she mutters, "But things aren't always that simple."

"It's exactly that simple." It's hard to pull my gaze from the evidence of her misery.

Her heavy sigh fills the kitchen. "Why did you come here, Boy Scout?"

"I'm earning my 'Helping A Neighbor' badge." I force a smile as she turns back to me.

She gives the tiniest lift at the corner of her mouth. I try to hide my disappointment; I really hoped she'd be doing better before I left.

"You can't stay locked up in here. Or in there," I add, pointing to her head. "You need to let your friends in. And I'd batter you until you cave, but I have to get out of town. So can I trust that you'll talk to someone?"

"Scout's honor." She holds up two fingers with a straight face, and although I've never been a boy scout, I'm still fairly certain whatever move she's trying to pull isn't accurate. I can't help but laugh. Her hand falls and she frowns. My laughing intensifies. "What the hell is so funny?" she asks, confused.

I pat my hidden vest to calm myself. "You just make me laugh."

She remains unamused. Smokey winds around her legs and throws himself onto his back, rubbing his fluffy coat along her bare feet.

I want nothing more than to wrap her in my arms and do whatever is needed to ease her pain. I hate to leave her like this. But it's not my place to stay, and she's not acting as if that's what she wants. "Please. Reach out to friends. You still have my card?"

She drops her eyes to the cat, nodding just enough to indicate her answer, and lifts a foot to rub at his belly. He wriggles his midsection to get more comfortable.

"Ok." I stand fully from the door frame. "Call or text me any time."

"Yeah. Ok." Her soft voice is still dismissive.

Something keeps tugging me to her. I have one more thing to try. "Leah. Look at me." My tone is firm, and she does so immediately as a different kind of tightness overtakes her features. I soften my voice and ask, "Do you need a hug?"

Her eyes bounce back and forth in indecision. Finally, her arms fall open at her sides, and I know it's the only invitation I'm going to get. I cross the kitchen and lean forward to scoop her into a hug.

She throws her arms around my neck and lifts her feet off the ground, wrapping her legs around my waist. And *fuck*, I do not want to leave. I squeeze her tightly, committing the feel of her soft body molded to me to memory, and I don't let go until her legs finally open and drop as she reaches with her toes for the ground.

Setting her softly to the floor, I study her face. There's a little more life in her eyes than when I arrived, a little more color in her cheeks.

A few strands of hair have come loose from her bun. They frame her face, and my brain screams at me to lean in. To taste her mouth and kiss away her hurt. Instead, I tuck the tempting locks behind her ear.

Her eyes widen and she licks her lips. "Thanks for stopping by," she says stiffly, taking a large step back. "Guess you were right to watch out for me. I'm more of a mess than I thought."

"You're not a mess," I argue softly. "You're going through some shit. But you don't have to do it alone."

Her head bobs, and I feel a little better about leaving. I turn for the door and she follows, stopping at the threshold. "Bye, Nick. Drive safe."

"Later, Wild Thing."

CHAPTER 23

LEAH

Maci:

Sutton and I are going to a livestock auction this weekend. Who wants to join?

Time to find cattle for the new herd.

Izzy:

Can't this weekend. I have family stuff.

Me:

Seen one cow, you've seen them all.

Maci:

We both know that's not true.

Me:

Do I get to bid?

Maci:

I don't think I even get to bid.

Me:

Sutton afraid you'll paddle him?

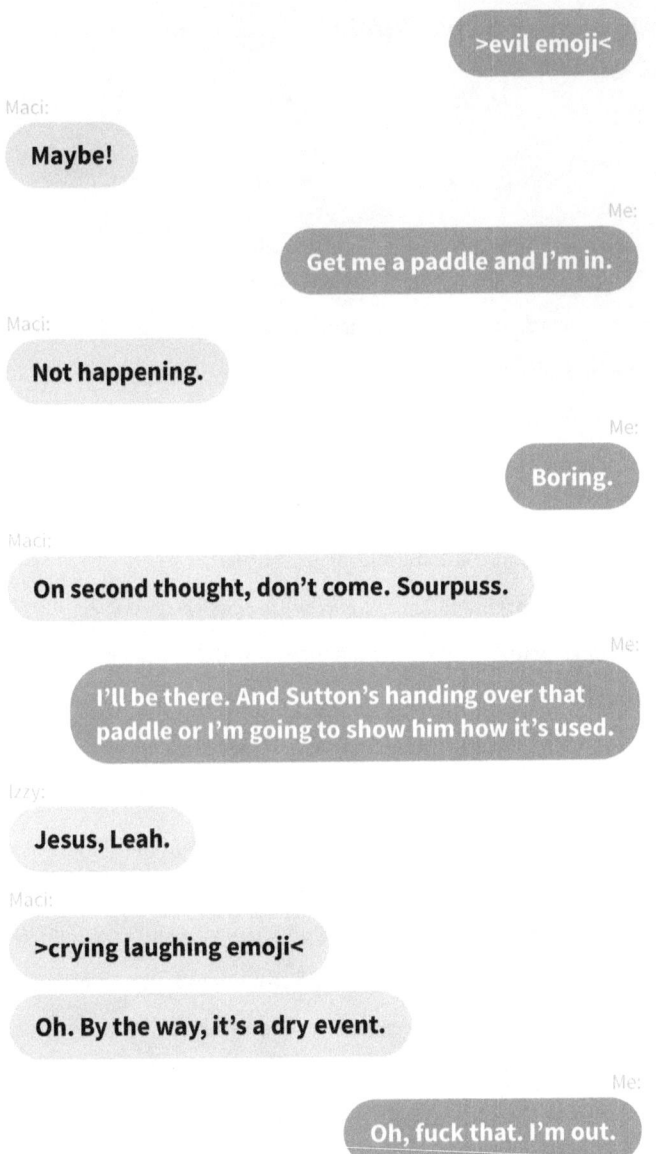

>evil emoji<

Maci:

Maybe!

Me:

Get me a paddle and I'm in.

Maci:

Not happening.

Me:

Boring.

Maci:

On second thought, don't come. Sourpuss.

Me:

I'll be there. And Sutton's handing over that paddle or I'm going to show him how it's used.

Izzy:

Jesus, Leah.

Maci:

>crying laughing emoji<

Oh. By the way, it's a dry event.

Me:

Oh, fuck that. I'm out.

I know she's kidding, but it's not the first time she and Izzy have said something about my drinking. Subtle or otherwise. Would she have mentioned it to Izzy if she was the only one going?

It doesn't matter. I can certainly go an evening without a drink.

True to his word, Sutton has not handed over the paddle to Maci or me. He didn't even balk when I promised to show him how to use it properly. Maci only snickered at me.

When the last herd is up for bidding, movement behind the pen catches my eye.

A familiar sand-colored uniform and cream hat. *Nick.*

My heart beats faster. *Isn't alcohol supposed to be a downer?*

He chats with a few of the ranchers, a wide, amicable smile plastered across his face.

As if called, his eyes shoot my way. I stare back at him like a deer in headlights, but I can't bring myself to smile or wave the way he does.

"Oh hey, there's Nick." Maci jumps up from her seat and waves.

"You're already engaged," I grumble.

She sticks her tongue out at me as Sutton briefly eyes me from her other side. I home in on him. Nothing Sutton does is casual. He's the most calculated, stoic person I've ever met. An endearing quality, honestly—when it's not directed at me.

"By the way, what's up with that?" Maci seats herself between us again.

I study her face. "What's up with what?"

"You and Nick," she says.

My fists tighten in my lap. "I'm not sure what you mean."

Sutton snorts. Maci's head snaps his way. "You saw it, too."

I wait for her to turn back. "Someone want to tell me what you saw?"

She purses her lips. "The tension between you and Nick. And don't even think about playing dumb with me."

I shake my head and feign major interest on the final bidding taking place. "No idea. He came to the show; I went to the auction with Izzy." I pull the pineapple-shaped flask from the inside pocket of my jacket, taking a swig. "This herd looks good."

Maci ignores my final comment. "Ok, yeah, but you bid on Nick at the auction. And you won. Are you telling me he didn't take you on the date? Because that's not the Nick I know."

"Then you must not know him as well as you think, because Nick Foster and I have not gone out on a date." I choose my words carefully.

It takes all my willpower, but I do not give in to Maci's narrowed eyes. Instead, I study the auctioneer like he's the most interesting person in a black cowboy hat that I've ever seen.

I clap my hands loudly after the gavel sounds. "So what's next!"

Sutton stands. "I need to go settle up."

Maci takes his extended hand. "Come on. I bet we can see Nick back there," she says, grinning at me.

I grunt toward the arena, ignoring the place I last saw Nick. "I'll come for moral support."

"Yeah. Ok," she retorts, her tone thick with sarcasm.

We hardly make it downstairs before Nick rounds from a different hallway and meets up with us. He shakes Sutton's hand with a friendly greeting and gives Maci a side hug.

Our greeting is stiff. "Hey, Boy Scout," I say, keeping back.

He winks.

Maci coughs a few times. "Liar," she spits out, then continues to cough.

Sutton snickers and Nick looks between us, happily oblivious to the joke. I scowl and nudge her in the ribs.

"On second thought, I'm really tired. You two have fun," I mutter.

"I'll walk you out," Nick offers without hesitation. Because of course he does.

"Bye!" Maci waves excitedly over her shoulder and Sutton guides her deeper down the hallway with an arm around her waist.

Nick falls in stride with me as we exit the building.

"I'm parked over there." I swing my hand in the direction of my car.

He gestures for me to lead the way and walks next to me, not filling the silence.

"How was your vacation?" I finally ask.

His answering chuckle sends a shot of electricity down my spine. "I enjoy visiting other counties. It was a good week."

"Good." *Great response, Leah.*

"How are you? Did you have a good week?" he asks, his voice softer. Expectant.

"It was fine. Thanks." We stop next to my car, and I turn fully to him for the first time tonight. "Listen, I appreciate you stopping by to check on me before you left, but it doesn't have to be a repeat occurrence."

His eyes roam my face, setting my skin on fire. "I didn't do anything I wouldn't do for any other friend."

"But are we friends, Nick? Really?" My words come out with a little more exasperation than I intend.

"Yes, we're friends," he says adamantly, his brows furrowing together. "Why would you ask me that?"

"You think we act like friends?" I cross my arms over my chest. "That we talk like friends? That you watch over me like a friend? Even if you try to kid yourself that you don't, you make a point to scare off anyone else."

"That's not true! Fuck, Leah. If you want to sleep with someone, do it." His jaw is stiff and his lids heavy, refusing to make eye contact now. I feel like an asshole. His bottom lip almost pops out in a pout, and I want to jump into his arms and tell him to stop playing like we both don't know what's going on.

But I don't. Because he's also made it clear that he doesn't want to sleep with me. Or date me. Or both. So whatever reason he has to feel protective, whatever it is that causes tension between us, it doesn't matter.

"I don't want to," I say anyway. His sullen face makes it hard to maintain my frustration, and my words come out more sincere than I want. "Ok, that's a lie. But not the way you think." I immediately regret spilling the rest.

His tense jaw releases as he studies me. "What does that mean?" he asks, then immediately shakes his head. "Never mind. It's not my business."

I want to argue. To tell him he's made it his business by inserting himself into my life over and over, but that wouldn't be fair. To me or him. Maybe I'm reading him wrong. Maybe to him everything is friendly, and he's acting the same as he would for any friend. Maybe I'm just so wildly horny that I'm willing something else to be there.

I really fucking need to get laid.

The tension rises between us as we continue to study each other without moving or speaking.

"I'm not trying to suffocate you." He rubs his hand back and forth across his mouth. Nick is so unflappable that just that little motion proves I'm not just imagining things.

"You're not." I lean against the car door. "Maybe I'm just not used to people looking out for me. My parents never did. My sister barely tolerates me. Izzy and Maci are always there, obviously. It's just me. I've never had a guy friend. I'll work on it. You've been clear I'm not what you're looking for anyway."

"That's not what I said," he argues, closing the space between us. "I told you that *I'm* not what *you're* looking for. You want something I can't give you."

"I didn't propose," I tease, leaning into him and pressing my hands against his chest. The Kevlar vest is an odd combination of hard and cushion beneath my hands.

He looks down at me tenderly. "I can't give you one night, Leah. That's just not who I am."

"That's all I'm good for," I whisper back, defeated.

"Are you crazy?" His eyes widen and his hands find my hips.

I shrug. "Maybe. My family is nuts. Doubt the apple falls far from—"

"You don't see yourself properly."

A bitter laugh forces itself from me. "What does that even mean? Is that some convoluted way of saying I need more confidence or something? Because I don't."

"I'm saying you're worth far more than one night."

Almost to myself, I shake my head the tiniest bit. "You have no idea what you're talking about."

"I could prove it to you." He says it like a promise.

"How?" I challenge. "You can't give me one night, and I can't give you anything more."

"You're wrong. You give so much more without even trying." After a moment, he releases my hips and steps back, swallowing deeply. His mouth tips to one side as he chews the inside of his lip.

I stare at him, dumbfounded. "What are you talking about?"

His eyes dart back and forth between mine. "Fuck it."

With one step forward, he grabs my face between his hands and covers my mouth with his. Despite the grip on my cheeks, his hungry kiss is soft, tender. Pressing into him, I reach up with a hand to hold the back of his head as he continues to explore my mouth with his. A scent that is all Texas in the spring floods my nostrils.

He releases one cheek, only to slide that hand around my back.

When he breaks the kiss, loosening his grip on me as he prepares to step away, I lean in hard, pressing my lips against his mouth again. I bring my other hand around his neck to hold him tighter. Whatever he's done, he's opened something inside me. I can't let him go.

He doesn't fight, instead teasing at my lips with his tongue, which I let in willingly. It brings the interaction to an entirely new level, and, like in my kitchen, I lift my legs to wrap around his waist. He presses into me, crashing me into the side of my car as he continues to explore, our tongues twisting and sliding together.

Of all the kisses I've had—hard, hungry, wet, devouring—none have ever come close to this. Maybe it's the months of building tension; I don't know. But I don't ever want a kiss that isn't like this one.

Eventually he releases my mouth, which feels gloriously swollen, and kisses my cheekbone and then my jaw. He pauses with his face against my temple, catching his breath. Each inhale and exhale heaves into my ear. My chest rises and falls in time with him.

When he pulls back, I drop my legs to the ground, and he settles his hands on my hips until he's sure I'm steady.

"What the fuck was that?" I say on a breath.

His eyes close slowly as he inhales once more. He backs up and I step forward to follow, but he reaches around me to open my door.

Was that the end? Did he realize I'm not what he wanted after all?

I slide into the driver's seat, keeping my eyes on him.

"Drive safe," he orders quietly, maintaining eye contact, and closes the door.

I hardly give myself time to think as I start the car and pull out of the parking lot while he stands watch. My fingers dance over my lips the entire ride home. I just had the best first kiss of my life. And I'm scared to death it will never happen again.

CHAPTER 24

NICK

Even though kissing Leah was everything I thought it would be and then some, a tiny part of me still thinks it was a terrible idea. She's deserving of more than a quick lay, but mind-altering kiss or not, she may decide that's still not what she wants. And I'm not sure I can go without doing it again.

If only she'd use the damn number I gave her. She's even more stubborn than I realized.

Mercifully, I don't have the opportunity to stew on it. It's my turn to have support, and Game Warden Jeffries from two counties over is with me. Today, we're on the water checking licenses. I can check the banks as frequently as I want or need to, but being on the open water isn't an option without someone with me, and it's been about five weeks since I've had the chance.

Our county has a small lake system. The water is high right now from spring showers, but the last few days have been calm and there are fishermen everywhere. A cool breeze gusts through the cockpit every other minute, making the day even more pleasant.

"How'd you end up in your own county?" Jeffries asks as we head back to shore.

"Coincidence. The warden here was retiring." Not everyone is so lucky to work in the county they want. The process to become a warden is long, and placement is determined by availability.

"That was a lucky break."

We've worked together a few times after the last year, so getting the boat in and out of the water has become a bit of second nature. When the time comes, he drops me at a dock near the truck and trailer, and I back it down the ramp.

Jeffries situates the boat onto the trailer, and I hop out to help him lock everything down. My phone vibrates in my shirt pocket.

"All right, I'll pull forward," I tell him once we're secure.

Jeffries climbs down from the boat when I've parked, and I pull out my phone to check the message. Most likely my mom asking about lunch this weekend.

Wrong.

It's actually fucking Leah.

Unknown:

Hey Boy Scout. Fuck up any fish's day today?

Of course she'd ask about the fish. I feel immediately lighter and respond after adding her info to my contacts.

Me:

Nope. Just fishermen.

Leah:

Buzzkill.

Me:

I've been called worse.

Leah:

Hopefully better, too.

Is she flirting with me? I feel so fucking out of my element. I'm a reasonably confident guy. I'm not afraid to ask women out. But I don't even know what the end goal is with Leah, so I have no idea how to traverse what it is we're doing. Or not doing. Or thinking of doing.

Fuck. I know what I've been thinking of doing. And it starts with—

Leah:

I'm having a birthday party for my niece this weekend.

You should come.

Me:

I have a family thing Sunday, but I can make Saturday work.

Leah:

Good. It's Saturday.

Me:

Your house? What time?

Leah:

Yes. Two.

Me:

Count me in.

I pocket my phone.

"Girlfriend?" Jeffries asks. He's buckled in the passenger seat, staring at me.

"Oh no, just a friend." I smile, feeling like I've been caught with my hand in the cookie jar.

"Right. Whatever you say, man."

I focus on my mirrors as I maneuver away from the boat ramp, ignoring his teasing grin.

When I pull up to Leah's on Saturday, I'm not the first one there. Trucks and cars line both sides of the street, leading me to wonder how big this two-year-old's birthday party really is.

The front yard houses several rectangular tables with bright colored, disposable tablecloths. It's littered with beach balls. Among the children running between the tables with various noise makers, I spot Savannah and Roman wearing party hats. A handful of people I'm loosely familiar with skirt the yard.

Just as I hit the driveway, Sutton and Maci emerge from the front door. Sammi, Justin, and Viviane follow them out. Sammi sets Viviane on the ground and she runs as fast as her tiny legs can carry her to meet up with the others.

"Hey, Nick!" Sammi sees me first.

"What are you guys doing here? This is a ways from Dallas," I ask before greetings go around.

Sammi smirks. "Viviane and Banana hit it off at Thanksgiving at Mom and Dad's house," she says, referring to Strickland Ranch. "We had to make it. Plus, it gives me more time to bond with my new sister." She reaches for Maci, who blushes but accepts the hug.

"That's cool. I'm going to drop this ice inside"—I hold the bag up as proof—"and then maybe I can snag the birthday girl for a minute."

"Leah's in the kitchen," Maci offers. Her raised eyebrow and pursed lips don't feel like a response to the ice.

Smokey's yowl is the first thing I hear when I pass through the storm door. It closes behind me and I scan the living room for him, but he's nowhere to be seen.

Leah pulls a tray from the oven when I enter the kitchen. Her head pops my way as she sets it on the counter. "How'd you know I needed ice?" She snatches the bag from me unceremoniously and drops it twice to the kitchen floor before shoving it into the freezer.

"Lucky guess."

Her hair is loose and wild, one of my favorite looks on her. She wears a pair of tattered denim shorts and a loose white top. It's casual, like she isn't out to impress anyone, but I find her alluring nonetheless.

She smiles, turning from the fridge. Her whole frame seems lighter than last week.

"Is your sister here?" I ask, and a small part of me hopes she isn't, because I may have a hard time not acknowledging what I know.

She snorts. "Not even. She said Savannah didn't need a party and she dropped them off to go work."

"Have things been better?"

Leah starts organizing food onto trays. "I guess. Her phone is finally on, so she sends me a text before she comes. That's the extent of our communication."

"What about what Roman said?" I don't mean to push, but it's more than she's said in weeks. I'm rolling with it, hoping it means she's ready to talk.

She grips one of the metal pans and her shoulders tighten. "She said she runs up to the corner store on occasion to get a soda."

I clamp my teeth together, my neck and shoulders tensing. "Do you believe her?"

She turns wildly, her frustration bleeding into her words. "It doesn't matter. Even if it *is* the truth, it's not ok. Not in my eyes. And if it's worse than she's letting on . . ." She stops talking and stares at me, sadness creeping in.

"Ok." I move closer, running my hands over her shoulders. "I'm not trying to dampen the mood. I just wanted to check on you. What can I help with?" I eye the counters like the food may start jumping off.

Her mouth hints at a smile. "Here," she says, handing me two platters. "Courtesy of Maci and Sutton. There's a table in front of the porch for food. I'll follow you out with the others."

"So I'm in charge of appetizers?" It feels unnatural to have her follow me and not the other way around. I push open the storm door and lean into it, letting her pass.

"I'm sure I could leave you in charge of a lot more than that and it'd be just fine in your capable hands."

Turning my head to one side, I blurt, "What do you know about my hands?" Instantly, heat rushes through my face.

"Are you flirting with me, Boy Scout?" I laugh as she smirks over her shoulder. "You're still wearing the bracelet I made." Her tone softens the tiniest bit.

A fire flares in my chest. I'm not especially sentimental, but I haven't removed the gift since I got it.

She keeps talking, quieter. "I know what to expect from your hands. They're strong and tender."

I let the spring breeze carry the echo of her words away. It's better than telling her that my hands ache to memorize the feel of her skin. Every curve and dip. Her warmth.

We arrange the platters on the table just the way she wants and encourage the kids to eat. They have pizza and decorate their own cupcakes before we sing the birthday song. There's even a bubble station, and all the kids leave with a goodie bag.

Aside from our core friend group, everyone departs after a couple of hours, including Sammi and her family who head out to relax with the Stricklands. Izzy and Liv follow shortly.

The sun is sinking when Maci and Sutton take Roman and Savannah into their room to play. It's not a huge space, and it's made even smaller by the toys strewn all about from party friends.

Leah and I clean up out front, moving all the extra food to the kitchen and filling several trash bags with tablecloths, plates, cups, and random trash that's accumulated.

The sky is hinting at dusk when Lily pulls in. She climbs out of the car, not bothering to acknowledge my existence. "Jesus, was it a kegger?"

Leah ties the strings of the trash bag in her hands. "Funny." Her voice doesn't hold an ounce of humor. "They had fun. Pizza and cupcakes."

Lily stops walking where the driveway meets the yard. "What do I need to load up?"

Leah's eyebrows lift slightly. "Load up?"

"Yeah. Gifts."

Leah laughs. Not a small chuckle, but a full belly laugh. She throws her head back and howls into the sky.

Lily's face tightens and she clenches her keys tighter.

Leah straightens herself and turns to steel before my eyes. "So let me get this straight. I offered to host a party for Savannah, which *you* told me she didn't need, and you would rather drop them off so you could go work. Then, I paid for the party setup and literally planned, coordinated, and executed the entire thing—by myself—and now you'd like to haul off with the gifts?"

Lily opens her arms wide and leans the top half of her body forward, her feet staying planted. Her voice is full of venom. "If you would have let us move in, you wouldn't have to do it all on your own. We could split it. But no. You're too good for that. You'd rather be a martyr, creating a scenario that's so hard that people applaud you for completing it."

I wonder if there was a time the sisters remember just loving each other. Because this, this is toxic.

"Why would I let you move in?" Leah cries. "You drop the kids on me every chance you get. I'd never see you if you were here. And honestly, that's not the point. You didn't think your own daughter deserved to be celebrated on her birthday."

"She's two! She's not going to remember this!" Lily shouts.

Leah takes a step forward. "She might not. But if she does, she's going to remember that she had fun. And that you weren't there."

Lily's lips pull back. "You're a bitch. I had to work."

I step forward. "Ok, maybe we need to take a breather."

"I would've rescheduled it," Leah says, ignoring me. Lily still hasn't acknowledged I exist. "That's why I told you about it in the first place. But you'd rather just show up for the loot."

Lily rolls her eyes and throws her hands up. "Yes, because I'm going to play with the toys and wear the clothes myself. The gifts are for her, Leah. And if you don't realize that, it's on you. You're the one being selfish."

"Yeah. I'm the selfish one." Leah crosses her arms over her chest and stares at her sister.

The storm door bangs open as Roman and Savannah burst into the yard. "Mommy, watch dis!" Roman holds one of the large bubble wands in his hand. A tray of the liquid still sits on an empty table. He coats the large wand while Savannah watches.

Just as his hand raises into the air with the coated wand, Lily speaks. "Come on, kids. We have to go."

Roman's face drops alongside his arm. The large bubble emerges and Savannah pops it with a squeal, but the defeat on Roman's face remains.

I want to punch something.

Lily gets in the car and Roman rounds to the other side to climb into the back. Leah scoops up Savannah and buckles her into her car seat.

"I love you," her muffled voice says. She blows kisses into the backseat at both of them. "Happy birthday, pretty girl."

She tickles Savannah's tummy one last time, earning a giggle, but my eyes are stuck on Roman's face illuminated in the dome light. He stares into his lap, his cheeks rounded in a pout. Fuck punching; I want to break something.

Leah closes the door and Lily backs out without another word.

I cross the space between us, wrapping my arms around her from behind. "I'm sorry. That entire thing was shitty."

She allows the comfort for a moment before pulling out of my arms and turning to face me. "I just wanted the kids to have a good day. But lately it feels like everything I want, I can't have."

I tap her under the chin with a knuckle. "That's not true. You wanted the kids to have a good day, and they did. You made that happen." I point into the street. "That. That moment. That doesn't override their day. You made it special. And you're right—they'll remember this day as being fun because of you."

She forces a small smile.

"Don't stop doing the things you want," I continue. "Because you can absolutely have them. And don't let Lily or anyone else convince you otherwise. You're a fucking badass."

Her smile widens. "Thanks, Boy Scout. I think you just earned your Supporting A Friend In Need badge."

I grin. "Are we friends?" It's a half tease, but part of me wants to know where we go from here. What did that kiss really mean and what are we doing now?

"You two going to stand out here in the dark all night?" Maci asks from the front porch.

Leah turns quickly. "Lily just picked up the kids. We're finishing cleaning up."

Maci walks into the yard and picks up a closed bag. "I'll take this one to the trash," she offers, heading around the side of the house. Sutton follows, grabbing two more filled bags.

When cleanup is finally complete, the four of us stand on the porch talking.

"Oh, I need to let Smokey out," Leah says. "Poor thing's been locked up since the party started." She hurries inside.

"We have dinner with the family," Sutton says, unlocking the truck with the key fob. The dome light illuminates the cab on the street.

"Y'all drive safe. I'll be out of here in just a minute, too." I open the storm door, but Sutton and Maci keep their curious eyes on me.

"Where'd Leah go?" Maci inquires.

I scan the living room. "I have no idea. I thought she was letting the cat out."

"I'll just text her later," Maci says, peeking past me. "Tell her bye for us."

"Will do."

I step inside and release the storm door to close between us. Maci waves as they walk away. Once she's in the truck and Sutton's rounding the front, I shut the main door and head for the kitchen.

I stop short in the doorway. Leah has changed from her party outfit to a T-shirt long enough that I can't tell what's beneath it. She's perched against the counter near the fridge, eating ice cream from a spoon. It's not a single-serve portion like earlier, but instead a pint.

"Needed something to cool off?" I ask playfully.

She dips the spoon into the container and places it into her mouth upside down then draws it out slowly. "I've been thinking about what you said," she murmurs, her tone husky.

My own mouth goes dry and my dick hardens. "What's that?" I manage.

"About wanting things I can't have."

"And?"

CHAPTER 25

LEAH

"I want you," I say firmly.

Nick stares at me from the kitchen entry. Even naked, I've never felt this exposed before. And it has nothing to do with the way my T-shirt barely covers my nether region.

Without turning, I open the freezer door and slide the ice cream back in, keeping my eyes on Nick the entire time.

He breathes deeply, his chest expanding and contracting heavily; there's an intensity in his gaze that threatens at being on the edge of something. He confirms, "You want me."

"Yes," I say again, my tone still adamant.

"Prove it." His voice is a command.

My chest heats. I hesitate. I want to ask what he means. Is he looking for words or something else as confirmation?

"Lift your shirt up and show me what I do to you," he orders.

Does he think he's calling my bluff? He must know I'm not afraid of a challenge—even a sexual one. It feels like more, though. Like a need.

I trail one hand along the hemline at my side. "You want to see what's under here, Boy Scout?" I lift my foot to take a step toward him.

"Don't," he says, with a little bite. Then softer, "Don't move."

His request should make me falter, not just physically, but emotionally. I stop moving, but his clenching fists don't warn me off.

Instead, I drag my hand to the center of the hemline, lifting it slowly. It may be evil of me, but I want the anticipation to be excruciating for him. I pause, closing my fist around the shirt, still covering what I know he wants to see.

"Higher," he strains. Then, swallowing, his gaze returns to mine and that same wild hunger is there. "Lift it. Spread yourself open and let me see how fucking wet you are."

"You think I'm wet?" I can't help the breathy tease from falling out.

"I know you are." He looks to the rising shirt again. "You better be."

I grin. "I better be?"

"Yes. You said you want me. You better be drenched."

Without looking, I reach behind my hips to grip the counter and lift myself up. Nick takes a half step forward before stopping, still just inside the door. I tug the shirt up over my hips and open my legs wide, sitting on the edge of the counter.

"Fuck," he breathes, the desire written all over his face battling with a type of wonder instead. "I can tell from here."

"I told you," I say quietly.

He glides his eyes over me from head to toe. Then he reaches for the closest chair of the new dining set, positioning it so it faces me head-on from the middle of the room. "Touch yourself."

I lift the shirt overhead and drop it to the floor. He groans and rubs a hand over his face. "You're gonna fucking kill me. I'm dying in this chair."

I know he's exaggerating, but the appreciation he's showing me increases my desire. I can't say I've felt unwanted when I've been naked, but no one has ever looked at me the way Nick is now. Like I'm a treasure, a masterpiece, something to worship.

Lifting a heel to rest on the top of a drawer, I glide my fingertips along the inside of my thigh. Slowly, back and forth. My pelvic muscles tighten in anticipation and I lean my head against the upper cabinet, my heartbeat stronger in my chest. I bring the other hand to my mouth, Nick watching intently. There's a light scent of chocolate ice cream as I wet two fingertips before dragging them down my chin and chest, and directly toward one peaked nipple where they dance in a circle.

The hand on my leg moves closer to my exposed center, but instead of diving in, I draw one finger up and down my hip joint.

"Do it," he whispers. "You're teasing yourself as much as me. Give in. Show me how you like to be touched."

So I do. I dip two fingers down, smothering them in wetness and then circling my clit gently. The moan I release is half satisfied, half aching; I arch my back slightly, lifting my breasts up.

I'm like a live wire. The current running through me is so built up, I know I'm going to crash into this orgasm in no time.

No one has ever watched me touch myself before, and the way Nick holds himself hostage from me, wanting to see me fall apart in front of him, has me slipping into ecstasy. My fingers move quickly and the moans become more insistent.

"Stop," Nick says suddenly.

My eyes pop open and I freeze, unsure where I went wrong. "What?"

He sits forward in the chair, leaning his forearms onto his thighs. "Take your hand away." He pins me with a predatory look.

I raise it in surrender, still holding my nipple between the other fingers. "What's wrong?"

"Nothing. Everything is right. You did as you were told, which given your track record is surprising. I got to see what I do to you. And now, you're going to see what you do to me."

He doesn't miss my eyes falling to his lap, releasing a chuckle and shaking his head. "No. No, no, no," he chides with a grin. He points to himself. "Not this. This." He points directly at my legs spread wide open on my counter. "You keep me right on the edge all the fucking time, and now I'm going to return the favor."

I'm stunned. "You're not gonna let me come?" How the fuck did I manage this? The one person I thought could release me from my sexual purgatory won't even let me finish.

He leans back in the chair, crossing his thick arms over his chest. "Not yet." Giving me only a split second, he says, "Now keep going."

I bite my lip, considering if I want to do what he's asking. "Not yet" isn't a no, but how long do I have to wait?

"Leah," he says tightly. "Keep going." He pins me with a focused, steady gaze, mirroring his verbal demands.

I release my nipple, bringing the second hand down near the first and fluttering two fingers over the engorged skin. Such a sweet ache. I press down with a finger on my outer labia and spread the skin, exposing myself further, before bringing more of my arousal up to my clit with the other hand.

This time, I work around my clit with slow, tender fingers before rubbing it directly. I increase my pace, another moan spilling into the kitchen and echoing off the walls.

Nick hisses through his teeth and I watch him watching me. Apparently needing his own friction, he shifts in the chair, rubbing a hand over the bulge in his pants.

Again my orgasm starts to build and I lean into it, anxious for relief.

"Stop." This time his command is a whisper, confident that I'll cease at just the hint of an order.

I still do, dropping both hands. "You've proven your point," I say on a breath.

"Hardly." He stands, setting his cap on the table and lifting his shirt over his head.

Holy hell.

I've imagined Nick's muscular body. But seeing it is completely different. His defined shoulders, chest, and abs are a work of art, perfectly sculpted. Without his shirt hugging his biceps tightly, he looks even broader than I thought.

I want to taste every inch of his exposed skin. Run my tongue over every line. Elicit more of those fucking groans and then some.

He unclasps his buckle and works the belt free, laying it on the table next to his hat and shirt.

"Again."

My fingers hover above the sensitive flesh. "Please, Nick," I say firmly.

He takes a large step forward and smirks at me. "Again."

"Fuck," I moan, but I do as I'm told. Why? Because I'm dying to orgasm and also because no one has ever told me what to do before. Not this way. There's something intoxicating about it, even if it's killing me.

Just as I reach the precipice again, he closes the remaining distance between us. "Stop." He stands just between my knees.

I drop my hands to the countertop, practically growling as I grip the edge and readjust to lean my chest toward him, almost close enough to touch. He's at the perfect level to kiss, and I lift my chin his way. If he wants to be the one to do it, that's fine. I just need relief.

He scans my face, pausing on my mouth in appreciation, then draws his eyes back up to mine. "Do you want me?"

"Yes." I'm exasperated by the question. "I told you." And then softer, "I showed you." Because isn't that what this was all about? Proving that I wanted him?

"I want you, too." His admission is low, and despite his steady tone, the smallest hint of vulnerability sneaks in. "But I only want you if I can have all of you. And not just for the night."

He pauses, letting the words sink in. My eyes are glued to his.

"I don't care what desires you have. You want pleasure? It comes from me. No one else." His face inches closer, and my body begs for release while my heart aches for him to rid the distance between us. One warm palm cups my cheek. "Do you understand? If you want me, you give me all of you. Every want, every need, every darkness."

I nod, because I can't formulate a response. Finally, he crashes his mouth against mine, searing the agreement between us. His lips are soft and hungry and tender. He's the driving force and I let him have his way with me, eagerly granting him access when he licks along my lips, throwing my arms around his neck as he explores my mouth. I roll my hips forward, seeking something, anything, to grant me the release I've been chasing.

Nick steadies my hip with a firm hand. When I can hardly breathe, he pulls back.

"Please, Nick," I whisper. He has me so wound up, I would give him just about anything he asked for at this point.

A wicked light returns to his eyes. "Do you want to come, Wild Thing?"

"Yes. Please, yes."

"All you had to do is say you wanted to come," he teases in a low voice. His hand leaves my side and dives between my legs. My hips buck at the warmth. "Fuck," he murmurs, slipping his fingers through the wetness and dragging them around. A thick finger slides inside me, and there's no stopping the way my body clenches around it. "Shit, you like that?"

"Mm hmm," I groan.

"What about this?" he whispers, pulling out the lone finger and sliding in two instead.

"Oh, god," I moan loudly, and my chest collapses forward onto his shoulder.

He kisses his way to my neck, slowly thrusting his fingers in and out of me. I ride his hand without a care, gripping tighter at his shoulders, trying to pull him closer and closer. "You're a fucking goddess. You deserve to be worshiped, cherished, pleasured."

His words and ministrations send me careening for the strongest climax of my life. "Nick, I . . ." My words turn to gasps as he plunges his fingers into me deeper and faster.

"Take it," he encourages.

"Harder," I whisper, and his finger-fucking intensifies. "Yes. So . . . good. Oh my god." My eyes squeeze shut, and everything goes black except for a starburst of white that explodes into my vision as I come.

When the spasming of my core calms, I release my grip on his neck. My fingers ache. He slowly pulls his own from within me and makes a show of sliding one into his mouth and licking it clean.

I swallow, which is hard to do with a dry mouth.

"Open," he says.

I drop my jaw and stick out my tongue. He offers the finger still coated in my cum. "Suck." His nostrils flare when I take his finger tightly into my mouth. After I release the digit, he kisses me hard on the mouth. "You should know, we're just getting started."

Again, he leaves me without the ability to protest as he slides a hand under each ass cheek and lifts me off the counter, hoisting me over his shoulder. I laugh as he spins on his heel, walking into the living room and dropping me onto the couch.

"Stay," he says firmly. I give him a tiny salute and watch as he disappears shirtless into the hallway, headed for my bedroom. I'm curious, but I stay put.

A few moments later, Nick returns with two pastel-colored objects. Adult toys. *My* toys. I look from his hands to his face, wondering how he could have known they were there.

As he stands before me at the end of the couch, he lifts one in each hand as if offering a choice. "This one or this one?" He raises them each slightly one after the other. The purple vibrator turns on as his fingers fiddle with the bases. Seeing the grin that crosses my face, he returns the look. "This one then."

Nick sets the dildo on the coffee table and sits in the center of the sectional with the vibrator next to his leg. He jerks his head. "Come 'ere."

I sit up and crawl toward him playfully, not waiting for directions as I lift a leg over his lap to straddle him. Each of his hands grips a hip, and I drop my mouth to kiss him, teasing my fingers through the hair at the base of his skull.

"Up," he says when I release his lips. He must see the confusion on my face, because he adds, "Stand."

Resting my hands on his shoulders, I shift to stand fully, my feet sinking into the soft cushions. I press my palms against the wall, keeping eye contact with him the whole way. His hands glide up the backs of my legs in a slow exploration, and every inch of me tightens. With my pussy directly in front of him, he inhales deeply.

One hand squeezes a thigh. "Put this one on the back of the couch."

His sure grip never leaves my leg as I lift it and place my foot on the flat top of the couch, eager to see where this is going. "I've died and gone to heaven," he says in a low voice, before nipping the inside of my thigh still near his face.

Maybe it's the overhead light in the living room, or because I'm used to having sex in the dark, but I feel completely on display.

"You're not going to tease me again, are you?" I ask, holding my breath.

He looks up at me wickedly. "You can't take what you dish out, Wild Thing?" He doesn't wait for my response before opening his mouth and leaning into me, dragging his flat tongue over my center. I inhale sharply, pressing my palms into the wall and praying my legs will support me.

His hands grip my ass as he buries his face in me. Despite the small break, everything is still sensitive from our start in the kitchen. It's not long before I'm moaning and rocking my hips against his mouth. One hand drops, and I wonder if he's undoing his pants, when something presses at my opening.

I tense briefly before realizing it's the vibrator, still off. He doesn't stop feasting on me as he presses the toy fully inside. My head falls back, and I gasp at the ceiling, the two sensations heightening my arousal.

Nick draws the tip of his tongue in circles around my clit before looking up at me. He pulls the vibrator out to the tip. "You like that?"

"Yes," I breathe, releasing the wall with one hand to grip his hair and push his mouth back toward my pussy. His chuckle rumbles through my core as he resumes both actions. Just when I think things can't get any better, the vibration turns on, causing me to cry out. My fist tightens in his hair. If he stops now to prove some point, I might cry.

Nick twists the base of the vibrator and the intensity increases. He pumps it in short pulses inside me. I squeeze my eyes shut, all the sensations driving me to overstimulation. "Nick," I gasp. "I can't."

He doesn't stop moving the toy inside me as he leans back to look up at me again. "You can and you will. If there's a badge for this, I'm earning it."

"A badge?"

"Yeah. Toys Are Teammates or something." He grins. I drop my head and laugh, which causes him to turn the vibrator up again, and the noise shifts to an appreciative groan.

"Now, I'm going to resume eating out your perfect cunt, and you're going to come all over my face and hand."

My mouth falls open. Who knew Nick Foster had such a dirty fucking mouth?

He leans forward, licking at my clit wildly, and his thrusts with the vibrator become firmer and faster.

I watch him as he fucks me. He looks completely in his element, and despite my initial hesitation, everything about this feels natural and comfortable. As if sensing my thoughts, his eyes raise to mine. They gleam, and I wet my lips.

My stupid heart tries to catapult toward him. I am not ok.

He turns the vibrator up again, and I can't take it anymore.

My climax slams into me and I almost crash against the wall, trying to grip with my fingers and surely hurting Nick with the force of my other hand. I can't form a coherent thought. My vision starts to go black, and something like "fuckfuckfuck" continuously exits my mouth before my legs turn to jelly.

Nick seems to sense the change, because he draws the vibrator out of me and drops it on the couch, reaching up quickly to grab my hips and lowering me down. My foot on the back of the couch gets caught, and he adjusts it as I melt into his chest.

I think I'm going to cry. And not out of embarrassment, but from pleasure, happiness. Nothing has ever felt this good.

Am I due for my period? My emotions seem entirely out of whack.

Nick strokes my back without speaking.

My vision returns to normal, and I start to register more than just euphoria. I was right earlier that Nick had undone his pants. His thick erection is tucked against my center. I shift my hips in a small circle to confirm, and he tries to stifle a groan.

His body relaxes beneath me, and I lift my head to take him in. His features have softened, and he looks more like the boy next door again. "Boy Scout, you haven't gotten yours," I murmur.

"Are you ok?" he asks, ignoring my statement.

"Yes." I brush his lips with a kiss. He's still eager, tugging me back for more. I circle my hips over his lap again. "You've been a good boy; you deserve a treat."

"Oh yeah?" He digs in his back pocket and retrieves a condom, which I snatch from him, tearing open the packet. His face tenses with hunger as I toss the wrapper to the side and shift my hips backward.

I stroke him with one hand, testing pressure. His head falls back onto the couch, and a moan slips free. Using the opposite hand, I roll the condom on. He lifts his head to watch as I raise my hips and adjust his cock between us.

When the tip slides inside me, we moan in tandem and I ease onto him while his hands hold my hips steady. Instead of raising up again, I rock my hips back and forth.

His mouth is warm against my neck as he kisses me while working his boots off and kicking them under the table. With a hand on each of his cheeks, I guide his mouth back to me, kissing him deeply as he shoves his jeans farther down his legs.

"You've ruined me," I say quietly.

Nick's eyebrows jump. "I doubt that very much."

"I'm not going to be able to give you the best ride. My legs are spent."

"Don't you worry about a thing. You've already got me on the edge." He wraps his arms around my back and shifts forward on the couch until his knees press against the coffee table, shoving into me in the process, and I moan loudly into his ear.

His palms splay along the back of my hips. "Lean back and put your hands on the table."

Maintaining eye contact that says if he drops me, I'll kill him, I readjust. "I've got you," he promises.

Something tells me it's not just about the position.

He pulls back and thrusts into me slowly. My eager pussy clamps on him hard, causing him to inhale sharply. He repeats the motion, faster this time, and I meet him with my hips.

One of his hands slides up the center of my chest and around my neck to grip the back. "Hold on." Then he sets his own pace, thrusting into me over and over. I'm at his mercy, and it's glorious. My breasts bounce with each movement, never quite catching up.

"You're even more staggering than I imagined. Watching you come on my cock is going to be sublime."

"I'm not coming again," I breathe.

"Oh yes you are," he argues sternly.

I shake my head with a breathy laugh. "No. I can't. Two is my max."

"Maybe it used to be, but you're coming with me." He lifts a hand to my mouth for the second time tonight, pulling my jaw down with his thumb. "Suck."

I let him in, swirling my tongue around his thumb and sucking until he pulls it out with a pop. Then he slides it down to my clit and begins rubbing in sweeping circles.

I gasp. "No, no. It's too much."

"You can take it," he demands.

"I can't," I moan as he continues.

"Do you want me to stop?"

My eyes pop open. He's staring at me, the question honest. "No," I whisper.

"No, what?" he prompts devilishly.

"Don't stop," I manage.

He grins. "Tell me what you need. Whatever it is, I'll give it to you."

I believe him, no matter what he means in the moment. I swallow. "Fuck me harder."

"You want it harder?" He does as he's told, picking up pace and thrusting into me deeper. "Like this?"

"More," I gasp.

"You can have it all, baby." We work together, keeping the strong, steady pace, and him rubbing firmly on my clit until I feel my body start to tense.

"There it is," he praises. "I told you that you could. Come for me, Wild Thing. Please. I want nothing more than to watch you come all over me."

And for the third time tonight, I climax harder than ever before. This time, my arms start to give, and Nick wraps his arm around my back and grips my neck tighter, crushing my body against him.

My hips continue grinding as he pumps into me, until his fingers dig into my neck and back. His breathing stutters and his forehead drops to my shoulder as he comes, his grip growing even tighter. His thrusts slow, and he drags his teeth along my shoulder with a satisfied groan.

He leans backward against the couch, keeping me close as we settle our breathing. Like earlier, his fingers dance over my back.

As soon as my nervous and respiratory systems are settled, my mind follows, seeming to come out of the haze that we dove into starting in my kitchen.

Nick apparently hasn't left the lusty fog, evident by him gripping an ass cheek per hand and lifting us both off of the couch.

"What are you doing?" I laugh.

"Getting you cleaned up," he says, as if it's a given.

He sets me down in the shower and turns on the water before turning and disposing of the condom.

At first, I think cleaning me up is a euphemism for another round—which I'm a little unsure about—but Nick makes a point to wash me from head to toe. Even tangled in my hair as he lathers and massages my scalp, his fingers feel amazing. He rubs my shoulders until the water runs clear of bubbles.

Once we're both clean, we towel off and he tucks me into bed, but instead of climbing in he begins to dress.

"Where are you going?" I slide back up into a sitting position, letting the blanket fall despite feeling suddenly vulnerable.

"I have to be up early for work," he says in a neutral tone, his mouth tipping up on one side.

"On Sunday." It's not a question, but I am trying to decipher if what he's telling me is the truth.

"Yes. Sometimes I work weekends," he agrees gently.

"Ok." I want to tell him he can stay, but I don't. I don't want to seem needy after being the one who asked for one night in the beginning.

Before leaving, he comes back to the bed and leans down, pressing a kiss to my forehead. "Sleep well."

"Bye," I whisper, my chest tightening as he leaves. Did he have any desire to stay? He didn't even ask or hint at it.

I've never wanted anyone to stay over before. In fact, I've never fucked anyone here.

It wouldn't be so bad to fall asleep with someone, though. Right?

CHAPTER 26

LEAH

I'm in completely new territory. I've never wanted a round two. Never needed someone to check in with me after. Certainly, I've never wanted to reach out to someone else.

And yet that's all I want. He played me like an award-winning musician. I need an encore.

The only texting or calls that we've exchanged were regarding Savannah's birthday. I don't know what his normal is when it comes to communication, and I've never had to navigate a morning after like this.

Do I call? He said he wanted more than a night.

Maybe he said all of those things to me in the heat of the moment, but now it's out of his system.

In an effort to distract myself from all of the what-ifs and maybes, I spend the morning reorganizing the second bedroom. Half-opened presents litter the space, and I sort through all of the clothing to see what Roman and Savannah have outgrown or worn out before adding Savannah's new items in.

Then I start working on the second round of custom orders that have rolled in. The demand has been higher than I anticipated, and I've had to add a workstation to keep up. A light, a desk, and some baskets to organize the influx of items are just a few of the new additions to the second bedroom.

Even after cleaning up, it's all starting to feel cramped. And I don't like that it's taking over space that I've previously dedicated to Roman and Savannah. Savannah is still small enough that I don't trust her not to put things in her mouth. And Smokey keeps being an asshole and knocking baskets of stones over. I need to figure out a different setup.

A few of the necklaces and earring sets have become second nature to make because of their popularity. Unfortunately, that means they don't require enough brain power to keep me from thinking about what the fuck happened with Nick.

Sex with him was the best I've ever had. And the aftercare? Fuck me. A girl could get spoiled by behavior like that.

But the words he said to me in my kitchen battle with the image of him leaving after a casual goodbye. I hate not knowing where we stand. This is just another reason why I don't do more than a night—I never have to be in limbo.

My phone chirps from the corner of the desk. I finish twisting the gold metal around a pink stone for a pair of earrings before checking it.

Nick:

Have a good day, Wild Thing.

I owe him more than a "you too," but I'm at a loss. I stare at the screen for far too long before I finally message back.

Me:

You too.

Be careful of fishermen not wearing orange.

Nick:

202

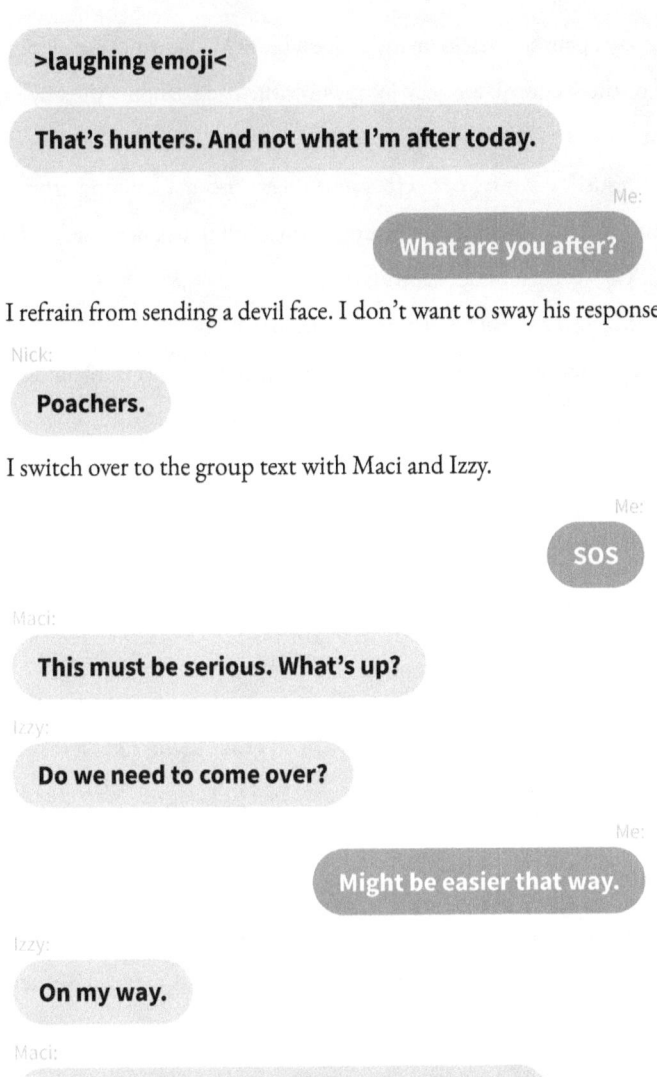

>laughing emoji<

That's hunters. And not what I'm after today.

Me:

What are you after?

I refrain from sending a devil face. I don't want to sway his response.

Nick:

Poachers.

I switch over to the group text with Maci and Izzy.

Me:

SOS

Maci:

This must be serious. What's up?

Izzy:

Do we need to come over?

Me:

Might be easier that way.

Izzy:

On my way.

Maci:

I'll be a little bit behind but I'm coming too.

Izzy arrives with snacks, letting herself in with a half knock. I've just finished deep cleaning the kitchen and plopped down on the couch in the living room.

Maci arrives a few minutes later.

Izzy opens the snacks on my coffee table as Maci throws herself onto the end of the sectional. Smokey jumps over the back, landing directly on her chest.

"Jesus!" she cries out. He ignores her outburst, sniffing around her mouth and sticking his tongue out the tiniest bit to lick her chin. "What the fuck? Get your cat under control, Leah."

"Maybe he smells the jizz on your mouth."

Izzy squeals and Maci starts laughing uncontrollably until Smokey gets half thrown off the couch. "You're so wrong for that," Maci says, laughing.

When our laughter calms, Izzy is the one to press. "So, what's going on?"

"I fucked up," I say, tucking myself into the couch and picking at a seam of one of the pillows.

"How bad?" Izzy asks at the same time that Maci asks, "What kind of fuck-up?"

A pit forms in my stomach. I haven't considered how they're going to take this. Sleeping with people in the friend group seems like an easy no-no, but until recently it wasn't something we had to navigate. We were basically the three amigos, plus Liv on occasion.

When I don't answer right away, Izzy presses, "Is it really that bad?" Color starts to drain from her face. She's gonna give herself an ulcer.

"I slept with Nick," I say, with far more confidence than I have internally.

"I knew it!" Maci cries, bouncing into a sitting position. "How was it?" Izzy's mouth hangs open.

The high of the night returns and my chest heats at the memory. Not in embarrassment, but in a reignited fire. "Amazing. Mind-blowing. It was everything I've needed for months. Or ever."

"So what's the problem?" Maci asks.

Izzy turns her disbelief on Maci. "Um, that Leah doesn't do strings and he's basically Velcro'd to our group?"

Maci frowns in thought. "Was it here? Did he stay over?"

"Yes. And no." I readjust my legs for something to do.

"Have you talked to him?" Izzy questions.

"We texted this morning. Nothing significant."

Quiet settles over us as our eyes bounce between each other.

"So maybe it's a non-issue," Maci offers. "It's not like you're quiet about your sex life."

"Oh yes, because I shout it from the rooftops."

My friends exchange a teasing look before Izzy says, "Basically. And there's nothing wrong with how you live, but everyone knows you're not looking for anything serious."

"Just give it some time. I'm sure it'll work itself out," Maci adds. Smokey jumps into her lap, sniffing at her chin again.

"Did you eat tuna before you came over or something?" I tease.

She grins. "I have no idea what's up with him."

"Speaking of what's up—what's going on with Lily?" Izzy picks at the veggie tray on the coffee table.

Guess it's time to spill all the details I've been keeping to myself. "We got into a fight."

"About her moving in?"

"No." I swallow. "I mean, she tacked that on at the end, but that's not what started us down this path. I think I'm going to have to report her."

"Report her?" Maci leans forward on the couch, as if the few inches will add clarity.

"For what?" Izzy stops chewing the half-eaten celery.

"She's been leaving the kids alone sometimes. She made it seem like it's just for a few minutes to run up to the store, but I don't think she's telling the truth."

"That's never been her strong suit," Maci mutters.

I purse my lips in agreement. "She thinks I'm being judgmental."

"Um, yeah. Neglect is something you absolutely get to be judgy about," Izzy scoffs, her temper flaring. "I know you haven't told us everything about your childhood, but we know enough. And you'd think after what you two have been through that Lily would want to do better for her own kids."

"Yeah. You would." It's all I can manage. Keeping the emotions bottled on the shelf is the only way I'm able to deal with everything. But it does feel like things are coming to a head. And I've put off doing something about Lily's behavior for too long.

"So, are you going to call?" Maci scratches Smokey's ears. His purrs nearly drown out her voice. "Yeesh, give it a rest." She gives his head a playfully rough shake. His mouth seems to tug into a smile and his eyes squish tighter together.

I study my cat and my best friend. "Are you pregnant?" I ask, my tone a little more accusatory than intended.

"No!" Maci cries. "I already told you that the last time you asked."

"Ok, well just because it wasn't true two months ago, doesn't mean it isn't true now." I raise an eyebrow at her.

Maci's jaw hardens as she stares at me in frustration. "I just got my depo shot renewed. It'll be good through the wedding," she grits out.

"Oh yes, because you've done everything else the right way," I tease.

Izzy snickers. "You're such a bitch sometimes, Leah," she says and laughs.

Maci shakes her head. "No wonder your cat likes me more." She sticks her tongue out at me. "It's not about doing things right. We just have a lot going on right now. The spring herd is calving, upgrades, the new herd—"

I put both my hands up to give in and to get her to stop talking. "Ok. I got it. My bad. You're not pregnant."

A text alert interrupts us, and I reach for my phone on the coffee table.

Nick:

Do you have dinner plans?

Me:

Does leftover birthday cake count?

"Is that him?" Maci perks up.

I roll my eyes. "Don't you have your own relationship to obsess over?"

"Oh, it's a relationship now," Izzy teases.

"Hey, you're the one who called us over here, panicking," Maci says with mock sass.

"I was not! I was just worried I fucked things up. Feels like I do a lot of that lately."

"Not even," Maci says gently. She sets Smokey on the floor and scoots close to me. "I know neither of us are good at talking about our feelings, but take it from me—we love you. There's nothing you could do that would change that. Not even if it involves a shovel." She winks. "And you don't have to do this on your own."

A smile creeps over my lips. I work to keep it subdued. "You're right. You fucked up way worse than me. I'm basically an angel compared to you."

"And, there she is." Izzy laughs and throws a baby carrot at me.

"Just have fun," Maci says, wrapping an arm around my shoulders. "Nick's a big boy, and a really damn good guy. I don't have to tell you two that; you saw how amazing he was after Colt attacked me. If something is too much for him, he'll find a way to say it."

"I am a lot." I return to picking at the couch cushions.

Izzy's brows pull together tightly. "That's not what she means, and you know it. And if anyone tells you you're too much, they can fuck all the way off." Her face hardens. "Guaranteed Nick never will."

My phone pings again.

Nick:

Girl dinner?

You should come out to my place.

I give the phone a little shake. "He's asking about dinner."

"Go get you some." Maci grins. "Dinner. Get you some dinner."

Our girlish giggles fill my living room.

CHAPTER 27

NICK

I told Leah she's worth more than one night, and I'm going to prove it to her. So when I invite her over it's with strict instructions to myself—specifically my dick—to behave. This is not a "Netflix and chill" situation.

After checking that she has no food allergies, I give Leah the address and tell her to come by whenever she's ready.

There's no way to miss hearing her pull in the drive, thanks to how secluded the house is. When I step out to meet her on the porch, I'm immediately reminded how she manages to make everything look good. From the flannel that's tied around her waist, covering her cutoff jean shorts, to the rock band T-shirt she wears knotted on one side, she's a knockout.

I descend the stairs for something to do as I repeat a mantra not to wrap her hair around my fist and take her straight to the bedroom.

She grins at me as she closes her car door. "This is *exactly* what I was expecting. Only better."

"How so?" I can't help myself; as soon as she's within arm's reach, I wrap a hand around her waist and pull her close to kiss her on the forehead. I want more than that, but I don't trust myself to stop.

She pauses, studying my face for a few seconds, before continuing. "I knew you'd have a piece of land, but the view out here is amazing."

"Just wait until you see the back porch," I promise.

"Can't wait."

I lead Leah inside. As soon as the door opens, she inhales deeply. "Are you actually cooking? It smells delicious."

"Am I actually cooking?" I laugh. "What does that mean? I said I was going to make you dinner."

She eyes me over her shoulder as she makes her way into the kitchen, inspecting the stove and oven, which beeps when she turns the oven light on. "Steak, shrimp, potatoes, and green beans," she murmurs to herself, then turns to me. "This is *not* what I was expecting."

I lean against the counter, watching her take it all in. "What were you expecting?"

Her eyes are soft and wide. "Spaghetti? Takeout? I don't know. Something easy."

"Why?" I can't decide if I want to laugh or not. She stares back at me. And then it hits me: of course she's used to the bare minimum. She barely got that. "Come on. I thought we could eat outside."

I lead her through the back door from the kitchen.

Her mouth parts in that perfect O as she peers into the distance. "This is gorgeous. How do you ever leave?"

She's right. The view from my back porch is one of the prettiest you'll see in the Texas Hill Country. Aside from the private pond and dock, the house sits somewhat elevated with an expansive view of untamed land. "It's hard. But since I get to spend so much time looking at all the wonderful things this state has to offer, it's a little easier to go."

"Yeah. Maybe the trade-off for sweating all day isn't so bad," she snickers.

"Oh, you want to spend some more time in nature after all, huh?"

"That is not what I said," she says with a smile. "For you, the trade-off is probably fine."

"So what trade-off would make it worthwhile for you?"

"I'll think on it and let you know." She continues to stare into the distance.

"I'm going to grab plates. I'll be right back," I say, and flip the porch light on as I head back in. When I return, Leah sits at the table, staring dreamily out at the expanse.

"Peaceful, right?"

She sits up straighter. "So peaceful. I'm in love."

I cough and she laughs.

The first minute or two of dinner is quiet, aside from Leah's appreciative moans over the food. "I can't believe you made all of this," she says more to herself.

"So what's the long-term plan for your jewelry business?" I ask, cutting into my steak.

"Honestly, it started as a way to change the monotony." She sets her silverware onto the plate. "I thought it would pick up slowly over time. And don't get me wrong, I'm not a multi-millionaire, but people are way more into it than I thought."

"That's a good thing."

"It is," she agrees. "Izzy, Maci, and I made a plan one day, but I'm just rolling with the punches. I finished a second round of custom orders and I'm going to drop them off with everyone tomorrow."

"All from the show?" I lean back in my chair, watching the way Leah lights up as she talks about something good in her life.

"Some. Some are word of mouth. A few repeat and a few new. It's really so surreal still."

"I told you you're talented."

She smiles softly at me. "Thanks."

Her eyes drop to my wrist and the green paracord bracelet. I give it a playful shake. "Still there."

"To answer your question, my only long-term goal is for stability. When the business is enough that I can quit Sadie's, I will. I want to build something of my own. So I'll keep growing, learning new techniques, offering new things, and just having fun." She smiles around a bite to punctuate the statement.

The Leah before me is so different from the party girl from that first night. They're still one and the same, but she's letting out the depth I knew she was hiding. Letting her dreams and desires out.

"What about you? What's your long-term plan?" she asks, shoving a shrimp in her mouth and waiting for my answer.

I look out at my property. "You're going to laugh at me. But all I want is a life I can be proud of. To help people, do good, and take care of this earth."

"That's beautiful. And deep." She pulls her legs into the chair, wrapping her arms around her knees. "I'm not laughing at you about that. I think it's the perfect dream for you."

The life I want seems so simple, it feels silly saying it out loud. "On a smaller scale, I'd like to complete training to add a K-9 to the county."

"Is it hard?"

"It's extensive. There's an approval process and training for the warden, the dog, and then the warden with the dog."

Her eyebrows rise. "Wow. That'd be cool, though. Having your own partner, since you're on your own so frequently."

I nod. "Yeah. I may get called out more frequently, too. But it'd be beneficial here."

A comfortable quiet passes between us.

"Thank you for dinner, and for inviting me out here." She squeezes herself tighter in the chair.

"Why do you do that?" I ask quietly.

Her head cocks to one side. "Do what?"

I motion to her positioning. "You wrap yourself up all tight. Is it comfortable?"

A tiny, embarrassed smile teases her mouth. "To behave," she murmurs.

"Behave?" I lean forward. "Do you actually know how to do that, Wild Thing?"

She laughs. "Very funny. Actually, it goes back to wanting things we can't have. I do it to remind myself not to reach."

I can't help how deeply my eyebrows pull together. "Not to reach? I think that's the opposite of what you should be reminding yourself."

She stares at me while she chews at her lip.

I lower my voice. "What are you keeping yourself from reaching for right now?"

"You." Her answer is immediate.

I lean back in the chair and beckon her with two fingers. She holds eye contact as she unfolds and walks around the table to me. I pat my leg, but instead of sitting sideways on my lap, she straddles me and places a hand on each side of my neck.

My cock twitches in my pants, and I have to remind myself again that tonight isn't about something physical. "Why are you stopping yourself with me?"

"This is just foreign," she whispers. Her breath skates over my lips and her fingers begin to play with my hair. "I've never wanted more than a night with someone."

"And now you do?"

"I'm at least interested. Last night was . . . incredible. I knew the last few months were bad for me, but now I can't figure out if it's supposed to be like that all the time or . . . I don't know. I don't know how to travel this road. I don't know what's too much or too clingy." She babbles her sweet brain dump, and I'm finding it harder and harder not to take her into the bedroom. Or fuck, even right here. How can she think anyone wouldn't want her advances?

"Leah."

Her eyes meet mine.

"You are not too much. Do you understand?" I wait for her to nod before continuing. "Don't hide yourself. Not from me." My thumbs rub along her hips, the only additional touch I allow myself.

She grips my neck tighter and leans down, pressing her lips firmly against mine. I let her lead, taking whatever she wants to give. The kiss turns deep quickly, and she seeks entrance to my mouth. I groan when her tongue dives in, my dick hardening.

Her hips rock forward once, and I plant my hands on the small of her back. Now that I've had her it's all I can think about.

She kisses me hard once more before she severs the connection to pull back. "Thank you."

I kiss her chest above the hem of her shirt before leaning my head back and looking into her eyes. "I need to be honest with you."

She stiffens, and I resume rubbing her back to soothe her.

"I want to fuck you. Badly. But I'm not going to." Her slowly spreading grin halts as I continue. "I fully believe that there is more to you than sex. I genuinely invited you out here to spend time with you. I enjoy talking to you. And fucking you. And believe me, I plan to do much more of the latter, but you're important. Your thoughts and feelings and dreams are important. I'm just as invested in those parts of you as I am the rest. And that is why I will not take you to bed tonight."

A light sheen covers her eyes, and I wait for any indication of how she's taken what I've said.

Finally, she smiles and her eyes close briefly. "You really are a fucking boy scout. You know how to use everything perfectly, do everything perfectly, and you're still a goddamned gentleman." She leans down and kisses my lips softly.

After the sun has set completely, we clean up the kitchen together and Leah thanks me again for dinner. Everything feels natural and easy.

I lean against the front porch post long after her taillights disappear into the dark. I'm a fucking idiot for not pushing more. But I have nothing to offer if not my word. And I need her to see I was serious—that she's worth everything.

CHAPTER 28

LEAH

This joint bachelor/bachelorette party at The Lodge may be a low-key event with a private chef, but that doesn't mean Izzy and I are letting anyone get out of party attire. She and I have nearly similar floor-length dresses, hers in blush and mine in black, paired with white and black felt hats, respectively. Both have a generous number of rhinestones. Liv, Maci, and Sammi also play along, dressing up in their best glitzy dresses, but skipping the hats.

Rooms have been assigned and Chef is working away in the kitchen as the bridal party congregates in the main room.

"Sit," I say firmly to Maci, as soon as we're all in The Lodge.

"You're not the boss of me," Maci says.

I turn to Sutton. "Tell your fiancée to sit before I spank her."

"If anyone's going to spank her, it's going to be me," he quips.

Liv turns pink, looking between them.

Maci puts a hand on her hip. "Are you going to spank me if I don't sit?"

"No, but I'll spank you if you do," he offers.

Maci sits immediately, causing the room to erupt in laughter. I press the tiny bridal crown and veil into her hair, attached to a plastic comb.

"Oh nooo," she says, laughing. "I thought I was going to miss out on these."

216

"Not even," Izzy adds. She pulls out several sashes and hands them around the women. Maci's reads "Bride" and the rest say "Bridesmaid."

"Did you think we were going to forget who's who tonight?" Casey jokes.

"Knowing you, maybe," I say over my shoulder. This causes more laughter.

What I love most about this group is the easy way that we all merged. One bonfire and our banter came together naturally, and without offense.

"Ok, so strip poker?" he suggests.

"Ew. I do not want to see my brother naked," Sammi says. "I didn't really need to hear about his affinity to spanking either."

"I read once that kinks are hereditary." I turn and look at Sammi pointedly.

A mixture of laughter, squeals, and groans move through the group. "I'm not going to think too deeply on that one," Sammi argues.

Chef Luca enters, smiling. "Appetizers are ready. I've also prepared a few cocktails."

"Thank you, Chef," Sutton says.

Izzy opens a bag near the couch and pulls out a set of ties.

"What is that?" Nick asks in concern.

"You didn't think you were getting out of wearing something, did you?" Izzy grins at him.

"Are those ties?" Casey leans over the coffee table in the middle of the room to assess what Izzy holds.

"They are." I grab half the stack and hand one to Liv to test a theory. "Here, put that on Shane."

Her eyes meet mine with a small hint of terror before she stows it away.

I move toward Nick, watching Liv and Shane in my periphery. He bends slightly at the knee so she can reach over his head. She moves quickly, tightening the simple knot and hurrying away.

"Eyes on me, Wild Thing," Nick whispers. There's enough chatter in the room that no one hears, but my eyes snap his way. "Ooh, you're getting better at listening."

I smack him on the shoulder. "Take your hat off."

He holds it in front of himself with a grin while I lift the tie over his head and take my time tightening the knot. I pat the blade and step back.

"Hey, this has a pocket," Casey says, assessing the tie.

Izzy and I grin at each other.

"What are we storing in here?" Nick asks as he holds up the end of the tie.

"Beer." I shrug.

"Well that's a pocket I didn't know I needed," Shane says.

"What now?" Sutton asks.

"No idea. That's all we got." I plop down on the couch.

Sammi laughs. "Of course it is. You nailed all the important parts."

Truthfully, Izzy and I planned a few light games, but we spend most of our time talking and enjoying each other's company.

Dinner from Chef Luca is to die for and dessert, a perfectly made tiramisu, is heavenly.

Eventually everyone starts dispersing to bed until Izzy and I leave Sutton and Sammi sitting in the living room, talking. I find it sweet that they're the last two up, maybe reminiscing about what life on the ranch was like growing up and happily looking forward to its future.

Sammi may not be fond of ranch life, but I know she's proud of her brother. And just like the night of the bonfire, everything is easy within the group. Even Nick and I manage to play friendly.

Izzy passes out in the bed next to me. But I can't follow suit. I toss and turn, but it's no use.

I grab a sweatshirt and pull it over my sleep shirt and shorts. The cut-out neck makes it especially comfortable.

The living room is empty when I walk out to the front porch and settle into one of the new rocking chairs. It squeaks quietly each time I rock it back, but not enough to truly split the air. The sky bleeds into the earth, stars covered in a fluffy haze.

I close my eyes and let the rhythm of the chair ease me into something more peaceful.

"Couldn't sleep?" Nick's voice causes me to open my eyes. He studies me as he approaches.

"No," I admit.

He sits in the rocking chair next to me. "Me neither."

"You need rockers at your house."

He chuckles. "I do."

I turn my eyes to the vastness ahead of us. "If I had something like that, I think I'd spend a lot of time rocking on the porch. Watching sunsets and shit."

He laughs. "And shit."

His mouth pulls to one side for a moment. "Would that shit include raising two-point-five kids and a house with a picket fence?"

I scrunch my nose. "No picket fence." I hesitate. "I'm not sure I want kids, honestly."

I don't know what to make of his returning silence.

"Really?" he finally asks with a skeptical tone.

My chair rocks harder as I use the momentum to process the emotions swimming within. "I've just never seen myself as the typical mom." He turns to look at me. "I know a lot of women think about it, but . . . I don't know. Maybe it's because the women in my family haven't shown they're especially capable of caring for children."

He rubs a hand over his mouth and my eyes focus there. "That's definitely your choice." His comment is so neutral.

"What about you?"

"Me?"

"Yeah. You want a gaggle of kids?" I grin to break what I'm sensing as tension, whether he feels the same or not.

He only rocks back and forth for a few seconds, seemingly lost in thought. "I think I've always seen myself in some kind of role with children."

"What does that mean? Some kind of role?"

He shrugs with a soft smile. "I guess I didn't get into the details. How those kids came to be."

"You like kids."

"Yeah." He meets my eyes. "So do you."

"Sure I do. Especially my niece and nephew. That doesn't make me good mom material."

He lifts a hand from the arm of the chair in surrender. "I'm not pressing. Just observing."

We let the sounds of the night fill the air between us for a few minutes.

"How are Roman and Savannah?" he asks after a minute.

My heart hurts. "They deserve more than what they get." I raise my eyes to meet his, and his returning expression is full of understanding. Like he doesn't want to put to words the truth we both know: my sister is failing as a mother.

I keep putting off calling someone because I know it's going to tear the final shreds of our family apart. And what will happen to my niece and nephew? Will they be removed from the home, maybe placed somewhere that's potentially worse?

My eyes catch on my new butterfly tattoo. I don't feel like a butterfly, light and free. I feel more like I'm still in transition. Maybe I should've gotten a chrysalis instead.

When Nick speaks, I'm surprised by his words. "You didn't drink tonight."

CHAPTER 29

NICK

Leah continues to stare at her wrist as if she didn't hear me. I wasn't that quiet, and there's hardly any other noise out here. I follow her gaze to land on the butterfly tattoo.

A warm wind whips through the porch, and Leah shudders. I'm about to lose my coat and offer it to her when she stands abruptly. She says nothing as she steps off the porch. She reminds me of a March hare. Like she's about to tear off through the spring flowers.

I've spent a lot of time at Strickland Ranch over the years, but I have no idea what's in this new area. Not really. "Where are you going?"

She takes the steps down to the makeshift driveway. I follow, leaving the light from the porch behind. It's dark as shit, so I can't anticipate her movements, but it's no question that I'll follow. I'm so gone for her I'd follow her anywhere.

When she turns back to me, smiling widely, her face is bathed in moonlight. She doesn't offer an answer, so I repeat my question. "Where are you going?"

Her eyes dart around the drive and land on the ATV, sitting with the keys in it at the edge of the car line. "To cool off." She drags her bottom lip through her teeth, then tears off through the darkness.

Without another thought, I take off after her. She jumps into the driver's seat and turns on the ATV, not waiting as I launch myself into the passenger side before she pulls off through the thick grass.

"There is a road!" I call loudly over the engine.

She throws her head back and laughs. "We don't need roads where I'm going."

I have no idea where she's headed, but I settle in for the ride. About two minutes later she's crossing the property line back into the original Strickland Ranch land, but it only serves to increase her speed. She winds from the new trail onto the main road and straight across the property, heading toward the build site of Maci and Sutton's house.

Just inside the pasture, she pulls to a stop. The quiet air is almost deafening when the engine cuts off. Leah scans the tree line as if looking for something. She leaves the keys when she jumps out, and darts into the trees. I jump out after her as she removes her light sweater and tosses it behind her as she runs. Does she even have shoes on?

I have no idea how she isn't tripping through the thick ground cover as we travel through the near-pitch-black area. Branches, new growth, and dense leaves in various stages of decomposition fill the area between the cedar and mesquite trees. As my eyes adjust, I tune into her steps through the foliage, following without issue. Soon, the sound of her movements mingle with running water.

There's a splash as I come to the edge of a creek.

Leah is chest deep in the middle, and nude, if her bare shoulders are any indication.

"What are you doing?" I can't help but chuckle at her. She's a wild beauty, framed in moonlight and splattered with water. Her eyes are bright and free, the happiest I've seen her in weeks. The hunger from before returns with a vengeance.

She beams at me. "Going for a swim."

"Why? It must be freezing."

She wets her lips and my cock twitches. I want to climb in after her.

"I had this English teacher in high school. He was my favorite. He loved to teach about symbolism using popular movies. I learned so much in his class, which is really saying a lot because I hated school as a whole." Her monologue turns introspective as her fingers dance across the water. "Anyway, one movie he talked about had a scene where a man escapes prison through the plumbing, and he drops into this water and it's raining. And our teacher talked about the symbolism of washing clean. A rebirth, maybe." Her eyes slowly rise to find mine.

My breathing is shallow, but I force the words to come out. "And you thought you needed to be reborn right now?"

Her mouth tugs up on both sides, begging to be kissed. "Not exactly. I was just thinking about Roman and Savannah, and what they deserve. What they've come from. What Lily and I have come from."

A large, partially covered stone creates a makeshift seat, and I settle in. She has more to say, even if she's quiet now.

The wind rushes across the water. "Mm, that breeze is the perfect addition." She lifts a few drops of water up to her collarbone, dribbling them across her skin. I want to lick it off. To taste every inch of her. To make her come underneath the moon.

But I don't move or speak, because what she's telling me is important.

"I think I need to be sober." She avoids my gaze as the quiet words slip out.

When she doesn't continue, I ask, "What makes you feel that way?"

She sinks lower in the water, presumably sitting on a rock. The water isn't that deep. "It's becoming too much. Too frequent. It's too easy to say 'It'll take the edge off,' or 'It's just one,' or 'I'm just having fun.'" Her words pick up in intensity as she shares. "I've been drinking before I go to work."

My eyebrows shoot up. I can count on a lot of wild comments and even behavior from Leah, but that one is a surprise. She's always seemed to pull it together.

"It's just getting out of control."

I scoot forward on the rock. "You have to do what you think is right. If the alcohol is starting to control you, then I think it's safe to say it's time to re-evaluate."

She nods, and her expression changes. Her focused eyes and slightly pursed lips warn of a challenge. "Why aren't you coming in?"

Caught off guard, I rake my tongue over my top teeth to compose myself. "Do you want me to?"

"If you want."

"I didn't come in because I was assessing the situation. If I had, I knew I'd want to fuck you until you screamed my name to the Texas sky. So, it was better I stay put."

She stands suddenly, with purpose. Exposed to her waist, water rushes down her body, her nipples hard in the cool air. "And now?"

"That depends. You look cold. Are you done?" I tease.

Leah runs her hands down her body, gliding over her perky breasts as she does. My eyes freeze on the movement, even as she says, "Yeah, I'm getting chilly."

My cock strains against my pants.

She moves closer in the water, rising up farther. Droplets trickle down her body, driving all my attention to her center. She climbs out of the creek gracefully, like a goddess of nature.

I need to be inside of her again. Now.

Untangling my legs, I stand. She's only inches from me, begging to be touched. Fucked.

"You didn't answer me," she says coyly. "What about now?"

I slide my coat off and wrap it around her shoulders. "Are you asking if I still want to fuck you?"

"Do you?" Her sultry gaze falls on my mouth.

I tuck my head, bringing our mouths closer together. "Did you make yourself come, thinking about me fucking you?"

Her chin bobs up and down. "More than once." She leans into me so the wind hardly has room to pass between us.

Without thinking, I lightly grip the base of her throat with my hand to stop her movement. Her eyes blow wide as they fly to mine. But when her lips part, it's not in fear.

"We're going to have to work on your listening skills. I told you they're all mine." I'm about to give in, taste her sweet mouth again, when she scoffs.

"You can't be serious, Nick."

My grip on her neck tightens. "I can't be?"

"You did not say 'every orgasm,'" she says more adamantly.

"Let me rectify that. You don't get to orgasm without me."

She reaches up and grips my wrist. "No."

I smirk. "We had a deal. You want me, you give me everything." Her smug smile drops. "Face it, I do it better anyway."

"Someone's cocky," she mutters.

"Says the woman naked in the woods begging me to fuck her."

"I'm not begging," she says firmly, but her body betrays her. Her chest heaves with full breaths and she presses into my hold.

"Maybe you should."

"Never going to happen."

I wonder if she realizes the challenge she's created. "What did you think about most? Tell me, and maybe I'll take care of you. Are you dying for me to touch you again, or bury my cock in your greedy pussy?" I let my fingers gingerly trace along her hip, up to her waist.

"Jesus," she breathes. Her eyes move between my mouth and eyes. "It's a tie."

"That's not enough," I murmur. My fingers drift across her stomach. I creep my mouth closer, and she leans up on her toes to reach me.

"It wasn't one specific thing," she replies, her voice just above a whisper. "You controlled my body. My orgasms. Anytime I thought about what you said to me, how you touched me . . ." Her eyelids flutter.

"You like when I edge you, Wild Thing?"

She drags her bottom lip through her teeth as she nods. "I like everything."

I capture her mouth with mine. She tastes like spring, fresh and cool. Her hips lean toward me, and I slide my hands up her slick sides until I reach her breasts. Her moan travels into my mouth as I tease and tug at her hardened nipples. When I let go, she presses into me, a few stray droplets seeping through my shirt.

I lick and bite my way down her neck and chest to her breasts. The combination of creek water and cool wind has made her hands feel like icicles, and I relish them against my skin as she grips my cheeks while I lick and suck a nipple.

"Good. Because I'm punishing you." I release her and take a step back, looking around the darkened area.

"What?" She stares at me, wide eyed.

"You decided to get off without me, so you don't get to again until you beg for it." I spot her shorts not far away and grab them, returning to help her step into them.

"Nick." She smiles despite herself.

I release the waistband with a snap of elastic and wink at her and then continue scanning the space. "Where are your shoes?"

She laughs, looking around as well. "I don't know. And I'm not begging for release."

"I'm making the rules, not you. You ran through all of this barefoot?" I'm all for bare feet, but mesquite thorns are dangerous.

She shrugs.

"Well, that solves that." I reach for her legs, and she steps back quickly.

"What are you talking about?"

"If you're going to act like a Wild Thing, I'm going to treat you like one." I sweep her legs up and toss her over my shoulder. She's too occupied holding my jacket around her to prohibit me from picking her up—not that she could.

"Nick!" she squeals, but it's dampened by a hysterical laugh, and I carry her the entire way back to the ATV. She's tear-streaked and breathless from laughter when I set her down. It's a sound I want to hear every day for the rest of my life.

CHAPTER 30

LEAH

Having Nick deny me at the ranch was the last thing I expected. I hadn't planned to fuck him while we were there, but the timing seemed to present itself. How was I supposed to know that he wanted to be a part of every single orgasm I have?

I could choose to ignore the request and continue to please myself on my own. But he is right that sex with him is far more enjoyable than sex on my own.

Unfortunately, Nick's been gone all week, so I haven't been able to pursue convincing him. Thankfully he's coming over tonight, and I'm bound and determined to get him to cave.

When he knocks, I answer in the nude. It seems like the best way to have him see the error of his ways.

"Fuck, Wild Thing," he says as his eyes pop, and he shoves me back, pushing into the house and slamming the door behind him. "What the hell are you doing?" He chuckles at me, running his eyes down my body.

I rock my head from side to side. "Well, I know it's been a long week out of town for you, and I'm sure you're pent. I figured we could get right to it, get you relaxed, and then chill." I keep my voice light, as if the entire idea is spurred on by a need to satisfy *him*. Which, in truth, I'd love to do. But the man has moves, and I need him to satisfy me, too.

His eyes narrow. "I'm not that pent. And I know what you're doing."

"Trying to fuck? Yeah. It's not a secret." I cross my arms and push my tits together in the process. "So what's the big deal?"

"Oh, now it's a deal?" He walks forward, pressing into me. Though I manage to stand firm, his cotton shirt brushes against my tight nipples, sending an ache south. God, I need this man inside of me. I don't care if it's his hand, tongue, or cock, but it's a visceral desire. "Also, last I remember, you thought I was being ridiculous."

I set my jaw briefly. "You were. But that's in the past."

"Is it?" He takes another step, and this time I have no choice but to yield my space. "I remember there being something else."

"I don't know what you mean." My arms fall and I shuffle my feet backward as he herds me toward the small hallway off the living room.

His voice lowers. "I think you do." The words almost vibrate over my lips and my pussy clenches, aching for something to fill it. "You're going to beg, like a good girl."

I've never wanted to *be* someone's "good girl" before, but fuck I do now. And yet the brat in me hates giving in to him. Why does he get to win all the time? "I told you," I breathe with as much force as I can muster, "I don't beg."

"Then it seems to me you might be in need of a cold shower." He stops moving at the entrance to the hallway. His fresh scent swirls between us, another layer of his arsenal against me.

I shake my head, the bun on top bumping the door behind me. "That's not what I need."

"It's all you get until you learn to behave."

"You're impossible," I grind out.

A proud smirk teases the corner of his mouth. He closes the space between us, tucking his mouth against my ear. His breath washes over my neck as he says, "Come on, Wild Thing. Be good and tell me what you need. Ask nicely and I'll fuck you so deep you won't know where you end and I begin."

My lower jaw falls slack. I'm going to be a puddle on this fucking floor.

When I don't move, don't respond, Nick brushes his nose along the lobe of my ear. My eyes flutter shut. "Are you a sleeper agent?" I whisper.

He leans back and chuckles. "What? Why would you ask me that?"

"That's not a no," I say more firmly. "You have all the qualities. You know: boy next door, good neighbor type, all the green flags. And then one day, you'll up and do something psychotic, and we'll all say 'Oh my god! Not Nick Foster!'" My words rise in pitch and intensity, thick with sarcasm and southern charm. I place a dramatic hand against my exposed chest. "'I knew him my whole life. There's no way he's capable of this.' But then if we think real hard, in a tiny, dark corner of our minds, we'll know . . . we'll know. He was so good at all the things. So. Fucking. Charming."

I reach my hands forward, fingers brushing his wrists as I run them up the outside of his forearms without breaking eye contact. Speaking slower I say, "So good with his hands, his words, his mouth. He fooled us all along. Had us eating out of his hand."

When I reach his elbows, I bring my hands forward, barely brushing the fabric that separates his chest from my touch.

"Do you want to eat out of my hand, Wild Thing?" he asks, his voice almost a purr. Not like a housecat, but like a wild cat. How I imagine a leopard would sound. Low, bold, and dominating. It's an odd thing to think about. Because who wants a man to purr to them? But fuck me, he can do no wrong. And the timbre has me slicking my thighs.

Somehow, I continue to hold his gaze. "If that's what you want."

"Not exactly the begging I had in mind." He leans forward, a hand rising to my waist, but instead of touching me, he reaches behind me, twisting the rounded doorknob and letting the door fall open. He doesn't move, doesn't say anything else, just stares.

"You're making me feel unwanted." I try for a pout.

He drops his chin. "On the contrary, I've told you how fucking badly I want you. So badly that I want you all to myself. Every piece. A real glutton." He grazes my lips with his. "And yet you deny me. So now I have to put my foot down. We can both have boundaries, Wild Thing."

"Begging is hardly a boundary." I glare. This whole thing is backfiring. Why won't he just touch me?

"You didn't have to beg to start. Only because you were selfish."

"Selfish!" I screech.

He brings a hand to my face, holding my chin on his first knuckle. "I promised you everything. You can't take and not give."

"I'll give," I promise.

His thumb presses against my chin. "Give me what I want."

I can feel my walls cracking. Nick isn't relenting. I can deny him again, but he won't fuck me. And more importantly, I don't want anyone else to. I want it to be him.

"Please." My lips barely move as I force the hushed word out.

"Please, what?" he asks, patient.

I close my eyes. "Please, fuck me. I need to feel your hands, and your mouth, and . . ." I can't believe I'm doing this. I've never begged before.

Nick's breath skates over my ear. "All you had to do was ask." His tongue traces the lobe and tingles rush through my neck and arms. As he lowers his head, nipping at my shoulders, he grips my thighs and lifts me off the ground, walking into the bathroom.

I'm already gasping from his hot mouth as he twists the dial for the shower. When he releases my thighs, I keep my legs tight around his waist, returning the kissing against his neck as he readjusts.

He chuckles. "If you want me to fuck you, you have to let me get undressed."

"This is bullshit," I mumble, but I back into the shower spray with a grin, careful to step over the side of the tub. Immediately my back arches from the too-cold water. "Aah!"

Nick lets out another small laugh. "See what happens when you're a brat?"

"Am I?" The water starts to warm quickly, and I step directly under the head so it streams down my body. I feign a light washing just to rub my hands over my stomach and breasts.

"Fuck, yes, you are. A total fucking brat," he says, undressing.

"What are you going to do about it?" A sense of success at getting Nick to give in—even if I did have to beg a little—courses through me, fueling my confidence enough to goad him.

Finally naked, he prowls into the shower with me, meeting me in the spray and kissing me hard. He grips my throat in my favorite way and presses me into the shower wall.

"Shit! That's freezing!" I arch again.

"Deal with it." His free hand rubs over my slick body, sliding between my legs.

"I did something while you were gone," I say quietly, the tiled walls still echoing my words.

Nick grips my center firmly. "I swear, if you tell me you fucked yourself without me again, I'm going to tie you up and make you watch me edge myself."

My mouth drops open before I laugh. "Ok, wait. I might need to lie now because that sounds incredibly fucking hot. But that's not what I was going to say."

Two of his fingers wiggle deeper. I open one leg, granting him more access. "Oh my—I really missed your hands."

"So what did you do?" he asks, his deep voice rumbling. I close my eyes, enjoying the water and the heat and his strong hands teasing me.

"I stopped by the clinic. Checked the—oh!" He drives a finger inside me, causing me to cry out, but I manage to regain myself. "Checked the goods."

"Anything to report?"

I shake my head back and forth against the wall. "No. All good."

"Look at me."

My eyelids open slowly.

"Are you asking me to fuck you raw, Wild Thing?"

Nick Foster's mouth is my favorite thing. Something about his ability to be calm, professional, and charming one minute, and then demanding, seductive, and sexually overt the next makes him all the more appealing to me. Like I get to see a piece of him no one else does.

"I'm telling you it's an option, should you want to." I let my eyes close again and rock my hips against his hand as he slowly fingers me.

His thumb presses deeper into my throat, and I open my eyes again at the silent command. "I haven't been checked out recently, but it's been over a year since I've slept with anyone. And never unprotected."

"I could never go that long. I would spontaneously combust."

"Doubtful." His erection is slick against my belly. He looks up at the shower head and smirks, removing his hand from my neck and detaching the disc from the base. "This could come in handy."

"I removed the pressure regulator for added benefit." I smile wickedly and lick my lips.

He removes his hand between my legs, toying with the various settings on the nozzle. "Of course you did, naughty girl." He holds eye contact, twisting the control slowly. Like with the vibrator and dildo, it's clear he's looking for an indication of what I like. I clamp down hard on my lip, attempting to hide any hints. "I'm not afraid to try them all, if that's what it takes. I've got nowhere to be," he promises.

Remaining silent, I drop my head to the side and close my eyes.

"Have it your way." His low words are almost a threat.

The water pressure increases to a powerful stream and Nick pulls back to create space between us, guiding the head between my legs. He sets a hand against my hip, coercing me to tilt my ass forward. The water pummels my clit immediately.

"Holy shit!" I cry out. I open my eyes, but instead of looking at him, I look down to where he's fucking my clit with the water. "That's . . ."

"Not what you normally use?" he teases.

"I build up," I admit.

"You begged." He leans his torso forward, reaching closer to me with his mouth. "You wanted me to fuck you, so I am."

I moan in response. To him, his words, the pressure, this entire event. I silently scold myself for ever thinking Nick wasn't exactly what I needed.

"Feel good?"

"Yes." My eyes rise to him. "Really fucking good."

"Want more?" His fingers tease the dial.

"No," I almost cry, following with a laugh.

He smiles, releasing my hip and reaching down to stroke himself instead. The head of his cock glistens, and I have half a mind to push the shower head away and drop to my knees for him. I'm not always a fan of oral, but giving to Nick, taking him into my mouth . . . The idea alone forces more arousal from my pussy.

His grip is tight as he works his hand in slow movements up and down his shaft. "See something you like, Wild Thing?"

"Fuck yes." I reach my hand forward to take his place, relishing the feel of his slick skin in my palm when he relinquishes himself to me.

"Oh shit," he groans, his hips thrusting forward. "Don't worry about being gentle."

I grip harder, alternating between watching his face and his cock as I continue to stroke him. He moves his free hand along my torso and breasts, teasing my nipples and causing my hips to jerk against the forceful stream of water.

The humidity is thick and our breathing deepens with the change in the air, the rise in temperature. It's also causing me to sweat, even more moisture trickling between my breasts.

"I need you inside me, Nick. Now."

"I love when you tell me exactly what you want." He moves closer again, with me refusing to stop pumping him with my hand, and shifts my hips, lifting one leg around his waist.

I lean the rest of my weight against the shower tiles, thankful for the non-slip floor design. Nick puts his free hand over mine while I stroke him, and I swear I'm going to come from the action. "Oh my god," I whimper. "Why is that so fucking hot?"

He squeezes tighter. "If you don't let me fuck your needy cunt right now, I'm gonna come all over you."

I meet his hungry gaze. "That's not the worst threat I've ever heard," I admit, but I release him.

He slides the tip against my aching core, hissing when the spray also reaches him. "That's powerful."

I nod vigorously, knowing it's only a matter of time before I come. My hands slide around his back, urging him to enter me. "Please, Nick. Please fuck me." He grants my wish in a forceful thrust, pulling out slowly and entering again just as hard. "Yes."

Both of us focus on where we're joined, the overspray teasing his cock every time he pulls back, as it continues to torture my clit. I bring one hand forward, feeling his abs as he tenses and relaxes.

The water, the sensation of him filling me hard and repeatedly, running my hands over his wet body, it brings me to the edge of my release in no time. My moans warn of my impending orgasm, and Nick's eyes rise to mine. "You're about to come like a good girl, aren't you?"

"Yes," I whine. "I want you to come with me."

"Beg," he orders with a pinch of my nipple.

I hold his stare. There's no going back now. "Please, Boy Scout. Come with me."

His jaw tightens, as do his abs. "You can do better than that, Wild Thing." His pace increases, my body bouncing against the wall.

"Shit. Please, please," I whisper. "Please come with me. I want you to fill me up." That familiar fire starts to rise within.

He then shifts to grab my throat. "Make me."

"If you don't come, I'm gonna wrench that shower head from your hand and turn that water pressure on your balls. Now fucking come, Nick."

"There she is." He grins. His hand shifts to the back of my neck, and we speed toward our orgasms, our movements becoming near erratic.

He tenses beneath my fingers when he comes, his jaw setting as he pins me with his piercing blue eyes. They threaten to close in bliss. His bottom lip slips open and the pure lust coating his features makes me fall apart, my core clenching tightly around him. My nails dig into his torso as my pussy clenches again and again.

"Holy fuck," he breathes.

I shove the shower head away from my clit and he laughs. Our breaths slow.

"Wow," I groan. "You were right. It's way better with you."

CHAPTER 31

NICK

I wake to knocking. Leah is wrapped tightly in my arms, her back tucked into my front and my head buried in her hair. I inhale deeply and she stirs. I didn't mean to fall asleep last night, but fuck, I'm glad I did.

Since the night she greeted me fully fucking naked, we've taken turns visiting each other's houses over the last week. Talking, getting to know each other's bodies more. But it's the first time I've stayed over.

The knocking continues.

"Shit." Leah rolls over, and even though I'd rather tighten my arms, I release her. "It's my sister."

"Were we expecting her?" I rub the sleep from my eyes and stretch. "Do I need to go?"

"*We* weren't expecting her, but I guess *I* always should be at this point. And no, you don't need to leave. But maybe get dressed." She looks coyly over her shoulder before swiping my T-shirt from the chair in the corner.

There's some commotion at the door as she opens it. An exchange takes place between Leah and Lily that's especially brief, because she's gone by the time I make it into the living room thirty seconds later.

"Hiya, Nick." Roman smiles up at me as Leah closes the door. "Where's your shirt?"

"Who's hungry?" Leah says a little loudly, smiling down at Savannah.

Savannah grabs Roman's hand, and he hisses. "Sowwy, bud." Her round face turns up to me. "Bud owie?" Her sweet voice rises at the end of her question, and she scrunches her nose.

Roman lifts a bandaged hand to his chest. Bandaged is a loose term; it's only covered in a large nude adhesive, but he's cradling it like it might need more.

Leah scrunches her brows. "What happened to your hand, bud?" She reaches for it, and he flinches. She hesitates. "Roman?"

Leah looks to me. I shrug without an answer, but I'm just as curious. I drop down on a knee. "How'd you get this, Roman?"

He continues to hold the hurt hand with the other. "The stove."

Leah sighs. "I told you, you can't touch the stove. It's dangerous."

"I know. I was just trying to make pasta like you." He bumps his bottom lip out for a moment.

"Where was Mommy?"

He hesitates. Savannah pipes up in a sing-song voice. "Mommy bye-bye."

"Yeah, she's at work." Leah smiles down at her niece and then her face goes blank. Her head snaps back to Roman. "Roman, did your mom leave you and Banana alone?"

He nods. "She went to see Carl."

Leah's eyes fix for a moment, her brain processing the information.

"When was this?" I scoot closer on my knee, hoping he'll loosen up and I can take a look at the burn.

He takes a tiny step back. "Yesterday."

Leah's eyes fly up to me. Fear and fury war on her face. She inhales and hides away whatever she wants to tell me. "Did Mommy put medicine on it?"

He shakes his head. "We don't have any. And no Spider-Man covers either. Just deez." He holds up the hand.

"Is that the same one from yesterday?" I ask.

"Mm-hm." His head drops and shoulders slump, appearing to feel the pressure of our continued questions.

"I'd really like to look at it. Maybe put some medicine on it so it feels better. What do you think about that?" I tilt my head, looking into his dark eyes.

"It hurts," he whimpers. His eyes fill with tears.

Leah drops down to our level, too. "What if Nick is really gentle? I promise he is." Roman studies her face, working to stop his quivering lip. "And I'll go get you Spider-Man Band-Aids. Promise." She offers him a pinky.

He looks between us, and Savannah squeezes closer to him, looking into his face hopefully. "You 'tay?"

Damn, that makes my chest ache.

Roman nods and leans into Savannah. He doesn't take Leah's pinky, but he offers his hand to me. When I pull the bandage back, my teeth clench tightly; I'll be damned if I let these kids see it. They don't deserve my fury at the treatment of his injury.

The skin is swollen and blistered on his entire palm and halfway up each of his little fingers. He needed to see a doctor immediately. How could someone let their child hurt like this?

Tears fall down Roman's cheeks, and Savannah leans up and tries to kiss at his cheek with exaggerated lips. He's too tall and doesn't lean down, so it's more of an air kiss.

"You're being so brave." I glance at Leah, her face stiffly blank as she pins me with an intense stare. "Why don't we leave this open until Aunt Leah gets you those Spider-Man Band-Aids?"

Roman doesn't look sold on the idea.

"Who likes pancakes?" I ask, hoping a distraction will give him a little confidence.

"Me! Me!" Savannah shouts, dropping her hold on her brother.

"I *do* like pancakes," Roman agrees hesitantly.

"Well, you're in luck, because I make the best pancakes in the county." I stand, and Leah follows with a smirk.

"What's a county?" Roman sits on the couch.

I purse my lips. "It's a large area, sometimes bigger than a town or city."

"Is it bigger dan Bull Creek?"

"Yep."

His eyes widen and he speaks slowly. "Whoa. Dat's big."

"You two put on some cartoons and I'll whip us up some breakfast." I nod toward the bedroom and Leah heads that direction as Roman picks up the remote control and flips on the television.

"How bad is it?" Leah turns on me as soon as we reach the bedroom. She reaches for the hem of my shirt along her thighs and begins to lift.

"What are you doing?"

"Getting dressed so I can go to the pharmacy."

"I'd prefer that he see someone, honestly." My voice is low in an effort to keep her calm and so the kids don't hear. The night Maci was attacked, Leah remained calm the entire time. But a small child that's part of her family could trigger her differently. Especially given the circumstances.

Leah pauses. "Are you serious?"

I nod. "The burn covers almost his entire hand. It's pretty significant and it's on a sensitive area. The skin is swollen and blistered. It could be fine, but because of his age, and the size and severity, better safe than sorry."

Leah's face is rapidly losing color. "Will they take him?" She grabs my arms to steady herself, and I grip the underside of her elbows. She whispers loudly, "If it's that bad, will the doctors call Child Protective Services? Will they take Roman? She left them! The kids are not going to be able to hide that. And I can't lie. I won't. It's too far, Nick. Too much."

This is getting uglier by the minute. "I'm not going to lie and tell you everything is going to be ok. This is not a good situation. He needs to be seen; it needs to be documented. Especially because she left them. And I can guarantee that they will call CPS. But there's a strong chance they'll let you keep them because you're family. That's always the first goal."

"She's going to hate me. What if she goes to jail?" Leah's palm hits her forehead, and she pushes the hair away from her face.

"Ok, one step at a time. Let's get the kids fed and then we'll head to the doctor. If they decide to call CPS, we'll deal with it. If they remove the kids, we'll deal with that, too. But you need to know, when that happens there's usually a waiting period where the parents can't see them. Or potentially under supervision."

Her panic is increasing, her eyes flitting around the room. "This isn't just something to deal with! They can't be in the system!" Her hazel eyes glaze over. "Lily's going to blame this all on me. She was so pissed when I confronted her before. She told me I was looking for a reason to pick on her. She'll think I did it on purpose."

I don't get the impression Leah is trying to talk us out of taking the kids to the doctor. I suspect she's so used to trauma and stress where her family is concerned that she can't help but anticipate the events that will come.

"Why?" I ask. "To steal her kids? She's the one who left them." I grip Leah's shoulders and pull her to me for a hug to keep her from spiraling. "I'm going to stay with you through this. Ok?"

She nods against my chest.

"Take a minute to calm down. I'll start breakfast. It's going to be ok." I kiss her forehead and wait for her to respond.

"Ok," she murmurs, staring blankly at the floor.

CHAPTER 32

LEAH

I t's absolutely not ok.

The moment the nurse sees Roman's hand and we explain what happened, I see the distrust in her eyes. Once he's been seen by a doctor, the nurse applies an antibiotic and wraps Roman's hand in a non-adhesive bandage. She explains the protocol until it's healed. "Wait here while we get paperwork together," she states.

I don't fault her no-nonsense approach. She's kind to Roman, matter of fact to me, and I expect nothing more.

A social worker arrives before we've left the emergency room. She introduces herself as Marsha Fenway, a caseworker for the state, and invites us to sit and chat. Nick stays at a puzzle table with Savannah, while Roman and I sit with Marsha in a set of uncomfortable, puffy chairs.

"Roman, can you tell me what happened to your hand?" Her voice is soft, and she even offers him the hint of a smile.

Roman looks at me, his tiny frame appearing smaller than usual.

"It's ok, bud. You can be honest." I hide my own worry behind a smile for him.

His mouth crushes into a flat line. He looks at the older woman. "I burned my hand."

"Oh no. I've done that before. It's very painful." She tucks her head lower. "Does it feel better now?"

Roman only bobs his head slightly.

"What did you burn it on?" she presses.

"Da stove," he says dejectedly.

"Were you helping your mommy make something yummy?"

Again, Roman looks up at me and I give him a gentle nod.

"No. My mom was gone. I was making pasta for me and my sister."

Marsha's eyes meet mine for a second. "Oh. Were you helping your auntie?"

I wrap an arm around my nephew, tucking him into my side.

He shakes his head. "No. Only me and Savannah were home."

Marsha nods. "Ok. Have you and Savannah been there alone before?"

Roman nods.

The guilt I feel is crushing. I should've called sooner, if only to prevent something like this from happening. Lily's wrath isn't what's held me back. It's hope. Hope that I could get through to her. Remind her of the shit we experienced and the vulnerability of her children.

This is on me as much as her.

After a few more questions, Marsha directs her words at me. "I know y'all want to get home and rest." She eyes Roman, indicating wanting to shield him from her next words.

I lean down and speak softly into his ear. "Hey bud, why don't you go play with Nick and Savannah. We'll leave in just a few minutes."

He hops off the couch and sprints for the others.

Marsha waits for him to be out of earshot. "We'll be opening a formal investigation. This situation is serious. Because the children were alone and injured, that's grounds for an emergency removal."

My heartbeat is painful. "You're taking them?"

"No. Not from you," she affirms. Hot tears pool in my eyes in relief, though my chest feels unbelievably tight as I prepare for what else Marsha will tell me. "In cases like this, we'd be trying to place the kids with family anyway. They can stay with you for the time being, assuming you'll take them."

"Of course I will." I peek over at my niece and nephew. Savannah has crawled into Nick's lap.

"Given the circumstances, you can take them for tonight, but you're going to have some paperwork to complete. I need it by 8 a.m. tomorrow. We need to conduct background checks and I'll be stopping by for a home visit."

"That's fine."

She continues to rattle off information. "I'll reach out to the children's mother after we leave here and make her aware of the situation. Until further notice, she cannot be left alone with them. If you think she'll be argumentative or combative, I would advise that you avoid any interactions until we've had a formal hearing."

I wrap my arms around myself. "How long will that take?"

"I'll get it scheduled tomorrow and let you know. We'll be trying for an initial hearing this week. There will also be an ad litem attorney or a Court Appointed Special Advocate appointed at that time."

"What's that?"

"They're a lawyer or volunteer who looks out for the interest of the children. If your sister wants an attorney, and I'd say she will, she'll need to secure one on her own. Same for you, if that's what you want."

An ache begins to form in my temples. "Ok."

She pauses. "Are there grandparents? We'll need to conduct background checks on them, too."

"Our mother lives in town. But I'm not taking the kids to her. She'll just hand them over to my sister." *Or worse.*

"Good to know," Marsha says.

She gives me a few more instructions and meets us in the parking lot with a stack of paperwork.

"I'll need all of this ready when I come by tomorrow." She looks over the top rim of her glasses at me. "This is not negotiable. I can leave the children with you for tonight, but if anything negative comes back on these when we complete the checks, or we have concerns tomorrow, we may have to find alternate placement for Roman and Savannah."

"Yes ma'am." I refuse to consider this task daunting. This may not be how I planned to help Roman and Savannah, but it's what I can do for now. I waited too long—I won't fail them again.

On the way home, we stop at the store for additional medicine and bandages and a replenishment of groceries. The kids crash in the spare room for a nap while Nick and I put everything away. Just as we sit on the couch, my phone rings.

I cringe, checking the caller ID.

"Lily?" Nick asks.

"My mom." This is going to suck. I answer the call. "Hey, Mom."

My mother's aggressive greeting is only made worse by her permanently fatigued voice. "What the fuck is going on, Leah? Lily just called and said social services showed up at the club." She doesn't allow me to answer as she continues relaying the story. "She said they told her they're opening a case because Roman got hurt at your house."

"Wait a second," I interject. "He didn't get hurt here. I'm the one who took him to the ER. Lily dropped him off and he was already hurt."

"So you called child services?" she accuses angrily.

"No!"

Nick sits ready to pounce on the edge of the sectional. He studies me carefully as the conversation continues.

"Well then how'd they know?"

I lean against the back of the couch and close my eyes. It doesn't matter how I frame this; it'll be seen as my fault. "The nurse called. You didn't see his hand, Mom. It's awful. And it happened because Lily left the kids alone."

"His hand? How bad can a hand injury be? Your generation is a bunch of fuckin' hypochondriacs. Always want something to whine about." The irony of my mom saying we complain too much when she's addicted to synthetic opioids isn't lost on me.

"Whatever you say, Mom. He needs topical antibiotics and regular bandage changes. And there's a chance he'll have permanent scarring. It wasn't a small burn."

She scoffs. "So now what? Her kids get put in foster care?" Once again, she keeps talking before I can answer, this time for herself. "This is all she needs. I told her to get on birth control after the first one. Now there's going to be court costs and who knows what else."

I release a long breath. "I don't know all the details yet. The kids are staying with me for now. There's a home inspection or something scheduled for tomorrow. I'll ask for more details then. It was a lot."

"What a damn mess." Despite her irritation, it's clear she doesn't understand the severity of this. And no amount of my arguing with her will change that. "I can't believe you let this happen."

"Once again," I say through clenched teeth, "I didn't leave *my* children. If anything, I've been enabling her. That's what I'm guilty of. Not reporting her when this first became an issue."

She scoffs. "I can't believe you'd even say that. Report your own sister. You oughtta be slapped. All of this could have been handled within the family, Leah."

"Oh, yeah. The way we handled the first baby that you all but forced her to give up for adoption. The way we handle caring for the kids. With her failing to have consistent phone service and you falling asleep when they're at your house. With me allowing her to do the bare minimum. We aren't *handling* anything in the family."

"You're so goddamned dramatic. People nap with kids. And she's doing her best," she manages as she coughs loudly into the phone, the result of a lifetime of smoking. It's only gotten worse over the last few years.

"You know what, I'm not the crazy one here. And I'm not going to let you convince me otherwise. If you want to coddle Lily, by all means, go for it. But I'm looking out for Roman and Savannah." I end the call and throw my phone across the couch.

"That seemed to go well," Nick says softly. He opens his arms for me, and I fall into his chest.

CHAPTER 33

LEAH

Despite Nick's argument that the social worker won't be looking at the cleanliness of the house, I still wake up early and give it a thorough once over. Smokey gets a brushing, the couches get vacuumed, I turn on a diffuser instead of a normal candle.

Being Nick, he offered to stay for support, but I declined. I want to do this on my own. It was my failure to intervene that got them to this point.

The kids and I are cleaning up a breakfast of cinnamon rolls, eggs, and fruit when the doorbell rings five minutes early.

I open the door with a forced smile and Marsha greets me on the other side with something similar. "Good morning," she says politely.

"Good morning. Come in." I work to keep my voice steady as nerves race through me.

Her serious eyes take in the living room. "This is very quaint." Her tone is pleasant, but is "quaint" code for something? Too small? Too old? I don't even know what they're looking for.

Roman and Savannah loiter in the doorway to the kitchen.

"Good morning," Marsha calls, with an even bigger smile.

Savannah waves as she takes a bite of the strawberry in her other hand, but Roman remains still.

"I have all of the paperwork completed. It's in here." I gesture toward the kitchen. "Do you want to look it over while I get the kids' teeth brushed? They just had breakfast."

Marsha presses her lips together as if to hide a smile. "That'll be fine." She follows me through the small, cased opening.

"I don't have any coffee, but I have orange juice if you'd like."

"Not to worry, I had two cups of coffee before I left home this morning. But I may need to use the facilities before I leave." She winks, and a nugget of relief settles inside me.

"Ok. Well, make yourself comfortable. I'll be right back." I turn to the kids still clinging to the doorframe. "Come on, you two."

After they're cleaned up, I settle them in their bedroom. I moved all of the baskets with stones, beads, wire, and other small items into the top of the closet last night. I'm not taking any chances. I hurry back to the kitchen to check on Marsha.

"These look good," she says, collecting the stack of forms and sliding them into a folder on her dark clipboard, and stands. "It'll take a day or so to get the checks back. We won't notify you of good news, but you'll definitely hear if there's anything concerning."

"Ok." It's the most useless response ever, but it's all I've got.

"Care to show me around?" she asks with an amused smile.

I jolt. I should have offered. "Of course. It's not much, but I'll be happy to give you a tour."

Marsha's warm hand grazes my shoulder. "Do not discredit the validity of a stable, warm home." Her words hit harder than she may realize. It was all I wanted growing up and something I worked hard to give myself, even if I was the only one who got to enjoy it.

Although, maybe Roman and Savannah also benefited from what I created here. My eyes sting.

"Lead the way, sweetheart," Marsha says with a squeeze, and then releases me.

I give her a short look around. She peeks into closets and cabinets, saying things like, "You need to put these medicines in a locked cabinet," or "You'll need a fire extinguisher." Simple things that didn't occur to me. Before we get too far, I grab a notepad and make a list of her suggested changes.

Roman and Savannah are building a city out of Lincoln Logs when we move through their room.

"What are these? Do you make things?" Marsha peers at the desk and tools without touching anything.

"I design jewelry." I finger the necklace I'm wearing.

"How lovely. Is it a hobby? I don't remember it from the intake form." Her tone is curious.

"It's been a hobby for a while. I recently started offering custom and made-to-order pieces."

Her face brightens. "Oh wait! I remember something about a show at The Spur. Was that you?"

"Yes," I admit sheepishly.

"I don't ever go there," she adds with a wide smile. "This old woman is way past weekends of drinking at bars. But I did see the flyers."

"Oh Marsha, you just need one night with me and I'll have you reliving your glory days." We both laugh, but then my face falls a little. It doesn't feel appropriate to joke about with the kids here now. At least for the present, responsibility takes precedence.

"Let's sit and chat." Marsha nods to the doorway and exits toward the living room with me following suit.

I sit stiffly on the edge of the couch.

"I know this is really scary," Marsha starts. "But everything seems fine here. All of the things I mentioned to you are items we would require in any prospective foster home. They're requirements for the program. It doesn't mean you've done anything wrong."

Her reassurance only helps a little.

"As far as what's next, we have a preliminary hearing tomorrow. This will be when we set a plan for Lily in order to successfully reunify."

"Reunify?"

"For the children to go home. That's always the primary goal." Her words hang in the air as if there's another option.

"I'm sorry—what's the alternative?" The curiosity in my words is thick; I don't know what other outcome there would be.

Marsha pats the clipboard absently. "We look at the safety and well-being of the children above all else."

"Of course," I agree.

"We'll set a plan in place for the parents to provide the best home they can. Sometimes that's parenting classes, assistance with substance abuse, anger management, therapy . . . Every path is different, because each family's needs are different. But ultimately, if the parents aren't able to complete the steps or it's not in the best interest of the children to return to the home, then we will look at other placement options. Or a more permanent situation."

"Permanent. You mean adoption." My heart rate increases. "How long does Lily have to complete what's needed?"

Marsha shifts on the couch. "Each situation is different. There is usually a sixty day minimum. Sometimes the family needs up to eighteen months."

"Eighteen!" I clamp a hand over my mouth. I can't imagine my sister losing eighteen months with her children. What that could mean for Roman and Savannah long term.

"We'll have more details tomorrow. But this is a somewhat fluid situation."

"I'm sorry. I understand." I work to curb the tidal wave of emotions I'm experiencing.

Marsha reaches across the cushion between us and places her hand on my knee. "It's ok to be emotional about this. We'll have meetings along the way, and you'll have support." She stands and again I follow as she walks toward the door. "Call me if you have questions."

I take the card she extends to me, which has a time and address for tomorrow written on the back.

"Thank you." Even after Marsha leaves, I stand staring at the card. Yesterday morning, I thought I was going to babysit for a few hours. Overnight even. And now, my sister may lose her children permanently.

After Marsha leaves, I call Sadie and let her know that I'll be taking the week off.

"Is everything ok?" she asks, her sunny voice filled with worry.

"Honestly, no. Not really. I have some family things I need to take care of." I'm already embarrassed enough of the situation; I can't say any more than that.

"You take all the time you need, sweet girl," she says, her southern charm thick.

"Thanks. I'll be in touch later this week." I can't bring myself to return the same emotion. I'm taking things hour by hour at this point.

My next call is Izzy.

"Hey, gorgeous!" she greets happily.

I wish her excitement over hearing from me helped my mood. "Hi, beautiful. I really need my sisters from another mister. Think you can reach Maci and come over?"

Her jovial tone turns worried. "Of course. I'll call her. Are you ok?"

"It's complicated. It's about Lily and the kids."

A tiny inhale travels through the line. "Are they ok?"

My throat constricts. "I'll explain everything when you get here."

"Ok, honey. We'll be on our way soon."

While I wait for my friends to show up, Roman, Savannah, and I have lunch and then I lay them down for a nap. Smokey curls between them in the bed, purring contentedly and making biscuits on Savannah's tummy.

I manage to slip out of their room at the same time Maci and Izzy arrive. Maci gives a short knock before they both walk in.

Izzy throws her arms around me. "Tell us everything."

We settle on the couch in the living room, squished together.

"Roman and Savannah will be staying with me for a while. There's a case open with Child Protective Services."

"You called?" Maci asks while Izzy looks on in horror.

"No. I should have, but I was too late. She left them alone and Roman burned himself on the stove trying to make them lunch." Summarizing out loud makes me sick to my stomach. Tears flood my eyes.

Izzy gasps. "How bad was it?"

"Nick and I took him to the ER. His whole hand was covered in blisters. They called social services. Lily can't be alone with the kids for now, and we have a hearing tomorrow morning. They did a home visit earlier, and I had to fill out a bunch of paperwork to run background checks and stuff."

"What's happening at the hearing?" Maci asks.

"I don't know all the details, but it sounds like we'll have a plan of action after we leave."

"Is Lily going? Are they arresting her?" Izzy continues coming up with more questions before I can answer. "Does she have a lawyer? Do *you* need a lawyer?"

"Hank does family law," Maci offers, referencing her own lawyer, who was originally the executor of her grandmother's estate. But when shit went down after she was attacked by her stepbrother, she talked him into representing her against any civil or criminal charges that came up because of her actions of self-defense.

"That's probably not a bad idea," I agree. "I wonder if he's handled many of these cases, since he focuses on family law?"

She shrugs. "I'll give you his number. I'd say this is more in his wheelhouse than what he did for me." She smirks, but it doesn't have the desired effect.

"How else can we help?" Izzy puts a hand on my knee.

Roman and Savannah have spent so much time at my house that I have a solid stash of clothes and toys. Toothbrushes and combs. All of the essentials. Those aren't the things I'm worried about.

"I need to figure out childcare. My mom isn't an option." One good thing that's come of this is that I can finally put my foot down when it comes to my niece and nephew being with my mom.

The room is quiet for a minute as the three of us contemplate.

Finally, Maci says, "It's out of the way, but maybe Andi could help? I don't really want to offer her without asking, but I think she's moving into a different phase of life."

Sure, it would add a much longer commute to work, driving the kids out to the ranch and coming back into town, but that's not even a concern for me. "I'd gladly make the drive. Can you give me her number, too?"

After discussing all the logistics with my friends, I feel like a weight has been lifted from my chest. We sit and chat, switching topics to wedding plans and things at Izzy's work, until the kids wake up.

The door to their bedroom opens with a click and the three of us quiet as tiny pitter-patters move toward us. Roman pokes his head around the corner. "Maci! Izzy!" He barrels through the room and launches onto us where we still sit side by side.

Savannah runs behind him on the balls of her feet, her sandy hair bouncing with each step. I scoop her onto the couch with us.

My friends love all over my niece and nephew like aunts are supposed to, and the room fills with giggles, and light, and happiness. It's a reminder of how friends can be the family you choose. This is my family. And I will protect them at all costs.

CHAPTER 34

LEAH

The next morning, Roman, Savannah and I head to the courthouse, where Marsha has an additional social worker who will keep them entertained while we're in the hearing.

Lily is already waiting outside when we arrive. She crouches down to them. "Hi babies. I miss you." Her tone isn't especially soft, but I've never seen her get down on their level. Maybe she needs this to remind her what she stands to lose.

I hang back and let them talk to her. Roman lets his mom hug him while Savannah stands to the side. "Look at my new bandage," he says quietly.

"That's big," Lily says, glaring over the top of his head at me. "I know you want to come home. I'm going to pick you up as soon as I can."

"It's ok," Roman says. "Aunt Leah has Lincoln Logs."

Lily doesn't respond to him. Instead, she stands and continues to stare daggers at me. "You really did it this time," she growls. "This is a new low."

"You only have yourself to blame." I keep my voice quiet before turning my attention to the kids. "Roman, Banana, this is Miss Gwen. She's going to hang out with you while Mommy and I talk."

Roman shrugs and Savannah waves. Gwen leads them to a shaded area, where she lays out a blanket and sits with them.

I ignore Lily as we head inside, and Marsha guides me to sit in the audience.

This skirt is too tight, and my hair itches when it's pinned up this way. The last time I pulled it up into an updo was at Nana's funeral. It didn't bother me then, probably because it felt like a choice instead of a necessity. Either way, it's doing nothing for my anxiety. I want to rip it all out.

A few minutes pass in near silence before the judge comes in. I haven't reached out to Hank yet, so I make a point to pay close attention.

The bailiff reads off a long number and a list of names as the judge gets situated.

"I looked over the details that were submitted. Please give me any updates," the judge says. He has a no-nonsense tone and eyes my sister down the bridge of his nose, where she sits on the opposite side of the court by herself.

"Good morning, your honor," Marsha says. She has someone with her I haven't been introduced to. "Your honor, we removed the two children in question due to an emergency situation. The injury described was sustained while the children were alone and no medical treatment was provided. At this time, the children are staying with their maternal aunt, Leah Van Hoff. The background check didn't turn up anything, and the children have stayed with her regularly. We feel this is the best placement for them at this time because of the stability it provides. A home visit has been conducted and there were no red flags."

The judge scans the pews to find me. "You're the aunt?"

I stand. "Yes, sir. Your honor," I amend quickly.

"You're comfortable with your niece and nephew living with you for the time being?"

"Yes, your honor. They already had their own room at my house. They're always welcome."

He continues without acknowledging my response one way or the other. "You'll be eligible for assistance, similar to a foster family. It's about fourteen dollars per day, per child."

This hadn't even occurred to me. "Oh. Uh, thank you."

He turns his attention back to Marsha. I sit and they begin outlining the expectations for Lily. Parenting classes, supervised visitations, a permanent childcare plan, and more.

Lily remains unfazed.

The judge finally addresses her. "Ms. Van Hoff, do you understand these requirements as outlined?"

"I do," she says flatly.

"And do you understand that if you do not participate in the requirements of this plan of service that you may be ineligible for reunification? That you may be forced to terminate your rights?"

"Yes." Neither her tone nor expression changes. I can't understand. She doesn't seem worried in the least.

"Do you have any questions at this time?"

"I do." Lily looks over her shoulder at me, disgusted. "Do I have a say in where my kids are? My sister has made it clear that she doesn't support my parenting, and I don't think she's going to put in the effort to help so I can get them back."

The judge looks toward Marsha.

Marsha stands again to respond. "Your honor, we considered Ms. Van Hoff's choice for placement of Roman and Savannah. In this case, this was her mother, Cheryl Courtland. Her background check did have some concerning charges and when we arrived to interview her, she was too inebriated to speak with us. The caseworker did notice various prescription bottles opened with items accessible. We do not feel this would be the best placement at this time."

"Of course," Lily mutters. Her jaws tightens. It's a wonder she hasn't thrown something yet—not that there's much within reach.

"What about paternity?" the judge offers, glancing at my sister from the corner of his eye.

Marsha speaks up. "There are two different fathers in this case. We've reached out to both but haven't made contact yet. Based on our initial interviews, the children don't know them and the fathers have not been present or financially supportive."

"Any other questions?" the judge asks, looking back to my sister.

"No." She crosses her arms in annoyance.

The hearing concludes without much more fanfare. Marsha agrees to stick around and let Lily spend an hour with the kids before bringing them to my house. Apparently, they maintain car seats for just these types of situations.

And it works in my favor, because the entire thing is crashing down on me. I barely make it to my car with a small smile on my face, so as not to worry Roman and Savannah.

My chest hurts and my eyes burn.

Somehow, I keep the furious tears at bay until I close my front door behind me. That's as far as I get before ripping bobby pins out of my hair and flinging them into the wooden bowl on my entry table. I unzip the side of my charcoal skirt and untuck my cream blouse with a furious yank.

This whole situation is so fucked.

Chapter 35

Leah

Maci:

Say hello everyone. This is our new group chat.

Me:

I did not agree to a room change.

Izzy:

Can you not be a pain in the ass for ONE minute?

Me:

OMG. Do you eat with that mouth?

Liv:

Hey everyone! Sorry, duty calls. I'll text after school lets out.

Sammi:

I'm so excited to be part of the chat now!

Me:

Oh yes! Fresh faces!

Me:

I was so tired of the old folks.

Izzy:

I'll take that as a no.

Maci:

I've decided we all need to embrace our village more—here's looking at you, Leah. So I'm expanding the chat for all of us.

Me:

You mean here's looking at you, mirror.

Maci:

>annoyed emoji<

Me:

Sammi, you're a little far, yeah?

Sammi:

You're so out of the loop.

We're moving back!

Izzy:

I'm so excited for this!!

Me:

You guys never tell me anything.

Maci:

You've been a little preoccupied.

Sammi:

BTW Leah, add me to the list.

Me:

List?

Maci:

For Roman and Banana.

Sammi:

Yeah. Justin and I are driving down this evening so we can look at houses over the next few days. If you need some help, Vivi and I can hang out with the kids.

Me:

Normally I'd say I got it, but I think I'll take you up on that.

By Friday morning, all of my girlfriends are able to get checked with CPS. Sammi comes by with Viviane on Friday morning to watch the kids, so I can stop by Hank Campbell's office for a consultation.

The Smith, Drummond, and Campbell Law Office looks like an average historical house on the corner of Main and Pecan. The house is a sage green with auburn trim, and mature magnolia trees surround it in a well-kept yard. I study the upstairs stained-glass windows as I ascend the steps to the front porch.

The front door opens directly to a set of stairs and a check-in desk. A middle-aged woman sits behind the desk with a dashing man talking to her from the front side. His crisp, navy-blue suit is perfectly tailored, matched with a white shirt and mulberry tie that has a muted filigree design.

He smiles brighter than the secretary when I walk in, like someone from a toothpaste commercial.

"Good morning. How can we help you?" the woman asks, standing.

"I'm Leah Van Hoff. I have an appointment with Mr. Campbell."

"That's me," he says stepping forward, his smile never faltering. "Hank. Nice to meet you."

I accept his extended hand and a sense of comfort washes over me. "Hi."

Maci mentioned that Hank was especially grounding each time she worked with him, and I can already see what she means. He has a warm demeanor, like nothing can rattle him. And yet, he's hardly said two words.

"Follow me," he says cordially. Hank turns to the right of the entrance, where wide French doors open up to a large sitting room. He continues through to the back, where another small sitting area has been turned into an office. It has modern leather chairs and cream walls above traditional, tall baseboards. "Have a seat."

"Thanks for seeing me on short notice," I say as we sit.

"Happy to. You mentioned on the phone that you have a Child Protective Services case. How can I help?" He clasps his arms so that one is facing up and one faces down, gripping near the opposite elbows.

"My sister has a pending case against her—let me back up; I have no idea what lingo to use, so if how I word things doesn't sound accurate, just interrupt." I squeeze my interlaced fingers together in my lap.

"Leah," Hank says, lowering his voice and holding my gaze with his bright blue eyes, "I am not here to judge you. I'm here to help. I'm not worried about what language you use. We'll figure it all out as we go." A gentle smile punctuates his statement.

I inhale and exhale heavily. "My nephew was injured when he and my niece were home alone. Child Protective Services determined it was an emergency, and both kids have been placed with me for the time being."

He nods and reaches for a pen. After writing a note on a legal pad, he looks to me again. "Have you had an initial hearing with them?"

"Yes."

"Go ahead and relay that to me."

I do as I'm told, sharing all that I remember.

Hank takes more notes as I talk. "How old are the children?" he asks when I've finished.

"Roman is four and Savannah is two."

He leans back in the chair, getting comfortable. I anticipate I may be in for a long speech. "Thank you for sharing all of this with me," Hank starts. "I know you're probably pretty overwhelmed right now, and you likely have a lot of questions. I'll do my best to answer and guide you."

I nod for him to continue.

"As you said, the goal right now is reunification—getting Roman and Savannah back home with Mom. Throughout the process, you're going to have check-ins with the social workers, both to see how the kids are faring and for you to be able to update them on any events they need to be aware of." He presses one pointer finger to the other as he starts listing examples of items to share. "Does your sister show up unannounced? Does she maintain scheduled visits and attend for the entire duration? What is her treatment of the children during these events and how does she behave?"

I'm not sure I like the use of "behave," but I get the gist.

"Likewise, you'll receive updates from family services." He starts counting again. "Is your sister completing the tasks that have been outlined? Is she supplying them with the plans they've asked for? Does the house pass inspection when the time comes?"

"This feels like a lot. I'm not used to being the big sister." I can't help feeling like a weight is coming down on me, even if it's what's best for the kids.

"That's fair. What you need to focus on is Roman and Savannah's needs and complying with the state. They will leave the kids in your care so long as they feel it's the best option."

"I can do that, no problem."

"Do you have a good support system? Because I'll be honest, that's one of the biggest factors in how well this goes. This may be your niece and nephew, and you may be very familiar with them, but you'll need to maintain your own well-being throughout this, too."

I nod. "Yeah. I have a great group of friends."

"All right," Hank says. "So best case scenario, in the eyes of the Department of Family and Protective Services, is to get Roman and Savannah back with their mom. Let's talk about what happens if that's not an option."

"They hinted at terminating Lily's rights if she doesn't comply."

Hank pauses, studying me briefly. "I know you said Maci is your friend. I suspect if she shared my name with you, it's because you're close with her, so I'm going to be honest with you. As honest as I was with her."

I sit up straighter. "I prefer honesty. I know I seem overwhelmed, but I just want what's best for Roman and Savannah. And I want to be able to prepare them in an age-appropriate way. I don't want anything sprung on them," I tell him adamantly.

He nods and continues. "There are a lot of reasons that these types of cases do not go to plan. That can be just needing more time for the parents to get things completed, or other complications all together."

My shoulders deflate a little. "My sister already has one child that she voluntarily put up for adoption. It's an open adoption, but I'm not aware that she's ever seen the baby—child."

"DFPS will consider that, but less so given that it was a voluntary adoption." He swivels his head back and forth. "They're going to consider her support system, as well."

"My sister wants support on her terms. And her communication skills are lacking."

Hank crosses his arms. "She'll need to work on that, or this is going to be a very hard process."

"Ok"—I take a steadying breath—"let's say reunification is off the table. What happens then?"

"Social services will try to place the children with family more permanently. I know you said they haven't reached the fathers, but they will make all efforts to make contact. Then they'll go down the line." He stares at me intently, like he's trying to communicate something telepathically. "You need to prepare yourself for the possibility that they will ask you about permanent placement."

I can't bring myself to respond, but he continues. "If they don't find a suitable family member, or if that person is unwilling to keep them, then they'll consider foster homes to place the children for adoption."

The idea of Roman and Savannah being with complete strangers makes me sick to my stomach. They're social kids, but that doesn't mean they would be comfortable. Roman already shared he feels guilty for hurting himself, even though I keep reassuring him that it's not his fault. If they were to get placed elsewhere, I imagine his guilt would increase tremendously. That's not something a four-year-old needs to deal with.

I was prepared for some homesickness, tantrums, and normal growing pains as we navigated this. But now I'm worried about more significant mental health issues for the kids. Marsha mentioned therapy support; I think it's time to call in reinforcements.

While Roman and Savannah nap, I call Andi to discuss the possibility of her watching the kids. Outright asking for help is such a foreign concept to me. As a child, my mother had a tendency to ask anyone and everyone for things, big and small. It always seemed so wildly inappropriate, because of non-existent relationships or the caliber of what she was asking for, that I was forever mortified. I'm having to unlearn the unnecessary embarrassment. But no matter how awkward, I'll do what's needed.

"Hello?" Andi's sunny voice greets.

"Hi Mrs. Strickland, this is Leah Van Hoff, Maci's friend."

"Hi sweetheart, how are you?" Enough compassion seeps into her voice that I know she's been briefed on the situation.

I pause to consider her question. I've been so focused on my niece and nephew that I haven't given myself much thought. "I'm hanging in there. Every day is something new I didn't expect."

"I can only imagine, honey. I'm so sorry your family is going through all this, but it sounds like there needed to be a bit of an intervention. How are the kids? They're so sweet."

"They're doing well, actually. I think I expected more questions about their mom and when they can go home, but they haven't asked at all." It almost hurts more to admit that truth. "I haven't spoken to my sister since the hearing. She was obviously upset. And my mom doesn't agree with any of it."

"Sometimes we have to have an outside perspective before we can see what's right in front of us," Andi says optimistically. She's not the kind of woman to judge, and again I think how lucky Maci is to have her as a mother-in-law.

"Maybe you're right." However, I can't see how any outside perspective would make Lily or my mom see anything more clearly. If the few conversations we've had this week are any indication, I'm more concerned they're going to double down.

"Anyway," I say on a deep inhale, "I was actually calling to see if you might be able to help me a little. And before I ask, please know that you are more than welcome to say no and it won't hurt my feelings at all. It's a big ask."

"Well, let's hear it," she says in an almost sing-song voice that puts me at ease again.

"Maci mentioned you may be looking at new ways to fill your time, and I wondered if you may be willing to babysit Roman and Savannah? I'd pay you, of course. And I can provide meals, too."

"Of course I can help. And don't you worry about food. I can handle that," she promises. "I won't always be available. But we can work on a weekly schedule if that's ok."

My response spills out quickly. "Sure, yes, of course! I make the store schedule so I can be flexible, too."

"You know I won't have them all to myself, right?" Andi giggles. "I imagine the kids are going to spend a lot of time helping around the ranch."

I grin. Roman and Savannah loved getting to ride Sutton's horse, Johnny Walker, at Thanksgiving, and Roman's been begging to visit again. "I don't think they'll complain. They may make more of a mess than help, though."

Andi laughs. "They'll learn."

"Thank you, Mrs. Strickland."

"Please, Leah. Call me Andi. And relax. You're doing great."

I nearly burst into tears at her kind words. I'm not used to being all in my feels; the support and stress is really getting to me.

"Thank you. I'll check my schedule for next week and get back to you."

"Ok, sweetheart. I'll talk to you soon," Andi says warmly before hanging up.

CHAPTER 36

NICK

My week out of town for April falls right after Roman's burn incident, so I've been doing my best to support Leah from afar. We're in contact all week. She updates me on the hearing, additional background checks, her meeting with the lawyer, and childcare plans.

I'm glad she's leaning on her friends, but I think she and the kids need a break from her house for a bit. So, I make sure to be available Saturday to get them out for a while.

The main door is open when I arrive at her house. I knock on the storm door and Roman runs in from the kitchen. "Hiya, Nick!" He pushes the door open to let me in.

"Hey, man! How are you?" I offer him a fist and he bumps it with his unbandaged hand. "How's your hand?"

"Better." He waves the bandaged hand in the air.

"It's a good thing he's so tough," Leah says, entering the living room behind him. She addresses Roman. "Can you help Savannah pick up the rest of the toys? Breakfast is almost ready."

"Yep!" Roman runs into the hallway.

I take the opportunity to give Leah a hug and kiss her neck. I don't know how she feels about affection in front of them—it's something we need to discuss. "Let's go for a hike," I mumble into her ear.

She shifts in my arms. "Nick, pinch me. I'm having a nightmare." I do as I'm told, and she squeaks.

"I'm serious. Let's get the kids out and do something fun," I continue.

She pulls back. "I don't know. That sounds like a lot of sweating. And Savannah's still pretty little."

"Have you forgotten what my career is? I would never suggest something that she can't handle. There are some short trails. We can pack lunch."

She chews her lip before quietly relenting. "Ok."

After breakfast, and with all the essentials in tow, we head out for one of the closer trailheads. It's not peak summer heat, but we've covered the kids with sunscreen and packed extra water bottles.

"Lead the way, Boy Scout," Leah says, once we're out and prepped to start.

I grin, and Roman asks, "Why do you call Nick a boy scout?"

Leah presses her lips together in thought. "It's a fun nickname. Kind of like how I call you 'bud' and we call Savannah 'Banana.'"

"Mmm." His face scrunches in thought. "Does Nick have a nickname for you?"

Leah and I stare at each other, trying to hide our smiles. "Sometimes he calls me 'Wild Thing.'"

"Like the book?"

"Sure," she says with a ruffle of his hair.

Roman reaches for her hand as she steps off the sidewalk onto the trail. "Where does dis go?"

"It's a trail to explore nature," I explain, holding Savannah's hand as we walk. Her free hand reaches out to the leaves as we pass shrubs. "You have to pay attention out here because there are some really pretty things. There are also some things you don't want to touch."

"Why?" ask Roman.

"They'll make you itchy. Or sick." I smile down at him.

He continues to pepper us with questions as we walk, taking the trail slowly so I can point out various plants and wildlife. When Savannah's pace slows, I crouch down. "Need a ride, Little Bit?" She doesn't answer right away. "Want me to carry you?"

"Up!" she says happily and reaches for me with both arms.

I stand and grab her waist, twisting her around and setting her onto my shoulders. She giggles and grips my hat with loose hands. "Hold on tight," I say, knowing good and well she won't.

Leah looks up at us, assessing the new arrangement. "You good, bud?" Her eyes fall to Roman.

"Yep."

We continue along the trail until we come to the lookout point at the end. It seemed like the best choice for their first hike, which has an awesome view for the kids to check out. Others offer more rocky trails and tree line views, but I doubted the kids would find as much interest in that.

We find a good place to stop for food, and Leah and I set up a thin blanket and the lunches we packed. Roman and Savannah play just off the trail, digging in the dirt and stacking rocks in short towers.

AMANDA MARQUARDT

"Come eat, you two," Leah calls. She pulls baby wipes from her backpack and cleans off their hands as we all sit together. They dig into the sandwiches and Leah looks over at me. "Maybe this wasn't a terrible idea."

"No?" I ask. "You don't have sweat in unmentionable places?"

She grins. "It's not bad. But don't ask me to do this in July. You'll definitely be on your own then."

"We'll see about that," I say, the corner of my mouth lifting.

In a blink, Roman and Savannah are finished eating. Roman hurries off to play, but Savannah lays with her head in Leah's lap. Leah drags her fingers through Savannah's hair, and in moments the toddler's eyes close softly.

"I'm going to check on Roman." I follow his path and call, "Can I play with you?"

"Sure." Roman pats the dirt next to him and I plop down. He continues stacking rocks on a tree stump. He remains quiet as he moves items around.

"A penny for your thoughts," I say gently.

He turns his brown eyes up at me. "What?"

"A penny for your thoughts. It means I want to know what you're thinking. If you want to tell me." I lean my head to one side.

"Oh." He remains quiet, so I find a stick nearby and begin to draw abstract lines in the dirt. Finally he says, "Do you think me and Savannah are going back with Mommy soon?"

"Do you miss your mom?" I ask, instead of answering him. I doubt he has a solid concept of time yet, and it doesn't seem helpful to give him information he's not able to process. Especially without anything solid.

"Yes and no." He keeps stacking small rocks without looking up at me. "I like Leah's house."

"Yeah, aunts are fun. They do special things with us."

Roman pauses his movement, considering my words. "No."

"No?"

"Leah does do fun tings with us," he starts. "But dat's not why I like her house."

"What is it?"

"It's happy," he says, and his tone matches. "My mom's house is angry." His voice drops.

"Angry at you?" I want to be careful with my questions, but it's also important to understand if there are concerning dynamics.

"Sometimes. Sometimes just angry. She doesn't talk to us a lot. She yells on her phone or at people who come over." Roman kicks at the dirt absently.

"That's no fun. I like to be where I'm happy, too."

Roman looks up at me with curious eyes. "Does Leah make you happy, too?"

Fuck, does she.

A smile spreads over my face. "Yeah, man. She really does."

CHAPTER 37

LEAH

Roman and Savannah have been with me for three weeks, and in that time, Lily has appeared for three of her scheduled visits. Three of nine. They've always been scheduled at the city park. Marsha suggested a neutral location, and that seemed like the best place.

When Lily arrived for the first, I made myself scarce, working on some jewelry within sight, but not too close. She played a little with the kids but spent a lot of time on her phone, which I couldn't understand for someone who hadn't seen their children in almost a week.

But then she didn't show to the second visit.

"Is Mommy coming? I thought we were meeting her here," Roman asked after we'd been at the playground for about twenty minutes.

"You know what? I'm sorry. She sent me a message that something happened with the car so she couldn't come. I'm sorry I forgot to tell you."

Roman nodded, though he didn't seem convinced. He didn't ask any further questions.

After that, I stopped telling the kids when she was coming. I couldn't lie for her again, and I couldn't bear for them to think that they were the reason she wasn't coming. So instead, we just made frequent trips to the playground. Sometimes she'd show and sometimes she wouldn't.

My weekly status call with Marsha falls during work. It also happens to be when Sadie is in the store.

She's sitting at the desk in the front counter area. It's a busier-than-usual day. Everyone is gearing up for summer, and our hat orders are through the roof. Another employee, Martin, is busy sizing and helping customers with hats.

I walk up to her, phone in hand. "Sadie, I have an important call I have to take. Abigail is fine, but I wanted you to know."

Sadie scans the store and then nods at me. Her concerned eyes tell me she doesn't agree with the choice, even if she chooses not to argue at the moment.

I make my way to the break room in the back of the store before dialing Marsha.

"Hello Ms. Leah," she says cheekily as a greeting.

"Hi, Marsha. How are you?" I settle in a chair facing the doorway.

"I'm doing well. How are you and the kids?"

"We're good. Roman's hand is mostly healed. The coloring on his palm isn't the same, but at the follow-up appointment the doctor said that's normal, and it could take a while to work itself out." Roman babied the hand for a bit after he was able to remove the bandage, but I didn't acknowledge it much. He grew more confident as his pain decreased.

"I'm so glad. Are the play therapy sessions helping?"

"Yes. I think they've been good for them. Roman has a lot of questions about emotions and things, and I think it's helping him to process. Encouraging him to talk to trusted adults," I explain. Nick shared his conversation with Roman to me. It hurt me to know his worries, but I'm glad he has healthy people to communicate with.

"That's wonderful," Marsha replies. "And how are the visits? It doesn't sound like Lily has been attending all of them, based on our last call."

279

I sigh. "That's still the case, unfortunately. She's attended two more of six since we spoke last."

"That's really no good, Leah." I don't take her comment as being directed at me. "Does she have anything to say about it?"

"I haven't pushed much. We only speak when the kids are around, and I do my best not to upset them when she's there." I push an errant hair away from my face. "My mom is really pushing me to get the kids home. She's called twice asking me to do what I can. I told her it's not up to me."

"It sounds like a very tense situation." There's clicking on Marsha's side, and I wonder if she's typing on a computer. "Let's stick to the same schedule for visits in terms of frequency and duration. Offer Lily other days or times if you can. We want to show we've worked with her as much as possible in trying to have her see the kids."

"Is this the only thing she's behind on?" I ask.

"No," Marsha says, annoyed. "She hasn't signed up for the parenting class yet, and it's a two-part series. Plus, she still needs to take the one on appropriate discipline techniques. And that doesn't include anger management."

I tap my fingers absently on the table. "We're a third of the way through this. Is she going to have time to finish?"

"If she doesn't sign up soon, she won't. If she can prove that it's due to a scheduling conflict with work, the judge *will* grant her more time. But she has to show a concerted effort to participate in the plan. So far, she has two strikes in that department."

Adrenaline threatens to surge through my veins, as if I'm subconsciously anticipating the worst.

Sadie steps into the doorway.

A part of me wants to hide the conversation, but she's aware Roman and Savannah are staying with me, just not the extent. It's probably time for that to come out.

"Keep me updated on everything," Marsha continues. "Let's chat again next week."

"Will do. Thanks, Marsha."

"Bye Leah."

I end the call.

"Are you ready to tell me what's going on?" Sadie asks softly. She enters the room and seats herself across from me at the tiny plastic table. "Is this about your niece and nephew?"

I drop my hands into my lap. "It is. My sister has a case pending with Child Protective Services. That's why they're staying with me."

Sadie's eyes widen and her mouth parts. "I'm so sorry, Leah Charlotte."

"I appreciate it," I reply, my voice steady despite how I feel.

"Are the children ok?" For once, I can't determine if her interest is genuine.

"They are. It's a tough situation, but they're handling it well." I don't offer more. Her lack of response to my show made me re-evaluate things, and as I sit here studying her, I realize we're only acquaintances—not friends. That, and I'm no longer afraid of upsetting her or what happens here at work. My family comes first. My well-being comes first.

"Let me know if there's anything you need." Her hand reaches halfway across the table, but with mine in my lap there's nothing for her to grab. She gives me a sad smile, leaving her hand out, all but asking for a connection. One I won't give her.

CHAPTER 38

NICK

Maci and Sutton haven't kept to all of the wedding traditions, but one they did agree on is not seeing each other prior to the ceremony. For that reason, and maybe for Andi's benefit, the rest of the groomsmen, Sutton, and I have breakfast in The Big House with Sutton's family, including Sammi and crew.

It's about as warm an atmosphere as there ever was. Surprisingly, Andi is happy and teary but not full-out crying. At least, not yet. Michael, Sutton's dad, wears a huge smile. Bigger than I've ever seen throughout our entire friendship.

After breakfast, we head out for a short horseback ride together. Over the past few months, we've had a chance to see the area that's been added to Strickland Ranch. And because of my job, I've had the opportunity to check wildlife on the property and keep an eye on things from a different perspective. But the ride is just us guys having some time with Sutton before he's married.

Back at the ranch manager's house, we shower and ready for the event.

"Nervous?" Casey asks Sutton playfully.

"Not a bit," he says. And I believe him.

"Not even a little?" Casey presses.

Sutton turns to him from a mirror in the hallway. "Not even a little. Maci and I already had a close call. I already imagined my life without her. This—building a life with her—is completely right."

"And she feels the same?" Casey doesn't mean anything bad by the question, but Shane shakes his head.

"You need to learn when to stop." Shane's deep voice could shut any comment down.

Sutton smiles at them. "I don't intend to ever give Maci a reason to want to leave. To doubt me." He straightens his jacket. "Everyone ready to head up to The Big House? The in-laws should be arriving soon." He grins at me.

I don't know how I'd handle having the President of a motorcycle club as a father-in-law, but Sutton and James seem to have an understanding. Although, we've never discussed if there are any concerns on the law enforcement side—and if there was something big, I know Shane would say something. I have an inkling that something is going on beneath the surface.

"I'll catch up with you guys," I say, as we all head for the door. "I'm going to check on the ladies before we're on the other side of the ranch."

Casey grins. "I wanna check on the ladies."

Shane rolls his eyes.

"Thanks, man," Sutton says, and the three of them head for his truck, leaving me to climb into mine.

I don't bother knocking at The Lodge. I have no idea which rooms they're in or if they'd hear it anyway.

"Hey! Anyone home?" I call into the high ceiling, hoping my words will carry to wherever they are. The last thing I need is to accidentally see my best friend's fiancée in her lingerie before their wedding.

"Oh, you naughty boy scout." Leah's low voice travels down from above, and I spot her looking over the cedar post banister. "Like a fox in the hen house."

I chuckle. "Not even. I just wanted to check on y'all before I head over to The Big House. Anyone need anything?"

A sly smile spreads over her delicious mouth. "Sure. I could use a hand. First door on the left." She turns and moves away from the railing.

At the top of the stairs, I spot Leah leaned against her closed door in a short black robe. I'd like to spread her open, but I promise to do my best to keep my head together and my dick put away. "Where are the kids?"

"Napping with Vivi in Sammi's room." She presses the door open with her back, and I follow, shutting it behind me. "I'm just getting into my dress."

"How's Maci?" I ask. It's easy to keep things casual when I focus on something genuine. I make my way to the large French door and look out at the ranch.

"She's calm, actually," she says, her voice muffled by fabric. "Izzy's still with her in Liv's room."

"So is Sutton. Calm, I mean." I laugh at the addition.

"They're made for each other." Her tone is matter of fact, like there isn't an argument in the world that would have them without each other. I have to agree.

She rounds to my front, slipping between me and the windows. "A little help?" she asks seductively, offering me her back and loosely holding the dress together where it needs to be zipped.

Fuck my life.

I mean to make it quick, but the teeth of the zipper tease us both as they connect piece by piece. She arches and shifts her shoulders like a chill just raced through her.

"I want this to go the other way," I murmur. The zipper reaches the top and I lightly drag my fingers down her sides.

She turns quickly, grinning. "Thanks."

"I'm not done." I slide a hand into her hair and drop my mouth to hers, kissing her just softly enough to tease us both. "I don't think I can keep my hands off of you all day."

She drags her bottom lip through her teeth and presses against my chest with her hand. "I used to think I was a bad influence, but I'm realizing it's you I have to watch out for."

I know when it comes to weddings, everyone focuses on the bride. A little on the groom, but always the bride. But I don't. I can't take my eyes off one of the Maids of Honor.

Leah moves around, mingling with everyone, and she's as effervescent as ever. She cracks jokes and offers hugs as if she's known people her whole life. Aside from Maci's mother, Stephanie, who looks at everyone with a large helping of disdain. As I stand observing from the sidelines, I realize that I was completely wrong about her not having anyone looking out for her. She's right smack dab in the middle of her village, and she may not even realize it.

Andi looks at her affectionately, James eyes her with amusement, even Sutton keeps tabs. She hardly moves without one of the other bridesmaids by her side—to her benefit or theirs, I'm not sure, but they're always there.

We stand before The Big House, greeting people coming in. Parking is easier up here, even if the ceremony isn't that large. And Michael ferries everyone over to the ceremony location in a decked-out trailer full of hay bales. It's all very Texas.

"How are you keeping Sutton from seeing Maci?" I ask when I get a moment alone with Leah.

"She's at The Lodge," she says, as if I've forgotten.

"Yes," I say, smirking, "but how's she getting to the ceremony site unseen?"

Leah offers me a pleased smile. "In this." She walks to the corner of the house and jerks her chin around the side.

I follow her and find that the ATV has been covered in what looks like panels to a deer blind. A space has been left open for the driver to see, but otherwise it's a camo utility vehicle. "Whose idea was that?"

"Mine." She places her hands on her hips.

"Why a deer blind?" I scrunch my eyebrows.

Her smile widens. "For fun." I sense there's something she's not telling me, but I'm not sure I want to know the details. "What time is it?" She looks at my watch.

"Twenty minutes to showtime."

She reaches for my opposite hand with her own, but instead of holding it, she lifts the cuff of my jacket and peeks underneath.

"Still there," I tell her, referencing the paracord bracelet.

Her eyes bounce between mine and she leans up on her toes. I drop my head, fully willing to kiss her here in front of everyone.

"Leah! We have to get the bride!" Izzy yells and scurries down the front steps of The Big House.

Leah jumps. "Coming!" she calls back, annoyed; I agree with the sentiment. She turns back to me briefly. "Wait for me at the entrance," she orders, as if I have an option but to wait on the two of them to return with Maci.

The ceremony goes off without issue. The kids all walk as instructed, the small crowd oohs and ahhs over them. Sutton stands the proudest I've ever seen. There isn't a dry eye in the audience—except for Stephanie. She smiles politely, but I get the impression she's putting on a show.

My least favorite part of the night is the toasts. Izzy and Leah cheat and produce a joint toast that everyone laughs and cries over. They talk about the day they met Maci and what a wonderful friend she is. How her passion for photography allows her to capture beautiful moments for other families, and they can't wait to see her and Sutton's new family grow. How even though she's an only child, she'll always have two sisters looking out for her.

Even I get a little choked up over that part.

And then they turn the microphone over to me. It's only half as bad as the auction because I'm not, in fact, being auctioned here.

"Hi everyone. I'm Nick, Sutton's Best Man." I adjust my grip on the microphone for something to do with my hands. "Sutton and I met when we played peewee sports. I've been friends with him longer than my own brother.

"He's always had a bit of a one-track mind. Once he makes a decision about something, he sees it through to the end. It was something I admired about him in sports, in school, and even as we became adults. It translated to him having a crazy work ethic, too.

"After he met Maci"—I smile at her where they sit at a tiny two-person table toward the middle of the room "—I got to see how that translated to a romantic relationship. I used to think that Sutton wouldn't marry anyone because he was married to the ranch." The crowd gives a light laugh at that. I smile and continue, "But he just hadn't found the one he had a one-track mind about yet.

"Maci and Sutton are perfect for each other. Leah and Izzy told you all the ways that's romantically true. All the sweet things. But they're perfect in practical ways, too. Maci challenges Sutton. She challenges him to think bigger than he has before and from a new perspective. She matches his work ethic and his drive to create a legacy. And she values family and integrity the same way he does. They're Bull Creek's own power couple, and I'm so happy to say they're my friends.

"I love you both, and I hope you have an amazing life together," I finish.

Everyone yells "Cheers" and "Hear, hear" and raises their glasses. Leah catches my eyes, lifting a glass of sparkling water.

Glad to slip into the small crowd again, I hand the microphone off to the DJ, who invites Maci and Sutton up for their first dance. Halfway through the song, movement on the opposite side of the tent catches my attention.

Leah slips out an open corner. The main entrance isn't far from me, so I sneak that direction, making my way out and around the tent and finding her on the other side. She stares up into the moonlight.

"Where are you running off to?" I ask.

"Just needed some air," she says, gazing into the sky.

"Things are just getting started," I say softly. "The dance floor is open."

She cocks her head to one side. "No one in there is going to miss me. Toasts are over; the blushing couple is making their rounds. Before long, tipsy people will fill that temporary dance floor and sway the night away." She lifts her hand as if to stop me from interrupting. "And don't worry, I'm not hurt or jealous. I'm so damn happy for Maci and Sutton; everything I said in there was true. They are going to have a beautiful life . . ."

Her voice trails off, and I don't prompt her to continue, even though I want her to. The partially hidden stars continue to draw her eyes up. "Sometimes, it's just too much," she finally says.

"What's that?" I stuff my hands into my pant pockets.

She scrunches her face like she has a bad taste in her mouth. "Being around happy people all of the time."

"You're not happy?"

Leah's eyes fall back to me. "I always considered myself happy. But maybe a false sense of happy. There was so much I was ashamed of growing up, and then when I moved out, I convinced myself that I would create my happiness."

"And what happened?"

"Nothing." She shrugs. "Don't get me wrong, I have happy moments. I love my friends, my niece and nephew, and for a while my job. I was proud of the stability I created for myself, and I was determined not to fall into the behaviors of my sister and mom. So I kept everything in my romantic life casual."

There's no room left in my pockets, but I shove my hands farther. Wanting to wrap her in my arms is a compulsion. It's not that I think she'll push me away; I just want her to be able to feel whatever she needs to without me interfering.

Her face softens. "I thought my own business would make me happy. And it has, in its own way. It's just overshadowed by the other stuff right now."

"So what comes after?" I move closer, wanting to keep her talking, keep her gorgeous hazel eyes on me.

"After Roman and Savannah? I have no idea. This could end up extended over a year. And so far, Lily isn't fully participating." She exhales heavily.

"What do you want?" I finally give in to temptation, sliding my hands from my pockets and allowing them to reach for her hips. She takes a step closer, and with more affection than usual, she traces the lapel of my jacket.

It's a simple gesture. Not seductive or teasing—just a connection. And it does things to my insides that I couldn't have predicted. It's a reassurance I didn't know I needed. That in some way, her own way, she wants to remain close to me. She wants more with me.

"Just stability. I think this situation with the kids and my sister has made fears from my childhood resurface. But this time I'm viewing it through a different lens. And from a different place of power." She stands straighter. "I'm trying to give them routine and consistency with me."

"I think you've done exactly that," I confirm.

Her eyes are glossy when she looks up again. "Thank you for all you've done. And don't say anything about it being for a friend. Because if you equate what we've been through to friends, I might puke."

I grin. "That's fair." I bring a hand up to her cheek, tracing my thumb over her mouth. A mouth I've been dying to taste all day. "I see you as more than a friend." Torturing us both, I drop my lips to her ear. "Especially when I get to taste your sweet cunt."

I hardly finish the sentence before Leah turns her head to kiss me hard, throwing her arms around my neck and shoving her tongue into my mouth. The kiss is passionate but relatively brief.

"I'm sorry we haven't had more time alone," she says when she's broken the kiss. "I know having the kids around puts a damper on sex."

"You don't need to apologize. I wasn't saying it to make you feel guilty. I can miss tasting you and also understand the situation. I'm not going anywhere."

She kisses me again, softer this time. And I can't tell if she believes me or not.

CHAPTER 39

LEAH

I am not ok.

Things with the kids are good. We're doing our best and working through all these big changes.

Things with Nick are great. He's supportive and amazing with Roman and Savannah. He completely respects our time, communicates well, and doesn't push for anything physical when they're around.

Or ever.

And that's what tells me this whole thing is moving too fast. What guy wants to jump into bed with someone, randomly add two kids to the mix, and lose all physical connection he once had?

Maybe he's fine with it now, but before long that will change. He'll resent the kids. He'll resent my boundaries.

He doesn't need the dumpster fire that my life is. That's on me. It's a choice I made.

What's shitty is that I miss him. He's out of town again this week, two counties over, and even though we talk most nights and text throughout the day, I just miss him.

Which is how I end up staring at his good morning message, contemplating this entire situation.

Nick:

Good morning, Wild Thing. I had a dream about you last night. We fell asleep under the stars. One night I'm going to show you what that's like. Have a good day.

"Is Nick coming over?" Roman asks, walking into the kitchen.

I stare at him. It's the first time he's asked to see Nick. "No. He's out of town."

"Oh."

My heart lurches at the idea of Savannah and Roman hurting when this all goes sideways. Savannah trails in, carrying Smokey around the belly. "Oh, come here, sweet boy," I coo, saving him from her tiny arms. He's patient, but I never like to put him in a position where he'd get annoyed. It wouldn't be fair to anyone if the kids got hurt for accidentally being too rough.

"Do you want to see Nick?" I inquire.

Roman shrugs while Savannah bobs her head up and down. She says, "Yyyes," drawing out the y.

"He's nice," Roman adds.

"He is," I agree. I set Smokey on the dryer to be safe and turn back to the kids.

"You like him, don't you?" Roman asks, as if he's worried I'll say no.

"Of course I do. He's a very good friend."

Roman's mouth pulls into a deep purse. "Is he family? Like Maci and Izzy?"

I crouch down. "Maci and Izzy are forever, huh? I've known them a *really* long time. I haven't known Nick as long." I don't like skirting the answer, but I hope it's enough for Roman to pause. He and Savannah deserve more than a revolving door of people, and I don't want him to get the wrong impression.

"Who wants sno-cones?" I ask to change the subject. "The place by the river just opened this weekend!"

"Oh, yes, me!" Roman bounces on his feet and Savannah follows suit, though it's evident she doesn't know why.

"Go get your shoes and we'll head out." When they run off, I text Nick back.

Me:

> Sleeping under the stars sounds wonderful. And maybe itchy and hot.

> >grinning emoji<

> Be safe.

We're on our way to the sno-cone stand when my phone rings. I answer on the dash. "Hey, Nick."

"Hi Nick!" Roman yells from the back as Savannah calls, "Nick!"

"Well, hello," he says, surprised. "I got a three-for-one special."

"We're on our way for sno-cones," I explain.

"Fun. You guys enjoy. Quick question. How do you feel about dinner with my parents?"

This is the opposite of boundaries. The opposite of backing off. Runaway train opposite. "Um, well, I think nothing is defined, so . . ."

"Do you want it to be defined?" he presses.

Downhill runaway train with no brakes.

"That's not what I meant, exactly." I almost fumble my words as I try to backpedal, but it's no use.

"It's whatever you want," he says simply.

"I just think parents say something big. Important." Being cryptic is also not working in my favor right now. This really isn't a conversation I want to have with my niece and nephew around.

"We've been through this. You are important," he says earnestly.

And my stupid insides warm because Nick has that ability to break through my walls.

One dinner doesn't tie us together forever. We can still have this conversation later. In person.

"Fine," I acquiesce. "Dinner with your parents."

"Ok. I'll tell Mom to make a reservation at the club."

My heart plummets. "The club?" I've never been to the country club.

"Yeah," he replies, clearly distracted. "I gotta run. I'll call you tonight. Have fun, guys!" He hangs up before I have a chance to say more.

A sour taste fills my mouth.

Chapter 40

Leah

A nna and I are locking up the store for the evening when I hear the sound of quick feet rushing toward us on the concrete sidewalk. I turn to check who thinks it's appropriate to run at two women in a mostly deserted parking lot at dusk.

Payton.

She's the absolute last person that I want to see. And frankly, the only one I have a problem with.

"Oh no! I'm too late," she cries, giving an exaggerated pout.

It's not like she missed our closing by a minute or two. It took us twenty minutes to wrap up and close drawers tonight.

"Oh, sorry. We open again at nine tomorrow morning," I say curtly.

Her returning smile is so sweetly fake I almost get a cavity. "Leah, right?"

I don't bother smiling. "Yeah."

She lays a hand against her chest. "Payton. I organized the charity auction."

"Yep," I say shortly.

Anna shifts on her feet.

"You can go, Anna. I'll only be a minute. Thanks for today; have a great night."

Anna's eyes ping-pong between Payton and me, but she settles on leaving. "Have a good night, Leah."

Payton and I watch as Anna walks deep into the parking lot.

"I was surprised to see you with Nick." Payton adjusts the designer bag resting on her elbow. "He and I went to high school together."

"I heard." I'm usually better at small talk, but I can't bring myself to engage fully in this conversation. Mainly because I have a bad feeling about where this is going.

She looks into the darkened store absently. "I always thought he'd end up with someone from our class." I don't miss the double entendre.

"Presumably you?" I tilt my head to one side.

Her head snaps my way again. "I wouldn't have been surprised about that. We came from the same circles." At that, her true colors break through, the smile falling and her lip curling slightly. "Old money. Not no-money."

"That's so funny. He's never mentioned your money. Or his." I cross my arms, bored of this conversation.

"He doesn't have to. That doesn't mean he wants to live without it." The condescension is thick in her chuckle. "You think he's serious about an assistant manager at a clothing store?"

"Oh, that's sweet. You've been keeping up with me." I offer her some of her own condescension.

She ignores my comment and continues on her tirade. "Does he know about your drug head mom? Or your stripper sister who can't keep her legs closed?"

Heat floods my face, but it's overrun with the need to defend my sister. She may be on my shit list right now, but no one is calling her out but me. "Don't be jealous that men pay to see her when you couldn't even get Nick's attention by paying for it."

"You're so stupid," she dismisses, rolling her eyes, but she's beginning to fume. "First of all, I couldn't bet on him. Your measly two hundred and fifty dollars is chump change. And secondly, do you think Nick needs your family drama anywhere near him? Sadie Kay told me about the pickle your sister has herself in now. Nick's law enforcement. If you cared about him, you'd stay far away." Her mouth tips smugly.

I step toward her and she backs up, bumping against the windows of the building. "For the record, he sought me out. Maybe he's sick of southern belles with no fucking class."

She hikes an eyebrow. "Nick is playing the long game. He may think he's too young to settle down, but he'll come to me when he's ready. You're an easy lay, not family material." Her face changes abruptly, her mouth opening aghast. "You didn't poke holes in the condoms, did you?"

I swallow to compose myself. "Well, this has been—"

"I know all about the baby your sister gave up as a teenager. My little sister was in her class, and it was big news when she showed back up in town with a newborn. I also know that before she left, she was sleeping around with some married guy who worked at the building supply store." Her lips purse. "Did she try to trap him? I bet that's where you learned—"

I step forward again, so that Payton's back is pressed into the front of the store. "You don't know *anything*. But I'm really concerned with your obsession with my sister. You may want to see a professional. Fair warning, though: keep my family out of your mouth. Maybe if you do, you'll still have all your teeth if Nick ever decides to come knocking. But I wouldn't count on that."

Saving face in a small town isn't new for me, but it doesn't make the cuts sting any less. I turn sharply and head for my car.

Even as I buckle in, Payton's words play on a loop. She's right. What do I have to offer Nick? A truck load of family drama, kids always around, a protective services case, a fear of commitment. None of those are Nick's problems, and I don't want to burden him with them.

After double checking the car doors are locked, I pull my phone from my purse and open the text message.

Me:

> **Feeling sick. Can't make it after all. Sorry.**

Immediately, bubbles appear on the screen.

Nick:

> **What's wrong? Do you want me to bring something over?**

Me:

> **Don't worry about it. I'll call you when I'm feeling better.**

CHAPTER 41

LEAH

R oman and Savannah are at Strickland Ranch having a sleepover with Vivi, thanks to Sammi, so they don't witness me losing my shit as I get home.

I'm in the kitchen, trying to force down a panic attack and ignore the alcohol still in my fridge when Nick knocks on my door.

God, I know his knock already. How stupid is that?

I don't answer. I'm a mess, and he doesn't need to comfort me.

He keeps knocking. I keep gasping.

He starts calling through the door, but I barely make out his words. "Leah, come on. Open the door. What the fuck happened?"

It actually hurts my heart to have him standing outside acting like a boyfriend who did something wrong. It's so far from the truth. Everything he does is right.

My heavy steps must alert him to my approach because he stops knocking. I open the door without wiping my face. "I'm fine, Nick. Just go home."

"Like fuck. What the hell is going on? Why are you crying? I missed something, and I'm not usually this dense. So please, tell me what went wrong." He steps inside, shutting the door behind him with one hand and grabbing one of mine with the other, like he thinks I'll bolt.

300

"I just said fuck it. We're just wasting time." Hot tears pour down my face. Why am I always fucking crying around him?

I've managed to replace the heaving breaths with despondence. He can't reject me if I do it myself.

He tips my chin up with his free hand. "You're not making any sense. Stop for one fucking second. Just be real with me. Please."

"We are at two completely different places in our lives. Two worlds almost. You're looking for someone to settle down with, have kids, and I'm . . . . I'm not. I'm not the settling down type, Nick. I have a shit ton to deal with. My sister is a royal fuck-up, my mom is a mess. I'm trying to start my own business like I have any sense for that. The kids are here for the foreseeable future. And I'm—I'm a walking disaster.

"I don't have money. I never went to the country club, or deb balls. I was hardly able to get to the rodeo to see Izzy compete when we were younger. And now, I'm hanging on by a fucking thread. We are so vastly different. I'm not the right fit."

I continue to stare at the ground as my words hang in the air.

"Goddamn, Wild Thing." He uses his large frame to press me into the wall next to the entry table. "Take a breath."

I do, but it doesn't help.

"Are you done?"

I almost feel small when he asks, but I manage to nod.

"Ok, good. Because I'm about to shed some light on this situation that you think you have all figured out—even though you didn't bother to ask me. At all." He releases my hands and thumbs away the tears under each eye. "I'm crazy about you. Everything about you. The way you take care of your family, your friends, the passion you have for your job and your new business. You have so much courage and it's sexy as fuck. I adore Roman and

Savannah. They've never bothered me. Honestly, I could give two fucks about your bullshit reasons why we don't belong together."

His hand slides along my cheek, drawing my eyes up. "I've never said one word to you about money. So why in the hell are you bringing it up now?"

I press my mouth tight.

"Oh, good. So you already know it's silly." His quip makes me smile.

"I ran into Payton at the store."

He scrunches his eyebrows. "Payton? What does she have to—" He pauses, his eyes moving rapidly as he considers, and his mouth forms a small o. "Money. Of course."

"I'll never be that, Nick."

"Good. I don't want you to be. Ever." His hands come to my hips, which he grips firmly. He leans back slightly to take full stock of my outfit. "What is this?"

"It's a blazer." I tip my head to one side. "I'm sure you've seen one before."

He grips my chin in his hand. "Not what I mean and you know it, Wild Thing. You're not dressed like you."

"These are all my things," I argue. I have on my own little black dress with a cream blazer and leopard-print heels. They happen to be my favorite heels; I just don't get a chance to wear them often.

He stares into my eyes. "Still not my point. You look stiff. You're not stiff."

"I just wanted to impress your parents," I whisper.

"Fuck. Just be you." He kisses my mouth softly. I want to lean forward, for him to press harder, but he maintains his hold on my chin, locking me in place. "I'm not bringing you for an inspection; I'm bringing you because you're important to me. And I want them to know who I'm spending my time with."

"Why would you—"

"Stop," he whispers. And it doesn't matter that it's soft; it's a command. "You've got yourself so worked up. Stop fucking thinking."

He releases my chin and begins unbuttoning his shirt. "First, we're going to settle you back down." He nuzzles into my neck, his breath hot against my skin as he nips at my ear. "And then, you're going to dress as you and we're going to have a nice dinner. Where I'm going to show you off, because you're fucking amazing and you deserve to be shown off." He slides the shirt off his shoulders and lays it neatly behind him on the back of the couch.

"We're going to be late," I whisper, as he reaches for my shoulders and tugs the blazer down my arms.

"Then we'll be late." His tone is low and a chill runs down my spine. He lays the blazer over his shirt. "Ten minutes ago you said you weren't going."

My breathing is shallow as I watch him remove his boots and jeans. I reach for my shoes. "Don't move," he orders, laying the jeans over the couch next to the others, and then continues until he's completely nude.

"I really like the angle these shoes create," he murmurs, running his hands up my thighs and under my dress. He reaches the black lingerie beneath the dress and slides them down, lifting one foot and then the other for me to step out of them.

They have to be soaked.

He looks at the scrap of fabric and then me. "These are staying nearby," he says, setting them on the entry table.

Then he drops to a knee, pushes the hemline up over my ass, and lifts one of my legs over his shoulder. "Now just relax." His eyes don't leave mine as he leans forward, inhaling deeply as he presses his face to my center.

My head thuds against the wall with the first swipe of his tongue. "Holy shit," I whisper. He starts slowly, teasing and tasting me, but he speeds up quickly. Before long, I'm rocking against his face as he groans into my pussy. His fingers dig deeper into my ass cheek, encouraging me to thrust against him.

All at once I come, shuddering repeatedly as I flood his mouth. He moans as he continues to eat me out.

My dress has bunched up to my hips, and he hikes it even farther as he stands.

"Now, are you ready for me to show you exactly how well we fit? Because we are a *perfect* fit." His eyes gleam as he looks down at me.

I nod.

"Good. I'm going to help you out of this dress, that I never want to see again, by the way, and then I'm going to fuck you with just these heels on. Got it?"

I absolutely love when Nick tells me what to do. There is something so comforting about trusting someone enough to control your body and pleasure. His confidence is sexy as fuck, and it makes me lean into the experience every single time.

"Yes," I whisper.

He grips my hips and spins me around to face the wall. The zipper loosens bit by bit, the dress releasing its angry hold on me.

"How did you—" I begin.

"You're thinking again," he interrupts. He slides the dress down my body, letting it pool to the floor, before I step out of it and he kicks it away. "Turn around."

I turn and press my back against the wall. Nick leans down enough to glide his hands up the backs of my thighs. His lips are soft as he presses them against mine. "I missed you." He kisses again. "I hate that you're upset, but I love that I get this time alone with you instead of sharing you right away."

Something like a whimper escapes my throat, and he swallows it as the kiss turns hungrier. He breaks long enough to say, "Hold on," and lifts me off the ground.

I throw my arms around his neck, hooking a leg around his waist as he adjusts to slide inside me. My chin falls to the side. "Nick," I breathe.

He kisses my chest. "Yeah, baby."

"I missed you, too."

He cups my cheek and turns my face to him. "Then I'll make it worth the wait." With one hand on my ass and the other still on my cheek, he fucks me hard into the wall.

At some point, I manage to do what he asked in the beginning and just relax, just feel. Nothing exists outside this room, this moment. My moans turn from pleasured to something more animalistic, and I lean forward and kiss him deeply to cover them.

I've never come from penetration alone. Always needed something extra to help me get there. But Nick has quickly learned exactly what I need. And yet somehow, I know I'm going to climax from just him thrusting into me this way.

There's an emotional component that I try not to consider. That he continues to be there for me even when I try to push him away. Even when I'm spiraling.

I shut it out, just giving in to the feeling.

"I'm so close," I whisper. More to myself than him, because I can't believe I'm on the edge right now.

His hand slides down to my throat, and he pushes me away from him, into the wall. He stares into my eyes as he fucks me. "Give it to me," he says.

It's right there. Right fucking there.

My jaw drops. It's not as bad as the night he edged me, but I want it bad and it's eluding me.

His grip on my neck tightens. "Come for me, Wild Thing."

And there it is, the little extra. My pussy spasms around his cock as I dig my nails into his neck. His grip loosens on mine, but I think I'm holding my breath, so it doesn't matter.

"You feel so good," he says as his forehead meets mine, his eyes closed. His thrusting increases in intensity. "So fucking good."

"Come for me, Boy Scout," I whisper, my orgasm subsiding. His eyes pop open, meeting mine, and I tighten a fist in his hair. "Be a good boy and give it to me." I let a teasing smile play across my lips.

Nick grins before covering my mouth in a heated kiss, his tongue brushing mine before his teeth clamp on my lip as he climaxes. His body tenses and his fingers dig into me, a moan working its way up his throat. "Fuck," he almost whines, and I think I'm going to come again. Holy shit.

He sets me back on the floor, but he whips me around again to face the wall and drops to a knee. "Spread your legs," he orders and jerks my hips from the walls, diving into my sopping core. His hands grip my ass, spreading me open.

"Jesus, fuck," I cry, and my head bumps against my hands supporting me on the wall.

"Just me," he murmurs and then licks me from front to back, his tongue toying with my asshole.

I shove into him, crying out again.

"You like that, Wild Thing?"

"Surprisingly, yes," I breathe to the wall.

One hand leaves my cheeks, and he slides two fingers inside me. My pussy squeezes them in appreciation. He begins thrusting slowly, gauging my response after the ride he gave me on the wall. As soon as his tongue teases my ass again, I clamp down hard and shove against him.

"Fuck that's hot," he grunts. He nips my other cheek. His fingers continue pistoning in and out of me as he says, "I could come just from watching you. Just from your pleasure."

"No," I breathe.

"Fuck yes." He bites harder and I jolt against his hand. "Fucking you is the greatest pleasure. Why do you think I never want to stop?" His thrusting intensifies along with my moans and he begins eating out my ass even faster.

I squeeze my eyes shut, fucking his hand and mouth, and careening into space. There's no warning or sign; I just fucking come. A long, continuous moan accompanies the orgasm.

The top half of my body leans against the wall for support, and I work to right my breath. Nick kisses up my back to my shoulder with a hot mouth. "I can't get enough of you," he whispers.

"The feeling is mutual," I breathe.

CHAPTER 42

LEAH

While I work on my hair, Nick steps out and calls his parents to let them know we're running late. I can't imagine what the other side of the conversation sounds like, because it takes more than a few minutes.

The thought threatens to raise my blood pressure all over again. Instead, I focus on my outfit. I feel like a million bucks after the way Nick handled me, and I go a completely different route with round two. White pants, a blush bralette and matching strappy blouse. But I do put the leopard-print heels back on, and I add a matching jersey kimono, plus layers of my necklaces and a pair of white feather earrings.

Nick enters my bedroom. "Fuck. Are you trying to have me start all over again?"

"Don't even think about it." I fluff my hair from underneath. "My hair is perfect and we're already too late."

He presses against me, having redressed himself. Luckily, he carries a "go bag" in his truck, so he had everything needed after showering. Almost like he'd planned it.

His hands slide under the satin shirt. "I'll cancel the whole fucking thing."

"This was your idea." I lean forward and place a chaste kiss on his mouth. "Now let's go. Show me off."

He grabs my hand in his, leading me toward the front door. At the entry table, he pauses, swiping my panties from earlier. A wicked grin crosses his face as he looks over his shoulder at me and brings the fabric to his nose for a deep sniff. Then he pockets them and says, "Let's eat."

The country club is about twenty minutes outside of Bull Creek. It features a mix of lush grasses and fountains, next to water-conservative Xeriscape. The low-maintenance shrubbery and rock designs give me inspiration for some new jewelry ideas as we pull up to the entrance.

A valet opens my door and I slide out, pulling my gold chain purse with me. My phone chimes from inside, and I check it to find a message from Sammi with a photo of Vivi, Savannah, and Roman feeding the pigs at Strickland Ranch. She was ridiculously excited to host them for a sleepover tonight after I asked for an evening of babysitting.

Nick's warm arm wraps around my waist, and he tucks his mouth against my ear. "Everything ok?"

I smile up at him. "Yeah. Sammi was updating me on the kids."

"They're good, right? Do we need to get them?"

I shift my weight against him. "I'm beginning to think it's you who wants to skip this dinner. They're fine." I pat his chest.

"Not even." He kisses my head. "Come on."

Nick's parents are waiting at a table in the back of a quiet restaurant when the hostess escorts us in. His father stands and shakes his hand.

"Hey, son. Glad you could make it." His tone is friendly, though his face is serious. I can see a bit of future Nick in the worry lines and softness of his chin.

Nick pulls a chair out for me. "Mom, Dad, this is Leah. Leah, these are my parents, Christine and David."

David offers me his hand from the seat next to me, and I shake it. Christine doesn't move. Her eyes home in on my jewelry. "What interesting necklaces," she comments. Despite her words, there's no kindness or admiration in her voice.

"Thank you," I say anyway.

"Leah designs jewelry," Nick says proudly as he sits beside me.

"How nice," his mother says stiffly. "The appetizer should be here any second. We took the liberty of ordering when you said you'd be delayed."

"Thank you," Nick says firmly.

"How's work?" David asks.

Nick exhales quietly. "Work is fine, Dad. I just got back from a week in Kimble."

"What do you do for work?" David turns to me.

"I'm the assistant manager at Sadie's." I sip from the water goblet on the table.

"The Western store?"

"That's the one," I say with a smile.

"Can't say I've ever been in there," David muses.

"You wouldn't wear anything they sell," Christine supplies. She drinks from a glass of red wine.

"So is the goal manager, then?" David continues to press.

Nick clasps his hand over mine on the table.

He's right that I worked myself into a frenzy, and Payton did the opposite of helping. But I can't start this relationship off being someone I'm not. It's not sustainable. So maybe my breakdown prepared me for this. I'm familiar with my parents judging me from when I was younger, and it's a sentiment I can handle, if the alternative is not being me.

"No, I have no desire to be the manager; I do all of that work already. But I'd like to build something of my own." I swallow following my admission.

"An entrepreneur." David rocks his head side to side as if it's an idea he never thought of before.

"That doesn't seem stable," Christine states. It's like she knows my Achilles' heel.

"Leah's growing quickly," Nick argues gently. "She had a show at The Spur recently and people all over town are ordering custom pieces from her. She's busy." He places emphasis on the final statement.

Christine smiles, but it's not pleasant or sweet. It's condescending. "Nicholas, The Spur is hardly a fashion mecca. And Bull Creek is far from New York or Paris."

"I don't need New York or Paris," I say sharply. "I need enough to be comfortable. I don't mind small-town life. I don't have big aspirations. I just want to be able to provide a consistent income for myself, and for my niece and nephew."

"Your niece and nephew?" David prompts.

"Yes. They're staying with me for now."

The waitress appears and sets the appetizer between us. "Can I get you two a drink?" She directs her question at Nick and me.

What I want, what I really want, is the strongest whiskey they have without the soda. I exhale long and slow. "I'll take a Shirley Temple."

Christine's eyes widen.

AMANDA MARQUARDT

"Simple pleasure," I say her way, with a smile on the corner of my mouth.

Nick squeezes my hand twice. "I'm fine with water."

The waitress gets our food orders and slips away.

"How long have your niece and nephew been with you?" David asks, picking up with the interrogation. His eyes slide over to Nick.

"About six weeks now."

"They're super sweet kids," Nick adds. "We went hiking a few weeks back and her nephew, Roman, asked me to take them again."

"I didn't know that." I study his face.

He smirks. "I don't tell you everything I talk about with Roman."

I breathe a laugh.

"How long will that be for?" Christine interrupts.

"I'm not sure yet," I reply, shifting in my chair. "It's a little out of my hands. My sister needs to work on herself right now. But I'm happy to have them as long as necessary."

"Permanently?" she asks in a challenge.

My eyes flit to Nick and then back. "If that's what's needed. I can't imagine them being with strangers."

Her chin lifts, though she says nothing.

The waitress returns with salads, and David shifts the conversation to Nick's brother, Eli. He talks fondly of his son's business dealings, and I don't miss the way Nick works out his neck part way through the discussion.

"He's really going places. Building something." David's pride is nearly as large as the restaurant we sit in.

"All parents should be as proud of their children as you are of both of yours." I smile at David and Christine in turn, but Christine's sharp eyes confirm that the jab isn't lost on her.

"Yes," she agrees, sitting taller, "I think it's every parent's dream for their children to attend college and find successful careers." Her head tilts the slightest bit, and she adds, "I'm not sure what I'd do if they were too focused on a hobby."

"Mom, don't." Nick pins his mom with his intense gaze. They share the same eyes, and it's a little unnerving to see them offer each other the same demanding look.

"I'm not sure—" Christine tries to argue, but Nick interrupts her.

"Do not dismiss what Leah does. She works hard and she's passionate about it. Don't demean her building something new as a hobby."

Her face turns the lightest shade of pink, and her mouth tightens as if she's never been talked to this way. "I'm sorry, Nicholas. You must have misunderstood me," she says too sweetly.

"I didn't and you know it. Drop it."

She stabs a crouton indignantly and shoves it into her mouth.

Though the remainder of dinner is stiffer, we finish the event mostly unscathed. I don't know what to think of Nick standing up for me against his mom. I started it with my own dig, but it felt nice for him to be so adamant about respect for my new business. He believes in me unconditionally—the same way Maci and Izzy do—even when I can't fully commit myself.

The four of us exit together, stopping on the front steps while two valets head for our respective vehicles.

"It was nice meeting you," Christine says, though she makes no move to shake my hand or otherwise engage as the valet opens her door. "We'll see you soon, Nicholas." She settles into the Mercedes and slams the door closed.

"Bye, Mom," he says with a smirk. The second valet pulls in with Nick's truck behind his parents' vehicle, and Nick opens the door for me to climb in.

"Nice to meet you," David says, offering me a hand again.

I shake it politely and maneuver into the truck. Nick closes the door, and I rest my elbow on the arm, accidentally hitting the window switch so that it slides down some before I jump.

"She's very attractive, Nick." David's voice seeps through the gap. "But taking on someone else's kids?" He twists his head to the side like the idea is concerning. "You really need to think about that."

"There's nothing for me to think about," Nick says firmly. "I don't have a single issue with the kids being a package deal. I adore them. Leah is smart, and funny, and driven. There's nothing about her that's too much or too little for me." I should close the window, but instead, I stare ahead with tears in my eyes. "If anyone needs to think about things, it's you two and your disgusting behavior tonight. I won't put her through that shit again."

I turn to look at them, a little shocked at Nick's words. David's eyebrows rise to his hairline.

Nick steps off the curb and rounds the truck. I hurry the window back up as his door shuts.

"Ready?" He gives me one of his boyish smiles, reaching for my hand and lifting it to his lips before I can respond. "I'm sorry about that. It will never happen again."

He pulls the truck around his parents' car and exits the club. I continue to stare at him. I thought he might be angry at me for instigating, but he protected me.

I'm speechless.

Chapter 43

Leah

Sammi has Roman and Banana.

I'm aware.

For a sleepover.

You catch on quickly.

Why?

I second this question.

Oh hey hi. I can answer this. I offered a sleepover.

What she said.

S ammi sends a photo of the kids playing with colorful dough. The countertops look like the ones from The Lodge, so I'm not even sure how Maci knows they're all there.

Sammi:

It's homemade and non-toxic!

Of course it is. I snicker to myself.

Liv:

Awww. Cousins sleepover!

Maci:

Yes. Sweet.

But also, I think you two are in cahoots.

Izzy:

Where are you, Leah?

Me:

What is this, the Spanish Inquisition?

Maci:

You don't get to use that phrase if you can't actually identify what happened.

Me:

That's like saying I can't wear Pink Floyd shirts if I can't name their songs.

Get fucked.

Liv:

>gasp emoji<

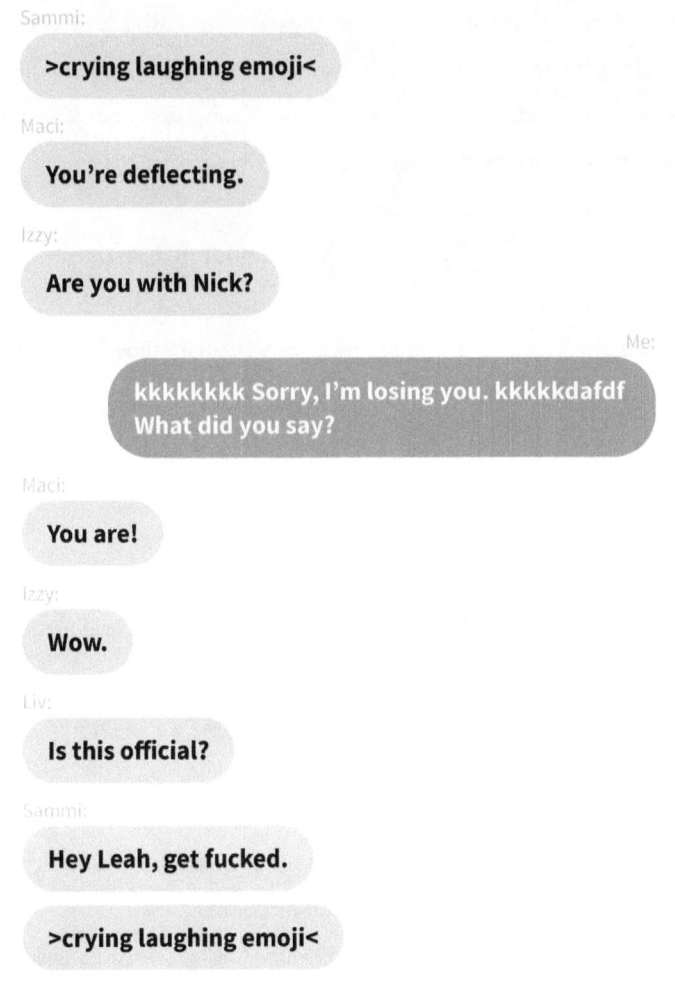

Sammi:

>crying laughing emoji<

Maci:

You're deflecting.

Izzy:

Are you with Nick?

Me:

kkkkkkkk Sorry, I'm losing you. kkkkkdafdf What did you say?

Maci:

You are!

Izzy:

Wow.

Liv:

Is this official?

Sammi:

Hey Leah, get fucked.

>crying laughing emoji<

"What are you doing over there?" Nick's hand rests on my leg as we head toward his house.

"Chatting with the girls." I smile over at him.

"What are they up to?"

"Being nosy," I mutter.

He squeezes my knee. "Something I should know?"

"I think the cat's out of the bag. Maci knows Sammi has the kids."

Nick takes the final turn onto his gravel driveway. It's a long, soft bend toward the house at the back of the property. He's quiet until he pulls to a stop near the house, and then he turns to me. "Leah, I don't care if all of Bull Creek knows. I already made my terms clear. You accepted the deal."

"No take backs, huh?" I laugh.

"Have you changed your mind?" His lips lift in amusement, but his question is sincere.

"I mean . . . no, but I didn't think it was written in stone." As the words leave my mouth, I stare into his deep blue eyes, grasping the magnitude of where we are.

He unbuckles and opens the truck door.

"Wait—" The door shuts firmly, cutting me off.

Nick rounds to my side and opens the door, pressing his forearms to the top of the frame and crowding me in the cab. "Let me ask you a question. If another man called you, would you entertain him?"

It's on the tip of my tongue to tease him. Breaking tension with humor comes as second nature to me. But I respect him, and I want him to know I take him seriously.

Before I can answer, he starts talking again. "Because earlier tonight you were ready to write me off over some bullshit reasons."

"That's not true." I tilt my head up to him. "Yeah, I was freaking out. I've never done anything serious before and I have so much going on right now. Men have dropped my mom and sister over far less. *Big* things are happening, Nick. You can't deny that plenty of people would freak the fuck out over them."

"You're right," he says, validating my point.

"But that doesn't mean I want someone else. Man or woman. It means that I don't want you to hurt me." My voice cracks at my admission. And like all the other times, once it's out I can't stop it. "I really like you. As more than a friend. But the tiny part of me that wants this to actually be something? I keep telling her to stop wanting more. Because if we keep going and you decide you don't want all of my baggage, I'm going to be devastated."

Nick's arms drop and he reaches for my face, but I stop him with a hand, wiping away my own tears as I continue. "You may not even realize how important you are to me. But over the past few months you've become someone I can lean on when I'm falling apart. And quite frankly, it feels like I'm doing that a lot lately." I pause as my words get caught and wipe again at the free-flowing tears.

"Sure, I have my friends, but you're different. You're . . . you." I smile through the tears. "You're my steady boy scout."

Nick leans across me, unbuckling my seat belt and lifting me out of the truck. My arms find their way easily around his neck, as if it's a natural resting place for them. His kisses are tender and insistent as he covers my face, before meeting my eyes again. "I've already told you where I stand on all of this. What I said in your kitchen wasn't just about your body. But apparently, I'm not getting through. So can you please tell me what I need to do to make you see that I want every"—he punctuates each word with a kiss—"single, beautiful, wild, battered piece of you?"

I capture his lips and kiss him firmly. It doesn't matter that I've opened up more over the last few months than ever before—I'm still better with physical communication. After everything I've said tonight, I think I can only show him how I feel.

"Prove it," I tell him, using his words.

Nick's eyes roam my face for a moment before his own turn molten. He slams the truck door closed with a hip and carries me into the house.

CHAPTER 44

LEAH

When I was here before, the only rooms I saw were the main rooms. And since Nick's kissing me furiously as we move through the house, I don't get a chance to see much more. We ascend the stairs, and he turns sharply back toward the front. He enters a room with an open door and sets me on the floor.

I hardly get a chance to observe the cozy, antique feel of the decor and the gorgeous original wood floors before Nick starts pushing my kimono off my shoulders and lifting the tiny satin blouse off me.

There's an undeniable hunger between us, a need to touch, feel, and connect, but our movements aren't frenzied. They're determined, insistent, and charged. His hands barely brush my skin as he undoes my pants, but the minimal contact is enough to have me drenched and needy.

Instead of ripping off his shirt, I unbutton it one button at a time, not bothering to watch my hands. Nick is good at talking, but he's also stellar at what he says without words. And if I had paid closer attention to his eyes before tonight, thought more about the subtle ways his attention lingers on me, I would've admitted to myself well before now that he wants me as more than just a warm body.

I think he might love me. And falling for him may have been gradual, but I have. So deeply and indisputably. In all the little moments he's been present, quiet, and steady. In all the simplicity of his affection for Roman and Savannah. Every time he's taken the time to learn something about my wants or desires, physical or otherwise. The way he's shared his own dreams with me.

As I think back to that first time he was on my couch, and how that quiet voice thought he might be easy to love, I realize I couldn't have been more right. He's everything I never knew I needed and then some. I just hope to be even half of that for him.

My hands graze his shoulders as I push his shirt down. I let my fingertips ghost against his skin on my way to start on his pants, when he stops me.

"Get on the bed," he demands, and my pussy pulses. My pants are already pooled on the floor—my arousal is next.

Instead of prowling across the bed in a seductive manner, I sit heavily, directly before him on the edge of the bed. It looks reminiscent of a bed in a cabin, with a gently rounded headboard made of thin, glazed logs and a short footboard made of the same, but they don't quite reach the top of the mattress.

His jaw remains tight and he stares down at me as he approaches, stopping just shy of touching distance.

Pressing back on my hands, I maintain eye contact, pressing the soles of my feet onto the bed and spreading my legs wide. Only a tiny lace thong prevents his full view of me.

"You like what you see?" I ask as chills race over my skin.

"Lay back." His words are quieter this time, less gruff.

The soft mattress diminishes my fall as I release my arms and plop back. In return, Nick unbuckles his belt and whips it loose in a single, swift motion. I nearly have a spontaneous orgasm; I've never seen something so fucking hot in all my life.

He crawls onto the bed to straddle me, caging me in with his jeans still on. The belt is pressed into the mattress in one hand. My breathing shallows and his eyes dart over my face before landing on my eyes.

"I'll never do anything to hurt you." His declaration seems misplaced. Ordering me to lay on the bed is hardly rough. "But I want you to come up with a safe word."

I blink, then laugh. "Nick, this is far from a sex dungeon. What are you talking about?"

"I'm not asking." Despite the fervor of his words, there's no malice. "Call it practice if you want. Choose something you wouldn't otherwise say."

My eyes ache to roam his face, but they're adhered to his like it's his will.

I scramble to think of something. It's a paradox really. How do you think of a word you'd never say? And then it hits me. "Safe word."

His mouth twitches the tiniest amount. "Safe word? That's what you're going with?"

I nod proudly.

"That's your only way out now."

Before I can respond, the hand holding the belt swipes my wrist upward, toward the head of the bed. I jerk my face in the same direction as he grabs the opposite wrist in his free hand and brings them together. My nipples tighten beneath the lacey bralette, and my core throbs with need.

He makes quick work of binding my wrists to his headboard before placing his hands on either side of my head. His mouth drops to mine and he kisses me softly. "I'll be back," he says, staring into my eyes with a hint of amusement, then leaves the room in just his jeans.

I tug against the belt to test the feel. The leather is firm and warm around my wrists. How long does he plan to leave me this way?

There's a rattle and a thump from downstairs and I close my eyes, listening carefully. What is he doing?

Footsteps approach on the stairs and my eyes pop open, focusing on the doorway. Nick enters with a bowl and a smirk.

"Did you bring me a snack?" I quip.

"Not quite," he says with a grin. He sets the ceramic bowl on the bedside table. It's full of ice.

I plant an amused smile on my face while my stomach clenches.

"I know your stance on sweat," he says, removing a single square and closing it in his hand. Anticipation builds as he doesn't open it again. "So I thought we'd play with cold instead."

My eyes shift from his fist to his face. I swallow, still smiling stiffly. "Ok."

He hovers his closed hand over my breast, still barely covered by my blush bralette. Nick opens the bottom two fingers of his fist and ice-cold water drips onto my chest.

I inhale, arching in reaction. He makes a circular motion over me, dribbling the water farther along my body. It's not enough to soak, but it's jarring.

"Cold, Wild Thing?" he asks in a low voice.

I raise my eyes to him, not giving a response through my smirk. Not that he's looking for one.

He pushes the bowl to the edge of the table, closer to the bed, and pops what remains of the cube into his mouth as he climbs between my legs. Resting on bent knees, he spreads my legs open, hooking them around his lap.

"You're not taking your pants off?" I ask curiously.

"Not yet," he says around the ice cube, then leans forward, maintaining eye contact as he moves to a covered nipple.

When his tongue slips beneath the flimsy fabric, I tense, letting out a short hiss preceding a moan. He teases the sensitive flesh around my rock-hard nipple with his icy tongue, never quite reaching where I want. A cold trail follows behind his mouth as he makes his way to the other side.

I twist, forcing myself closer to his mouth, but he pulls back.

"No fair," I whisper in a whine, my eyes squeezing shut. I want more.

One hand reaches beneath me, rubbing along my covered back, searching. After a moment, Nick's eyebrows pull together in confusion.

I giggle. "There's no clasp."

He smiles widely, the boy next door breaking through for a moment, pushing it up my chest to rest against the belt and my wrists. He's face to face with me, playful and hungry, mirroring my own emotions.

My body arches, trying to reach him; I lift my head to access his mouth. To my surprise, he gives in, opening willingly and rolling his tongue against mine. It's cool, but the iciness is wearing off.

He kisses across my cheek to my neck and down, as he reaches out with a hand toward the table. I'm torn between anticipating where I'll feel cold next and enjoying his warming mouth on my body. His eyes light with mirth as he pulls back enough for me to witness him push another piece of ice into his mouth. He rolls it around with a closed grin, and he is completely the boy-next-door image. Soft, and gorgeous, and subtly proud.

But his eyes narrow in a small challenge, warning me of his plan. He drops his mouth toward my chest again and draws the ice caught between his teeth around and around my nipple. I jerk at the cold, my hips bucking upward in his lap.

He returns pressure with his hips to my core and sucks the ice back into his mouth.

"You like torturing me," I whisper.

"You've already told me you like it," he says around the ice.

"I don't think that's what I said." I turn my head away playfully, closing my eyes before peeking at him from one.

He grins again and takes the ice to my other breast, repeating the motion. It's melting quickly against my skin, chilly water dripping down my side and onto the comforter.

"Fuck," I whisper as the two sensations increase the building wetness at my center. My rocking hips seek friction.

Who knew ice could be so fucking hot?

Nick sucks the cube back into his mouth, chuckling against my skin. He leaves a cold path up my chest and neck until he's close enough to kiss again.

He rubs his chilled lips on my mouth briefly, keeping me locked in his gaze. Then he pulls his lips back with just the tip of the cube between us. An offering.

I open and stick my tongue out enough to accept, and he slides his own along mine, sharing what's left of the icy chip. It rolls and melts between our tongues.

Once it's gone, Nick bites my bottom lip. It's sharp and just as arousing as everything else.

I rock my hips against him again. "How long are you going to tease me with ice?"

"As long as I want," he says in a low voice. "I haven't used much of the bowl, yet." He indicates what remains with a glance.

"You can't be serious," I argue. "It'll melt before you can use it all."

"Then we'll play with cold water instead," he taunts with a grin.

I only smile and shake my head.

He reaches out for another cube and pops it in his mouth like candy. I expect more of the same torture, but he sits back onto his feet and slides his hands behind my knees, pressing my legs straight into the air. I relish the feel of his palms sliding back down to my ass, where he grabs my thong on both sides, pulling it up and off my legs.

Spreading me wide again, and resting them over his hips, he leans forward and drags the melting ice down my sternum to my belly button.

"Shit, that's cold," I cry, and his quiet laugh vibrates into my stomach as he draws lower. At my belly button, he removes the ice from his mouth and drags it in circles, letting the water pool inside. A tremor rocks through me, and I raise my head again. "You're killing me," I groan.

"If you have something specific to say, say it. Otherwise, enjoy the ride. I told you it's the only way you're getting out." He nips my stomach.

"I said 'prove it,' not tease me to death," I grumble. I pull against the restraints uselessly.

Nick rises up to meet my eye. "I told you if you wanted me you had to give me everything. It's only fair that I do the same. This is what you're in for. Take it or leave it." There's a gleam in his eye. He's calling my bluff.

"Give me all you got." I pull against the belt, using the resistance to lift my torso off the bed and kissing him hard. He grabs the back of my neck and deepens the kiss.

When he releases me, he grabs another ice cube and I fall against the soft bed. This time he keeps the icy assailant between his fingers, drawing down my body in abstract lines and whirls. It's about half melted when he dangles it over my exposed center, droplets of icy water hitting my skin. A large drop falls onto my clit, and I gasp.

Nick rubs his fingers over the ice, encouraging it to melt faster. It drips against my skin in a cold, light rain, my body moving outside of my control. It's just a tiny piece by the time he pushes it into his mouth and drops to my pussy, licking my clit.

My startled thrust encourages him, and I barely get out a surprised cry when it turns into a pleased moan. He goes slowly, torturously, just like everything else. His palms grip my ass, one warm and one chilled, pushing me higher for him to feast on.

I want to rock, but he controls my hips. I want to grab him, grip his hair, something, but my wrists remain bound. I don't know what to do with myself being completely at his whim.

His tongue warms, and the change brings forth a new sensation as he continues to explore and devour me. At some point, I relax into the bed, letting him have his way, releasing control. And like a reward, my building orgasm greets me, swirling up from my core. Everything tightens and I whimper. "Nick," I warn softly.

He doesn't respond, completely focused. His appreciative groans fill the space around us.

My nipples harden again and I come, arching into Nick's mouth and gripping the post of the bedframe I'm attached to.

As my climax subsides, Nick's licking and sucking slows, but he doesn't retreat.

"Hey Boy Scout, you got the badge," I say playfully.

He hums against me, and the stimulation causes me to gasp.

"Nick," I say more insistently, laughing as I swivel my hips, trying to pull away from his mouth.

His grip tightens on my legs. He releases my pussy long enough to say, "I'm not done yet," and dives back in. His tongue softens, but he pauses to say, "Just enjoy the ride, Wild Thing."

I rest into the pillows as he continues, closing my eyes and trying to ignore how sensitive my clit is. His tongue works in wider circles, dipping inside me and teasing around my entrance before working his way back up. He slows again, playing me like a fucking fiddle.

Like a switch, something inside turns on again. My pussy clenches and my hips rise on their own. It's all the cue he needs to pick up the pace.

It's another slow rise until he brings me to the brink of another orgasm. Only this one hits me like lightning, and I come so hard I can't breathe or make a sound. As it subsides, Nick continues moaning and lapping at me.

This time he pulls back, wiping at his glistening mouth. He smiles like the cat that ate the canary before pressing my legs closed and turning them to one side so he can roll off the bed.

He approaches the pillows, the hunger returning to his eyes as he leans down and kisses my mouth. The belt loosens around my wrists and my hands slip free. An ache lingers and Nick's hands skate over my skin, rubbing up and down in a featherlight motion, before returning to the top and massaging gently.

"Too much?" he asks against my mouth.

"There's no such thing," I mumble back, sucking his bottom lip in between my teeth and earning an appreciative groan.

He stands fully and I study his body. "What?" he asks, amused.

"You've never let me suck your cock." It's almost a question. I've never slept with a guy who hasn't made oral a priority.

His mouth tips up on one side. "Do you want to?"

"I do. I'm just curious why it hasn't come up before now."

He swivels his head back and forth. "It's selfish. Well—actually, I guess oral has always felt selfish because it's only about my pleasure. But in reality, I get just as much, if not more, from making you come undone."

My brows pull together. "You don't want me to give you head because you'd rather give me head?"

He laughs. "Sure, you can put it that way. But, to be clear, I've never not wanted you to. It's just not what I want most."

"So, I can?" I narrow my eyes from my place on the bed.

"Yes."

"Good." I roll onto my side, reaching for his pants, and thank god he steps forward willingly, because I still almost feel like I'm coercing him. Making quick work of the button, I slide his pants and boxers down in one motion, his dick rising up to my lips.

I grip his shaft and spit onto the head, working the saliva over the tip before I take him into my mouth. "Jesus." He groans, and his face transforms in a way I've never seen. It's base, less calculated than anything else he's done. I'm immediately turned on again.

Pressing onto my elbows for better reach, I continue to suck and bob, making sure to add to the lubricant as I go. When he hits the back of my throat, he grunts a curse and reaches into my hair, gripping a handful.

Maybe we're both selfish, because I want him to get pleasure from me. And not from doing things to me, but from what I do to him. Moaning around him, I press my head into his hand, encouraging him to take what he wants.

He presses once on my head, testing the limit. His cock hits the back of my throat again, and I give him a happy moan before pulling back to say, "Take what you want," as I stare up at him.

"I already have what I want," he says. But his mouth hangs open after in pure lust, lips puckering the slightest bit.

"Take more." I lick his head, swirling my tongue around and maintaining eye contact as I take him into my mouth again.

The hand in my hair grips tighter, and he shoves me down his shaft. This time I almost gag but recover. He does it again and then something unleashes, and he uses my hair as a guide.

"Shit, Wild Thing," he groans, not stopping his glorious assault on my mouth. "I'm about to come down your fucking throat."

I keep my eyes pinned on his, his pace picking up, and moan my approval. Sliding an arm out from under me, I reach between his legs and grab his scrotum tightly, squeezing around the top of his sack with two fingers and massaging his balls with the rest.

"Oh, fuck," he murmurs, and this time his head falls back. It feels like a win, watching his composure break. It's only a few seconds before he rights himself, looking down on me again. "Are you gonna swallow like a good girl?"

I feel the flirty smile that meets my eyes, and I suck harder. I know he's close.

This time his "Shit!" comes out through gritted teeth, the veins in his neck appearing, and he comes into my throat. He narrows his eyes at me as I watch him hungrily. I swallow as promised and wait until he slides himself from my mouth.

"I think we might have to rock, paper, scissors for giving in the future, because that was fucking hot," I tell him.

I press up onto my knees and Nick leans down to kiss me. "I'll just keep you tied up until you beg like you're supposed to."

CHAPTER 45

NICK

The next morning, Leah's phone ringing wakes us.

"That might be Sammi," she mumbles and rolls out of my arms to find her phone on the floor by her pants. "Hello?" Her voice is groggy and rough; she's barely opened her eyes.

I roll onto my back, fluffing a pillow against the bedframe and tucking an arm beneath my head as I watch her.

"Oh, hi Marsha. We're well. I wasn't expecting to hear from you today." She seems to perk up at the social worker's call.

She's quiet as Marsha continues to speak on the other end of the line. Leah's eyes roam the hardwood floors, her jaw slackening. She sits slowly on the hope chest at the end of the bed.

The fingers of her free hand move to her mouth, tracing her lips in deep thought. "So, what does that mean? Now we . . ." Her voice trails off as Marsha picks up again.

"Can they see them later?" Leah asks, and as Marsha answers, she turns her face to me, sadness creeping into her features. "Will you tell Lily?"

She stands again. "Ok."

I sit up, not knowing what to do with myself because it's obvious she's getting big news, but I don't want to interrupt. She loosely paces the floor at the end of the bed.

"I'm not going to tell the kids. They won't understand and it's not fair to them." She waits for a few seconds and then, "No, we have visitation scheduled tomorrow. I'll let you know if she comes . . . Ok, talk to you soon. Bye."

After ending the call, Leah stares at me unseeing for a long moment. "Their dads terminated their rights."

"Roman and Savannah's?" There's no one else we'd be talking about, but I can't help but confirm.

"Yes. Marsha said they finally made contact with both of them."

"Have they ever met the kids?" I ask, wondering how you can write off a child so easily.

She shakes her head. "Not that I know of, and they seemed to relay as much to social services."

Still naked, she climbs on top of the covers next to me.

"They're not even curious to meet them? I don't understand." My own brain is pouring over what I might do if I was told I had a child somewhere.

"Lily has a tendency to find men looking for mistresses. The daughter she gave up was conceived with a married guy here in town. If Roman and Savannah's fathers were too, I'm not surprised they don't want to be involved."

"You don't know who they are?" I ask. "If Eli ever knocked someone up, I guarantee he'd call me before anyone else. Don't sisters tell each other things like that, too?"

"Sure, normal sisters, I guess." Leah looks at me with a sad smile. "Lily was happy to share her sex life with me, in the sense of adventure. Something new she experienced—a threesome, double penetration. But she didn't share the details of longer-term things. Roman even mentioned that she was visiting a guy named Carl the day he got hurt, and I have no clue who that is."

"Fuck. I'm sorry." I open my arms to her, and she leans against me, wrapping her arms around my chest from the side. Her face is cool against my shoulder. "So now what?"

"Now, we hope that Lily gets her shit together and starts doing what she needs to do. Best case scenario, the judge may give her more time to complete the tasks she was assigned to do. I don't know the likelihood of that." She shakes her head as much as she can leaning against me. "She hasn't been coming to the visits though, and I think that's pretty significant in their eyes. How can we reunify if she won't even come see Roman and Savannah?"

"I have to agree. If it were up to me, that'd be a screaming red flag," I admit.

"Marsha is going to notify Lily about the paternal rights. We have a visitation tomorrow. She only has a couple weeks to turn things around."

We sit quietly together, with me stroking her shoulder as both of us consider what's to come. She leans over after a minute, kissing me on the cheek. "I'm sorry we got woken up. But I do need to go get the kids."

I miss her already as she rolls away, looking for her clothes around the room. She finds her pants first and steps into them.

I follow, moving to the end of the bed. Her lacy thong dangles over the end, and I offer it to her. "How would you feel if I came with you?"

Leah stops moving and looks at me. "To get Roman and Savannah?"

"If that's ok. Unless y'all have something going on today."

"I was going to get the stuff for Roman's party next weekend." Her uncovered breasts tease me as she stands in only her white pants. Leah has insecurities, but not about her body. At least not in any way that I've witnessed. She embraces her body and sexuality wholeheartedly, and it only fuels my desire for her.

She reaches for the extended clothing as I step closer, keeping her eyes on me. "You can come if you want." A smile tugs at one corner of her mouth. "I know the kids would love to see you."

"That settles it then," I say, grinning.

Her heavy exhale almost seems amused. I debate tying her to the bed again before we go. "This should be good," she mutters.

"You said the cat's out of the bag," I retort.

Sucking her bottom lip between her teeth, she nods. I close the distance between us, pulling her to me by her hips. "What could go wrong?"

"It's not them I worry about."

"You don't need to worry about anything." I kiss her softly.

She pecks me again. "Ok. I'm going to head home and clean up before we go over."

"I'll meet you at your place in just a bit. I can leave my truck there for later." I kiss her forehead. "I guess I'll shower, too. Although being covered in your scent isn't the worst thing in the world."

CHAPTER 46

LEAH

Sammi and Justin are staying at The Lodge for now, so Nick and I bypass The Big House when we arrive at Strickland Ranch. It feels secretive to ignore my best friend, and guilt creeps in as we take the caliche road.

I don't have too much time to dwell on it, because as Nick parks next to the house, Maci and Sutton follow Roman and Savannah onto the porch. Sammi hurries after them with Justin and Viviane in tow.

"Here goes nothing," I say sarcastically.

Nick winks at me before opening his door and climbing out.

"Nick!" Roman yells and runs full speed out from the house.

Maci crosses her arms with a hip kicked out. Savannah remains on the porch by her, while Sammi helps Viviane down the stairs.

"What's up, hot stuff?" I say to Maci and scoop Savannah up, asking her, "Did you have fun?"

"No," she says blandly; it's her new favorite word even if she hasn't figured out the right context in which to use it.

"What are y'all doing here?" I ask my friend, throwing a glance over my shoulder to find Nick setting Roman on the ground with the others nearby.

"What's Nick doing here?" Maci's position hasn't changed, and she throws all of her sass at me.

Savannah reaches for my sunglasses, putting them on her own face.

335

"I think this is actually something." My voice comes out quieter than intended.

"Shit!" Maci jolts at her own curse before placing her hands over Savannah's ears and loudly whispering, "He must be really fucking good in bed."

A loud laugh bursts from me, drawing Savannah's attention momentarily. "God, it's so much more than that." It was hard enough to tell Nick what he means to me. It doesn't matter that I told Maci to fuck what everyone else thought about her quick fall-in with Sutton. My relationship with Nick has been building for months, but it seems so counterintuitive to everything I ever thought of for myself.

"Told you he's a good one." Maci leans forward, hugging me and Savannah as one. "I'm happy for you."

"Thanks. It just feels like counting my chickens before the eggs have hatched."

"The eggs have hatched!" she cries. "Count them. Love them, name them, cuddle them. Nick Foster is as good as they come, and you only deserve the best."

I grin at her excitement, her support. I was stupid to think she'd be anything but. "We're just so different."

"You're yin and yang, not oil and water."

Nick approaches with Roman and Sutton. "Hey, Little Bit," he says, tickling Savannah's round face.

"Aunt Leah, can we come back here again?" Roman places himself between Maci and me.

The "aunt" part is growing on me. Lily and my mom never referred to me that way, so the title never stuck. But the more time he spends with Nick and the others who do refer to me that way, the more he's embraced it.

"I take it you had fun." I smile down at him as he nods. "Of course we can come back. This family is practically our family." And it couldn't be more of the truth. This is the family I've chosen—who've chosen me. Who accept all my harsh, rough cuts and prickly comments, alongside my partying ways.

In the week between our reveal to the family and Roman's party, Nick, the kids and I spend almost every evening together. Twice he's been closer to Strickland Ranch than me and picked up Roman and Savannah on his way back into town. Since I've been leaving the car seats at the ranch in case something comes up, it's been that much easier.

Friday evening, after Roman and Savannah are in bed, Nick is stationed with me on my living room floor, prepping goodie bags for the party. Savannah's were all toddler-friendly, but I've gone a little bigger this time since Roman's turning five. It's hard to believe he'll be starting kindergarten in the fall.

For once, Smokey is with us instead of Roman and Savannah, purring loudly from the center of the sectional.

"Is Smokey afraid of dogs?" Nick asks randomly.

I look at him from the corner of my eye, stuffing a pair of sunglasses into the bag I'm holding. "He's never met a dog."

"Never?" he asks skeptically.

"No. My family never had pets, and none of my friends do. It's not like I walk him around on a leash." My voice is thick with sarcasm.

Nick knots the ribbon on the bag he's closing.

"Is that a specialty knot?"

"Specialty?" He sets the completed bag in a pile with the others and shifts his torso to face me.

"Yeah. Don't you have to earn a Knot Tying badge or something? Maybe a specific one? Fisherman's knot or maybe the—Oh! Oh, oh! The Trucker's Hitch!"

A wide, confused smile spreads across his face. "Wild Thing, are you making knots up now?"

I burst into laughter. The kind of laughter you can't recover from, where your face pulls hideously and tears stream and you can't breathe. I tuck my head into my lap to curb the noise. Finally, the fit subsides and I sit up, wiping under my eyes and grinning ear to ear.

Nick has that wondrous look in his eyes again. He reaches a hand out and cups my cheek. "I really need you to do that more."

"Make up knot names?" I tease.

He ignores the joke, leaning forward slowly.

"Are you gonna kiss?" Roman's voice makes us both jump.

"Hey bud, why aren't you sleeping?" I twist around and open my arms to him. "You ok?"

He approaches with a smile and sits in my lap, wrapping his little arms around my neck. "You have a funny laugh," he says, ignoring my question.

"It sounds weird?" I ask playfully.

"No, it makes me laugh, too." He rubs his nose against my jaw.

"Me, too," Nick agrees. His fingers dance along my shoulder while I cuddle Roman.

"Are those for my party?" Roman asks, and his accurate pronunciation makes my heart ache. Like when he was younger and switched "booberry" to "blueberry," one night recently he switched to a proper th sound without prompting.

"Yeah," I whisper. "But can't you just stay four forever?"

"No way!" he shrieks, smiling.

"Pleeeease," I plead, squeezing his frame tighter. "Five is too old."

He pushes away to look me straight in the face. "I'm getting bigger. Like Savannah."

I fake pout. "I know. Can you at least promise to stay my sweet bud?"

He smiles happily. "Promise." And then he lifts a tiny pinky to me. I take it, kissing my fist as he does—it's painfully beautiful.

"You want me to tuck you back in?"

Roman shakes his head. "No." He kisses my cheek and stands. "Night." And just like that, he turns for the bedroom.

When I turn back to Nick, he's still staring at me.

"What?"

"I love you," he says plainly. Like a universal truth.

My mouth falls open.

He continues. "I'm completely and utterly in love with you. Every fucking beautiful, broken, crazy, adorable thing about you. I love every piece." He leans forward and slides a hand into my hair, pulling me to him in a staggering kiss.

It rivals our first. As if in each breath, each movement, he's pouring all the love he's kept quiet.

His thumb rubs the apple of my cheek as he pulls back.

"I love you, too," I whisper, and I climb into his lap so he can kiss me again.

#

After Roman goes back to bed, Nick and I fill the hallway between the two bedrooms with blown-up balloons. The squeals of my niece and nephew wake me in the morning. Nick is already out for his run.

"Who's ready for breakfast cake?" I cry, opening my bedroom door.

"Cake!" Savannah yells at the same time Roman bounces up and down saying, "Mememe!"

We make our way to the kitchen, balloons spilling from the hallway into the entry and living room as we maneuver. I make a big deal of letting them help prepare the pancake batter. We spread it on a sheet pan with their favorite fruits mixed in and honey on top.

While it bakes, they dress and I check my phone for messages from Lily. She still hasn't told me if she's coming to the party today. She did attend visitation the day after Marsha and I spoke, but she missed the one schedule later in the week.

"Is my mom coming to my party?" Roman asks, entering the kitchen again. He seats himself at the table while Smokey winds around the legs of the chairs, stopping to sniff for crumbs occasionally.

"I'm not sure, bud. I don't know if she has to work." I smile to cover what feels like another lie. It's infuriating and disappointing.

He nods. "Can I have some milk?"

"Yep." I pull two cups down and fill them halfway. Savannah is still practicing using a cup and frequently spills more than she gets in her mouth.

"I don't think she likes us," he says solemnly.

I freeze with a cup in each hand and stare at the kitchen window. "Who doesn't like you?"

"Mommy."

Taking a deep breath, I turn and move to the table, setting the cups at their place settings. "That's not true, bud." I sit in the chair next to him.

"Mommy just . . . she's . . . she has big feelings sometimes. And I don't think she remembers to take a big breath. Or remember that it's ok to cry."

"She needs to use her words," Roman says flatly.

"Yeah. She does." The timer beeps and I ruffle Roman's hair as I stand. But something occurs to me, and I squat next to him. "Roman?"

"Yeah?" His head turns sharply at the irregular use of his given name.

"You know I love you, right?"

"Yeah," he says with a giggle as if it's a given, and he twists to wrap his arms around my neck. "I love you, too."

I head for the oven, calling, "Savannah, breakfast."

She hurries in from the bedroom.

I plate the sheet of pancake and set them on the table as a knock sounds on my door. I listen carefully. It's too early for partygoers.

"I'll be right back." I make my way to the door, opening it without checking as usual, and am surprised to find my mom standing on the other side. "Mom."

"It's fucking hot out here," she grumbles and pushes into the entry with me.

"I didn't know you were coming." I take a large step back. She holds a plastic grocery bag and hefts her fat purse over her shoulder.

"I'm not staying. I just came to give Roman his gift from me and Lily." She doesn't make eye contact, scanning my living room, then plops down on the end of the sectional closest to the kitchen entry. "Where is he?"

"Roman, Savannah," I call into the kitchen. "Bunny's here."

My niece and nephew enter from the doorway. Neither jump into her lap or seem eager to see her. "Well come 'ere," she says roughly. "I brought yer present."

Roman approaches with Savannah a half step behind. My mom shoves the bag at him unceremoniously.

He opens the plastic and peers in. When he doesn't reach in, Mom grabs the bag to pull out the contents. Two plastic water guns, which I'm guessing she got from the corner store, given their size and assumed durability.

"What are they?" he asks, taking the guns and flipping them over in his hands.

"Water guns," she tells him gruffly. She pops the orange stopper of one open with a dirty fingernail. "You fill it up there and put the cap back on. Then you and your sister can spray each other."

"Oh. Thanks." He looks at her with a small smile. "I'm gonna go finish breakfast cake." He sets the toys on the couch and leads Savannah back to the kitchen.

"Cake for breakfast?" my mom asks, standing. She adjusts her heavy purse.

"Please, spare me any kind of judgment. They're pancakes, and I'm not in the mood to fight with you."

"You can't keep these kids from their mother, Leah." She lets loose a heavy cough, thanks to her aggressive tone.

To calm myself, I take a slow breath and study the items on my built-in shelves. I wet my lips. "I'm not keeping them from her. She isn't coming to the visits."

"Supervised visits!" my mother hollers. "As if she can't be trusted with her own kids."

I lean forward, my voice coming out in a whispered yell. "She can't! She left them alone and Roman got hurt trying to take care of them. A four-year-old trying to take care of a toddler? Yeah, there's something really fucking wrong there."

She opens her mouth to speak, but I put a hand up. "And let me be crystal fucking clear," I continue in my hushed rage, no longer whispering but not at full volume, "this is the last time you come into my house and raise your voice at me. I'm not a child anymore. I'm doing what's best for Roman and Savannah. And if you don't see that, then see yourself out my fucking door."

"You've lost your goddamn mind, talking to me like that," my mother says angrily, but she walks right out the entry and lets the door slam behind her.

Seconds later, Nick opens the storm door, looking into my driveway. His hair is covered in sweat and his cheeks are red. "What the heck is going on out here?" he asks breathlessly.

"My mom stopped by." I slam the door shut. "Guaranteed that's the last time that happens."

CHAPTER 47

NICK

Just like Savannah's, Roman's party goes off without a hitch. Leah rented a water slide and the small group of kids has a blast going up and down the slide a zillion and a half times.

The rest of us sit nearby in lawn chairs, soaking up the summer sun and enjoying each other's company.

Lily hasn't shown by the time the party is over. Sadly, her kids hardly seem aware of her absence. Leah, on the other hand, scans the street almost as many times as the kids go up and down the inflatable.

When the moment's right, I lean over and whisper in her ear, "Are you checking for your other boyfriend?"

Leah throws her head back and laughs. "I hardly have one. Certainly not two." She composes her face into something more serious, her mouth tight. "I keep checking for Lily; I can't help it. I can't believe she didn't come to her son's birthday party."

"I hate to be inconsiderate here, but she's shown what she's like."

Leah nods sadly. "It doesn't mean I won't keep wishing she'd show up for her kids."

"They had a great day. Roman had a blast. Can you say that they would've had the same experience with her here?" I slip my hand under hers,

344

tangling our fingers together. It's not a move to show off, but I'll be damned if I'm going to avoid a moment of pride over her being mine.

"Fuck," she whispers. "When you put it that way."

"Exactly. Stop worrying about her. You can't make her want to do what's right."

It's not long before everyone begins to dry off and eat. The kids fill themselves with too many chips and too much ice cream cake. But their peals of laughter are what summer days are made of, what joy is made of. The adults soak it up willingly. None of us stop them from indulging in a single thing, as if all of us are in silent agreement that there are far bigger things for their little minds to stress about. It's better they remain uninhibited.

Eventually, everyone leaves and Leah gets the kids into baths. Roman is first out. Once he's dressed, he carries Smokey to the couch and sits down next to me. Smokey purrs at the rubs.

"Cookie for your thoughts," he says to me.

I burst into laughter and he smiles, happy but confused. "Oh man, that's a great trade." I ruffle his clean hair, still damp to the touch. "It's actually a penny for your thoughts."

He frowns. "A cookie is way better."

It's the simplest mindset, and it's beautiful. I don't tarnish it by trying to explain the origin of the phrase. "I was thinking how much I love spending time with you and your sister and your aunt."

Roman's face spreads in a wide smile. He looks down at the cat and rubs the soft fur of his belly. "And Smokey?"

"And Smokey." I give the cat's head a solid rub.

"Do you think my mom loves me?" Roman asks suddenly.

I twist on the couch to face him. "I can't say how other people feel. But I don't know how anyone could not love you. You're an amazing big brother—and I know what it takes, because I'm a big brother. And you're a super helper to your Aunt Leah. Plus, you take great care of Smokey. You're really funny, and smart, and you make great stone towers." I try to keep things on a five-year-old's terms. It's not my place to explain to him that a parent's love should be unconditional, paramount.

Roman looks up and grins. "Can we go hiking again?"

"Yep. But you have to convince Aunt Leah."

I consider my own parents; I haven't spoken to them since our dinner with Leah. It's not that they haven't tried. They've each called a few times. But I was so fucking angry after how they treated her that I haven't trusted myself to have a civil conversation. To see if they realized how fucked up they were.

"We can go to my house, too. I have a dock into the water and a lot of room to run and play." Roman slumps into my side as I finish speaking. I look down at him. His small hand isn't rubbing anymore, though you wouldn't know it from Smokey's constant purring. Angling my head forward, I find Roman's face soft. He's out like a light.

Leah walks in. "Savannah hardly had pajamas on before she passed out—" Her eyes narrow on Roman as she says more quietly, "Ok so maybe the sun kicked their asses today."

"Water and sun are the perfect sleep combo," I agree. "I'll move him."

Smokey protests when I place him on the couch, but his eyes remain shut anyway. Roman transfers easily to bed. Savannah is already snoring away.

It's only when I hear noise from the kitchen that I realize Leah hasn't followed me into the room. I'm stuck in the doorway, staring into the dimly lit room.

If someone had asked me six months ago if I'd be entertaining the idea of marriage, or loving kids who aren't even mine, I'd think they were on drugs. But the people in this house have done a one-eighty on my world.

Leah hums a dance song as I enter the kitchen. Like in the kids' room, I stand in the doorway and watch. She just keeps rolling with the punches and doing a fucking badass job at it.

"You done in here, Wild Thing?"

She turns her face from the sink, water halfway up her arms as she washes the large dishes, her eyes twinkling like I'm crazy. And I am. So fucking crazy about her.

"No, actually I'm not." Her laugh is sarcastic, but she doesn't turn away from me.

I approach anyway, wrapping my arms around her middle and kissing her neck. "Let me rephrase. You're done in here."

"Nick, these dishes won't wash themselves," she half argues, turning her head to give me better access.

"And they won't get up and walk away either," I mumble against her skin, nipping gently.

"What's so pressing?" She rubs her ass against my dick mischievously.

"Actually, it's you I need to be pressing. Into your bed while I make you come repeatedly." She groans quietly, and I slip a hand between her legs. "But you have to be quiet because I just got the kids to sleep, and I don't need you waking them up screaming for me to fuck your pussy harder."

Leah jerks in my arms and splashes soapy water over her shoulder. The droplets splatter my face. I grip the damp cotton between her thighs tighter. "How rude. I'm trying to be nice and look out for your needs."

"Sure, charmer. My needs." She splashes again.

"That's it. You need a spanking." I spin her to face me completely, before throwing her over my shoulder.

Her hands beat against my back as I carry her to the bedroom, but she stays silent. Miraculously, she manages to stay quiet—not silent—for what comes after, too.

CHAPTER 48

LEAH

Izzy:

What's going on with the hearing?

Sammi:

I would also like to know.

Me:

The status hearing is Monday.

Izzy:

Has Lily completed everything?

Me:

No. We haven't seen her for visitation since before Roman's birthday.

Sammi:

So what now?

Me:

The social worker says this judge has been known to extend cases like ours.

> So maybe just another cycle of the same.

It'll all work out.

Unlike the first hearing, I feel far more equipped for this one. Not because I know what the outcome will be, or what to expect, but because I know that I've done what I can to help my sister. More importantly, I've done everything in my power to help Roman and Savannah.

They don't know any of it. And I've made a point to keep it that way. We never acknowledge that Lily's missing, unless Roman brings it up. Savannah has asked for her once but dropped the subject when I said she was at work.

This weekend is Independence Day, and I would love to get together with everyone, let the kids play in the water and have a weekend of fun in the sun. But it's already raining and the forecast calls for more of the same for the foreseeable future. Nick even cancelled his work trip out of town this week, because flooding is likely in the area and he wants to be available. He and some other wardens from local counties started work early this morning to prepare. He hasn't given me all the details of what that entails, but he said to be on alert for any notifications coming in.

Our area is prone to flash flooding. The combination of hard, dry ground from extended droughts, and the rugged, rocky terrain full of valleys and basins means when it volleys down on us, there's no chance for moisture to soak in. Depending on the severity, the creeks and small rivers rise quickly, creating impassable low-water crossings, and sometimes even the bridges are underwater.

I've already gotten several notifications on my phone warning of the potential for flooding. So the kids and I are cuddled on the couch under a blanket, watching a movie, with Smokey curled in between. He's loved all of the extra affection over the last few weeks.

My phone rings on the coffee table and I peek at the caller ID to find it's Marsha.

"I'll be right back." I slip out from under Savannah and grab my phone, answering on my way to the kitchen. "Hi, Marsha."

"Hi, Leah. Do you have a minute?"

The chairs at the dining table are hardly big enough, but I curl myself into one cross-legged. "Sure. Everything ok?"

"Ok is subjective," she says dryly. "I have some news."

"Ok..."

"Lily reached out to me. She's terminating her rights to Roman and Savannah," Marsha says somberly.

My heart stutters. "What?" My mind, heart, and gut war over bodily functions, sending a panicked spasm throughout my nervous system and threatening for me to burst into tears or puke at any second.

"She let me know that she's not interested in completing the courses and doesn't feel like she's able to provide them with what's needed." Marsha lets her words sink in before continuing. "We will still have our hearing Monday. At that time, we'll notify the judge of her request. He'll have the option to deny it, but I don't see that happening."

My face feels tingly. I scrub it with a hand. "What now? Are you taking the kids from me?" My lungs threaten to seize.

"No. Not immediately," she offers. "But you have some decisions to make. Or a decision, I should say. If you want to continue caring for the children, you'll need to complete the program to become a kinship foster. We'll complete another home study, and they can stay with you for the time being. If you don't want to do that, then we'll start looking for a permanent foster family for them."

"No!" I nearly shout, before lowering my voice. "No. I'll do the training."

"Ok. A majority of the front-end steps have been completed. There's a six-week course that you'll attend. The sessions are all online post-Covid."

"Ok," I agree again.

"Don't worry about anything tonight. We just need to get through Monday. We'll work out the rest later this week." Marsha waits for a response. "Leah?"

"Yeah," I croak.

"Everything's gonna be all right, darlin'. Those kids are where they need to be. I'll see you Monday."

"Bye." After hanging up, I set the phone on the dining table and stare out the kitchen window. Noise from the television picks up in the living room, and I take the time while Roman and Savannah are distracted to cry for their loss.

There's no coming back from this. The decision is permanent.

I want to reach out to Lily. To tell her I can help her more, that her children are worth more, but I won't. Because the more tears that fall, the more I'm reminded of all the ways I've tried to help over the years.

My sister might not be equipped to be a mother, but I will never let her kids think she didn't love them. Whatever conclusion they come to later on is one thing, but I won't place blame on her now.

Now, all they'll know is love. Even if it takes spending every moment pouring all the love I have into them, they will never feel forgotten or alone again.

Maci:

> **Sorry, just catching up. We just got the last herd moved up closer to the main part of the ranch.**

Liv:

> **Do y'all need any help?**

Maci:

> **No. Andi and Michael helped. With everyone out there, it wasn't too terrible. But the cattle don't give a shit. They just take their sweet-ass time walking.**

> **It's all going to work out the way it needs to, Leah. And come hell or high water, we're all here.**

Maci's texts come just before dinner. The rain seems to sit directly over us for the entirety of the day before picking up around midnight. The combination of thunder and lightning from the storm, and not hearing from Nick, keeps me in an anxious state overnight. Getting sleep is next to impossible. I check the street and backyard repeatedly for any signs of flooding, before tossing and turning on the couch.

The next morning, I still don't have any messages from Nick. It's the first time I'm forced to face the reality of his career in law enforcement and the daily risk. But I refuse to panic. So much of the last few months has taught me about my strength, and Nick has been a huge part of that. So the last thing I need is to be a distraction from whatever he's dealing with. I know he'll reach out when he can.

Liv sends a text just after eight in the morning. I wasn't far off from checking on everyone myself.

Liv:

Sound off, ladies. Everyone ok?

Me:

Just trying to keep Roman and Banana occupied. I'm over this rain.

Sammi:

Vivi is a little moody with the weather, too.

Maci:

Sutton and the hands are out checking on the cattle. We're beyond saturated.

Izzy:

All good here.

A few minutes later, my phone rings and Maci's name flashes on the screen.

"Hi gorgeous," I answer cheerfully.

"Have you heard from Nick?" Maci's clipped tone has me on immediate alert.

"No, have you?"

Her hesitation lasts too long.

"Maci?" I prompt.

"No," she says softly. "Do me a favor and take a breath before I continue."

I couldn't inhale right if I wanted to. It's like when people tell you not to move, but instead you panic and bolt. "Just tell me."

"The flooding has been far worse than predicted. Washed away cars, water rescues, the whole nine yards," she explains softly.

My cold fear rapidly turns to panic. I'm reminded of the night Maci was attacked. I told myself at the time that there was nothing I could do besides let the professionals handle it, and I resolved to keep Izzy in one piece while we waited for answers.

"Is he there? Where is this happening?" I have more questions, like how does she know this, but I try to limit them.

"Kerr County. I don't know. I'm only going on the information I have. I wanted you to know first, if you didn't already." Her voice softens. "Do you want me to come over?"

"No." My mind races with possibilities. "I'll let you know if I hear from him. Are you guys ok?"

"Yeah. Sutton and his dad are out checking the cattle with the ranch hands. Andi's making enough food to feed a large army. I think she's panicking a bit, but I have a feeling we're going to jump in and help where we can." I'm not surprised at this. Sutton and Nick always help in the community, and I imagine Sutton's family nurtured that desire.

I take a peek at Roman and Savannah. They're a little pent from being cooped up, so I planned some indoor games to keep them occupied today. "How do the roads look out there?" I ask tentatively.

"Mmm, I'm not sure yet," Maci muses. "None of us have left."

"I'm going to check the county website. If the low-water crossings look ok, I may try to drive out your way with the kids. Maybe they can occupy Vivi, and we can find some other ways to help."

"Ok. Just please be careful. I'm going to call Izzy."

It isn't until the kids and I get to the ranch that we all begin to find out the extent of the flooding. The destruction of property, the loss of life, and the aftermath of this event will live with us forever.

I don't hear from Nick until late in the evening, when Roman, Savannah, and I are back home. His voice is tired and he seems distracted. I want to ask if he's ok, but the obvious answer is no, so I refrain.

Our phones have been ringing constantly with people sharing news of what's happening all around us. I don't know if Nick was involved in water rescues, but I feel a little selfish that I'm relieved he's ok. Though, ok is subjective—like Marsha said—because being in the thick of this is probably going to have a lasting impact on him.

"How are you and the kids?" Despite the fatigue in his voice, it's clear he's genuinely interested in the answer.

"We're good. We were at the Stricklands' earlier. Before Michael loaded the tractor up."

"Mmhmm. There will be a lot of cleanup," Nick agrees absently. Sometimes he'll tell me funny stories about work, but on the few occasions something serious has come up, I've noticed he always compartmentalizes it.

"I know it's not the time," I start slowly, "but when you're ready, I'll be here. Not physically, but . . . if you want to talk."

He remains quiet for a few seconds before responding. "Yeah. I guess I need to be better about that."

"I don't expect for you to put everything into words." This is the worst thing to happen here for as long as any of us can remember. There may be things Nick sees or experiences that he'll never want to voice again, but I need him to know he can. "But if you want to, no matter how ugly, you have a place to fall apart."

"I love you, Leah." His voice catches and mine tightens in response. "I'm so glad you and Roman and Savannah are ok."

"I love you," I answer. "And the feeling is mutual."

The rest of the weekend carries on with us filling our time helping in any way we can, and not hearing from Nick until well after dark. The tragedy of it all mounts, and although Nick shares more of what's happening, it's clear he's still keeping the emotions of it all closed up.

Nick:

We're starting early this morning. Missing you.

Nick:

I know you're worried about the hearing today, but everything is going to work out.

Me:

Just be careful. Don't worry about me.

Nick:

That's what happens when you love people.

It feels dissociative to carry on with our life as if an unimaginable catastrophe didn't happen over the weekend. But here in Bull Creek, the flooding was minimal and everything is on track on the courthouse.

I texted Marsha yesterday afternoon and told her I wouldn't be bringing Roman and Savannah. If my sister couldn't be bothered to show for visitations or birthdays, and now she's relinquishing rights, it's not my responsibility to bring them to see her. The last thing they need is some dramatic scenario with her.

Sammi greets me at the house instead, Viviane on her hip. "You look like a boss," she says appreciatively just as I'm leaving.

"Fake it till you make it, right?"

"You are a boss. You've got this."

Thanks to the continued rain, everyone is waiting inside today. I wave to Marsha as movement from my left pulls my attention.

Lily approaches quickly. "Where are Roman and Savannah?" Her face is an odd mixture of anger and boredom, with heavy lids and a tight face.

"Are you serious right now?" I scan the crowd around us. "I didn't bring them."

Her eyes widen in shock. "You're not even going to let me say goodbye to them? Are you kidding me?"

I lean forward, lowering my voice. "You had weeks—months—to visit them when you couldn't be bothered—"

"I was working! Do you know I had to get a lawyer to keep me out of jail, thanks to you? For neglect?"

"Explain how I did that to you," I grit out.

She rolls her eyes. "Oh yeah, I forgot, nothing's your fault."

"You're right. Glad you're finally catching on." I'm past arguing with her. She's made her bed and her decisions. I brush past her, but turn sharply. "Oh, and don't think about having Mom come after me again."

Lily gapes as I turn and continue walking.

I sit with my head held high at the hearing. The judge grants Lily's request to relinquish rights. Marsha updates that I'll be completing kinship foster training. This doesn't seem to affect him one way or the other, and the hearing concludes quickly.

I call Sammi in the parking lot.

"Hey, is everything ok?" she whispers.

"Yeah, are you ok?" I ask, confused.

"Yeah. We're just playing hide and seek. I'm in the laundry room."

I snicker. "Ok, well after this round, let's go get sno-cones. I'm on my way back."

"Yes! The kids will love that."

Maybe throwing around the word "love" isn't a bad thing. Somewhere along the way, I've learned to embrace my village and, more importantly, create a bigger village for Roman and Savannah.

CHAPTER 49

NICK

S aturday, Roman and Savannah play in the yard, while Leah and I sit at the end of my dock. The pond water is a little murky from the rain over the last week, but my house saw far less of what hit our neighboring counties.

Leah's feet swish forward and back in the water, leaving ripples in their wake.

There's no world where she isn't endgame for me. She has to know that. Even before this past weekend, which solidified the importance of the people in my life.

"A penny for your thoughts," she almost whispers.

My head snaps her way. The sun dances on her exposed shoulders so that she's glowing as she basks in the warmth. Her smile is wild and free, teasing, just how I like it. Her eyes are bright, inquisitive, trusting. She's the most incredible sight I've ever seen. She is everything.

"Marry me, Wild Thing."

Her cheeks turn pink and not from the sun. I can't think of a time I've seen her blush.

She studies me silently, her hazel eyes bouncing between mine before running over my face.

I never want a day to go by where I don't get to see her.

"I'm not ready," she whispers, and her eyes pool. She swallows uncomfortably.

"I don't mean today," I joke, reaching my hands to hers and tangling our fingers.

"Nick, I don't even know if I want kids. And Roman and Savannah aren't going anywhere. Not if I have anything to say about it."

"I don't want them to go anywhere," I promise. "Well, maybe somewhere. And Smokey, too."

She frowns. "I'm not getting rid of my cat. I thought you liked Smokey? And you're crazy if you think I'm letting them go to a different foster home. I'm doing the training."

"Not what I mean," I say, looking over my shoulder. "The yard is too empty."

"What?" She jumps up and turns, looking for Roman and Savannah, who run in circles around a tree. "They're right there."

I laugh and stand. "I want to get a swing set or something for them."

"That's kind of a big thing," she argues.

"Not if they use it all the time."

"But they won't. We—"

"But they could. If you lived here," I interrupt, waiting for everything to sink in.

Leah's face morphs from confusion to disbelief. "You want us to live here?"

"Yes. Your house is too small. Your business is expanding and you're hardly even working at it. Imagine if you could actually focus on it. And I don't like the idea of Lily knowing where y'all are. I know she's your sister, and I would never keep you from her. That's completely up to you. But wouldn't you feel better if you had a place to escape to that she didn't know about? Especially with what happened at the courthouse?"

Her face softens. "It's not the worst idea. It's just a big change."

"I'll admit, I'm being selfish again." I reach for her hands. "I just want as much time with you as possible. And Roman and Savannah. It just makes sense."

"Ok." She nods and then leans up to kiss my mouth, her lips tender and warm from the sun. "But I'm not saying yes to marriage."

"Yet." I lean forward, pressing my lips to her forehead for a long moment and then mumbling against them, "I'll wait." I pull back and grin at her. "But Smokey has to play nice when I get a dog."

Leah's eyebrows scrunch.

"I'm filling out the paperwork for the K-9 request. It'll be a few months still, but I want to move forward on it."

"And you should," she agrees, before looking over to the kids. Savannah lies on her belly, picking flower petals, while Roman digs in the dirt.

"We'll have a lot of changes coming up. A move, a dog, foster training. Roman starts school in the fall," she muses.

"And we'll figure it all out. Together."

Epilogue

Nick

February

Smokey stretches out along the back of the couch with a pleased mewl and digs his front paws into my shoulders, making biscuits with mostly closed eyes. He climbs down using Leah's chest, where she rests with her head in my lap, as a bridge to the floor. Ryder, our German Shepard and most recent family addition, raises his head as Smokey walks slowly through his vision. They've done well together, but Smokey's kind of a slut for attention from the canine. His gray tail swishes behind him as he enters the kitchen.

Leah lets out a soft moan as my fingers continue running through her hair. She hated it the first time I tried, but she's grown fond of the affection over the months. "What is it, Boy Scout?" she asks quietly.

Savannah and Roman are fast asleep upstairs, which is surprising since they recently moved into separate rooms. It's not unusual for us to find Roman in Savannah's bed, their two hands clasped together in the mornings.

"Thinking," I muse.

"That's never good," she jests.

Ryder alerts to something Smokey's gotten into. He checks in with me, his keen amber eyes softening when he sees I'm aware, and then rests his head against his paws again.

My fingers leave Leah's hair, lowering to her rib cage, which I've discovered is her most ticklish area. I dance my fingers along her side, brushing the soft cotton of my stolen T-shirt. She hides a giggle, shimmying back and forth before pushing into sitting. "No fair," she says, with no frustration and a big grin.

"Marry me, Wild Thing," I say calmly. I haven't brought it up since the day on the dock, waiting for her to acclimate to all of the changes. To feel settled and comfortable in the new roles we've chosen.

She chews the inside of her lip. "I've been thinking, too," she says in response. It's not what I'm hoping for, but I wait. I've always seen myself as patient, but Leah has taught me so much in that regard. It's never been a bother to wait for her comfort, though.

She tucks her legs beneath her so that she sits back on her heels and places her hands in her lap.

"I want to adopt Roman and Savannah." She doesn't rush her words, nor does she give me a chance to respond. "I don't like this being in limbo, where they don't belong to anyone. Because they belong to me. They deserve to feel wanted and stable. Not waiting for more changes."

Her eyes are glassy, a hint of fear creeping across her tight mouth. As if she thinks I'll have something negative to say. It still surprises me all the ways she's been let down, and how she's still coming to terms with accepting my support at every turn. "I think you're right. They do deserve to feel wanted. You only got one thing wrong."

Her lips pucker, distracting me from the importance of the conversation. Nothing overshadows the kids, but my appetite for every bit of Leah is insatiable. She is fire in my veins, driving me every day to be better than I was the one before. She's the light that makes even the darkest day seem a little brighter.

"They belong to *us*." I lean toward her. "I want to adopt them with you. They can call me whatever they want, but I want them to know without a shadow of doubt that they'll never be alone again. That someone will always be in their corner. No matter what, I'm there."

Tears leak from Leah's eyes and her bottom lip quivers. She has immense strength, even if she considers crying a weakness. "You really want to?"

"More than anything. Please. Let me be a permanent part of their life, in a way that no one can argue."

"Ok," she says, nodding, and her mouth tugs into a smile even as the tears flow faster. She shifts, climbing astride my lap as she tucks a leg on each side of me. Her lips press tenderly against mine and her cool hands cup my cheeks. "Yes."

"Thank you—wait, yes?" I hold my breath.

She smiles wider. "Yes, I'll marry you, Nick Foster."

"Holy fuck." I slam my mouth against hers again, wrapping both arms around her tighter than necessary. Her own arms encircle my neck, and she laughs through our kiss. "Tomorrow," I breathe when I pull back.

She laughs again. "Hold your horses, Boy Scout. I'm not backing out." Her fingers thread through my hair at the back of my neck. "I want to talk to the kids about the adoption, and then we can tell them about us."

"Ok." I kiss her again. "That's fair." And again. "I've been patient this long."

EPILOGUE II

LEAH

November

Savannah's and Roman's adoptions were finalized in September, and together they walked with me down the aisle to Nick two weeks later—almost exactly two years from when he and I first met.

Our ceremony was even simpler than Maci and Sutton's. Just our immediate friends and Nick's family on our property. His parents seemed to take Nick's words from our dinner to heart, and while they haven't been overly welcoming, they also haven't made any further belittling comments about me. His brother, Eli, and his family have been very welcoming. They're busy building Eli's business and Erica is pregnant again, so we don't see them much. But they've been nothing but kind.

Our vows included the kids, our promises to them, which Roman understood far better than Savannah. And then life continued on as perfectly as before.

"You ready to go, kiddos?" Nick calls up the stairs.

Roman shouts back, "Almost!"

Most mornings, Nick packs Ryder, Roman, and Savannah up with him when he leaves, dropping Roman at school and Savannah at daycare.

After quitting my job at Sadie's upon finding out that she had been sharing personal information with Payton, I dove headfirst into jewelry making. It was a stretch at first, but by the time we moved in with Nick, I was making enough in orders to squeak by on the bills. We've converted the fourth bedroom into a work room, and I've hosted shows at The Spur as well as two salons in Bull Creek.

Nick laughs and shakes his head as he pulls out items to make a lunch for the day.

"I'm so proud of them," I say quietly, putting the last of our breakfast dishes into the dishwasher. "They've taken everything in stride."

Nick smiles at me, pulling his favorite meat from the container for a sandwich. "That's because they have you. And me."

If someone had told me that first night that Nick came over that I'd be this domestic in such a short time, I would have said they were insane. And yet, it's felt so natural. Nick never tries to change me. He embraces all of the wildness within as we all grow together.

A foreign smell infiltrates my nose, and my face scrunches.

"You ok?" Nick closes up the lunch box as Roman's and Savannah's footsteps descend the stairs.

"Yeah," I lie.

His eyes narrow.

"Can I pick the music today?" Roman bounces into the kitchen, hurrying to the fridge and pulling out his plastic lunch box.

"You bet!" Nick says. "Ready, Little Bit?" He grins at Savannah.

"I'm not little!" she argues with faux anger. Terrible twos were nothing. Three has given us a bit of a run for our money.

"Bye, Aunt Leah!" Roman squeezes my legs and rushes out the front door before I have a chance to hug him back. Ryder bounds after him.

I crouch before Savannah. "Have a good day, Banana."

She wraps her arms around me in a tight hug. "Bye, Aunt Leah." Her little munchkin voice is probably my favorite sound in the world, and I will never get over the way she's started to willingly show affection.

My sister's struggles had taken an even bigger toll than we thought. Once they got settled with me, Savannah's interactions with people, her speech, and Roman's confidence all seemed to blossom before our eyes.

She releases me and runs after her brother and the dog.

"Have a good day, Wild Thing," Nick says as I stand. He kisses me firmly. We've slowly introduced more affection in front of the children, and we agree that both their comfort and witnessing healthy romantic relationships are important.

I watch from the window as Nick's truck departs the driveway, and then I hurry up the stairs. When Nick's lunch made me queasy yesterday for the second time, I went and got a pregnancy test. I've convinced myself that it was nothing, and simply having the test would make the anomaly disappear. But now it's happened for the third time.

After taking the test, I set the timer and make myself busy in the bathroom—which is already clean and perfectly stocked. I don't manage to wait for the timer to go off before retrieving the test from the counter. My hand shakes as I stare at the white stick displaying two pink lines.

It's not the darkest pink I've ever seen, and I've seen them dark on Lily's old tests. But it's not faint, either. A clear positive. I'm pregnant.

I splash water on my face and stare into the mirror. It's not like I didn't know this could happen. Nick and I had several discussions about having a child together. And although he's been reassuring about my ability to mother, he's never pressured me. Always told me I'm enough.

We agreed that we'd be fine if I ended up pregnant. I came off birth control just before the wedding in October, but we haven't gone out of our way to make anything happen.

And yet, staring at the reality, my insides spiral. What's going to happen to my body? Is Nick going to be repulsed by me? Am I going to have massive hormonal changes? I don't want Roman and Savannah to ever feel pushed aside.

Holy shit. I have to push a baby out my fucking vagina. My eyes widen at my reflection.

We barely manage to keep the pregnancy news a secret until Thanksgiving. It's a beautifully crisp day with all of our favorite people at Strickland Ranch. Andi still hosts, and we're all crammed into The Big House for the final Thanksgiving there. She's agreed to move it to The Lodge starting next year.

"Time for grace!" Andi calls into the living room, and before long we've all congregated around the large dining room table. Our imperfect circle of people overflows into the living room.

Nick squeezes my hand and winks.

"Um, really quickly," I interrupt, causing all eyes to shift to me. "I just, I know I said something similar last year, but I want to thank you all for being a part of our lives. You're all so special to us, and we're so thankful that Roman and Savannah have you as family, too."

Nick squeezes again, urging me on as people coo and agree.

"And also, we are excited to share that we're expecting a baby next year." My cheeks flood with heat, and Izzy squeals next to me, releasing my hand and whoever's she had on the other side to wrap her arms tightly around me.

Maci grins over the top of Finn, strapped to her chest. Sutton kisses the top of her head. "We're so happy for you," she says lovingly. She smiles widely and looks up at her husband, who winks. "And that's perfect, because we're expecting next year, too."

"What?!" Andi cries, and the cheers in the room increase.

Having a baby at the same time as my best friend is the only thing that could make this entire thing any better.

Roman smiles, a single upper tooth missing, between Maci and I. "More cousins? This is gonna be great!"

"I couldn't agree more," I say, ruffling his hair with a proud smile.

Thank You For Reading!

Thank you so much for reading *A Penny For Your Thoughts*! If you enjoyed Leah and Nick's story, would you consider taking a minute to post a review on your favorite platform? A few words and a star rating go a long way! Thank you for all of your support!

Also by Amanda Marquardt

The Fallout Duet

When Sparks Fly

When the Smoke Clears

Bull Creek Series

A Penny For Your Thoughts

Book Two – Coming 2026

Falcons MC

Untamed – Coming 2026

Additional Considerations

As mentioned in the content notices, the list below contains a few organizations you may want to support for continued and future disaster relief efforts in Texas.

The last entry on the list is for Heroes for Children. While the bachelor auction that took place was fictitious, Heroes for Children is an organization based in Texas, which provides financial relief, social support, and items for children going through cancer treatment and their families.

TEXSAR (Texas Search and Rescue)
texsar.org/donate/

Kerr County Flood Relief Fund
https://cftexashillcountry.fcsuite.com/erp/donate/create/fund?funit_id=42
01

Travis County CARES Fund
https://ctxcf.networkforgood.com/projects/255420-travis-county-cares-flo
od-relief

Spirit of Giving Fund (HEB Disaster Relief Funding)

https://spiritofgiving.org/

Heroes For Children

https://www.heroesforchildren.org/

ACKNOWLEDGEMENTS

I t's crazy to think I'm publishing my third novel, and my first isn't even a year old yet. Doing this while raising four children, managing a household, and moving halfway across the country, has been a wild ride. So when I say the following people have been crucial to Leah and Nick's story being in the wild, it's the truth.

First and foremost, my husband who understands nothing about publishing but is unequivocally convinced that I can do anything, and more, while simultaneously reminding me that I don't have to be 'Superwoman'.

My amazing friend and editor, Megan. Everyone needs a Megan, but you can't have her because she's mine. Megan, I can't begin to count the ways you have been instrumental to not only this book, but all of my published titles thus far. You have gone above and beyond at every chance and I'm so proud, and thankful, to call you my friend.

My alpha readers: Stacey, Emily, and Stephanie, thank you for your time and dedication to Leah and Nick. Your initial feedback of my very rough, largely incomplete ideas and chapters helps more than you realize!

My beta readers: Tabitha, Chloe, and Mel, your commentary on this story was crucial in reaching a finished product that I am incredibly proud of. Thank you for loving these two as much as me!

Oh my goodness, my street team. Your love for Leah & Nick, as well as Maci & Sutton, your continued desire to hype these stories, and your conversations along the way have been so incredibly special. As some of my biggest fans, your input has been pivotal in decision-making and bringing this story to life. Thank you for being on this journey with me.

A huge thanks to Dani for helping create graphics as we got closer to release!

Tabitha, girl, there are no words. Your friendship is so grounding. You probably don't even know the number of times you've casually popped up when I'm one step from a full-blown spiral. Our conversations reminds me that I'm not crazy, as an author, reader, mother, and wife. I couldn't have created a better friend if I had tried to design you myself. Thank you for your constant, unwavering support, from the bottom of my heart.

Chloe, I am so incredibly thankful for you! As a reader, as my PA, as a friend, you are so important to me. You have seen Leah and Nick so clearly from the very beginning, and being able to bounce those raw ideas off you was so validating and integral to their story. Your creativity is inspiring, and I appreciate all the ways you push me whether you know it or not. Thank you!

Alex, my cover designer, you were so receptive to my jumbled ideas, and pulled this gorgeous girl out of a hat. I can't wait to show off the rest of the series!

To the ARC readers, thank you for taking a chance on Leah and Nick. Your enthusiasm for honesty and a good book is so important, especially for indie authors. Thank you!

And to all of the readers, you're literally making dreams come true. Thank you for being here!!

I wouldn't be here without all of you, so once again, thank you for your love and support, and for the time you've spent in Bull Creek!

AMANDA MARQUARDT